From the Pages of the Odyssey

Tell of the storm-tossed man, O Muse, who wandered long after he sacked the sacred citadel of Troy.   (page 1)

"Yet is my heart distressed for wise Odysseus, hapless man, who, long cut off from friends, is meeting hardship upon a sea-encircled island, the navel of the sea."   (page 2)

"Few sons are like their fathers; most are worse, few better."   (page 18)

"Many a grief the son of an absent father meets at home, when other helpers are not by. So with Telemachus; the one is gone, and others there are none in all the land to ward off ill."   (page 40)

Athene passed away, off to Olympus, where they say the dwelling of the gods stands fast forever. Never with winds is it disturbed, nor by the rain made wet, nor does the snow come near; but everywhere the upper air spreads cloudless, and a bright radiance plays over all; and there the blessed gods are happy all their days.   (page 71)

"Better to be the hireling of a stranger, and serve a man of mean estate whose living is but small, than be the ruler over all these dead and gone."   (page 142)

"Friends, hitherto we have not been untried in danger."   (page 152)

"Afterwards a man finds pleasure in his pains, when he has suffered long and wandered long."   (page 191)

"Half the value of a man far-seeing Zeus destroys when the slave's lot befalls him!"   (page 215)

Odysseus aimed an arrow and hit him in the throat; right through his tender neck the sharp point passed. He sank down sideways; from his hand the goblet fell when he was hit, and at once from his nose ran a thick stream of human blood.   (page 271)

"For all humankind immortal ones shall make a joyous song in praise of steadfast Penelope."   (page 297)

THE ODYSSEY

HOMER

Edited with an Introduction and Notes by Robert Squillace
Translated by George Herbert Palmer

GEORGE STADE
CONSULTING EDITORIAL DIRECTOR

JB

BARNES & NOBLE CLASSICS
NEW YORK

ℬ
BARNES & NOBLE CLASSICS
NEW YORK

Published by Barnes & Noble Books
122 Fifth Avenue
New York, NY 10011

www.barnesandnoble.com/classics

Published in 2003 by Barnes & Noble Classics with new Introduction,
Note on the Translation, Notes, Biography, Chronology, Inspired By,
Comments & Questions, For Further Reading, and Index.
Hardcover edition published in 2004.

Introduction, A Note on the Translation, Notes, and For Further Reading
Copyright © 2003 by Robert Squillace.

Note on Homer, The World of Homer and *the Odyssey*,
Inspired by *the Odyssey*, Comments & Questions, and Index
Copyright © 2003 by Barnes & Noble, Inc.

the Odyssey
ISBN 1-59308-167-7
LC Control Number 2004100772

Produced and published in conjunction with:
Fine Creative Media, Inc.
322 Eighth Avenue
New York, NY 10001
Michael J. Fine, President and Publisher

Printed in the United States of America
QM
3   5   7   9   10   8   6   4

Homer

We know very little about the author of the *Odyssey* and its companion tale, the *Iliad*. Most scholars agree that Homer was Greek, most probably from Smyrna, now the Turkish city known as Izmir, or from Chios, an island in the eastern Aegean Sea. According to legend, Homer was blind, and we have no scholarly evidence that suggests otherwise.

The ongoing debate about who Homer was and when, and even if, he wrote the *Odyssey* and the *Iliad* is known as the "Homeric question." Classicists do agree that these tales of the fall of the city of Troy (Ileum) in the Trojan War (the *Iliad*) and the aftermath of that ten-year battle (the *Odyssey*) coincide with the ending of the Mycenaean period (also known as the Bronze Age), around 1200 B.C. The Mycenaeans were a society of warriors and traders; beginning around 1600 B.C., they became a major power in the Mediterranean. Brilliant potters and architects, they also developed a system of writing known as Linear B, based on a syllabary, writing in which each symbol stands for a syllable.

Scholars do not agree on when Homer lived or when he might have written the *Odyssey*. Some place Homer in the late-Mycenaean period, which means he would have written about the Trojan War as recent history. Close study of the texts reveals aspects of political, material, religious, and military life of the Bronze Age and of the so-called Dark Age, as the period of domination by the less-advanced Dorian invaders who usurped the Mycenaeans is known. But how, other scholars argue, could Homer have created works of such magnitude in the Dark Age, when there was no system of writing? Herodotus, the ancient Greek historian, placed Homer sometime around the ninth century B.C., at the beginning of the Archaic period, in which the Greeks adopted a system of writing from the Phoenicians and widely colonized the Mediterranean. And modern scholarship shows that the most recent details in the poems are datable to the period between 750 and 700 B.C.

No one, however, disputes the fact that the *Odyssey*, and the *Iliad* as well, arose from oral tradition. Stock phrases, types of episodes, and repeated phrases—such as "early, rose-fingered dawn"—bear the mark of epic storytelling. Scholars agree, too, that this tale of the Greek hero Odysseus's journey and adventures as he returned home from Troy to Ithaca is a work of the greatest historical significance and, indeed, one of the foundations of Western literature.

CONTENTS

WANDER
OF
ULYSSES AN

- - - - - - - - Tra
- · - · - · - · - · - Tra

45°

o Patavium   o Timavus
Verona
o Mantua
R. Padus   *Illyrian-Bo*
LIGURIA   A
E   A
Padua o   D
o Pisa   R
Corythus o   I
Clusium o   A
Mt. Soroct   T
ETRURIA   I
Caere o   *R. Tiber*   C
Nomentum   S
o Tibur
R. Anio o Praeneste
Alba Longa
Laurentum LATIUM o
Ardea o CAMPAN Panthchope Arpi o
Aquelanum
Cumae L'Avernus
40°   C Mise o   Tarent
BIREN
CIPREÆ

SARDINIA   T Y R R H E N I A N   Velia o
S E A   *Cape Palinur* us Telopylus   Bay of
Tarentum

*Sallentinian
Fields* o Retilia
o Lacini
ÆA   Temese o
OGYGIA   Scylaceum
LIPARI IDS.   I O
M   E   ID. OF ÆOLUS *Peloria Sti*   o Caulon
D   Ery o   Scilla
I   Drepanum   *Peloria Stra*
Selinus   Mt. Ætna
Lilybeum o   TRINACRIA   Thapsus
Carthage o   Agrigentum o OR SICILY ORTYGIA
T   o Gela o
E   Syracuse *Plemmyrium Pr.*
R   *Pachynum Pr.*
R   ID OF THE SUN
A
35°   N

*Land of
Lotus-eaters*

10°   15°   Longit

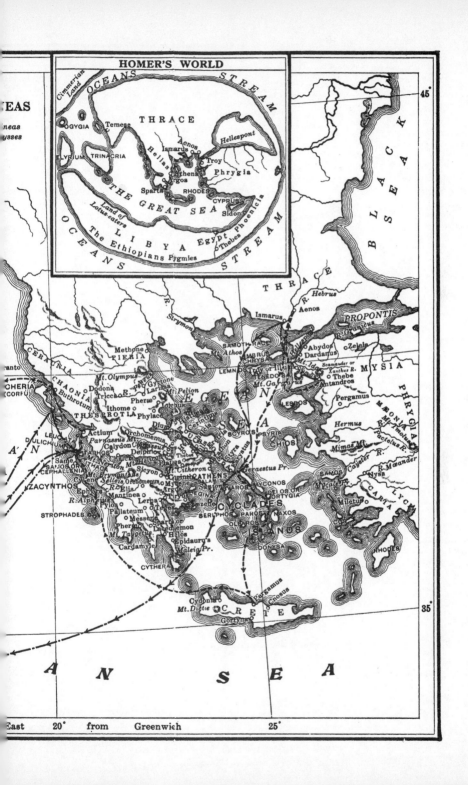

The World of Homer and the Odyssey

B.C. (approximate dates)

1650–
1400
The Mycenaean period, also known as the Bronze Age because bronze is widely used in weaponry, comes into flower. Pylos and Mycenae, city-states mentioned by Homer in his writings about this period of Greek history, are powerful and wealthy centers of Aegean trade.

1200–
1100
The fall of Troy ends the Trojan War, which Homer describes so vividly. Dorians invade, the Mycenaean culture declines, and the so-called Dark Age ensues. Linear B, the Mycenaeans' system of writing, is lost. The Homeric epics survive as oral legends.

1100–
700
Troy is uninhabited, suggesting that Homer's observations of life in the city predate the twelfth century B.C.

800–
750
The Greeks adopt the Phoenician alphabet and set down the *Iliad* and the *Odyssey* in writing for the first time.

500–
400
Threatened with a Persian invasion, the Greek city-states turn to Homer as a guide to banding together in the face of a common enemy.

30–19
The Roman poet Virgil writes the *Aeneid*, borrowing heavily from Homer.

A.D.

450
With the decline of the Roman Empire, interest in Greek texts and in Homer becomes dormant in the West until learning resurges in the Middle Ages.

600–700	Homeric figures begin to appear in the Arabic tales of Sindbad.
1870	Heinrich Schliemann, a retired German businessman with a passion for the Homeric epics, begins excavations at Troy.
1876	Schliemann excavates a grave circle at Mycenae and proves that the Mycenaean civilization of which Homer wrote indeed existed, inspiring other archaeologists to excavate in the region.
1900–1950	Sir Arthur Evans excavates ancient Knossos, on the island of Crete. Among discoveries relating to the Mycenaean culture are clay tablets with Linear B script. The findings help prove that Homer's works record historical events in the Mycenaean period.
1920s	Based on observations of contemporary verse composition in the Balkans, American scholar Milman Parry determines that the Homeric legends survived for many generations as oral stories.

INTRODUCTION

The Many Worlds of the Odyssey

The only other book to which the Western imagination owes so much of its stock of heroes, monsters, images, and tales as it does to the *Iliad* and the *Odyssey* is the Bible. At the same time, these epic poems attributed to Homer, like the Bible, are not originally Western or even European texts; in fact, even to call them Greek is misleading. Telling the full story behind this apparent contradiction sets the *Odyssey* firmly in its historical context, clarifying its relation both to its own time and to ours.

Before embarking on this tale, however, one must recognize the three basic layers of the poem's creation. First, the setting for the events the Homeric epics describe (to the extent such incidents as the Trojan War ever occurred in the first place) is a wealthy era known as the Mycenaean period. The dominant leaders of the most important city-states on the Greek peninsula, the Mycenaeans were speakers of an early form of Greek who made war with weapons of bronze. This period ended sometime between 1200 and 1100 B.C. Second, the characters, plots, and settings that appear in the epics, however much their origins may belong to the Mycenaean era, continued to develop during a period of oral transmission that spanned the so-called Grecian "Dark Age," namely, the centuries from 1100 to 800 B.C. The level of physical culture declined so markedly at this time that most historians believe a separate tribe speaking a different Greek dialect, the Dorians, conquered and sacked all but a few of the Mycenaean city-states. Iron replaced bronze, and the art of writing, known to the Mycenaean world, was lost, leaving the period utterly without written records. Third, the *Iliad* and the *Odyssey* were among the earliest works to be written down when the

Greeks reacquainted themselves with literacy in the early eighth century B.C.—the *Iliad*, most scholars agree, around 750 B.C., and the *Odyssey* twenty or thirty years later.

The modern concepts of "Europe" and "Greece" do not apply to such early periods. When the long story of the wanderings and homecoming of Odysseus was first committed to writing, no one regarded the disparate lands now identified on maps by the word "Europe" as a unified geographical entity, nor did any shared cultural inheritance (let alone the consciousness of one) unite those lands. Indeed, Homer unambiguously depicts the states of Phoenicia (Biblical Canaan; roughly, modern Lebanon) and Egypt as the most vital partners and rivals of the Greek-speaking world. While Homer does perceive a cultural and linguistic identity that distinguishes speakers of Greek from other peoples, the language was divided then into almost mutually unintelligible dialects. Also, though in making this distinction, Homer predates the formation of a politically unified Greece by something like 400 years (and that was a temporary union effected by Phillip II of Macedon and his son, Alexander the Great, representatives of a northern tribe whom the cultural leaders of Athens regarded as semibarbarous). The illiterate centuries of the Grecian "Dark Age," when the tale of Odysseus began to take form in the mouths of storytellers, were, of course, even earlier before the advent of a unified Greek nation.

Tellingly, Homer lacks a word that corresponds to the modern term "Greek" as a simultaneous designation of a language, a culture, and a state. He refers to what we might call Greeks as "Danaans" or "Argives," or "Achaeans," all three of which relate to the names of places from which some Greek-speakers happened to come, a usage loosely akin to referring to people born in the United States by randomly selecting any one of the designations "Southerners," "Yankees," or "Californians."

Unusual care is required to speak of Homer's world, as distinct from the conditions and assumptions of the later Hellenized, Romanized, and finally, Europeanized eras that unconsciously influence the ways most contemporary readers experience the poems. For that matter, the phrase "Homer's world" is problematic: To which of the very different layers of the poem's formation does such a phrase refer? In some respects, the materials of which the poem is composed seem to originate in the Mycenaean period. The city-states of Pylos and Mycenae, for instance, identified by Homer as the seats of the mighty kings Nestor and Agamemnon, reached the pinnacle of their power and wealth sometime between 1650 and 1400 B.C. The latter is the approximate date at which the magnificent artifacts of the Mycenaean tombs were assembled. (The self-trained archaeologist Heinrich Schliemann unearthed them in A.D. 1879 and naively assumed they came from Agamemnon's resting place, a view no contemporary scholar holds.) The former date, 1650 B.C., is about the time by which the Minoan city of Knossos, on the island of Crete and formerly the leading power of the northeastern Mediterranean, seems to have been at least eclipsed and likely conquered by the Mycenaeans. Moreover, if the Trojan War ever took place, the best candidate for the date falls in the Mycenaean period; the archaeological evidence suggests that a prosperous era in the history of Troy was violently terminated—whether by war or misfortune has yet to be determined to the satisfaction of all scholars—in the late thirteenth century B.C. Since the site of Troy remained uninhabited from about 1100 to 700 B.C., at least some of the memories that inform the poems, which depict the city as a rich and powerful place, must reach back to the Mycenaean era.

But one cannot accurately describe the Mycenaean world as the Homeric nor assert without qualification that the poems were "set" in that time. After 1200 B.C., when Mycenaean culture went into its steep decline, the system of writing it had employed, Linear B, was forgotten (and, in fact, no literary texts have yet been found in that script, which apparently served mainly to record palace business). In this womb of historical silence, the Homeric epics gestated. So how—and to what extent—could the Mycenaean past have been preserved in the poems?

The answer lies in the nature of what has come to be called oral-formulaic verse. A young American scholar named Milman Parry deduced, by observing this form of poetic composition still being practiced in the Balkans during the 1920s, that the *Iliad* and the *Odyssey* had been composed and circulated as oral-formulaic verse for indeterminate generations before they were at last written down. In this method of poetic composition, a bard intimately familiar with the details of a traditional legend or set of legends improvises, often for hours at a time, night after night, a metrical chanting of the story. The bard often relies on a great many prefabricated phrases and lines that fit the metrical pattern conventional to the culture—in Ancient Greek, the pattern of long and short syllables. (The musical forms of calypso and hip-hop often work in roughly similar fashions.) Frequent repetition of such phrases as "early, rosy-fingered dawn" and "earth-shaking Poseidon," as well as the tendency of characters to repeat word-for-word any message or description given them to repeat, demonstrates the origin of the *Odyssey* in oral-formulaic verse. Presumably, the same metrical phrases might be repeated in reference to the same characters, places, or incidents for centuries.

At the same time, it would be a mistake to imagine that the poem remained so little altered that Homer's tale reflected the basic social facts of life in the time of the Mycenaeans. Oral-formulaic verse changes by nature. Not only does each retelling subtly alter the previous incarnations, but bards must appeal to the audience seated before them in order to earn their bread. Their incentive is to create a world that is meaningful to their listeners, not to preserve accurately the ways of life that belong to their ancestors. Homer, to be sure, clearly sets his tale in the golden age of what, even to his first readers, was the distant past, being careful to include archaisms such as chariot warfare and bronze weaponry that had vanished from the world of his own time. His gestures in this direction, however, are precisely what provide modern archaeologists with the proof that the Homeric poems reflect the Mycenaean world very imprecisely. Warriors in the *Odyssey* essentially fight as they did in Homer's time: on foot, throwing and thrusting spears and, at close quarters, lunging with swords. When a Homeric hero steps into a chariot, he does so merely to arrive at the battlefield in high style, dismounting before drawing any of his weapons. The Mycenaeans, however, used their chariots as moving gunnery platforms from which to fire arrows. Indeed, some scholars believe they conquered the Grecian peninsula primarily by their mastery of chariots, part of a wave of victories by mainly Indo-European-speaking charioteers in India (the Aryan invasion), the Fertile Crescent (the misnamed "Hittite" Empire), and even Egypt (the Hyksos conquest). In Homer, the honored dead receive cremation; had this been the case in Mycenaean times, there would have been no tombs for Schliemann to open. Indeed, Homer's poems record no suspicion that a major cultural and political disruption separated his own era from that of the Trojan War heroes. Certain Mycenaean fictions may survive in the poem, but few identifiable realities.

So the world of the *Odyssey* does not precisely reflect the Mycenaean period, in that Homer, coming at the end of 300 years without written records, knew little of this vanished way of life. Nor does the *Odyssey* reflect the world of the late eighth century B.C., when the epic was likely written down, since the poet introduced purposeful archaism and the poem accumulated undatable story elements during its years, decades, or even centuries of oral transmission. Rather, Homer creates a mythic past—perceptible as imaginary to us, but regarded as the authentic voice of tradition by its original audience—in order to translate the customs of his own time into a vision of universal values and eternal meaning. Homer evokes a sense of great but indefinite temporal distance in order to provide a metaphor for the idea of timelessness. Homer's past is "always."

Simply to attribute the poem's intentions to Homer, though, hides another nest of complexities. While the poem circulated in oral form for some time, and at least certain elements of it reach back centuries, our *Odyssey* is and has long been a written text. Most scholars agree that it was first written down some time in the second half of the eighth century B.C., which makes it one of the earliest literary works to be committed to paper (or, more accurately, parchment) after the Greeks adapted the Phoenician alphabet to transcribe their own language. No manuscripts from that era survive, however; in fact, the oldest complete copies of the poem still in existence are little more than a thousand years old. These texts preserve a poem in absolutely finished form, varying only negligibly from each other; essentially, what one reads in any modern English edition of the poem, including this one, is a translation of those manuscripts. Many scholars believe the first truly authoritative text of the epic was established at the great library of Alexandria in the first few centuries A.D., giving those anonymous editors at least a small share in the identity of "Homer." A similar editorial effort may have occurred at the behest of the Athenian ruler Peisistratus even earlier, during the sixth century B.C., but no physical evidence to confirm this supposition has survived; only a few sentences of ancient historians attest to the possibility.

On the most crucial question concerning the poem's authorship, though, no one has any evidence of any kind: How did a poem that normally would have been orally improvised on the spot become a written manuscript in the first place? Tradition invariably identifies the author of the poem as a blind bard named Homer, but at precisely what point in the creative process might this figure enter? The poetry of the *Odyssey* shows clear roots in oral-formulaic composition, but it shows just as clearly that the poem is not simply the transcript of a particular oral performance or set of performances. No scribe squatted at the blind poet's knee hurriedly copying the 12,110 lines of the poem as he chanted them. The poem uses far fewer formulaic lines and phrases than any oral composition possibly could. The simplest solution is to assume that a literate poet intimately familiar with the materials and techniques of oral-formulaic poetry composed the poem in written form to sound as if it were orally composed, in keeping with tradition; one might as well call this figure "Homer" as anything else. Many scholars, however, regard "Homer" as a purely oral poet, relegating the scribe who reworked his poem into written form to secondary status. In any case, neither these half-invented Homers nor any other imaginable author of the texts that have survived can receive full credit for the contents of the poem, since the extent of its coalescence prior to the first appearance of any written text cannot be determined. The Homer of modern scholarly imagination, the poet on the cusp between oral and written composition, would not have invented the Trojan War or created the character of Odysseus or concocted his confrontation with the Cyclops—perhaps not even crafted the smaller details of his hero's victory. Rather, he would have inherited these incidents more or less fully imagined from his unknown predecessors. Just as the poem speaks from an indefinite time, it speaks with a composite voice.

Regarded as the authentic record of the earliest pan-Hellenic history and the repository of age-tested wisdom, the Homeric epics soon came to be regarded almost as sacred texts in the Greek city-states. Part of the appeal was political: Faced with invasion by a vast Persian military in the sixth and fifth centuries B.C., the rival Greek states sought precedent in myth for laying aside their differences to face a common enemy. When Athenians rebuilt the Parthenon in marble after the Persians razed its wooden predecessor during the occupation of Athens in 480 B.C.—ended only by the combined efforts of a largely Athenian navy, a largely Spartan army, and the contributions of many smaller allies—they carved images of the mythical conflicts by which the Lapiths had subdued the Centaurs and Theseus the Amazons into the stone. Like the Centaurs and Amazons—and unlike the Greeks—the Persians fought from horseback; the Greeks self-servingly imagined their victories over Centaurs, Amazons, and Persians alike as an imposition of order on chaos, a reassertion of "natural" hierarchies against the "savage" ambitions of animal instincts, women, and foreigners. Similarly, Greek unity in the Trojan War became a rallying point. When Herodotus wrote his history of the Greco-Persian conflict, he included a pointed anecdote (of very dubious historicity) relating how Xerxes, the Persian ruler, visited the ruins of Priam's palace (the nerve center of Troy) before embarking on his ill-fated invasion of the Greek mainland. In case the analogy escaped anyone's perception, Herodotus noted that the Persian soldiers suffered unaccountable dread during the night they spent within the ruined walls.

But the poem's influence far outstripped its momentary propaganda value. Not everyone considered Homer's influence to be salutary. Judging by the *Republic*, Plato regarded the Homeric epics as his most dangerous rivals in teaching Athenians how to regulate their lives, tell good from evil, and know the truth of gods and humans. The immorality of Homer's gods particularly troubled the philosopher, who in any case had little sympathy with what he envisioned (and condemned) as the essentially feminine act of poetic creation, with all the messy emotions it inspired in its audience. As thorough a literalist as any intellectual before the rise of empirical science, Plato often seems almost deaf to figurative meanings. He complains in his dialogue *Ion*, for instance, that a fisherman must surely be a better judge of the success of those Homeric passages in which a character attempts to catch fish than a rhapsodist (a dramatic reciter of poems also expected to explicate them ably).

The questionable morality of the poem's eponymous hero, as much as the foibles of its gods, troubled the Romans. Or, perhaps more accurately, Roman poets attempted to distinguish the virtues of their people from those of the Greeks to whom they obviously had so great a cultural debt by unfavorably comparing the behavior of the brawling, self-absorbed Odysseus with the self-restrained Aeneas, a Trojan supposed to have escaped the ruin of his city and wandered for many years before landing near the Tiber and founding Rome. Virgil's *Aeneid*, in fact, implicitly offers an almost point-by-point comparison of the Greek ethos with the Roman—curiously, always to the Roman advantage. Odysseus endangers his men by his curiosity to see a Cyclops, while Aeneas avoids the island altogether (pausing only to rescue a member of Odysseus's crew heartlessly marooned in the great trickster's haste to escape); Odysseus slaughters all the suitors besieging his home in order to reclaim his own property, while Aeneas unites his crewmen with the native tribes of Italy (even those who at first offer armed resistance) to create a new state, and so forth. Virgil does not directly depict Odysseus (or Ulysses, to use the Latin form of the name). But those Roman poets who did—most influentially, Ovid in his *Metamorphoses*—transformed the great warrior, the man of many devices, into something closer to a con man—and an unsympathetic one at that, always willing to take any unfair advantage that might present itself to bilk the weak or the stupid. The very qualities that made Odysseus so secure a guide to behavior in the Greek world of the eighth through the fifth centuries—a world of dangerous independence of city from city, estate from estate, and rulers from ruled—rendered him a virtual outlaw in the regulated precincts of philosophical reason and Roman polity, as purely theoretical as the rule of law may often have been in both those lands.

In the West, after the Roman Empire disintegrated in the last half of the fifth century A.D., the preservation of Greek manuscripts and the study of the Greek tongue so declined that Homer's voice went unheard until the fifteenth century A.D. No manuscripts of the epic poems were available in any European library throughout the Middle Ages. Indeed, no Greek literature of any kind, and very little else of the classical world's immense literature, survived in Western Europe, aside from what the scribes of Charlemagne's court happened to save. The Eastern (or Byzantine) Empire, centered on the citadel of Constantinople, conducted all its business in Greek and preserved the poems throughout its existence. Indeed, as Islam encroached farther and farther onto the older Empire's lands between the seventh and the fifteenth centuries A.D., the *Odyssey* entered the Arabic tradition as the antecedent of Sindbad's seven voyages, on one of which he defeats a cannibalistic giant by first intoxicating then blinding him. In his *Inferno*, meanwhile, Dante assigns Homer to an honored place among the five great epic poets (prior to himself) purely on the basis of reputation; his own guide being Virgil, he places Ulysses prominently in the eighth circle of damnation, the circle of deceivers. In sum, the poem that would later be claimed as a pillar of European civilization was absent from the long centuries that saw the foundation of European culture, except by its indirect influence over Roman poets with very different aesthetic and moral ideals. It took the colonizing hubris of the Renaissance to claim the poem as "European."

Since chivalric codes of behavior are utterly foreign to the ethos of the *Odyssey*—when Odysseus settles his score with the suitors, he scrupulously avoids a fair fight, surprising his most dangerous foe with an arrow through the neck while the man is innocently raising a goblet to his lips—its appeal to the Middle Ages would likely have lagged far behind that of the *Aeneid*. Virgil seemed to anticipate Christian theology so closely that some pressure for his canonization ensued, a fate his Greek forebear never risked. But the rediscovery of Homer, after the flight of scholars from the Ottoman conquest of the last strongholds of the Byzantine empire in A.D. 1453, struck a chord in Renaissance Italy that echoed across the continent and still resonates today. As the fifteenth century rolled into the six-teenth, the universal Christian church fragmented into factions that were always in figurative and often in literal combat with each other. Europeans expanded into both geographical and scientific spheres for which their inherited world view seemed to offer inadequate explanation, and the checkerboard of localized feudal governments coalesced into the modern landscape of nation-states. As the plays of Shakespeare demonstrate, the nature of identity and authority became acute questions in such a world; the old criteria by which people determined who they were and what role they filled in their community no longer seemed reliable. The problems of self-definition and the maintenance of social order would so define the five hundred years between then and now that the designation "early modern Europe," which stresses our continuity with the period, has replaced "Renaissance" in the vocabulary of many historians. In many ways, the newer term acknowledges, the fifteenth century is the beginning of now, of modernity. The *Odyssey*, in a sense, was reborn at the moment of the modern world's own hard birth; reading it today, its discourse on the matters of authority and identity remain one of its chief fascinations.

The poem begins, in fact, with a four-book segment known as the Telemachy, an overture that announces the intertwined themes of identity and authority that reappear throughout the epic. Telemachus, the son of a father he has never seen, stands on the threshold between adolescence and adulthood. He is so unsure of his own identity that he refuses to affirm without qualification his relationship to Odysseus: "My mother says I am his child; I myself do not know; for no one ever yet knew his own parentage" (p. 6). The means by which Telemachus determines who he is and confirms his parentage to his own satisfaction establishes a model for self-formation that nearly every subsequent episode of the work will test, refine, or challenge. Separation from home and an independent encounter with the challenges of the outside world—in short, an odyssey—is the first requirement. Homer indicates the absolute necessity of this separation by putting the impetus for Telemachus's journey in the mouth of Athene, the goddess of wisdom. The young man's transformation as a result of his experience suggests that the literal journey he takes through space stands for his interior journey in time from adolescence to adulthood.

Nor does Telemachus literally find what he seeks—his father or trustworthy news of his whereabouts; instead, he discovers his progenitor in himself. For Athene does not send him on some flight of escape to a new land that will be wholly his own and from which he will never return—a romantic discovery of selfhood in utter freedom, in isolation from the lowering authority of all fathers, predecessors, and precedents. Instead, she sends him into the country of the past, from which he must return to confirm his new identity. Actually, this identity is not new at all, but is a repetition of his father's great example. Repetition and revisiting the past, in fact, are the patterns on which the whole work is cut.

Telemachus's adventure both parallels and contains his father's longer excursion. We read little of Odysseus before book V, and he returns to Ithaca several books before Telemachus himself does. The sequence of events reinforces the epic's narrative structure of repeated loops and circles. The *Odyssey* visits Athene and Zeus on Olympus in its first and last books, follows Odysseus onto the island of Scheria, circles back to his earlier travails on the return from Troy, then returns to Scheria, and so forth. Indeed, Telemachus returns almost to the days before the Trojan War began when he leaves Ithaca. He visits Nestor enthroned in Pylos, just as he had been before the conflict; Menelaus is eerily reunited with Helen, almost as if nothing had ever happened to separate them. In meeting his father's old friends, Telemachus learns not only of the man's heroism, but also of his own resemblance in both face and character to the lost hero, attested equally by Nestor, Menelaus, and Helen. He starts to claim his future by immersing himself in the past; he starts to become himself by learning how he replicates his father.

The identity Telemachus seeks, then, does not arise from any spring of unique selfhood inside him. He learns what sort of man he ought to be by seeing his situation from the outside, by stepping out of the distorted nightmare of Ithaca to see life from the perspective of his father's generation, equally distant in place and time. The custom of unremitting hospitality, which attains a hypertrophic monstrosity on Ithaca when the all-consuming suitors occupy the household of the absent Odysseus, regains its proper dimension as the guarantor of peaceful and orderly conduct in the lands of Pylos and Sparta. Here, both Telemachus and the poem's audience quietly receive an education in the traditions of civility. Telemachus sees a grimmer potential in the mirror of Orestes, held constantly before his eyes by virtually everyone he meets on his journey. While explicitly offered to Telemachus in his quest to know his progenitor (and so himself) as a model of generational loyalty, the Orestian precedent implicitly raises a possibility too horrible ever to be named outright. Just as Orestes kills his mother, Clytaemnestra, to avenge her betrayal of his father, Agamemnon, so may Telemachus need to enforce Penelope's fidelity with the sword, should she falter in her long struggle to hold the suitors at bay. To be held a man, the analogy of Orestes implies, requires a son to identify himself absolutely with his father's affairs.

Indeed, while never literally required to slay his mother, Telemachus must nevertheless kill her influence over him in order to claim an adult male identity—kill her, that is, as a mothering figure.

The point of his little odyssey seems to be as much to escape his mother as to find his father, for the two actions are symbolically the same. Hiding the fact of his departure behind the robes of the old nursemaid Eurycleia instead of declaring his intentions to Penelope may indicate an imperfect degree of separation. But Telemachus shows, even before he sets foot on his hollow ship, that he is ready to assume the burdens and privileges of patriarchy by commanding his mother rather than being commanded by her. He does so by permitting the bard Phemius to sing the fates of the returning heroes of the Trojan War, affirming the value of the male, warrior's world of his father. He insists upon masculine control over language itself, in contrast with the woman's sphere of "the loom, the distaff" (p. 9), making the point both acutely and, for most modern readers, chillingly in its casual repressiveness. The text also suggests several times that Telemachus exhibits a lingering childishness in his very anxiety to demonstrate his maturity by rejecting the feminine so determinedly. Late in the work, he turns upon the slave maids who have made themselves the suitors' mistresses with more savagery than his father has sanctioned, killing them by the cruel and dishonorable means of hanging rather than dispatching them with the quick sword. More comically, he condemns with boyish heat his mother's failure to accept Odysseus as her returned husband on sight, at which "royal Odysseus smiled, and said . . . 'Telemachus, leave your mother in the hall to try my truth'" (p. 286). At the same time, the young man's journey toward identity demands that he take his place in a hierarchical structure that elevates men over women and leaders over followers. The fact that Telemachus takes command of a ship, planning and accomplishing an adventure in which his fellows acknowledge his leadership, establishes him as the true son of Odysseus with equal if not greater force than what he finds on his voyage. To know oneself in the Telemachy is to know one's place.

Such a system requires Penelope not only to know her place but virtually to become a place. Confined as Greek wives generally were to the interior life of the home, she can exercise no leadership even there. She cannot administer her missing husband's property; were she to admit his death, she would have to marry one of the suitors and be carried off to provide the foundation of his household, to bear his heirs and superintend the spinning of his cloth. Instead, she must maintain her identity with the home or risk the fate of Clytaemnestra. She must be the unaltered place to which Odysseus may return, just as women, nymphs, and witches give being to the destinations between which he travels: ten years in pursuit of Helen at Troy, nine years as Calypso's consort, a year of dalliance with Circe, a few final days as Nausicaä's potential fiancé. As little of the Trojan War as the epic recounts, Helen's flight from home and husband shadows every inch of its ground: The whole tragedy of combat and frustrated homecoming follows from the consequences of just one woman's mobility. That the reviled Clytaemnestra, who betrays her husband's bed and conspires with her lover to murder him, is also Helen's sister suggests that their twin offenses stem from a single root.

If male identity follows lineally in descent from father to son, if the son ideally inherits his father's exact slot in the social hierarchy, only the mother's fidelity can guarantee the legitimate succession of a male child who is genuinely his father's offspring. Indeed, in Greek medical theory, the mother's womb merely supplied the ground in which the male seed took hold and grew; again, the woman slipped from person to place. Any feminine movement, whether of Helen's body or Clytaemnestra's heart, undermines the system. Penelope, by contrast, demonstrates her transcendent worth by a brilliantly creative act of annulment: She delays the suitors by secretly unweaving in the concealing night the strands of the burial shroud of Läertes, which she has begged time to finish before she chooses her new mate. In the past thirty years or so, the image of Penelope endlessly weaving and unweaving the same garment, going no place and completing nothing, has come to serve as a cautionary symbol for the frustration of women's creativity, so powerfully does it encapsulate the consequences of the logic of gender hierarchy. In contrast to her son's challenge of becoming what he is not, Penelope must continue always to be what she has been.

Introduction

As Virginia Woolf noted, modern sympathies fall more easily on Clytaemnestra's side than on that of Agamemnon—who, after all, took the sacrificial knife to their daughter Iphigenia in order to satisfy oracles for the departure to Troy. While the Telemachy's assertion of hierarchical authority against the rule of chaos may have appealed to the uncertainties of the educated elite of the Renaissance (and after), it may well repel contemporary readers, however engaging they find the tale in other respects. But the *Odyssey* does not end after four books. The small odyssey of Telemachus takes the boy from his home island—all he has ever known—and reveals by contrast the nature of the conditions prevailing back on Ithaca. The great odyssey of his father carries the poem's audience entirely outside the realm of normal human reality—all we have ever known—and casts us into a series of inhuman worlds, some beautiful and some terrifying, against which we come to judge the values of the human community itself. The work thus sets the pattern of fabulous travel narratives from Dante's *Commedia* to *The Wizard of Oz* to the revealingly titled *2001: A Space Odyssey*.

The tale suggests the upper and lower bounds of (particularly masculine) behavior when Odysseus carries human custom into the semidivine worlds of the Phaeacians and the Cyclopes, whose common descent from Poseidon emphasizes their equal but opposite distance from normal reality. The victory Odysseus wins over the much larger, much stronger herdsman Polyphemus reflects the widespread belief of ancient agricultural societies that tilling the land marked the boundary between the civilized and the savage, superior and inferior. Indeed, the work constructs Cyclopean "society" in contrast with human society as utterly lacking not only farming, but any governmental or communal structures, any unit larger than the family. The Cyclopes see only half so well as humans, who live in social union with each other; hence, the single eye proves the downfall of Polyphemus. That Odysseus overcomes the giant largely by the use of words, whose meaning comes from a shared act of communication between people using a system communally inherited rather than individually created—that is, a language—further attests to the power of shared culture against the mere brute force of the mountainous Cyclopes, who defy even the gods. (Of course, the suitors, who show little respect for custom or for the council of elders that represents government on the island of Ithaca in the absence of its king, demonstrate the human capacity for monstrosity when men's eyes close to social responsibility.)

More tellingly, the episode ultimately reveals a fissure within the values set forth in the Telemachy. Despite his triumph, Odysseus cannot stand to remain a "Noman" to Polyphemus and reveals to the monster his true identity and lineage—in modern terms, practically giving away his home address, phone number, and ATM code. This act not only nearly allows the blinded Polyphemus to capsize the hero's ship by hurling boulders toward the sound of his voice, but directs the curse of Poseidon onto Odysseus as the self-confessed culprit in the maiming of the sea god's descendant. Thus, in his zeal to affirm his heroic identity, the very deed that seems to promise Telemachus a way to cure his land's disorder, Odysseus courts discord. He doubly endangers his crew by asserting himself at the expense of their safety from Polyphemus and Poseidon, reversing the relation of individual to communal needs that had seemed to be integral to his victory over the Cyclops. Examined in this distant mirror, a contradiction that is suppressed when Homer looks directly at his culture emerges: The hero's responsibility to demonstrate his greatness ill-suits the role of hierarchical leader for which his heroism is supposed to guarantee he is fit.

If, in his barbaric individualism, Polyphemus disguises what is finally a very human face behind a mask of monstrosity, then his cousins the Phaeacians conceal a virtual divinity in what seem to be merely human features. Sympathetic and generous, they accept the wrath of their father, Poseidon, to land the stranger Odysseus safely on Ithaca, first enriching him with greater treasure than he had obtained in the sack of Troy and lost in the wreck of his last ship before he washed up on Ogygia, the island of Calypso. The values of the Phaeacians' orderly, productive realm quietly challenge those even of the kingdoms Telemachus has visited on the Greek mainland, the epic's prior images of well-regulated society, throwing into question the whole heroic ethos of connecting masculine worth to military leadership. When the son of Alcinoüs goads Odysseus into showing his athletic prowess, he offers, in effect, to lick any man in the house. But his host gently reminds him of that house's different nature: "We are not faultless boxers, no, nor wrestlers; but in the foot-race we run swiftly, and in our ships excel. Dear to us ever is the feast, the harp, the dance, changes of clothes, warm baths, and bed" (p. 94). Rivalry without violence, bravery without warfare, peace without conquest: The paradise of Scheria may lie beyond human capacity, just as Poseidon finally removes the land itself from human access, but the achievements of the Grecian kings still diminish in its distant light.

Through the figure of Arete, the Phaeacian Queen, the episode particularly reconsiders the traditions into which the Telemachy initiates the youthful son of Odysseus. While Telemachus must turn from his mother to prove his maturity, Athene advises Odysseus to humble himself before the Phaeacian woman, whose status so differs from anything known in the Grecian world: "For of sound judgment, woman though she is, she has no lack; and those whom she regards, though men, find troubles clear away" (p. 80). Though Homer subsequently seems unable actually to depict Arete wielding power, so foreign a concept is this, his mere nod in this direction raises the possibility that not all is right with his own world's gender divisions. In particular, Arete's position is juxtaposed with those of Penelope and Helen. Like Arete, Helen surpasses her husband by reason of her descent from a major god; like Arete, Penelope shows surpassing wisdom, establishing herself as her husband's sole equal in stratagems (or he as hers). But neither of the Greek women has any public charge over men, exercising their powers only privately, even secretly. Helen's value lies in her beauty, not in her intelligence—indeed, the guile she employs while among the Trojans to coax the Greek warriors hidden in the belly of the wooden horse to reveal themselves makes her seem a dangerous figure. Penelope is driven to the lonely heroism of her silent resistance, misread even by her own son, precisely because she can render no judgments that the public world of men will respect: She cannot make the suitors quit the home she ostensibly controls. The reaction of Odysseus, when he later awakens alone and dazed on the shore of a home island he at first fails to recognize, measures to the inch how far Ithaca lies from paradise, even with its king at last restored. His reaction is at once comical and ugly: He abuses the Phaeacian sailors he immediately assumes have marooned him on some distant land, and even takes the outlandish precaution of counting the gifts they have themselves given him to ensure he has not been robbed.

Of all the strange worlds Odysseus visits—and I leave my readers the pleasure of exploring many of them without a map—the land of the dead, the voyage to which is known as the Nekyia (from *nekos*, dead body, corpse), apparently stands furthest from ordinary life. This voyage leaves Homer's audience with much greater knowledge than the manner of Odysseus's homecoming, its ostensible purpose, does. In narrative terms, a trip among the ghosts of the past would be far out of proportion to such limited returns; a story could more easily dispatch its hero to some oracle for such information. No, the Nekyia represents an encounter with ultimate knowledge, the knowledge of endings—of the story, of the hero's life, of human life itself. Most strikingly, the Homeric dead declare both directly and indirectly the final sovereignty of bodily existence. The fact that they cannot speak without a fresh infusion of the blood they lack shows the utter dependence of the bodiless dead on the embodied living. In contrast to later theologies that regarded the soul as the true essence of being, in the *Odyssey* the soul survives as a mere reminder of real existence, insubstantial as memory. As Anticleia, mother of Odysseus, informs her son, "like a dream the spirit flies away" (p. 136), an image that draws its power from the reality the dead commonly assume when we dream of them, only to vanish from our sight at waking.

For Homer, the departed intervene in present life only as shades cast in the minds of those whose hearts still beat. The way a poet envisions the afterlife reveals his or her (or his or her culture's) sense of the timeless, of what survives death. In the *Odyssey*, nothing of the individual remains when breath leaves the body, reputation and lineage alone outlasting time: All the spirits to whom Odysseus speaks bear great names, children, or both. The ordinary dead are not even acknowledged. And yet, the Nekyia reveals, fame lacks the value from the perspective of finality that it carries in the living world; again, the alternative reality forces a reevaluation of cherished assumptions. Meeting Achilles in the underworld, Odysseus proposes that even death can make little difference to so mighty a hero; just as his fame was secure among the living, so must he be a king among the dead. But the intangible reward of glory offers little consolation for an early death: "Better to be the hireling of a stranger," Achilles answers, "and serve a man of mean estate whose living is but small, than be the ruler over all these dead and gone" (p. 142). The Greek word translated as "hireling" is *thes*, which refers specifically to a laborer employed for a daily wage, a position even lower than that of a slave, who at least belonged to a household that had some concern for his or (usually) her welfare. To live as a *thes*, the antithesis of heroic glory, meant an almost total social exclusion, a faceless, unremembered anonymity. From the perspective of the dead—that is, taking the unavoidable fact of death into full account—the rage for identity typified by Odysseus's exultant declaration of self as he departed the island of the Cyclopes is not only dangerous, but fruitless. The immortality of fame is an empty bubble.

This leaves a son as the sole means to continue a man's existence beyond his own end. The poem's insistence on women's fidelity takes on new meaning from this perspective, being revealed as the consequence of male fears of annihilation. A man's children must positively have sprung from his own being if his real afterlife comes only through the continuation of his lineage, as both Agamemnon and Achilles affirm. The long catalogue of famous women who greet Odysseus at the gates of Hades all owe their fame—that is, the element of their existence that survives death—to their role as life-givers to male children. This fact emphasizes the idea that only passage through the gates of the womb balances passage through the gates of Hades, that women's power lies in their special connection to sexuality and birth. Paradoxically, such a system assigns women an equal association with death, as they are analogized to the productive earth from which life comes and to which it returns. Significantly, the episode makes continual reference to Persephone, the Queen of the Underworld, while entirely neglecting her husband. The periodic disappearance and reappearance of the goddess, daughter of the agricultural deity Demeter, creates the seasons, the dead months of the year corresponding with the time when Persephone's mother mourns her daughter's departure and the earth's revival with their joyous reunion.

The fact that Anticleia dies from the absence of her son shows how purely women's identity was bodily defined—the very existence of Anticleia, it seems, collapses when the prop of her motherhood is withdrawn. By so firmly tying women to the body, the poem avoids recognizing the idea that women might themselves possess less tangible identities whose continuation after death would concern them. Odysseus actually *talks* to none of the famous women who have won a kind of immortality through the success or failure of their children. Their importance, unlike that of Odysseus's old Trojan War companions, lies strictly—and probably, for most modern readers, depressingly—in the products of their bodies, not in their own ambitions and accomplishments (of which none are recorded). The poem fails even to remark that Leda bore Helen and Clytaemnestra, recording only her achievement in presenting her husband with sons who earned themselves a portion of immortality. While the Nekyia does far less than the Phaeacian episode to question the gender hierarchy that formed an inextricable part of the heroic code, it reveals the nature of male anxiety for women's sexual faith.

When Odysseus awakens from his dream-like voyage on the shore of his own island, he fails to recognize the place, asking: "To what men's land am I come now? Lawless and savage are they, with no regard for right, or are they kind to strangers and reverent toward the gods?" (p. 162). While the mists of Athene have produced the mariner's confusion, his questions do not vanish with their dissipation. Is Ithaca the ordered kingdom he left behind or a new realm of incurable savagery? And, after all the alternative worlds through which we have passed, to what land have we finally come? After meeting Arete and Polyphemus and Anticleia and Achilles and Circe and Calypso and the Sirens and the Lotus-eaters and many others, how do we now perceive Ithaca? The poem offers no unified answers, instead multiplying the complications it has engaged since Telemachus set sail for Pylos.

The first surprise of the Ithacan episode, at least to many modern readers, is its length; the landfall of Odysseus on his home shore marks only about the halfway point of the tale. Homer's buildup to the battle with the suitors is one of the slowest and most suspenseful in literature—even though his original audience knew the outcome from the start. As Alfred Hitchcock once observed, the sudden explosion of a bomb of which viewers know nothing generates a half-second's shock, while the slow ticking of a bomb of whose existence they do know generates a quarter-hour's suspense. Moreover, Homer fills the delay with its own significance. In the period between Odysseus's landing and the fight with the suitors, a series of recognition scenes unfolds, of disguises adopted and then penetrated or let fall. Odysseus reveals himself to his son, Telemachus, and to his loyal swineherd and cowherd. The old dog Argos, who had known his master as a pup, and the old nurse Eurycleia see on their own through the guise of age and poverty that Athene has helped the man of strategies don. To recognize Odysseus means more than simply to know who this particular individual is—or was, for if Odysseus remains unrecognized as the island's patriarch, if he cannot reclaim his old identity, he will become the old beggar he appears to be. To acknowledge the identity of this stranger as Odysseus is, in effect, to acknowledge authority itself, to demonstrate one's acquiescence to the whole system that legitimizes a king's rule. After all, no one who opposes the rights of Odysseus learns who the old beggar really is until he puts an arrow through Antinoüs's throat.

Not even such old, disloyal servants as Melantho and Melanthius show the slightest suspicion that the mysterious stranger they enjoy abusing is their dangerous master returned. Only those who submit themselves to the hierarchical system, who recognize their own places, can also recognize Odysseus. Indeed, Argos not only recognizes but directly mirrors his master, who also risks consignment to the dung heap in his disregarded age if he can no longer prove himself the man he used to be, bend the great bow he once wielded, and, in an image suggestive of continued sexual prowess, fire an arrow through a dozen axes.

The Telemachy's emphasis on the twin values of authority and identity dovetail with particular neatness in the token by which Odysseus is known. An old scar received years earlier in a boar hunt, the first heroic episode that vaulted the youth toward his maturity, made him who he is, written into his body so long as he lives. As in the Nekyia, bodily existence—bodily prowess and endurance— measure the value of life; indeed, the scar suggests that one defines oneself by exterior, bodily deeds, not by any individual interior psychology. The violence of Odysseus's reaction to his old nurse's discovery of the scar, a symbol of his passage from boyhood to maturity, even recalls the curt rejection of Penelope by her son, a parallel reinforced by the nurturing role Eurycleia has played for both father and son. In these respects, the return to Ithaca seems also to be a return to the familiar, hierarchical values presented to Telemachus on his miniature odyssey.

And yet identity is never so fluid as it is in the second half of the epic, authority never so elusive. Though the scar represents the absolute fixity of self, what saves Odysseus on Ithaca is his capacity not to be who he is. This same ability to reconstruct himself in accordance with the demands of circumstance freed him from the cave of Polyphemus and taught him how to approach Nausicaä. Were Odysseus merely to weave these impostures to overcome imminent danger, little sense of contradiction with the idea of a solid core of self would result. But such shifting marks Odysseus's character even more deeply than the scar does. So habitually does he transform himself into someone else that by the time he approaches his father, the aged Laërtes, in the guise of yet another wandering stranger, the excuse that he needs to test the old man's loyalty has worn nearly transparent. The hero's tendency to assume other selves has not only come to define him, it connects him most nearly with the divine. For the gods can be anything, as Athene's transformations into man, woman, child, and bird affirm; to be stuck as oneself is to be merely human. Odysseus reaches his apogee not by his glorious force of arms, but by his lies and fictions. In one of the most charming moments of the work, Athene recognizes their unity in owning the divine gift of the creation of what is not: "Bold, shifty, and insatiate of wiles, will you not now within your land cease from the false misleading tales which from the bottom of your heart you love? . . . you are far the best of men in plots and tales, and I of all the gods am famed for craft and wiles" (p. 165). When Odysseus acknowledges of his patron that "You take all forms" (p. 165), he might as well be talking about himself. Nor does the scar suffice to confirm the hero's identity to his feminine alter ego, Penelope. She acknowledges her husband only when he shows that he remembers the secret of their bed. Such a test of identity—with all the erotic overtones that a private, mutual knowledge of the bed evokes, an implicitly carnal knowledge—depends not on the exterior, public reputation preserved in that reminder of past deeds, the scar, but on a private, intangible, even unspeakable knowing of who someone is. Nowhere does the work come closer to identifying the interior sense of desire as the heart of selfhood.

The poem also equivocates in its rhetorical support for the hierarchical system by which the man at the top of the ladder, so long as he acts justly, exercises complete authority to enforce order down to the bottom rung. The careful differentiation the poem makes between the really vicious, the merely weak, and the nearly sympathetic suitors transforms the hero's slaughter of his foes from exultant triumph to, at best, regrettable necessity. While Homer never challenges the morality of Odysseus's actions, this differentiation modulates the emotional tone of his victory. Even more tellingly, the poem refuses to allow the killing of the suitors and their mistresses to be a resolution. Since the first book, the confrontation of Odysseus and the enemies occupying his house has been anticipated as a climax, a final judgment between chaos and authority. Surprisingly, it is nothing of the kind. Indeed, Odysseus's victory lasts only the length of a single night, after which he must embark on a new journey, leaving Penelope yet again to escape the vengeance of his victims' families. In the hills, he gathers fresh support from his father's household; the suitors' families pursue and the fighting begins all over again. Since what the poem seems to have advertised as Odysseus's greatest triumph fails to bring peace, the human capacity to enforce order by strength of arms falls into grave doubt. The killing only stops when the gods command it, forestalling its resumption by blacking out the bitter memories of the survivors. If memory itself leads men to war, how can it be in any king's power to make a lasting peace?

So Ithaca appears after the Odyssean tour of alternative worlds. And yet in a sense we remain in an alternative world even after the hero of the epic has come among the familiar scenes of his homeland: the alternative world of fiction. The second half of the epic makes readers more conscious of storytelling than ever, virtually offering a seminar on the nature and uses of fiction. When Odysseus spends his first night with his wife, he tells her the whole tale of the *Odyssey* in compressed and chronological form (p. 291). This condensation neatly contains the epic and at the same time alerts us by contrast to the complexities of the tale's nonchronological, expansive construction. For that matter, little occurs in the poem that is not also narrated; even the suitors tell the story of their slaughter amid the shades of the underworld, delighting Agamemnon. What is real, what lasts, it seems, is the story, not the event. Fictions may, of course, be simple lies; the disguised Odysseus deceives both Eumaeus and Penelope by claiming to be a Cretan veteran of the Trojan War who suffered difficulties among the Phoenicians and Egyptians—and who has encountered the great Odysseus himself. Every detail of this moonshine rings true, the tale confining itself to plausible circumstances among well-known peoples of the Mediterranean coast; as the narrator observes about his surrogate story-teller: "He made the many falsehoods of his tale seem like the truth" (p. 239). No monsters haunt the tracks of Aethon—the name Odysseus adopts in deceiving Penelope—no one hears the Sirens sing, no one changes form, and no one speaks to the dead. Within the confines of the poem, then, the apparently impossible (the actual voyage of Odysseus) is true and the entirely plausible (the journey Odysseus makes up) is false, implicitly suggesting that the truth of a story is not to be found in the accuracy of its events to what we perceive as daily reality, but in their significance, their capacity to show us some previously unknown way of understanding the world.

Most vitally, though, in a work that dwells so continually on the borders—it explores the intersection of living and dead, the flimsy barriers between human and inhuman, the double natures of authority and identity, and so on—the ideal of storytelling is to erase the boundary between the characters within the tale and the listeners outside it. When, in book XIV, a disguised Odysseus tells his swine-herd a story of a night he spent outside the gates of Troy when he was cold, the man recognizes the present relevance in the narrative of the past and hands the old beggar a coat. By his reception of the story, Eumaeus proves more than his loyalty to his absent master or the customs of hospitality; he shows his humanity, his willingness to recognize that another man's story is also his own, another man's discomfort his responsibility. To see themselves in the tales of others is precisely what Antinoüs and the other suitors fail to do, despite the explicit invitation of Odysseus, who warns them (in his beggar's rags) that he too prospered once but was brought low. The suitors fail to acknowledge their image in the old man's words—"What god has brought us this pest?" is the substance of Antinoüs's answer—and in so doing exclude themselves from humanity. It comes as little surprise when one of their number mocks poetic diction in aiming an empty jest at the old beggar's baldness (p. 232). The song reserved for those who fail to read themselves in another's story is only that sung by the bowstring, an analogy the poem makes explicit: "even as one well-skilled to play the lyre and sing stretches with ease round its new peg a cord, securing at each end the twisted sheep-gut; so without effort did Odysseus string the mighty bow" (p. 268). To rule oneself outside the common circle of humanity, in other words, is to die.

Each reader today faces the suitors' choice: to read the story as if it concerns himself—or herself—or to turn it aside as an extraordinarily old man's babble. No arrow will pierce the throat of those who make the latter choice. But a contracted sense of humanity may follow. Whether one regards the conflicts that the poem relates as fundamentally the same as or fundamentally different from those of our own time makes little difference. The poem largely does not offer an argument for the validity of the civilization that produced it, but instead allows the reader to view from different angles that world's ideas of life and death, women and men, order and chaos, war and peace, wealth and poverty, and so on. In this way, the *Odyssey* makes room for many sympathies. Its enduring wisdom is that only by encountering what seems unlike oneself does one come to gain any self-knowledge at all.

Robert Squillace teaches Cultural Foundations courses in the General Studies Program of New York University. He has published extensively on the field of modern British literature, most notably in his study *Modernism, Modernity and Arnold Bennett* (Bucknell University Press, 1997). His recent teaching has involved him deeply in the world of the ancients. He lives in Brooklyn with his wife, the medievalist Angela Jane Weisl.

A Note on the Translation

The text of the *Odyssey* found in this edition is substantially George Herbert Palmer's esteemed 1921 translation, one of the first to dispense with the archaisms, the "thees" and "thous," dear to earlier translators, in favor of a closer approximation to Homer's often colloquial tone. English itself, however, has continued to change since 1921, and usages that bordered on the everyday in Palmer's time now themselves sound antiquated. I have updated such language while doing my best to preserve the rhythmic force of Palmer's cadenced prose.

—Robert Squillace

THE ODYSSEY

BOOK I

The Council of the Gods and the Summons to Telemachus

Tell of the storm-tossed man, O Muse, who wandered long after he sacked the sacred citadel of Troy.[1] Many the men whose towns he saw, whose ways he proved; and many a pang he bore in his own breast at sea, while struggling for his life and his men's safe return. Yet even so, despite his zeal, he did not save his men; for through their own perversity they perished, having recklessly devoured the cattle of the exalted Sun, who therefore took away the day of their return. Of this, O goddess, daughter of Zeus, speak as thou wilt to us.

Now all the others who were saved from utter ruin were at home, safe both from war and sea. Him only, longing for his home and wife, the potent nymph Calypso, a heavenly goddess, held in her hollow grotto, desiring him to be her husband. Yet, when the time had come in the revolving years at which the gods ordained his going home to Ithaca, even then, among his kin, he was not freed from trouble. Yet the gods felt compassion, all save Poseidon, who steadily strove with godlike Odysseus till he reached his land.

But Poseidon now was with the far-off Ethiopians, remotest of mankind, who form two tribes, one at the setting of the Exalted one, one at his rising; awaiting there a sacrifice of bulls and rams. So sitting at the feast he took his pleasure. The other gods, meanwhile, were gathered in the halls of Zeus upon Olympus when thus began the father of men and gods; for in his mind he mused of gallant Aegisthus, whom Agamemnon's far-famed son, Orestes, slew. Mindful of him, he thus addressed the immortals:

"Lo, how men blame the gods! From us, they say, comes evil.

1

But through their own perversity, and more than is their due, they meet with sorrow; even as now Aegisthus, pressing beyond his due, married the lawful wife of the son of Atreus and slew her husband on his coming home. Yet he well knew his own impending ruin; for we ourselves forewarned him, dispatching Hermes, our clear-sighted killer of Argus, and told him not to slay the man nor woo the wife. 'For vengeance follows from Orestes, son of Atreus, when he comes of age and longs for his own land.' This Hermes said, but though he sought Aegisthus' good, he did not change his purpose. And now Aegisthus makes atonement for it all."

Then answered him the goddess, clear-eyed Athene: "Our father, son of Kronos, most high above all rulers, that man assuredly lies in befitting ruin.[2] So perish all who do such deeds! Yet is my heart distressed for wise Odysseus, hapless man, who, long cut off from friends, is meeting hardship upon a sea-encircled island, the navel of the sea. Woody the island is, and there a goddess dwells, daughter of evil-minded Atlas who knows the depths of every sea and through his power holds the tall pillars firm which keep earth and sky asunder. It is his daughter who detains this hapless, sorrowing man, ever with tender and insistent words enticing him to forgetfulness of Ithaca. And still Odysseus, through longing once to see the smoke of his native land would gladly die. Nevertheless, your heart turns not, Olympian one. Did not Odysseus pay you honor by the Argive ships and offer sacrifices on the plain of Troy? Why then are you so wrathful with him, Zeus?"

Then answered her cloud-gathering Zeus, and said: "My child, what word has passed the barrier of your teeth? How could I possibly forget princely Odysseus, who is beyond all mortal men in wisdom, beyond them too in giving honor to the immortal gods, who hold the open sky? No, but Poseidon, who encompasses the land, is ceaselessly enraged because Odysseus blinded of his eye the Cyclops, godlike Polyphemus, who of all Cyclops has the greatest power. A nymph, Thoösa, bore him, daughter of Phorcys, lord of the barren sea, for she within the hollow caves united with Poseidon. And since that day earth-shaking Poseidon does not indeed destroy Odysseus, but ever drives him wandering from his land. Come then, let us all here plan for his turning home. So shall Poseidon lay by his anger, unable, in defiance of us all, to strive with the immortal gods alone."

Then answered him the goddess, clear-eyed Athene: "Our father, son of Kronos, most high above all rulers, if it now please the blessed gods that wise Odysseus shall return to his own home, let us send Hermes forth—the Guide, the killer of Argus—into the island of Ogygia, straightway to tell the fair-haired nymph our steadfast purpose, that hardy Odysseus shall set forth upon his homeward way. I in the meanwhile go to Ithaca, to rouse his son yet more and to put vigor in his breast; that, summoning to an assembly the long-haired Achaeans,* he may denounce the band of suitors, men who continually butcher his huddling flocks and slow-paced, crook-horned oxen. To Sparta will I send him and to sandy Pylos, to try to learn of his dear father's coming, and so to win a good report among mankind."

So saying, under her feet she bound her beautiful sandals, immortal, made of gold, which carry her over the flood and over the boundless land swift as a breath of wind. She took her ponderous spear, tipped with sharp bronze, thick, long, and strong, with which she vanquishes the ranks of men,—of heroes, even,—when this daughter of a mighty sire is roused against them. Then she went dashing down the ridges of Olympus and in the land of Ithaca stood at Odysseus' gate, on the threshold of his court. Holding in hand his brazen spear, she seemed the stranger Mentes, a Taphian† leader. Here then she found the haughty suitors. They were amusing themselves with games of draughts before the palace door, seated on hides of oxen which they themselves had slain. Near by were pages and busy squires, some mixing wine and water in the bowls, others with porous sponges washing and laying tables, while others still carved them abundant meat.

By far the first to see Athene was princely Telemachus. For he

---

*Who would now be called Greeks.
†From the Greek island of Taphos.

was sitting with the suitors, sad at heart, picturing in mind his noble father,—how he might come from somewhere, make a scattering of the suitors, take to himself his honors, and be master of his own. Thus thinking while he sat among the suitors, Athene met his eye. Straight to the door he went, at heart disturbed to have a stranger stand so long before his gate.³ So drawing near and grasping her right hand, he took her brazen spear, and speaking in winged words he said: "Hail, stranger, here with us you shall be welcome; and by and by when you have tasted food, you shall make known your needs."

Saying this, he led the way, and Pallas Athene followed. When they were come within the lofty hall, he carried the spear to a tall pillar and set it in a well-worn rack, where also stood many a spear of hardy Odysseus. Athene herself he led to a chair and seated, spreading a linen cloth below. Good was the chair and richly wrought; upon its lower part there was a rest for feet. Beside it, for himself, he set a sumptuous seat apart from all the suitors, for fear the stranger, meeting rude men and worried by their din, might lose his taste for food; and then that he might ask him, too, about his absent father. Now water for the hands a servant brought in a beautiful pitcher made of gold, and poured it out over a silver basin for their washing, and spread a polished table by their side. And the grave housekeeper brought bread and placed before them, setting out food of many a kind, freely giving of her store. The carver, too, took platters of meat, and placed before them, meat of all kinds, and set their golden goblets ready; while a page, pouring wine, passed to and fro between them.

And now the haughty suitors entered. These soon took seats in order, on couches and on chairs. Pages poured water on their hands, maids heaped them bread in baskets, and young men brimmed the bowls with drink; and on the food spread out before them they laid hands. So after they had stayed desire for drink and food, then in their thoughts they turned to other things, the song and dance; for these attend a feast. A page put a beautiful harp into the hands of Phemius, forced to sing among the suitors; and touching the harp, he raised his voice and sang a pleasing song. Then said Telemachus to clear-eyed Athene, his head bent close, that others might not hear:

"Good stranger, will you feel offense at what I say? These things are all their care,—the harp and song,—an easy care when, making no amends, they eat the substance of a man whose white bones now are rotting in the rain, if lying on the land, or in the sea the waters roll them round. Yet were they once to see him coming home to Ithaca, they all would pray rather for speed of foot than stores of gold and clothing. But he, instead, by some hard fate is gone, and naught remains to us of comfort—no, not if any man on earth shall say he still will come. Passed is his day of coming. But now declare me this and plainly tell, who are you? Of what people? Where is your town and kindred? On what ship did you come? And how did sailors bring you to Ithaca? Whom did they call themselves? For I am sure you did not come on foot. And tell me truly this, that I may know full well if for the first time now you visit here, or are you my father's friend? For many foreigners once sought our home; because Odysseus also was a rover among men."

Then said to him the goddess, clear-eyed Athene: "Well, I will very plainly tell you all: Mentes I call myself, the son of wise Anchialus, and I am lord of the oar-loving Taphians. Even now I put in here, with ship and crew, when sailing over the wine-dark sea to men of a strange speech, to Temesê, for bronze.[4] I carry glittering iron. Here my ship lies, just off the fields outside the town, within the bay of Reithron under woody Neïon. Hereditary friends we count ourselves from early days, as you may learn if you will go and ask old lord Laërtes. He, people say, comes to the town no more, but far out in the country suffers hardship, an aged woman his attendant, who supplies him food and drink whenever weariness weighs down his knees, as he creeps about his slope of garden ground. Even now I came, for I was told your father was at home. But, as I see, the gods delay his journey; for surely nowhere yet on earth has royal Odysseus died; living, he lingers somewhere still on the wide sea, upon some sea-girt island, and cruel men constrain him, savage folk, who hold him there against his will. Yet, I will make a prophecy as the immortals prompt my mind and as I think will happen; although I am no prophet and have no skill in birds.[5] Not long shall he be absent from his own dear land, though iron fetters bind him. Some means he will devise to come away; for many a trick has he. But now, declare me this and plainly tell, if you indeed—so tall—are the true son of Odysseus. You surely are much like him in head and beautiful eyes. So often we were together before he embarked for Troy, where others too, the bravest of the Argives,* went in their hollow ships. But since that day I have not seen Odysseus, nor he me."

Then answered her discreet Telemachus: "Yes, stranger, I will plainly tell you all. My mother says I am his child; I myself do not know; for no one ever yet knew his own parentage. Yet would I were the son of some blest man on whom old age had come amongst his own possessions. But now, the man born most ill-fated of all human kind—of him they say I am, since this you ask me."

Then said to him the goddess, clear-eyed Athene: "Surely the gods meant that your house should never lack when they allowed Penelope to bear a son like you. But now declare me this and truly tell, what means the feast? What company is this? And what do you do here? Is it a drinking bout or wedding? It surely is no festival at common cost. How rude they seem, and wanton, feasting about the hall! A decent man must be indignant who comes and sees such outrage."

Then answered her discreet Telemachus: "Stranger,—since now you ask of this and question me,—in former days this house had promised to be wealthy and esteemed, so long as he was here; but the hard-purposed gods then changed their minds and shut him from our knowledge more than all men beside. For were he dead, I should not feel such grief, if he had fallen among comrades in the Trojan land, or in the arms of friends when the skein of war was

---

*Another word for Greeks.

wound. Then would the whole Achaean host have made his grave, and for his son in after days a great name had been gained. Now, silently the robber winds have swept him off. Gone is he, past all sight and hearing, and sighs and sorrows he has left to me. Yet now I do not grieve and mourn for him alone. The gods have brought me other sore distress. For all the nobles who bear sway among the islands,—Doulichion, Same, and woody Zacynthus,—and they who have the power in rocky Ithaca, all woo my mother and despoil my home. She neither declines the hated suit nor has she power to end it; while they with feasting impoverish my home and soon will bring me also to destruction."[6]

Stirred into anger, Pallas Athene spoke: "Alas! in simple truth you greatly need absent Odysseus, to lay hands on the shameless suitors. What if he came even now and here before his house stood at the outer gate, with helmet, shield, and his two spears,—even such as when I saw him first at my own home, drinking and making merry, on his return from Ephyra, from Ilus, son of Mermerus. For there on his swift ship went Odysseus, seeking a deadly drug in which to dip his brazen arrows. And Ilus did not give it, for he feared the immortal gods; my father, however, gave it, for he held him strangely dear. If as he was that day Odysseus now might meet the suitors, they all would find quick turns of fate and bitter rites of marriage. Still, on the gods' lap it lies if he shall come or no and if within his hall he shall find vengeance; but yours it is to plan to thrust these suitors from the hall. Give me your ear and heed my words. Tomorrow, summoning to an assembly the Achaean lords, announce your will to all and call the gods to witness! Bid the suitors all disperse, each to his own. And for your mother, if her heart inclines to marriage, let her go hence to her rich father's house. They there shall make the wedding and provide the many gifts which should accompany a well-loved child. Then for yourself I offer wise advice, and you should listen. Man the best ship you have with twenty oarsmen, and go in quest of your long-absent father. Perhaps some man may give you news or you may hear some rumor sent from Zeus, which oftenest carries tidings. First go to Pylos, and question royal Nestor. Then on to Sparta, to light-haired Menelaus; for he came last of all the armed Achaeans. And if you hear your father is alive and coming home, then, worn as you are, you might endure for one year more. But if you hear that he is dead,—no longer with the living,—you shall at once return to your own native land, and pile his mound and pay the funeral rites, full many, as are due, and you shall give your mother to a husband. Moreover, after you have ended this and finished all, within your mind and heart consider next how you may slay the suitors in your halls, whether by stratagem or open force. You must behave no longer like a child, being the man you are. Have you not heard what fame royal Orestes gained with all mankind, because he slew the slayer, wily Aegisthus, who had slain his famous father? You too, my friend,—for certainly I find you fair and tall,—be strong, that men hereafter born may speak your praise. Now I will go to my swift ship and to my comrades, who tire at my delay. Rely upon yourself. Heed what I say."

Then answered her discreet Telemachus: "Stranger, in this you speak with kindness, even as a father to a son. Never shall I forget it. But tarry now, though eager to be gone. Bathe, and refresh yourself; then glad at heart turn to your ship, bearing a gift of price and beauty, to be to you a keepsake from myself, even such a thing as dear friends give to friends."

Then answered him the goddess, clear-eyed Athene: "Keep me no longer now, when pressing on my way. And any gift your kind heart bids you give, give when I come again, for me to carry home. Choose one exceeding beautiful; yours in return shall be of equal worth."

Saying this, clear-eyed Athene passed away, even as a bird—a sea-hawk—takes its flight. Into his heart she had brought strength and courage, turning his thoughts upon his father more even than before. As he marked this in his mind, an awe came on him. He perceived it was a god. At once he sought the suitors, godlike himself.

To them the famous bard was singing, while they in silence sat and listened. He sang of the return of the Achaeans, the sad return, which Pallas Athene had appointed them on leaving Troy.

Now from her upper chamber, there heard this wondrous song the daughter of Icarius, heedful Penelope, and she descended the long stairway from her room, yet not alone; two slave-maids followed her.[7] And when the royal lady reached the suitors, she stood beside a column of the strong-built roof, holding before her face her delicate veil, while a faithful slave-maid stood upon either hand. Then bursting into tears, she said to the noble bard:

"Phemius, many another tale you know to charm mankind, exploits of men and gods, which bards make famous. Sit and sing one of these. The rest drink wine in silence. But cease this song, this song of woe, which harrows evermore the soul within my breast; because on me has fallen grief not to be appeased. So dear a face I miss, ever remembering one whose fame is wide through Hellas* and mid-Argos."

Then answered her discreet Telemachus: "My mother, why forbid the honored bard to cheer us in whatever way his mind is moved? The bards are not to blame, but rather Zeus, who gives to toiling men even as he wills to each. And for the bard, there is no ground for blaming if he sings the Danaäns'† cruel doom. The song which men most heartily applaud is that which comes the newest to their ears. Then let your heart and soul submit to listen; for not Odysseus only lost the day of his return at Troy, but many another perished also. No, seek your chamber and attend to matters of your own,—the loom, the distaff,—and bid the women ply their tasks.[8] Words are for men, for all, especially for me; for power within this house rests here."

Amazed, she turned to her own room again, for the wise saying of her son she laid to heart. And coming to the upper chamber with her maids, she there bewailed Odysseus, her dear husband, till on her lids clear-eyed Athene caused a sweet sleep to fall.

---

*A region in central Greece.
†Homer's third general term for Greeks.

But the suitors broke into uproar up and down the dusky hall, and longed to win her favor. Then thus discreet Telemachus began to speak: "Proud suitors of my mother, let us now enjoy our feast and have no brawling. For a pleasant thing it is to hear a bard like this, one who is like the gods in voice. But in the morning we will have a meeting of the assembly—let every man be there—and I shall tell you then in plainest terms to quit my halls. Seek other tables and eat what is your own, changing from house to house! Or if it seems to you more profitable and pleasant to spoil the substance of a single man without amends, go wasting on! But I will call upon the gods that live forever and pray that Zeus may grant me requital for your deeds. Then beyond all amends, here in this house you shall yourselves be spoiled."

He spoke, and all with teeth set in their lips marveled because Telemachus had spoken boldly. Then said Antinoüs, Eupeithes' son: "Telemachus, surely the gods themselves are training you to be a man of lofty tongue and a bold speaker. But may the son of Kronos never make you king in sea-encircled Ithaca, although it is by birth your heritage!"

Then answered him discreet Telemachus: "Antinoüs, will you feel offense at what I say? Willingly would I take the rule, if Zeus would grant it. Do you suppose a kingship is the worst fate in the world? Why, it is no bad thing to be a king! His house grows quickly rich and he himself receives more honor. Still, here in sea-encircled Ithaca are many other lords of the Achaeans, young and old, some one of whom may take the place, since royal Odysseus now is dead. But I myself will be the lord of our own house and of the slaves which royal Odysseus brought as prizes home."

Then answered him Eurymachus, the son of Polybus: "Telemachus, in the gods' lap it lies to say which one of the Achaeans shall be king in sea-encircled Ithaca. Your substance may you keep and of your house be lord; may the man never come who, heedless of your will, shall strip you of that substance while men shall dwell in Ithaca. But, good sir, I would ask about this stranger—whence the man comes, and of what land he calls himself. Where are his kinsmen and his native fields? Does he bring tidings of your father, or is he come with hope of his own gains? How hastily he went! Not waiting to be known! And yet he seemed no low-born fellow by the face."

Then answered him discreet Telemachus: "Eurymachus, as for my father's coming, that is at an end. Tidings I trust no more, let them come whence they may. Nor do I heed such divinations as my mother seeks, summoning a diviner to the hall. This stranger is my father's friend, a man of Taphos; Mentes he calls himself, the son of wise Anchialus, and he is lord of the oar-loving Taphians."

So spoke Telemachus, but in his mind he knew the immortal goddess. Meanwhile the suitors to dancing and the boisterous song turned merrily, and waited for the evening to come on. And on their merriment dark evening came. So then, desiring rest, they each departed homeward.

But off the beautiful court where a chamber was built high upon commanding ground, Telemachus now went to bed with many doubts in mind. And walking by his side, with blazing torch, went faithful Eurycleia, daughter of Ops, Peisenor's son, whom once Laërtes bought for himself when she was but a girl, and paid the price of twenty oxen. He gave her equal honor with the mistress of his house, but never touched her person or annoyed his wife.

She it was now who bore the blazing torch beside Telemachus; for she of all the handmaids loved him most and was his nurse when little. He opened the doors of the strong chamber, sat down upon the bed, pulled his soft tunic off, and laid it in the wise old woman's hands. Folding and smoothing out the tunic, she hung it on a peg beside the well-bored bedstead, then left the chamber, and by its silver ring pulled to the door, drawing the bolt home by its strap. So there Telemachus, all the night long, wrapped in a fleece of wool, pondered in mind the course Athene counseled.

Book II

The Assembly at Ithaca and the Departure of Telemachus

Soon as the early, rosy-fingered dawn appeared,[9] the dear son of Odysseus rose from bed, put on his clothes, slung his sharp sword about his shoulder, under his shining feet bound his fair sandals, and came forth from his chamber in bearing like a god. At once he bade the clear-voiced heralds summon to an assembly the long-haired Achaeans.[10] Those summoned, and these gathered very quickly. So when they were assembled and all had come together, he went himself to the assembly, holding in hand a bronze spear,—yet not alone, two swift dogs followed after,—and marvelous was the grace Athene cast about him, that all the people gazed as he drew near. He sat down in his father's seat; the elders made him way.

The first to speak was lord Aegyptius, a man bowed down with age, who knew a thousand things. His dear son Antiphus, a spearman, had gone with godlike Odysseus in the hollow ships to Ilios, famed for horses. The savage Cyclops killed him in the deep cave and on him made a supper last of all. Three other sons there were; one joined the suitors,—Eurynomus,—and two still kept their father's farm. Yet not because of these did he forget to mourn and miss that other. With tears for him, he thus addressed the assembly, saying:

"Listen now, men of Ithaca, to what I say. Never has our assembly once been held, no single session, since royal Odysseus went away in hollow ships. Who is it calls us now so strangely? Who has such urgent need? Young or old is he? Has he heard tidings of the army's coming and here brings news which he was first to learn? Or has he

12

other public business to announce and argue? At any rate, a true, good man he seems. Good luck attend him! May Zeus accomplish all the good his mind intends!"

As thus he spoke, the dear son of Odysseus rejoiced at what was said and kept his seat no longer. He burned to speak. He rose up in the midst of the assembly, and in his hand a herald placed the sceptre,—a herald named Peisenor, discreet of understanding. Then turning first to the old man, he thus addressed him:

"Sir, not far off is he, as you full soon shall know, who called the people hither; for it is I on whom has come sore trouble. No tidings of the army's coming have I heard, which I would plainly tell to you so soon as I have learned; nor have I other public business to announce and argue. Rather it is my private need, ill falling on my house in twofold ways. For first I lost my noble father, who was formerly your king,—kind father as ever was,—and now there comes a thing more grievous still, which soon will utterly destroy my home and quite cut off my substance. Suitors beset my mother sorely against her will, sons of the very men who are the leaders here. They will not go to the house of Icarius, her father, let him name the bride-gifts of his daughter and give her then to whom he will, whoever meets his favor; but haunting this house of ours day after day, killing our oxen, sheep, and fatted goats, they hold high revel, drinking sparkling wine with little heed. Much goes to waste, for there is no man here fit like Odysseus to keep damage from our doors. We are not fit ourselves to guard the house; attempting it, we should be pitiful, unskilled in conflict. Guard it I would, if only strength were mine. For deeds are done not to be longer borne, and with no decency my house is plundered. Shame you should feel yourselves, and some respect as well for neighbors living near you, and awe before the anger of the gods, lest it chances they may turn upon you, vexed with your evil courses. No, I entreat you by Olympian Zeus, and by that Justice which dissolves and gathers men's assemblies, forbear, my friends! Leave me to pine in bitter grief alone, unless indeed my father, good Odysseus, ever in malice wronged the armed Achaeans, and in return for that you now with malice do me wrong, urging these people on. Better for me it were you should yourselves devour my stores and herds. If you devoured them, perhaps some day there might be payment made; for we would constantly pursue you through the town, demanding back our substance till all should be restored. Now, woes incurable you lay upon my heart."

In wrath he spoke, and dashed the sceptre to the ground, letting his tears burst forth, and pity fell on all the people. So all the rest were silent; none dared to make Telemachus a bitter answer. Antinoüs alone made answer, saying:

"Telemachus, of the lofty tongue and the unbridled temper, what do you mean by putting us to shame? On us you would be glad to fasten guilt. I tell you the Achaean suitors are not at all to blame; your mother is to blame, whose craft exceeds all women's. The third year is gone by, and fast the fourth is going since she began to mock the hearts in our Achaean breasts. To all she offers hopes, has promises for each, and sends each messages, but her mind has different schemes. Here is the last pretext she cunningly devised. Within the hall she set up a great loom and went to weaving; fine was the web and very large; and then to us said she: 'Young men who are my suitors, though royal Odysseus now is dead, forbear to urge my marriage till I complete this robe,—its threads must not be wasted,—a shroud for lord Laërtes, against the time when the sad doom of death that lays men low shall overtake him. Achaean wives about the land, I fear, might give me blame if he should lie without a shroud, he who had great possessions.' Such were her words, and our high hearts assented. Then in the daytime would she weave at the great web, but in the night unravel, after her torch was set. Thus for three years she hid her craft and cheated the Achaeans. But when the fourth year came, as time rolled on, then at the last one of her slave-maids, who knew full well, confessed, and we discovered her unraveling the splendid web; so then she finished it, against her will, by force. Wherefore to you the suitors make this answer, that you yourself may understand in your own heart, and that the Achaeans all may understand. Send forth your mother! Bid her to marry whomever her father wills and him who pleases her! Or will she weary longer yet the sons of the Achaeans, mindful at heart of what Athene gave her in large measure, skill in fair works, shrewd wits, and such a craft as we have never known even in those of old, those who were long ago fair-haired Achaean women,—Tyro, Alcmene, and crowned Mycene,[11]—no one of whom in judgment matched Penelope: and yet, in truth, this time she judged not wisely. For just so long shall men devour your life and substance as she retains the mind the gods put in her breast at present. Great fame she brings herself, but brings on you the loss of large possessions; for we will never go to our estates, nor elsewhere either, till she shall marry an Achaean—whom she will."

Then answered him discreet Telemachus: "Antinoüs, against her will I cannot drive from home the one who bore and reared me. My father is far away,—living or dead,—and hard it were to pay the heavy charges to Icarius which I needs must, if of my will alone I send my mother forth. For from her father's hand I shall meet ills, and Heaven will send me more, when my mother calls upon the dread Avengers* as she forsakes the house; blame too will fall upon me from mankind. Therefore that word I never will pronounce; and if your hearts chafe at your footing here, then quit my halls! Try other tables and eat what is your own, changing from house to house! Or if it seems to you more profitable and pleasant to spoil the substance of a single man without amends, go wasting on! But I will call upon the gods that live forever and pray that Zeus may grant me requital for your deeds. Then beyond all amends, here in this house you shall yourselves be spoiled!"

So spoke Telemachus, and answering him far-seeing Zeus sent forth a pair of eagles, flying from a mountain peak on high. These for a time moved on along the wind, close by each other and with outstretched wings; but as they reached the middle of the many-voiced assembly, wheeling about they briskly flapped their wings,

---

*The Furies, who emerge from the underworld to haunt criminals.

glared at the heads of all, and death was in their eyes. Then with their claws tearing each other's cheek and neck, they darted to the right, across the town and houses. Men marveled at the birds, as they beheld, and pondered in their hearts what they might mean. And to the rest spoke old lord Halitherses, the son of Mastor; for he surpassed all people of his time in understanding birds and telling words of fate. He with good will addressed them thus, and said:

"Listen now, men of Ithaca, to what I say; and to the suitors especially I speak, declaring how there rolls on them a mighty wave of woe. Odysseus will not long be parted from his friends, but even now is near, sowing the seeds of death and doom for all men here. Yes, and on many others too shall sorrow fall who dwell in far-seen Ithaca! But long before that, let us consider how to check these men, or rather, let them check themselves, at once their wiser way. And not as inexpert I prophesy, but with sure knowledge. For this I say: all that comes true which I declared the day the Argive host took ship for Ilios, and with them also wise Odysseus went. I said that after suffering much, and losing all his men, unknown to all, in the twentieth year he should come home; and now it all comes true."

Then answered him Eurymachus, the son of Polybus: "Go home, old man, and play the prophet to your children, or else they may have trouble in the days to come! On matters here I am a better prophet than yourself. Plenty of birds flit in the sunshine, but not all are fateful. As for Odysseus, far away he died; and would that you had perished with him! You would not then be prating so of reading signs, nor would you, when Telemachus is hot, thus press him on, looking for him to send your house some gift. But this I tell you, and it shall come true; if you, who know all that an old man knows, delude this youth with talk and urge him on to anger, it shall be in the first place all the worse for him, for he shall accomplish nothing by aid of people here, while on yourself, old man, we will inflict a fine which it will grieve you to the soul to pay. Bitter indeed shall be your sorrow. And to Telemachus, here before all, I give this counsel. Let him instruct his mother to go to her father's house. They there shall make the wedding and arrange the many gifts which should accompany a well-loved child; for not, I think, till then will the sons of the Achaeans quit their rough wooing. No fear have we of any man, not even of Telemachus, so full of talk. Nothing we care for auguries which you, old man, idly declare, making yourself the more detested. So now again, his substance shall be miserably devoured, and no return be made, so long as she delays the Achaeans in her marriage. Moreover we will wait here many a day, as rivals for her charms, and not seek other women suitable for each to marry."

Then answered him discreet Telemachus: "Eurymachus and all you other lordly suitors, this will I urge no longer; I have no more to say; for now the gods and all the Achaeans understand. But give me a swift ship with twenty comrades, to help me make a journey up and down the sea; for I will go to Sparta and to sandy Pylos, to learn about the coming home of my long-absent father. Perhaps some man may give me news or I may hear some rumor sent from Zeus, which oftenest carries tidings. If I shall hear my father is alive and coming home, worn as I am, I might endure for one year more. But if I hear that he is dead,—no longer with the living,—I will at once return to my own native land, and pile his mound and pay the funeral rites, full many, as are due, and then will give my mother to a husband."

So saying, down he sat; and up rose Mentor, who was the friend of gallant Odysseus. On going with the ships, Odysseus gave him charge of his whole house, that all should heed their elder and he keep all safe and sound. He with good will addressed them thus, and said:

"Listen now, men of Ithaca, to what I say. Never henceforth let sceptered king be truly kind and gentle, nor let him in his mind heed righteousness. Let him instead ever be stern, and work unrighteous deeds; since none remembers princely Odysseus among the people whom he ruled, kind father though he was. No charge I make against the haughty suitors for doing deeds of violence in insolence of heart; for they at hazard of their heads thus violently devour the household of Odysseus, saying he will come no more.

But with you other people I am angered, because you all sit still, and, uttering not a word, do not resist the suitors,—they so few and you so many."

Then answered him Evenor's son, Leiocritus: "Mischievous Mentor, crazy-witted, what do you mean by urging these to put us down? Hard would it be, for many more than we, to fight with us on question of our food! Indeed, should Ithacan Odysseus come himself upon us lordly suitors feasting in his house, and be resolved to drive us from the hall, his wife would have no joy, however great her longing, over his coming; but here he should meet shameful death, fighting with more than he. You spoke unwisely! Come, people, then, turn to your own affairs! For this youth here, Mentor shall speed his voyage, and Halitherses too, for they are from of old his father's friends; but I suspect he still will sit about, gather his news in Ithaca, and never make the voyage."

He spoke, and hastily dissolved the assembly. So they dispersed, each to his home; but the suitors sought the house of princely Odysseus.

Telemachus, however, walked alone along the shore, and, washing his hands in the foaming water, prayed to Athene: "Hear me, thou god who camest yesterday here to our home, and badst me go on shipboard over the misty sea to ask about the coming home of my long-absent father. All thy commands the Achaeans hinder, chiefly the suitors in their wicked pride."

So spoke he in his prayer, and near him came Athene, likened to Mentor in her form and voice, and speaking in winged words she said:

"Telemachus, henceforth you must not be a base man nor a foolish, if in you stirs the brave soul of your father, and you like him can give effect to deed and word. So shall this voyage not be vain and fruitless. But if you are not the very son of him and of Penelope, then am I hopeless of your gaining what you seek. Few sons are like their fathers; most are worse, few better. Yet because you henceforth will not be base nor foolish, nor do you wholly lack the wisdom of Odysseus, there is good hope you will one day accomplish all. Disregard, then, the mind and mood of the mad suitors, for they are in no way wise or upright men. Nothing they know of death and the dark doom which now is near, nor know how all shall perish in a day. But for yourself, the voyage you plan shall not be long delayed. So truly am I your father's friend, I will provide you a swift ship and be myself your comrade. But you go to the palace, mix with the suitors, and prepare the stores, securing all in vessels,—wine in jars, and barley-meal, men's marrow, in tight skins,—while I about the town will soon collect a willing crew. The ships are many in sea-encircled Ithaca, ships new and old. Of these I will select the best, and quickly making ready we will sail the open sea."

So spoke Athene, daughter of Zeus. No longer then lingered Telemachus when he heard the goddess speak. He hastened to the house, though with a heavy heart, and at the palace found the haughty suitors flaying goats and broiling swine within the court. Antinoüs laughingly came forward to Telemachus, and holding him by the hand he spoke, and thus addressed him:

"Telemachus, of the lofty tongue and the unbridled temper, do not again grow sore in heart at what we do or say! No, eat and drink just as you used to do. All you have asked of course the Achaeans will provide,—the ship and the picked crew,—to help you quickly find your way to hallowed Pylos, seeking for tidings of your noble father."

Then answered him discreet Telemachus: "Antinoüs, I cannot, putting by my will, sit at the feast with you rude men and calmly take my ease. Was it not quite enough that in the days gone by you suitors wasted much good property of mine, while I was still a helpless child? But now that I am grown and hear and understand what people say, and in me too the spirit swells, I will try to bring upon your heads an evil doom whether I go to Pylos or remain here in this land. But go I will—nor vain shall be the voyage whereof I speak—go even as a passenger with others, since I can have command of neither ship nor crew. So seemed it best to you."

He spoke, and from the hand of Antinoüs quietly drew his own. Meanwhile, the suitors in the house were busy with their meal. They mocked him, jeering at him in their talk, and a rude youth would say:

"Really, Telemachus is plotting for our ruin! He will bring champions from sandy Pylos; or even from Sparta, so deeply is he stirred; or else he means to go to Ephyra,* that fruitful land, and fetch thence deadly drugs to drop into our wine-bowl and so destroy us all."

Then would another rude youth answer thus: "If he goes off upon a hollow ship and wanders far from friends, who knows but he too may be lost, just as Odysseus was! And that would make us still more trouble; for all his goods we then must share, and to his mother give the house, for her to keep—her and the one who gets her."

So ran their talk. Meanwhile Telemachus passed down the house into his father's large and high-roofed chamber, where in a pile lay gold and bronze, clothing in chests, and stores of fragrant oil. Great jars of old delicious wine were standing there, holding within pure liquor fit for gods, in order ranged along the wall, in case Odysseus, after toil and trouble, ever came home again. Shut were the folding-doors, close-fitting, double; and here both night and day a housewife stayed, who in her watchful wisdom guarded all—Eurycleia, daughter of Ops, Peisenor's son. To her now spoke Telemachus, calling her to the room:

"Good nurse, come draw me wine in jars, sweet wine, the mellowest next to that you keep, thinking that ill-starred man will one day come—high-born Odysseus—safe from death and doom. Fill twelve and fit them all with covers. Then pour me barley into well-sewn sacks. Let there be twenty measures of ground barley-meal. None but yourself must know. Get all together, and I tonight will fetch them, so soon as my mother goes to her chamber seeking rest; for I am going to Sparta and to sandy Pylos, to try to learn of my dear father's coming."

As he said this, his dear nurse Eurycleia cried aloud and sorrow-

---

*The location of this land has not been determined.

fully said in winged words: "Ah, my dear child, how came such notions in your mind? Where will you go through the wide world, our only one, our darling! High-born Odysseus is already dead, far from his home in some strange land. And now these men, the instant you are gone, will plot against you harm, that you by stealth may be cut off, and they thus share with one another all things here. No, you stay here, abiding with your own! You have no need to suffer hardship, roaming over barren seas."

Then answered her discreet Telemachus: "Courage, good nurse! for not without the gods' approval is my purpose. But swear to speak no word of this to my dear mother till the eleventh or twelfth day comes, or until she shall miss me and hear that I am gone, that so she may not stain her beautiful face with tears."

He spoke, and the old woman swore by the gods a solemn oath. Then after she had sworn and ended all that oath, she straightway drew him wine in jars, and poured him barley into well-sewn sacks. Telemachus, meanwhile, passed through the house and joined the suitors.

Now a new plan the goddess formed, clear-eyed Athene. In likeness of Telemachus, she went throughout the town, and, approaching one and another man, gave them the word, bidding them meet by the swift ship at eventide. Noëmon next, the gallant son of Phronius, she begged for a swift ship; and this he gladly promised.

Now the sun sank and all the ways grew dark. Then she drew the swift ship to the sea and put in all the gear that well-benched vessels carry; she moored her by the harbor's mouth; the good crew gathered round about, and the goddess heartened each.

Then a new plan the goddess formed, clear-eyed Athene. She hastened to the house of princely Odysseus, there on the suitors poured sweet sleep, confused them as they drank, and made the cups fall from their hands. They hurried off to rest throughout the town, and did not longer delay, for sleep fell on their eyelids. Then to Telemachus spoke clear-eyed Athene, calling him forth before the stately hall, likened to Mentor in her form and voice:

"Telemachus, already your armed comrades sit at the oar and wait your word to start. Let us be off, and not lose time upon the way."

Saying this, Pallas Athene led the way in haste, he following in the footsteps of the goddess. And when they came to the ship and to the sea, they found upon the shore their long-haired comrades, to whom thus spoke revered Telemachus:

"Up, friends, and let us fetch the stores; all are collected at the hall. My mother knows of nothing, nor do the handmaids either. One alone had my orders."

So saying, he led the way, the others followed after; and bringing all the stores into their well-benched ship they stowed them there, even as the dear son of Odysseus ordered. Then came Telemachus aboard; but Athene led the way, and at the vessel's stern she sat down, while close at hand Telemachus was seated. The others loosed the cables, and coming aboard themselves took places at the pins. A favorable wind clear-eyed Athene sent, a brisk west wind that sang along the wine-dark sea. And now Telemachus, inspiring his men, bade them lay hold upon the tackling, and they listened to his call. Raising the pine-wood mast, they set it in the hollow socket, binding it firm with forestays, and tightened the white sail with twisted oxhide thongs. The wind swelled out the belly of the sail, and round the stem loudly the rippling water sang as the ship started. Onward she sped, forcing a passage through the waves. Making the tackling fast throughout the swift black ship, the men brought bowls brimming with wine, and to the gods, that never die and never have been born, they poured it forth—chiefest of all to her, the clear-eyed child of Zeus. So through the night and early dawn did the ship cleave her way.

BOOK III

At Pylos

And now the sun, leaving the beauteous bay, rose in the brazen sky, to shine for the immortals and for mortal men upon the fruitful fields; and the two drew near to Pylos, the stately citadel of Neleus. The townsfolk here were offering sacrifice upon the shore, slaying black bulls to the dark-haired Earth-shaker.* Nine groups there were, five hundred men in each, and nine bulls were presented for each group. The inward parts were tasted and the thighs were burning to the god, when the two ran swiftly in, hauled up and furled their trim ship's sail, brought her to anchor, and came forth themselves. So from the ship came forth Telemachus, but Athene led the way, and thus began the goddess, clear-eyed Athene:

"Telemachus, no shyness now! For to accomplish this you crossed the sea, to make inquiry for your father and to learn where he lies buried and what fate he met. Go then straight forward to the horseman Nestor, and let us know what is the wisdom hidden in his breast. Beg him yourself to tell the very truth. Falsehood he will not speak, for just and wise is he."

Then answered her discreet Telemachus: "Mentor, how can I go? How importune him? In subtleties of speech I am not practised. Shyness befits a youth when questioning his elders."

Then said to him the goddess, clear-eyed Athene: "Telemachus, some promptings you will find in your own breast, and Heaven will send still more; for, certainly, not unbefriended of the gods have you been born and bred."

---

*Poseidon.

Saying this, Pallas Athene led the way in haste, he following in the footsteps of the goddess. So they approached the gathering of the men of Pylos and the group where Nestor sat among his sons. Round him his people, making the banquet ready, were roasting meats and putting pieces on the spits. But as they saw the strangers, all the men crowded near, gave hands in welcome, and asked them to sit down; and Nestor's son Peisistratus,[12] approaching first, took each one by the hand and placed them at the feast on some soft fleeces laid upon the sands, beside his brother Thrasymedes and his father. He gave them portions of the inward parts, poured out some wine into a golden cup, and, offering welcome, said to Pallas Athene, daughter of aegis-bearing Zeus:

"Here, stranger, make a prayer to lord Poseidon. It is his feast you find at this your coming. Then, after you have poured and prayed as is befitting, give this man too the cup of honeyed wine for him to pour; for I suppose he also prays to the immortals. All men have need of gods. But he is the younger, young as I myself; so I will give you first the golden cup."

Saying this, he placed the cup of sweet wine in her hand. And Athene was pleased to find the man so wise and courteous, pleased that he gave her first the golden cup. Forthwith she prayed a fervent prayer to lord Poseidon:

"Listen, Poseidon, you who encompass the land, and count it not too much to give thy suppliants these blessings. First upon Nestor and his sons bestow all honor; then to the rest grant gracious recompense, to all the men of Pylos, for their splendid sacrifice; and grant still further that Telemachus and I may sail away having accomplished that for which we came upon our swift black ship."

Thus did she pray, and was herself fulfilling all. To Telemachus she passed the goodly double cup, and in like manner also prayed the dear son of Odysseus. But when the rest had roasted the outer flesh and drawn it off, they divided out the portions and held a glorious feast. And after they had stayed desire for drink and food, then thus began the Gerenian* horseman Nestor:

---

*From a region of Sparta.

"Now, then, it is more suitable to prove our guests and ask them who they are, now they are refreshed with food. Strangers, who are you? Where do you come from, sailing the watery ways? Are you upon some business? Or do you rove at random, as the pirates roam the seas, risking their lives and bringing ill to strangers?"[13]

Then answered him discreet Telemachus, plucking up courage; for Athene herself put courage in his heart to ask about his absent father and to win a good report among mankind:

"O Nestor, son of Neleus, great glory of the Achaeans, you ask me whence we are, and I will tell you. We are of Ithaca, under Mount Neïon. Our business is our own, no public thing, as I will show. I come afar to seek some tidings of my father, royal hardy Odysseus, who once, they say, fought side by side with you and sacked the Trojan town. For as to all the others who were in the war at Troy we have already learned where each man met his sorry death; but this man's death the son of Kronos left unknown. No one can surely say where he has died; whether borne down on land by foes, or on the sea among the waves of Amphitrite.* Therefore I now come here to your knees to ask if you will tell me of my father's sorry death, whether you saw it for yourself with your own eyes, or from some other learned that he was lost; for to exceeding grief his mother bore him. Use no mild word nor yield to pity out of regard for me, but tell me fully all you chanced to see. I do entreat you, if ever my father, good Odysseus, in word or deed kept faith with you there in the Trojan land where you Achaeans suffered, be mindful of it now; tell me the very truth."

Then answered him the Gerenian horseman Nestor: "Ah, friend, you make me call to mind the pains we bore in that far land, untamed in spirit as we sons of the Achaeans were—all we endured on shipboard on the misty sea, coasting for plunder where Achilles led; and all our fightings round the stronghold of King Priam, where so many of our bravest perished. There warlike Ajax lies, and there

---

*Sea goddess; wife of Poseidon.

Achilles. There too Patroclus, the peer of gods in wisdom. There my own son, so strong and gallant, Antilochus, exceeding swift of foot, a famous fighter. And many other woes we had, added to these. What mortal man could count them? No, should you tarry five or six years here to ask what woes the great Achaeans suffered, you would return to your own land, wearied before I could tell.

"For nine years long we plotted their destruction, busy with craft of every kind; yet still the son of Kronos hardly brought us through. With one man there none sought to vie in wisdom; for far beyond us all in craft of every kind was royal Odysseus, your father,—if you are indeed his child. I am amazed to see. And yet, how fitting are your words! One would not say a youth could speak so fitly. Well, all that while, royal Odysseus and I never once differed in the assembly or the council; but with one heart, with will and steadfast purpose, we planned how all might best be ordered for the Argives.

"Yet after we overthrew the lofty town of Priam, when we went away in ships and God dispersed the Achaeans, ah, then Zeus purposed in his mind a sad voyage for the Argives! For in no way prudent and upright were all. So, many a one came to an evil end, through the fell wrath of the dread father's clear-eyed child, who caused a strife between the two sons of Atreus. For these two summoned to an assembly all the Achaeans, in haste, not in due order, at the setting sun; and heavy with wine the young Achaeans came. Then each declared the reason why he called the host together. Now Menelaus exhorted all the Achaeans to turn their thoughts toward going home on the broad ocean-ridges; but this pleased Agamemnon not at all. He wished to stay the host and offer sacred hecatombs, that so he might appease the dread wrath of Athene,—ah, fool! who did not know she might not be persuaded; for a purpose is not lightly changed in gods who live forever. Thus stood the brothers exchanging bitter words, while up sprang other armed Achaeans in wild din, and both the plans found favor. That night we rested, nursing in our breasts hard thoughts of one another. Zeus was preparing us the ill that comes from wrong. At dawn we dragged our ships into the sacred sea, and put therein our goods and the low-girdled women. Half of the host held back, remaining with the son of Atreus, Agamemnon, the shepherd of the people; while we, the other half, embarked and sailed. Swiftly our ships ran on; God smoothed the billowy deep. Arrived at Tenedos,* we offered sacrifices to the gods, as homeward bound; but Zeus had not yet willed our coming home,—cruel! to waken bitter strife a second time. Part turned their curved ships back and sailed with Odysseus, keen and crafty, again to proffer aid to Agamemnon, son of Atreus. I, with the company of ships which followed me, pressed onward, for I knew some power intended ill. On pressed the warlike son of Tydeus, too, inspiriting his men. Later upon our track came light-haired Menelaus, who overtook us while at Lesbos we debated on the long sea voyage, doubtful if we should sail above steep Chios, by way of the island Psyria, with Chios on our left, or under Chios and past windy Mimas. We therefore begged the god to show some sign; and he made plain our way, bidding us cut the centre of the sea straight for Euboea,† if we would soonest flee from harm. The whistling wind began to blow, and swiftly along the swarming water sped our ships, and touched at night Geraestus, where on Poseidon's altar we laid many thighs of bulls, thankful that we had compassed the wide sea. It was the fourth day when the crews of Diomed the horseman, son of Tydeus, moored their trim ships at Argos. I still held on toward Pylos, nor did the breeze once fall after the god first sent it forth to blow.

"And thus it was I came, dear child, bringing no tidings; nothing I know about the rest of the Achaeans, which were saved and which were lost. But all that I have learned while sitting here at home, this, as is proper, you shall know; I will hide nothing from you. Safely, they say, returned the spearmen of the Myrmidons, whom the proud son of fierce Achilles led; safely, too, Philoctetes, the gallant son of Poias;[14] and back to Crete Idomeneus brought all his men,—all who escaped the war, the sea took not a man. About the

*An island off the Trojan coast.
†A Greek island in the Aegean Sea.

son of Atreus you yourselves have heard, though you live far away; how he returned, and how Aegisthus plotted his sorry death. And yet a fearful reckoning Aegisthus paid! When a man dies, how good it is to leave a son! That son took vengeance on the slayer, wily Aegisthus, who had slain his famous father. You too, my friend,—for certainly I find you fair and tall,—be strong, that men hereafter born may speak your praise."

Then answered him discreet Telemachus: "O Nestor, son of Neleus, great glory of the Achaeans, stoutly that son took vengeance, and the Achaeans shall spread his fame afar, that future times may know. Oh, that to me, as well, the gods would give the power to pay the suitors for their grievous wrongs, for they with insult work me outrage! But no such gift the gods bestowed on me and on my father. Now, therefore, all must simply be endured."

Then answered him the Gerenian horseman Nestor: "Friend,—since you turn my thoughts to this by your own words,—they say that many suitors of your mother, heedless of you, work evil in your halls. Pray tell me, do you willingly submit, or are the people of your land adverse to you, led by some voice of the gods? Who knows but yet Odysseus may return and recompense their crimes, either alone, or all the Achaeans with him? Ah, might clear-eyed Athene be pleased to be your friend as formerly she aided great Odysseus, there in the Trojan land where we Achaeans suffered! For I never knew the gods to show such open friendship as Pallas Athene showed in standing by Odysseus. If now to you she would be such a friend and heartily give aid, perhaps some of these men would cease to think of marriage."

Then answered him discreet Telemachus: "No sir, not soon, I think, will words like these come true. Too great is what you say; I am astonished. Hope what I might, such things could never be, not if the gods should will them."

Then said to him the goddess, clear-eyed Athene: "Telemachus, what word has passed the barrier of your teeth? Easily may a god, who will, bring a man safe from far. Yes, I myself would gladly meet a multitude of woes, if so I might go home and see my day of coming, and not return and fall beside my hearth as Agamemnon fell, under the plottings of his own wife and Aegisthus. Yet death, it is true, the common lot, gods have no power to turn even from one they love, when the hard doom of death that lays men low once overtakes him."

Then answered her discreet Telemachus: "Mentor, let us talk of this no more. It makes us sad. For him no real return can ever be; long time ago the immortals fixed his death and his dark doom. At present I would trace a different story and question Nestor, since beyond all men else he knows the right and wise. Three generations of mankind they say that he has ruled, and as I now behold him he seems like an immortal. O Nestor, son of Neleus, tell me the story true! How did the son of Atreus die, wide-ruling Agamemnon? And where was Menelaus? What was the deadly plot wily Aegisthus laid to kill a man much braver than himself? Was Menelaus absent from Achaean Argos, traveling to men afar, that so Aegisthus, taking courage, did the murder?"

Then answered him the Gerenian horseman Nestor: "Well, I will tell you all the truth, my child. Indeed, you yourself guess how it had fallen out if the son of Atreus, light-haired Menelaus, had found Aegisthus living in the palace when he returned from Troy. Then over dead Aegisthus, men had heaped no mound of earth, but dogs and birds had feasted on him lying on the plain outside the town, and no Achaean woman had made lament for him; for monstrous was the deed he wrought. At Troy we tarried, bringing to fulfillment many toils, while he, at ease, hidden in grazing Argos, strove hard to win the wife of Agamemnon by his words. At first, indeed, she scorned ill-doing, this royal Clytaemnestra, being of upright mind. Moreover, a bard was with her whom the son of Atreus strictly charged, on setting forth for Troy, to guard his wife. But when at last the doom of gods constrained her to her ruin, then did Aegisthus take the bard to a lone island and leave him there, the prey and prize of birds, while her, as willing as himself, he led to his own home.

And many a thigh-piece did he burn upon the sacred altars of the
gods, and many an offering render, woven stuffs and gold, at having
achieved a deed so great as never in his heart he thought to see.

"Now as we came from Troy, the son of Atreus and myself set
sail together full of loving thoughts; but when we were approaching
sacred Sunion, a cape of Athens, Phoebus Apollo smote the helms-
man of Menelaus and slew him with his gentle arrows while he held
the rudder of the running ship within his hands.[15] Phrontis it was,
Onetor's son, one who surpassed all humankind in piloting a ship
when winds are wild. So Menelaus tarried, though eager for his
journey, to bury his companion and to pay the funeral rites. But
when he also, sailing in his hollow ships over the wine-dark sea,
reached in his course the steep height of Maleia, from that point on
far-seeing Zeus gave him a grievous way. He poured forth blasts of
whistling winds and swollen waves as huge as mountains. Dividing
the ships, he brought a part to Crete, where the Cydonians dwelt
around the streams of Iardanus. Here is a cliff, smooth and steep
toward the water, at the border land of Gortyn, on the misty sea,
where the south wind drives heavy waves against the western point
toward Phaestus, and this small rock holds back the heavy waves.
Some came in here, the men themselves hardly escaping death; their
ships the waves crushed on the ledges. But the five other dark-bowed
ships wind and wave bore to Egypt.[16] So Menelaus gathered there
much substance and much gold, coasting about on ship-board to
men of alien speech; and all this time at home Aegisthus foully
plotted. Slaying the son of Atreus, he reigned seven years in rich
Mycenae. The people were held down. But in the eighth ill came;
for royal Orestes came from Athens and slew the slayer, wily Ae-
gisthus, who had slain his famous father. The slaughter done, he
held a funeral banquet for the Argives, over his hateful mother and
spiritless Aegisthus, and on that self-same day came Menelaus, good
at the war-cry, bringing a store of treasure, all the freight his ships
could bear.

"You too, my friend, wander not long and far from home, leaving
your wealth behind and persons in your house so insolent as these;

for they may swallow all that wealth, sharing with one another, while you are gone a fruitless journey. And yet, I say, go visit Menelaus. Indeed, I bid you go; for he is lately come from foreign lands and from those nations whence one could not really hope to come, when once the storms had swept him off into so vast a sea,—a sea from which birds do not travel in a year, so vast and terrible it is. Go then at once with your own ship and crew, or if you like by land; chariot and horses are ready for you, and ready too my sons to be your guides to sacred Lacedaemon, where lives light-haired Menelaus. Beg him yourself to tell the very truth. Falsehood he will not speak, for just and wise is he."

As he thus spoke the sun went down and darkness came, and the goddess, clear-eyed Athene, said to them:

"Sir, certainly these words of yours are fitly spoken. But come, cut up the tongues and mix the wine, that after we have poured libations to Poseidon and the rest of the immortals we may seek our rest, since it is time for rest. For now the day has turned to dusk, and surely it is not well to stay long at the gods' feast; rather to rise and go."

So spoke the daughter of Zeus; and they listened to her saying. Pages poured water on their hands; young men brimmed bowls with drink and served to all, with a first pious portion for the cup; they themselves threw the tongues into the flame and, rising, poured libations. So after they had poured and drunk as their hearts would, then would Athene and princely Telemachus set off together for their hollow ship. But Nestor checked them and rebuked them, saying:

"Zeus and the other immortal gods forbid that you should leave my house and turn to a swift ship! As if I were a man quite without clothes and poor, a man who had not robes and rugs enough at home for himself and friends to sleep in comfort! But in my house are goodly robes and rugs. And never, surely, shall the loving son of our Odysseus lie on ship's deck while I am living, or while within my halls children remain to entertain such guests as visit house of mine."

Then said to him the goddess, clear-eyed Athene: "Well have you said in this, kind sir, and good it were Telemachus should obey, for it is far more fitting so. Yes, he shall now attend you and sleep within your halls. But as for me, I go to the black ship to cheer my men and tell their duties, for I am the only man of years among them all; the others, younger men, follow me out of friendship, and all are of the age of bold Telemachus. There would I lie down by the black hollow ship tonight; but in the morning I will go to the bold Cauconians where there are debts now due me, not recent ones nor small. As for Telemachus who stays with you, send him upon his way by chariot with your son, and give him horses that have swiftest speed and best endurance."

Saying this, clear-eyed Athene passed away, in likeness of an osprey. Awe fell on all who saw. The old man marveled as he gazed, grasped by the hand Telemachus, and said as he addressed him:

"Dear friend, you will not prove, I trust, a base man, lacking spirit, if when so young the gods become your guides. This is none else of those who have their dwelling on Olympus than the daughter of Zeus, Tritogeneia,* who honored your good father too amongst the Argives. Ah, queen, be gracious and vouchsafe me fair renown,— me and my children and my honored wife,—and I will give to thee a glossy heifer, broad of brow, unbroken, one no man ever brought beneath the yoke. Her I will give, tipping her horns with gold."

So spoke he in his prayer, and Pallas Athene heard. Then the Gerenian horseman Nestor led sons and sons-in-law to his fair palace. And they on reaching the far-famed palace of the king, took seats in order on couches and on chairs; and the old man mixed for all his comers a vessel of sweet wine, which, now eleven years old, the housewife opened, unfastening the lid. A bowl of this the old man mixed, and fervently he prayed, pouring libation to Athene, daughter of aegis-bearing Zeus.†

Then after they had poured and drunk as their hearts would,

---

*Another name for Athene; its meaning is obscure.
†Zeus' aegis was a divine protective shield.

desiring rest, they each departed homeward; but in the house itself the Gerenian horseman Nestor prepared the bed of Telemachus, the son of princely Odysseus, upon a well-bored bedstead beneath the echoing portico. By him he placed Peisistratus, that sturdy spearman, one ever foremost, he who was still the bachelor among the sons at home. But Nestor slept in the recess of the high hall; his wife, the Queen, making her bed beside him.

Soon as the early rosy-fingered dawn appeared, the Gerenian horseman Nestor rose from bed, and coming forth sat down on the smooth stones which stood before his lofty gate, white, glistening as with oil. On them in former days Neleus had sat, the peer of gods in counsel; but long ago he met his doom and went to the house of Hades, and now Gerenian Nestor sat thereon, as guardian of the Achaeans, holding the sceptre. Round him his sons collected in a group, on coming from their chambers,—Echephron and Stratius, Perseus, Aretus, and gallant Thrasymedes, and sixth and last came lord Peisistratus. Then they led forward godlike Telemachus, and set him by their side, and thus began the Gerenian horseman Nestor:

"Hasten, dear children, and fulfill my vow; that first of all the gods I seek the favor of Athene, who came to me in open presence at the gods' high feast. Go one among you to the field and have a heifer quickly brought, and let the cowherd drive her. One go to the black ship of bold Telemachus, and bring here all his crew. Leave only two behind. Let one again summon the smith Laerces hither, to tip with gold the heifer's horns. The rest of you stay here together. But tell the maids within our famous palace to spread a feast, to fetch some seats, some logs of wood, and some fresh water."

He spoke; away went all in breathless haste. And now there came the heifer from the field; there came from the swift balanced ship the crew of brave Telemachus; there came the smith, with his smith's tools in hand, his implements of art, anvil and hammer and the shapely tongs, with which he works the gold; there came Athene, too, to meet the sacrifice. Then the old horseman Nestor furnished gold, and so that other welded it round the heifer's horns, smoothing it till the goddess might be pleased to view the offering.

Now by the horns Stratius and noble Echephron led up the heifer; Aretus brought purifying water in a flowered basin from the store-room, and in his other hand held barley in a basket; and dauntless Thrasymedes, a sharp axe in his hand, stood by to fell the heifer, while Perseus held the blood-bowl. Then the old horseman Nestor began the opening rites, of washing hands and sprinkling meal. And fervently he prayed Athene at beginning, casting the forelocks in the fire.

So after they had prayed and strewn the barley-meal, forthwith the son of Nestor, ardent Thrasymedes, drew near and dealt the blow. The axe cut through the sinews of the neck and broke the heifer's power. A cry went up from the daughters of Nestor, the sons' wives, and his own honored wife, Eurydice, the eldest of the daughters of Clymenus. The sons then raised the beast up from the trodden earth and held her so, the while Peisistratus, ever foremost, cut the throat. And after the black blood had flowed and life had left the carcass, they straightway laid it open, quickly cut out the thighs, all in due order, wrapped them in fat in double layers and placed raw flesh thereon. On billets of wood the old man burned them, and poured upon them sparkling wine, while young men by his side held five-pronged forks. So after the thighs were burned and the inward parts were tasted, they sliced the rest, and stuck it on their forks and roasted all, holding the pointed forks in hand.

Meanwhile to Telemachus fair Polycaste gave a bath, she who was youngest daughter of Nestor, son of Neleus. And after she had bathed him and anointed him with oil and put upon him a goodly robe and tunic, forth from the bath he came, in bearing like the immortals; and he went and sat by Nestor, the shepherd of the people.

The others, too, when they had roasted the outer flesh and drawn it off, sat down and fell to feasting. Picked men attended them, pouring the wine into their golden cups. So after they had stayed desire for drink and food, then thus began the Gerenian horseman Nestor: "My sons, go fetch the full-maned horses for Telemachus and yoke them to the car, to bring him on his way."

So he spoke, and willingly they heeded and obeyed. Quickly they harnessed the swift horses to the car. The housewife put in bread and wine and delicacies, such things as heaven-descended princes eat. And now Telemachus mounted the goodly chariot, and Nestor's son Peisistratus, ever foremost, mounted the chariot too, and took the reins in hand. He cracked the whip to start, and not unwillingly the pair flew off into the plain, left the steep citadel of Pylos, and all day long they shook the yoke they bore between them.

Now the sun sank and all the ways grew dark, and the men arrived at Pherae, before the house of Diocles, the son of Orsilochus, whose father was Alpheius. There for the night they rested; he gave them entertainment.

Then as the early rosy-fingered dawn appeared, they harnessed the horses, mounted the gay chariot, and off they drove from porch and echoing portico. Peisistratus cracked the whip to start, and not unwillingly the pair flew off. So into the plain they came where wheat was growing; and through this, by and by, they reached their journey's end. So fast their horses sped them. Then the sun sank and all the ways grew dark.

BOOK IV

At Lacedaemon

Into the low land now they came of caverned Lacedaemon and drove to the palace of famous Menelaus. They found him holding a wedding feast for all his kin in honor of the son and gentle daughter of his house. To the son of Achilles, that breaker of the line, he gave his daughter; for long ago, at Troy, he pledged himself to give her, and now the gods brought round their wedding. Accordingly today with horses and with chariots he sent her forth to the famed city of the Myrmidons, whose king her bridegroom was. Then for his son, stout Megapenthes, he took to wife Alector's daughter out of Sparta, his son a favorite, though born of a slave mother. The gods gave Helen no more issue after she in the early time had borne her lovely child, Hermione, who had the grace of golden Aphrodite.[17]

Thus at the feast in the great high-roofed house, neighbors and kinsmen of famous Menelaus sat and made merry. Among them sang the sacred bard and touched his lyre; a pair of dancers went whirling down the middle as he began the song.

Now at the palace gate two youths and their horses stopped, princely Telemachus and the proud son of Nestor. Great Eteoneus came forth and saw them,—he was a busy fighting man of famous Menelaus,—and hastened through the hall to tell the shepherd of the people, and standing close beside him he said in winged words:

"Here are two strangers, heaven-descended Menelaus, and they are like the seed of mighty Zeus. Say, shall we unharness their swift horses, or shall we send them forth for some one else to entertain?"

Then, deeply moved, said light-haired Menelaus, "You were no fool, Boëthoüs' son, Eteoneus, heretofore, but now you chatter folly like a child! Why, we ourselves are here through having oftentimes had food from strangers; and we must look to Zeus henceforth to keep us safe from harm. No! take the harness from the strangers' horses and bring the men themselves within to share our feast."

He spoke, and Eteoneus hastened along the hall and called on other busy fighting men to follow. They took the sweating horses from the yoke, tied them securely at the mangers, threw them some corn and mixed therewith white barley, then tipped the chariot up against the bright face-wall, and brought the men into the lordly house. And they, beholding, marveled at the dwelling of the heaven-descended king; for a sheen as of the sun or moon played through the high-roofed house of famous Menelaus. Now after they had satisfied their eyes with gazing, they went to the polished baths and bathed. And when the maids had bathed them and anointed them with oil, and put upon them fleecy coats and tunics, they took their seats by Menelaus, son of Atreus. And water for the hands a servant brought in a beautiful pitcher made of gold, and poured it out over a silver basin for their washing, and spread a polished table by their side. Then the grave housekeeper brought bread and placed before them, setting out food of many a kind, freely giving of her store. The carver, too, took platters of meat and placed before them, meat of all kinds, and set their golden goblets ready. And greeting the pair said light-haired Menelaus:

"Break bread, and have good cheer! and by and by when you have eaten, we will ask what men you are. Surely the parent stock suffers no loss in you; but you are of some line of heaven-descended scep-tered kings. For common men have no such children."

So saying, he set before them fat slices of a chine of beef, taking up in his hands the roasted flesh which had been placed before him as the piece of honor; and on the food spread out before them they laid hands. But after they had stayed desire for drink and food, Telemachus said to Nestor's son,—his head bent close, that others might not hear:

"O son of Nestor, my heart's delight, notice the blaze of bronze throughout the echoing halls, the gold, the amber, silver, and ivory! The court of Olympian Zeus within must be like this. What untold wealth is here! I am amazed to see."

What he was saying light-haired Menelaus overheard, and speaking in winged words he said: "Dear children, no! No mortal man may vie with Zeus; eternal are his halls and his possessions; but one of humankind to vie with me in wealth there may or may not be. Through many woes and wanderings I brought it in my ships, eight years upon the way. Cyprus, Phoenicia, Egypt, I wandered over; came to the Ethiopians, Sidonians, and Erembians, and into Libya, where the lambs are full-horned at their birth. Three times a year the flocks bear young. No prince or peasant there lacks cheese, meat, or sweet milk, but the ewes give their milk the whole year round. While I was gathering thereabouts much wealth and wandering on, a stranger slew my brother when off his guard, by stealth, and through the craft of his accursed wife. Therefore I have no joy as lord of my possessions. But from your fathers you will have heard the tale, whoever they may be; for great was my affliction, and desolate the house which once stood fair and stored with many goods. Would I were here at home with but the third part of my wealth, and they were safe today who fell on the plain of Troy, far off from grazing Argos! But no! and for them all I often grieve and mourn when sitting in my halls. Now with a sigh I ease my heart, then check myself; soon comes a surfeit of benumbing sorrow. Yet in my grief it is not all I so much mourn as one alone, who makes me loathe my sleep and food when I remember him, for no Achaean bore the brunt as did Odysseus, and came off victor. And still on him it was appointed woe should fall, and upon me a ceaseless pang because of him; so long he tarries, whether alive or dead we do not know. For him now mourn the old Laërtes, steadfast Penelope, and Telemachus, whom he left at home a new-born child."

So he spoke, and stirred in Telemachus yearnings to mourn his father. Tears from his eyelids dropped upon the ground when he heard his father's name, and he held with both his hands his purple cloak before his eyes. This Menelaus noticed, and hesitated in his mind and heart whether to leave him to make mention of his father or first to question him and prove him through and through.

While he thus doubted in his mind and heart, forth from her fragrant high-roofed chamber Helen came, like golden-shafted Artemis. For her, Adraste placed a carven chair; Alcippe brought a covering of soft wool, and Phylo a silver basket which Alcandra gave, the wife of Polybus, who lived at Thebes in Egypt, where there is wealth in plenty. He gave to Menelaus two silver bath-tubs, a pair of kettles, and ten golden talents. And then, besides, his wife gave Helen beautiful gifts; she gave a golden distaff and a basket upon rollers, fashioned of silver, and its rim finished with gold. This her attendant Phylo now brought and set beside her, filled with a fine-spun yarn; across it lay the distaff, charged with dark wool. Seated upon her chair, with a footstool for her feet, she at once questioned thus her husband closely:

"Do we know, heaven-descended Menelaus, who these men visiting our house assert themselves to be? Shall I disguise my thought or speak it plainly? My heart bids speak. None have I ever seen, I think, so like another—no man, no woman; amazed am I to see!—as this man here is like the son of brave Odysseus, even like Telemachus, whom his father left at home a new-born child, when you Achaeans, for the sake of worthless me, came under the walls of Troy, eager for valorous fighting."

Then, answering her, said light-haired Menelaus: "Now I too note it, wife, as you suggest; such were Odysseus' feet and hands, his turn of eye, his head, and hair above. And even now, as I began to call to mind Odysseus and to tell what grievous toils he bore in my behalf, this youth let fall a bitter tear from under his brows and held his purple cloak before his eyes."

Then Nestor's son, Peisistratus, made answer: "O son of Atreus, heaven-descended Menelaus, leader of hosts, this is in truth his son, as you have said; but he is modest and too bashful in his heart to make display of talk on his first coming here, before you too, whose voice we both enjoy as if it were a god's. The Gerenian horseman, Nestor, sent me forth to be his guide; for he desired to see you, hoping that you might give him aid by word or deed. Ah, many a grief the son of an absent father meets at home, when other helpers are not by. So with Telemachus; the one is gone, and others there are none in all the land to ward off ill."

Then, answering him, said light-haired Menelaus: "What! Is there then within my house the son of one so dear, one who for me bore many a conflict! I used to say I should rejoice over his coming home far more than over that of all the other Argives, if through the seas Olympian far-seeing Zeus let our swift ships find passage. In Argos I would have granted him a city, and would here have built his house, and I would have brought him out of Ithaca,—him and his goods, his child, and all his people,—clearing its dwellers from some single city that lies within my neighborhood and owns me as its lord. So living here we had been much together; and nothing further could have parted then our joyous friendship till death's dark cloud closed round. But God himself must have been envious of a life like this, and made that hapless man alone to fail of coming."

So he spoke, and stirred in all a yearning after tears. Then Argive Helen wept, the child of Zeus;[18] Telemachus too wept, and Menelaus, son of Atreus; nor yet did Nestor's son keep his eyes tearless. For in his mind he mused on good Antilochus, whom the illustrious son of the bright dawn had slain.* Remembering whom, he spoke in winged words:

"O son of Atreus, that you were wise beyond the wont of men old Nestor used to say, when we would mention you at home, and raise questions. But now, if you will, give ear to me; for after a feast I do not like to sit and grieve. Tomorrow's sun shall shine. Not that I think it ill to weep for one who dies and meets his doom. It is the only honor sorrowing men can pay, to cut the hair and let the tear fall down the cheek. A brother of mine once died, and not the meanest of the Argives. You must have known him. I never looked

---

*Memnon, son of the Dawn, killed Antilochus at Troy.

upon his face and never knew him; but Antilochus, they say, was swift of foot, a famous fighter."

Then answering him said light-haired Menelaus: "Friend, you have said just what a man of understanding might say and even do, were he indeed your elder; for sprung from such a father you talk with understanding. Easily is his offspring known to whom the son of Kronos allots good luck in birth and marriage. And thus has he blessed Nestor, continually, all his days, granting him hale old age at home and children who are youths of wisdom, mighty with the spear. Let us then check the lamentation which arose a while ago and turn once more to feasting. Let them pour water on our hands. Again, tomorrow, for Telemachus and me there will be tales to tell."

He spoke, and Asphalion poured water on their hands,—he was a busy fighting man of famous Menelaus,—then on the food spread out before them they laid hands.

Now elsewhere Helen turned her thoughts, the child of Zeus. Straightway she cast into the wine of which they drank a drug which quenches pain and strife and brings forgetfulness of every ill. He who should taste it, mingled in the bowl, would not that day let tears fall down his cheeks although his mother and his father died, although before his door a brother or dear son fell by the sword and his own eyes beheld. Such cunning drugs had the daughter of Zeus, drugs of a healing virtue, which Polydamna gave, the wife of Thon, in Egypt, where the fruitful soil yields drugs of every kind, some that when mixed are healing, others deadly. There every one is a physician, skillful beyond all humankind; for they are of the race of Paeon.* So after she had cast the drug into the bowl and bid them pour, then once more taking up the word, she said:

"Heaven-descended son of Atreus, Menelaus, and you too, children of worthy men, though Zeus to one in one way, to another in another, distributes good and ill and is almighty, yet now since you

---

*That is, of Apollo in his character as healer.

are sitting at a feast within our hall, amuse yourselves with tales. One suiting the occasion I will tell. Fully I cannot tell, nor even name the many feats of hardy Odysseus. But this is the sort of deed that brave man did and dared there in the Trojan land where you Achaeans suffered. Marring himself with cruel blows, casting a wretched garment round his shoulders, and looking like a slave, he entered the wide-wayed city of his foes; and other than his own true self he made himself appear in this disguise, even like a beggar, far as he was from such an one at the Achaean ships. In such a guise, he entered the Trojans' town; they took no notice, one and all; I alone knew him for the man he was and questioned him. He shrewdly tried to foil me. But while I washed him and anointed him with oil and brought him clothing, after I swore a solemn oath not to make known Odysseus to the Trojans till he should reach the swift ships and the camp, then he told me all the Achaeans had in mind. So, slaying many Trojans with his sharp-edged sword, he went off to the Argives and carried back much knowledge. Thereat the other Trojan women raised a loud lament. My soul was glad; for my heart already turned toward going home, and I would mourn the blindness Aphrodite brought when she lured me thither from my native land and bade me leave my daughter, my chamber, and my husband,—a man who lacked for nothing, either in mind or person."

Then, answering her, said light-haired Menelaus: "Yes, all your tale, my wife, is told right well. I have in days gone by tested the wisdom and the will of many heroes, and I have traveled over many lands; but never have I found a soul so true as that of stout Odysseus. Consider what that brave man did and dared within the wooden horse where all we Argive chiefs were lying, bearing to the Trojans death and doom. Erelong you passed that way,—some god must have impelled you who sought to bring the Trojans honor; godlike Deïphobus was following after. Thrice walking round our hollow ambush, touching it here and there, you called by name the Danaän chiefs, feigning the voice of every Argive's wife. Now I and the son of Tydeus and royal Odysseus, crouched in the middle, heard your call, and we two, starting up, were minded to go forth, or else to answer straightway from within; but Odysseus held us back and stayed our madness. So all the other sons of the Achaeans held their peace. Anticlus only was determined to make answer to your words; but Odysseus firmly closed his mouth with his strong hands, and so saved all the Achaeans. All through that time he held him thus, till Pallas Athene led you off."

Then answered him discreet Telemachus: "O son of Atreus, heaven-descended Menelaus, leader of hosts, so much the worse! All was of no avail against sorry death, though an iron heart was his. Yet, bring us to our beds, that so at last, lulled in sweet sleep, we may get comfort."

He spoke, and Argive Helen bade the maids to set a bed beneath the portico, to lay upon it beautiful purple rugs, spread blankets over these, and then place woolen mantles on the outside for a covering. So the maids left the hall, with torches in their hands, and spread the bed; and a page led forth the strangers. Thus in the porch slept prince Telemachus and the illustrious son of Nestor. But the son of Atreus slept in the recess of the high hall, and by him long-robed Helen lay, a queen of women.

Soon as the early rosy-fingered dawn appeared, Menelaus, good at the war-cry, rose from bed, put on his clothes, slung his sharp sword about his shoulder, under his shining feet bound his fair sandals, and came forth from his chamber in bearing like a god. Then seating himself beside Telemachus, he thus addressed him, saying:

"What business brings you here, my lord Telemachus, to sacred Lacedaemon on the broad ocean-ridges? Public or private is it? Tell me the very truth."

Then answered him discreet Telemachus: "O son of Atreus, heaven-descended Menelaus, leader of hosts, I came to see if you could give me tidings of my father. My home is swallowed up, my rich estate is wasted; with men of evil hearts my house is filled, men who continually butcher my huddling flocks and slow-paced, crook-horned oxen,—the suitors of my mother, overbearing in their pride. Therefore I now come here to your knees to ask if you will tell me of my father's sorry death, whether you saw it for yourself with your own eyes or from some other learned that he was lost; for to exceeding grief his mother bore him. Use no mild word nor yield to pity out of regard for me, but tell me fully all you chanced to see. I do entreat you, if ever my father, good Odysseus, in word or deed kept faith with you there in the Trojan land where you Achaeans suffered, be mindful of it now; tell me the plain truth."

Then, deeply moved, said light-haired Menelaus: "Heavens! In a very brave man's bed these sought to lie, the weaklings! As when in the den of a strong lion a hind has laid asleep her new-born sucking fawns, then roams the slopes and grassy hollows seeking food, and by and by into his lair the lion comes and on both hind and fawns brings ghastly doom; so shall Odysseus bring on these a ghastly doom. Ah, father Zeus, Athene, and Apollo! if with the power he showed one day in stately Lesbos, when he rose and wrestled in a match with Philomeleides, and down he threw him heavily, while the Achaeans all rejoiced,—if as he was that day Odysseus now might meet the suitors, they all would find quick turns of fate and bitter rites of marriage. But as to what you ask thus urgently, I will not speak deceitfully, misleading you; but what the unerring old man of the sea reported, in not a word will I disguise or hide from you.

"At the river of Egypt, eager as I was to hasten home, the gods still held me back, because I did not make the offerings due; and the gods will us to be ever mindful of their laws. Now in the surging sea an island lies,—Pharos they call it,—as far from the river as in a day a hollow ship will run when a whistling wind blows after. By it there lies a bay with a good anchorage, from which they send the trim ships off to sea and get them drinking water. Here the gods kept me twenty days; not once came the sea breezes which guide the course of ships on the broad ocean-ridges. So all my stores would have been spent and my men's courage, had not a certain goddess pitied and preserved me. This was Eidothea, daughter of mighty Proteus, the old man of the sea; for I deeply touched her heart as she met me on my solitary way apart from my companions; for they were ever roaming round the island, fishing with crooked hooks as hunger pinched their bellies. She, drawing near me, spoke and thus she said: 'Are you so witless, stranger, and unnerved, or do you willingly give way, taking a pleasure in your pains? So long you have remained upon the island, unable to discover an escape, while fainter grows the courage of your comrades.'

"So she spoke, and answering her said I: 'Then let me tell you, whatsoever goddess you may be, that I remain here through no will of mine, but I must have given offense to the immortals, who hold the open sky. Rather tell me,—for gods know all,—which of the immortals chains me here and bars my progress; and tell me of my homeward way, how I may pass along the swarming sea.'

"So I spoke, and straight the heavenly goddess answered: 'Well, stranger, I will plainly tell you all. There haunts this place a certain old man of the sea, unerring and immortal, Proteus of Egypt, who knows the depths of every sea, and is Poseidon's minister. He is, men say, my father, who begot me. If you could only lie in wait and seize on him, he would tell you of your course, the stages of your journey, and of your homeward way, how you may pass along the swarming sea. And he would tell you, heaven-descended man, if you desire, all that has happened at your home, of good or ill, while you have wandered on your long and toilsome way.'

"So she spoke, and answering her said I: 'Instruct me how to lie in wait for the old god, lest he foreseeing or foreknowing may escape. Hard is a god for mortal man to master.'

"So I spoke, and straight the heavenly goddess answered: 'Yes, stranger, I will truly tell you all. When the sun reaches the mid-sky, out from the water comes the unerring old man of the sea at a puff of the west wind and veiled in the dark ripple. When he is come, he lies down under the caverned cliffs; while round him seals, the brood of a fair sea nymph, huddle and sleep, on rising from the foaming water, and pungent is the scent they breathe of the unfathomed sea. There will I bring you at the dawn of day and lay you in the line. Meantime choose carefully for comrades the three best men you have among the well-benched ships. And I will tell you all the old man's wicked ways. First he will count the seals and go their round; and when he has told them off by fives and found them all, he will lie down among them like a shepherd with his flock. As soon as you see him sleeping, summon all your heart and strength and hold him fast, although he strive and struggle to escape. He will make trial of you, turning into whatsoever moves on earth, to water even, and heaven-kindled fire; yet hold unflinchingly and clasp the more. But when at length he questions you in his own shape,—in the same shape as when you saw him sleeping,—then, hero, cease from violence and set the old man free, but ask what god afflicts you, and ask about your homeward way, how you may pass along the swarming sea.'

"Saying this, she plunged into the surging sea. I to the ships which lay along the sands turned me away, and as I went my heart was sorely troubled. But when I came to the ship and to the sea and we had made our supper and the immortal night drew near, we lay down upon the beach to sleep. Then as the early rosy-fingered dawn appeared, along the shore of the wide-stretching sea I went with many supplications to the gods. I took three comrades with me, men whom I trusted most for any enterprise.

"She, in the meantime, having plunged into the sea's broad bosom, brought from the deep four skins of seals; all were fresh-flayed; and she prepared the plot against her father. She had scooped hollows in the sand, and sat awaiting us. Near her we drew. She made us all lie down in order and threw a skin on each. Then might our ambush have proved a hard one; for the pestilent stench of the sea-born seals oppressed us sorely. Who, indeed, would make his bed by a monster of the sea? But she preserved us and contrived for us great ease. Under the nose of each she set ambrosia,* sweet of smell, and this destroyed the creature's stench. So all the morning did we wait with patient hearts. At last the seals came trooping from the sea and by and by lay down in order on the beach. At noon out of the sea came the old man, found his fat seals, went over all, and

---

*The food of the gods is called ambrosia; their drink, nectar.

told their number, telling us first among the creatures, and never in his heart suspected there was fraud. At length he too lay down. Then with a shout we sprang and threw our arms about him, and the old man did not forget his crafty wiles: for first he turned into a bearded lion, then to a serpent, leopard, and huge boar; he turned into cascading water, into a branching tree; still we held firm, with steadfast hearts. But when the old man wearied, skillful though he was in wicked ways, at last in open speech he questioned me and said:

" 'Which of the gods, O son of Atreus, aided your plot to seize me here against my will, by ambush? What would you have?'

"So he spoke, and answering him said I: 'You know, old man,—why put me off with questions?—how long a time I have remained upon this island, unable to discover an escape, while fainter grows my heart within. Rather tell me,—for gods know all,—which of the immortals chains me here and bars my progress; and tell me of my homeward way, how I may pass along the swarming sea.'

"So I spoke, and straightway answering me said he: 'But certainly to Zeus and to the other gods you should have made good offerings on setting forth, if you would quickly reach your land, sailing the wine-dark sea; for now it is appointed you to see your friends no more nor reach your stately house and native land till you have gone again to Egypt's waters, to its heaven-descended stream, and offered sacred hecatombs* to the immortal gods who hold the open sky. Then shall the gods grant you the course which you desire.'

"As thus he spoke, my very soul was crushed within me because he bade me cross again the misty sea and go to Egypt's river, a long and weary way. Yet still I answered thus and said: 'Old man, all that you bid me I will do. Only declare me this and plainly tell, did all the Achaeans with their ships return unharmed, whom Nestor and I left on our setting forth from Troy? Did any die by grievous death at sea or in the arms of friends when the skein of war was wound?'

"So I spoke, and straightway answering me said he: 'Son of

---

*Strictly speaking, a hecatomb was the sacrifice of 100 animals.

Atreus, why question me of this? Better it were you should not see nor comprehend my knowledge; for you will not long be free from tears after you learn the truth. Yes, many were cut off and many spared. Of leaders, only two among the armed Achaeans died on the journey home,—as for the battle, you yourself were there,—and one, still living, lingers yet on the wide sea. Ajax was lost, he and his long-oared ships. At first Poseidon wrecked him on the great rocks of Gyrae, but saved him from the sea. And so he might have escaped his doom, though hated by Athene, had he not uttered overbearing words, puffed up with pride; for he said he had escaped the great gulf of the sea in spite of gods. Poseidon heard his haughty boasting, and straightway, grasping the trident in his sturdy hands, he smote the rock of Gyrae, splitting it open. One part still held its place; the broken piece fell in the sea. It was on this Ajax at first had sat, puffed up with pride. It bore him down into the boundless surging deep. So there he died, drinking the briny water.

" 'Your brother escaped his doom and came in safety, he and his hollow ships; for powerful Here saved him. But when he was about to reach the steep height of Maleia, a sweeping storm bore him once more along the swarming sea, loudly lamenting, to the confines of that country where Thyestes dwelt in former days, but where now dwelt Thyestes' son, Aegisthus. And when at last from this point on his course was clear of danger, and the gods changed the wind about and home came all, then with rejoicing did he tread his country's soil, and he kissed and clasped that soil; while from him many hot tears fell at seeing the welcome land. But from a tower a watchman spied him, whom wily Aegisthus posted there and promised him for pay two golden talents. He had been keeping guard throughout the year, lest unobserved the king might come and try the force of arms. He hastened to the house to tell the shepherd of the people, and soon Aegisthus contrived a cunning plot. Selecting twenty of the bravest in the land, he laid an ambush; and just across the hall bade that a feast be spread. Then he went to welcome Agamemnon, the shepherd of the people, with horses and with chariots, while meditating crime. He led him up unheeding to his death and slew him at the feast, even as one cuts the ox down at his stall. Not a follower of the son of Atreus lived, nor a follower of Aegisthus; all died within the hall.'

"As thus he spoke, my very soul was crushed within me, and sitting on the sands I fell to weeping; my heart would no more live and see the sun. But when of weeping and of writhing I had had my fill, then said the unerring old man of the sea: 'Do not, O son of Atreus, long and unceasingly thus weep, because we know there is no remedy. Seek rather with all speed to reach your native land; for either you will find Aegisthus still alive, or Orestes will have slain him, so forestalling you, and you may join the funeral feast.'

"So he spoke, and the heart and sturdy spirit in my breast through all my grief again grew warm; and speaking in winged words I said: 'Of these men then I know, but name the third who still alive lingers on the wide sea; or if he is dead, despite my grief I want to hear.'

"So I spoke, and straightway answering me said he: 'It is Laërtes' son, whose home is Ithaca. I saw him on an island, letting the big tears fall, in the hall of the nymph Calypso, who holds him there by force. No power has he to reach his native land, for he has no ships fitted with oars, nor crews to bear him over the broad ocean-ridges. As for yourself, heaven-favored Menelaus, it is not destined you to die and meet your doom in grazing Argos; but to the Elysian plain and the earth's limits the immortal gods shall bring you, where fair-haired Rhadamanthus dwells. Here utterly at ease passes the life of men. No snow is here, no winter long, no rain, but the loud-blowing breezes of the west the Ocean-stream sends up to bring men coolness; for you have Helen and are counted son-in-law of Zeus.'[19]

"Saying this, he plunged into the surging sea. I with my gallant comrades turned to our ships, and as I went my heart was sorely troubled. But when we came to the ship and to the sea, and we had made our supper, and the immortal night drew near, we lay down to sleep upon the beach. Then as the early rosy-fingered dawn appeared, we in the first place launched our ships into the sacred sea, put masts and sails in the trim ships, the men embarked themselves, took places at the pins, and sitting in order smote the foaming water with their oars. So back again to Egypt's waters, to its heaven-descended stream, I brought my ships and made the offerings due. And after appeasing the anger of the gods that live forever, I raised a mound to Agamemnon, that his fame might never die. This done, I sailed away; the gods gave wind and brought me swiftly to my native land. But come, remain awhile here at my hall until eleven or twelve days pass. Then I will send you forth with honor, giving you splendid gifts, three horses and a polished car. Moreover, I will give a goodly cup, that as you pour libations to the immortal gods you may be mindful all your days of me."

Then answered him discreet Telemachus: "O son of Atreus, keep me no long time here, though I could be content to stay a year, and no desire for kindred or for home would ever come; for I take astonishing pleasure in hearing your tales and talk. But already friends at hallowed Pylos are uneasy, and you still hold me here. As for the gift that you would give, pray let it be some keepsake. Horses I will not take to Ithaca, but leave them as an honor here for you; for you rule open plains, where lotus is abundant, marsh-grass and wheat and corn, and the white broad-eared barley. In Ithaca there are no open runs, no meadows; a land for goats, and pleasanter than grazing country. Not one of the islands is a place to drive a horse, none has good meadows, of all that rest upon the sea; Ithaca least of all."

He spoke, and Menelaus, good at the war-cry, smiled, patted him with his hand, and said:

"Of noble blood you are, dear child, as your words show. Yes, I will make the change; I can with ease. And out of all the gifts stored in my house as treasures I will give you that which is most beautiful and precious: I will give a well-wrought bowl. It is of solid silver, its rim finished with gold, the work of Hephaestus.* Lord Phaedimus, the king of the Sidonians, gave it to me, when his house received me on my homeward way. And now to you I gladly give it."

---

*The divine metalsmith of the gods.

So they conversed together. But banqueters were coming to the palace of the noble king. Men drove up sheep, and brought the bracing wine, and their veiled wives sent bread. So busy were they with the feast within the hall.

Meanwhile before the palace of Odysseus the suitors were making merry, throwing the discus and the hunting spear upon the level pavement, holding riot as of old. Here sat Antinoüs and godlike Eurymachus, the leaders of the suitors; for they in manly excellence were quite the best of all. To them Noëmon, son of Phronius, now drew near; and questioning Antinoüs thus he spoke:

"Antinoüs, do we know, or do we not, when Telemachus will come from sandy Pylos? He took a ship of mine and went away, and now I need her for crossing to broad Elis where I keep my twelve brood mares. The hardy mules, their foals, are still unbroken; one I would fetch away and break him in."

So he spoke. The others were amazed. They had been saying Telemachus was not gone to Pylos, to the land of Neleus; they thought he still was somewhere at the farm, among the flocks, or with the swineherd.

Then said Antinoüs, Eupeithes' son: "Tell me precisely when he went and what young men were with him. Picked men of Ithaca, or did he take his hirelings and slaves? That indeed he might do! And tell me truly this, that I may rest assured; did he with violence, against your will, take the black ship? Or did you give it willingly, because he begged?"

Then answered him Noëmon, son of Phronius: "I gave it willingly. What else could anybody do when one like him, with troubles on his heart, entreated? Hard would it be to keep from giving. The youths who next to us are noblest in the land are his companions. I marked their captain as he went on board, and it was Mentor or a god exactly like him. Yet this is strange. Here I saw noble Mentor yesterday in the morning; and there he was embarking on the ship for Pylos."

So saying, he departed to his father's house. But the proud spirits of the two were stirred. They made the suitors seat themselves and stop their sports. And then Antinoüs, Eupeithes' son, addressed them in displeasure. With fierce anger was his dark soul filled. His eyes were like bright fire.

"By heavens! Here is a monstrous action impudently brought to pass, this journey of Telemachus. We said it should not be; and here in spite of all of us this young boy simply goes, launching a ship and picking out the best men of the land. Before we think, he will begin to be our bane. But may Zeus blast his power before he reaches manhood! Come then, and give me a swift ship with twenty comrades, and I will lie in wait upon his way, and guard the strait between Ithaca and rugged Samos. So to his grief he cruises off to find his father." He spoke, and all approved and urged him on. And presently they rose and entered the hall of Odysseus.

But now Penelope, no long time after, learned of the plans on which the suitors' hearts were brooding. For the page Medon told her, who overheard the plot as he stood outside the court, while they within it framed their scheme. He hastened through the palace with the tidings to Penelope; and as he crossed her threshold Penelope thus spoke:

"Page, why have the lordly suitors sent you here? Was it to tell the maids of princely Odysseus to put by work and lay their table? Oh that they had not wooed or gathered here, or that they here today might eat their last and latest meal! You troop about and squander all our living, even all the estate of wise Telemachus. To your fathers of old you gave no heed when you were children, nor heard what sort of man Odysseus was among your elders, how he did no wrong by deed or word to any in the land. And that is the common way with high-born kings; one man they hate and love another. But he wrought no iniquity to any man. Yet what your disposition is, and what your shameful deeds, is plain to see. There is no gratitude for good deeds done."

Then Medon spoke, a man of understanding: "Ah, Queen, I would that were our greatest ill; but weightier matters yet, a sorer evil, the suitors now propose—which may the son of Kronos hinder! They have resolved to slay Telemachus with the keen sword, as he sails home. He went away for tidings of his father, to hallowed Pylos and to sacred Lacedaemon."

As he thus spoke, her knees grew feeble and her very soul. Long a speechless stupor held her; her two eyes filled with tears, her full voice stopped. But at the last she answered thus and said: "Page, why is my child gone? What need had he to mount the coursing ships, which serve men for sea-chariots and cross the mighty flood? Was it to leave no name among men here?"

Then answered Medon, that man of understanding: "I do not know whether a god impelled him, or if his own heart stirred within to go to Pylos, to gather tidings of his father's coming or there to learn what fate he met."

So saying, he departed along the hall of Odysseus. But upon her heart-eating anguish fell. No longer had she strength to sit upon a chair, though many were in the room, but down she sank upon the floor of her rich chamber, pitifully moaning. Round about, her slave-maids were sobbing—all her household, young and old. And with repeated cries, Penelope thus spoke:

"Listen, dear maids! Surely the Olympian gave me exceeding sorrow, beyond all women born and bred my equals. For I in former days lost my good husband, a man of lion heart, for every excellence honored among the Danaäns—good man! his fame is wide through Hellas and mid-Argos. Moreover now my darling son the winds have snatched away, silently, from my halls; I heard not of his going. Hard-hearted maids! No one of you took thought to rouse me from my bed, though well your own hearts knew when he embarked on the black hollow ship. Ah, had I learned that he was purposing this journey, surely he would have stayed, however eager for the journey, or else he should have left me dead within the hall. But now let some one hurry and call old Dolius, the slave my father gave when I came here, who tends my orchard trees; that he may quickly go, seat himself by Laërtes and, telling all, learn if Laërtes can devise a way to come before the people and cry out against the men who seek to crush his race and that of great Odysseus."

Then answered her the good nurse Eurycleia: "Dear lady, slay me with the ruthless sword or leave me in the hall; I will not hide my story. I knew of all. I gave him what he wanted, bread and sweet wine. But he exacted from me a solemn oath to speak no word to you until twelve days were past, or until you should miss him and hear that he was gone, that so you might not stain your beautiful face with tears. Now therefore bathe, and putting on fresh garments, go to your upper chamber with your maids, and offer prayer to Athene, daughter of aegis-bearing Zeus; for thus she may preserve him safe from death. Vex not an old man, vexed already. Surely I cannot think the Arceisian line* is wholly hateful to the blessed gods. Nay, one shall still survive to hold the high-roofed house and the fat fields around."

She spoke, and lulled the other's cries and stayed her eyes from tears. Penelope bathed, and putting on fresh garments went to her upper chamber with her maids, took barley in a basket, and thus she prayed Athene:

"Hear me, thou child of aegis-bearing Zeus, unwearied one! If ever wise Odysseus when at home burned the fat thighs of ox or sheep to thee, thereof be mindful now; preserve me my dear son. Guard him against the cruel suitors' wrongs."

Thus having said, she raised the cry, and the goddess heard her prayer. But the suitors broke into uproar up and down the dusky hall, and a rude youth would say: "Ha, ha! at last the long-wooed queen makes ready for our marriage. Little she thinks that for her son death is in waiting." So they would say, but knew not how things were.

And now Antinoüs addressed them, saying: "Good sirs, beware of haughty talk of every kind, or some one may report it indoors too. Come, rather let us rise and quietly as we may let us effect the scheme which pleased the hearts of all."

So saying, he chose the twenty fittest men, who went to the swift ship and to the shore. They in the first place launched the ship into

---

*The line of Laërtes and Odysseus.

deep water, put mast and sail in the black ship, fitted the oars into their leathern slings, all in due order, and up aloft spread the white sail. Stately footmen carried their armor. Out in the stream they moored the boat, they themselves disembarked, took supper there, and waited for the evening to come on.

But in her upper chamber heedful Penelope still lay fasting, tasting neither food nor drink, anxious whether her gallant son would escape death, or by the audacious suitors be borne down; as doubts a lion in a crowd of men, in terror as they draw the crafty circle round him. To her in such anxiety sweet slumber came, and lying back she slept and every joint relaxed.

Now a new plan the goddess formed, clear-eyed Athene. She shaped a phantom fashioned in a woman's form, even like Iphthime, daughter of brave Icarius, her whom Eumelus married, that had his home at Pherae. And this she sent to the house of princely Odysseus, that it might make Penelope, mourning and sighing now, cease from her griefs and tearful cries. It came into the chamber past the bolt-strap, stood by her head and thus addressed her:

"Are you asleep, Penelope, dear troubled heart? No, never shall the gods that live at ease leave you to weep and pine; for still your son is destined to return, since in the gods' sight he is no trangres-sor."

Then answered heedful Penelope, very sweetly slumbering at the gates of dreams: "Why, sister, have you come? You never before were with me, because your home is very far away. And you bid me cease from grief and all the pangs that vex my mind and heart, me who in former days lost my good husband, a man of lion heart, for every excellence honored among the Danaäns—good man! his fame is wide through Hellas and mid-Argos. Moreover now my darling son is gone on a hollow ship, a mere boy too, but little skilled in cares and counsels. Therefore for him I mourn even more than for that other. For him I tremble, and I fear that he may meet with ill, either from those within the land where he is gone, or on the sea. For many evil-minded men now plot against him and seek to cut him off before he gains his native land."

And answering her, said the dim phantom: "Take heart, and be not in your mind too deeply afraid. So true a guide goes with him as other men have prayed for aid—for powerful is she—Pallas Athene. Seeing you grieve, she pities you, and it was she who sent me here to tell you so."

Then heedful Penelope said to her: "If you are a god and have obeyed some heavenly bidding, come tell me also of that hapless one, if he still lives and sees the sunshine; or is he now already dead and in the house of Hades?"

And answering her, said the dim phantom: "Of him I will not speak at length, be he alive or dead. To speak vain words is ill."

So saying, it glided past the door-post's bolt into the airy breezes. And out of sleep awoke Icarius' daughter, and her very soul was warmed, so clear a dream was sent her in the dead of night.

Meanwhile the suitors, embarking in their ship, sailed on their watery journey, purposing in their minds the speedy murder of Telemachus. Now in mid-sea there is a rocky island, midway from Ithaca to rugged Samos—Star Islet called—of no great size. It has a harbor, safe for ships, on either side; and here it was the Achaeans waited, watching.

BOOK V

The Raft of Odysseus

Dawn from her couch by high Tithonus rose to bring light to immortals and to men;[20] and now the gods sat down to council. With them was Zeus, who thunders from on high, whose power is over all; and to them Athene, ever mindful of Odysseus, told of his many woes; for she was troubled by his stay at the dwelling of the nymph.

"O Father Zeus, and all you blessed gods that live forever, never again let sceptered king in all sincerity be kind and gentle, nor let him in his mind heed righteousness. Let him instead ever be stern and work unrighteous deeds; since none remembers princely Odysseus among the people whom he ruled, kind father though he was. Upon an island now he lies, deeply distressed, at the hall of the nymph Calypso, who holds him there by force. No power has he to reach his native land, for he has no ships fitted with oars, nor crews to bear him over the broad ocean-ridges. Now, too, men seek to slay his darling son, as he sails home. He went away for tidings of his father, to hallowed Pylos and to sacred Lacedaemon."

Then answering, said cloud-gathering Zeus: "My child, what word has passed the barrier of your teeth? For was it not yourself proposed the plan to have Odysseus crush these men by his return? As for Telemachus, aid him upon his way with wisdom,—as you can,—that he may come unharmed to his own native land, and the suitors in their ship may be turned back again."

He spoke, and said to Hermes, his dear son: "Hermes, since you in all things are my messenger, tell to the fair-haired nymph our steadfast purpose, that hardy Odysseus shall set forth upon his homeward way, not with gods' guidance nor with that of mortal man; but by himself, beset with sorrows, on a strong-built raft, he shall in twenty days reach fertile Scheria, the land of the Phaeacians, who are kinsmen of the gods. There shall they greatly honor him, as if he were a god, and bring him on his way by ship to his own native land, giving him stores of bronze and gold and clothing, more than Odysseus would have won from Troy itself, had he returned unharmed with his due share of spoil. Thus, then, it is his lot to see his friends and reach his high-roofed house and native land."

So he spoke, and the guide, the killer of Argus, did not disobey; forthwith under his feet he bound his beautiful sandals, immortal, made of gold, which carry him over the flood and over the boundless land swift as a breath of wind. He took the wand with which he charms to sleep the eyes of whom he will, while again whom he will he wakens out of slumber.[21] With this in hand, the powerful killer of Argus began his flight. On coming to Pieria, out of the upper air he dropped down on the deep and skimmed along the water like a bird, a gull, which down the fearful hollows of the barren sea, snatching at fish, dips its thick plumage in the spray. In such a way, through the multitude of waves, moved Hermes. But when he neared the distant island, there turning landward from the dark blue sea, he walked until he came to a great grotto where dwelt the fair-haired nymph. He found she was within. Upon the hearth a great fire blazed, and far along the island the fragrance of cleft cedar and of sandal-wood sent perfume as they burned. Indoors, and singing with sweet voice, she tended her loom and wove with golden shuttle. Around the grotto, trees grew luxuriantly, alder and poplar and sweet-scented cypress, where long-winged birds had nests,—owls, hawks, and sea-crows ready-tongued, that ply their business in the waters. Here too was trained over the hollow grotto a thriving vine, luxuriant with clusters; and four springs in a row were running with clear water, making their way from one another here and there. On every side soft meadows of violet and parsley bloomed. Here, therefore, even an immortal who should come might gaze at what he saw, and in his heart be glad. Here stood and gazed the guide, the killer of Argus.

Now after he had gazed to his heart's fill on all, straightway he entered the wide-mouthed grotto, and at a glance Calypso, the heavenly goddess, failed not to know it was he; for not unknown to one another are immortal gods, although they have their dwellings far apart. But sturdy Odysseus he did not find within; for he sat weeping on the shore, where, as of old, with tears and groans and griefs racking his heart, he watched the barren sea and poured forth tears. And now Calypso, the heavenly goddess, questioned Hermes, seating him on a handsome, shining chair:

"Pray, Hermes of the golden wand, why are you come, honored and welcome though you are? You were not often with me before. Speak what you have in mind; my heart bids me to do it, if I can do it and it is a thing that can be done. But follow me first, and let me give you entertainment."

So saying, the goddess laid a table, loading it with ambrosia and mixing ruddy nectar; and so the guide, the killer of Argus, drank and ate. But when the meal was ended and his heart was stayed with food, then thus he answered her and said:

"Goddess, you question me, a god, about my coming here, and I will truly tell my story as you bid. Zeus ordered me to come, against my will. Who of his own accord would cross such stretches of salt sea? Interminable! And no city of men at hand to make an offering to the gods and bring them chosen hecatombs! Nevertheless the will of aegis-bearing Zeus no god may cross or set at naught. He says a man is with you, the most unfortunate of all who fought for Priam's town nine years and in the tenth destroyed the city and departed home. They on their homeward way offended Athene, who raised ill winds against them and a heavy sea. Thus all the rest of his good comrades perished, but wind and water brought him here. This is the man whom Zeus now bids you send away, and quickly too, for it is not ordained that he shall perish far from friends; it is his lot to see his friends once more and reach his high-roofed house and native land."

As he said this, Calypso, the heavenly goddess, shuddered, and speaking in winged words she said: "Hard are you gods and envious beyond all to grudge that goddesses should mate with men and take without disguise mortals for lovers. Thus when rosy-fingered Dawn chose Orion for her lover, you gods that live at ease soon so begrudged him that at Ortygia chaste Artemis from her golden throne attacked and slew him with her gentle arrows. Again when fair-haired Demeter,* yielding to her heart, met Jason in the thrice-ploughed field, not long was Zeus unmindful, but hurled a gleaming bolt and laid him low.²² So again now you gods grudge me the mortal tarrying here. Yet it was I who saved him, as he rode astride his keel alone, when Zeus with a gleaming bolt smote his swift ship and wrecked it in the middle of the wine-dark sea. There all the rest of his good comrades perished, but wind and water brought him here, I loved and cherished him, and often said that I would make him an immortal, young forever. But since the will of aegis-bearing Zeus no god may cross or set at naught, let him depart, if Zeus commands and bids it, over the barren sea! Only I will not aid him on his way, for I have no ships fitted with oars, nor crews to bear him over the broad ocean-ridges; but I will freely give him counsel and not hide how he may come unharmed to his own native land."

Then said to her the guide, the killer of Argus: "Even so, then, let him go! Beware the wrath of Zeus! Let not his anger by and by grow hot against you!"

So saying, the powerful killer of Argus went his way, while the potent nymph hastened to brave Odysseus, obedient to the words of Zeus. She found him sitting on the shore, and from his eyes the tears were never dried; his sweet life ebbed away in longings for his home, because the nymph pleased him no more. Yet being compelled, he slept at night within the hollow grotto as she desired, not he. But in the daytime, sitting on the rocks and sands, with tears and groans and griefs racking his heart, he watched the barren sea

---

*The goddess of grain.

and poured forth tears. Now drawing near, the heavenly goddess said:

"Unhappy man, sorrow no longer here, nor let your days be wasted, for I at last will freely let you go. Come, then, hew the long timbers and fashion with your axe a broad-beamed raft; build a high bulwark round, and let it bear you over the misty sea. I will supply you bread, water, and the ruddy wine you like, to keep off hunger; I will provide you clothing and will send a wind to follow, that you may come unharmed to your own native land,—if the gods will, who hold the open sky, for they are mightier than I to purpose or fulfill."

As she said this, long-tried royal Odysseus shuddered, and speaking in winged words he said:

"Some other purpose, goddess, you surely have in this than aid upon my way, when you thus bid me cross on a raft that great gulf of the sea—terrible, toilsome—which trim ships cannot cross, although they speed so fast, glad in the breeze of Zeus. But I will never, notwithstanding what you say, set foot upon a raft till you consent, goddess, to swear a solemn oath that you are not meaning now to plot me further woe."

He spoke; Calypso, the heavenly goddess, smiled, caressed him with her hand and spoke thus, saying:

"A cunning rogue you are, never inclined to folly! How could you think of uttering such words! Hear this, then, Earth, and the broad Heaven above, and thou down-flowing water of Styx,—which is the strongest and most dreaded oath among the blessed gods,—I am not meaning now to plot you further woe. No, I have that in mind, and that I here propose, which I would seek for my own good were such need laid on me. Indeed, my thoughts are upright: no iron heart is in my breast, but one of pity."

So saying, the heavenly goddess led the way in haste, and he walked after in the footsteps of the goddess. And now to the hollow grotto came the goddess and the man, who sat him down upon the chair whence Hermes had arisen. The nymph then set before him all food to eat and drink which are the meats of men, and took her seat facing princely Odysseus, while maids set forth for her ambrosia and nectar; then on the food spread out before them they laid hands. So after they were satisfied with food and drink, then thus began Calypso, the heavenly goddess:

"High-born son of Laërtes, ever-scheming Odysseus, do you so wish to go at once home to your native land? Farewell, then, even so! But if at heart you knew how many woes you must endure before you reach that native land, you would remain with me, become the guardian of my home, and be immortal, despite your wish to see your wife, whom you are always longing for day after day. Yet not inferior to her I count myself, either in form or stature. Surely it is not likely that mortal women rival the immortals in form and beauty."

Then wise Odysseus answered her and said: "O lady goddess, be not wroth at what I say. Full well I know that heedful Penelope, compared with you, is poor to look upon in height and beauty; for she is human, but you are an immortal, young forever. Yet even so, I wish—yes, every day I long—to travel home and see my day of coming. And if again one of the gods shall wreck me on the wine-dark sea, I will be patient still, bearing within my breast a heart well-tried with trouble; for in times past much have I borne and much have I toiled, in waves and war; to that, let this be added."

As he thus spoke, the sun went down and darkness came; and going to the inner chamber of the hollow grotto, they stayed together for the happy night.

Soon as the early rosy-fingered dawn appeared, quickly Odysseus dressed in coat and tunic; and the nymph dressed herself in a long silvery robe, finespun and graceful, she bound a beautiful golden girdle round her waist, and put a veil upon her head. Then she prepared to send forth brave Odysseus. She gave him a great axe, which fitted well his hands; it was an axe of bronze, sharp on both sides, and had a beautiful olive handle, strongly fastened; she gave him too a polished adze. And now she led the way to the island's farther shore where trees grew tall, alder and poplar and sky-stretching pine, long-seasoned, very dry, that would float lightly. When she had shown him where the trees grew tall, homeward Calypso went, the heavenly goddess, while he began to cut the logs.

Quickly the work was done. Twenty in all he felled, and trimmed them with the axe, smoothed them with skill, and leveled them to the line. Meanwhile, Calypso, the heavenly goddess, brought him augers, with which he bored each piece and fitted all, and then with pins and crossbeams fastened the whole together. As when a man skillful in carpentry lays out the deck of a broad freight-ship, of such a size Odysseus built his broad-beamed raft. He raised a bulwark, set with many ribs, and finished with long timbers on the top. He made a mast and sail-yard fitted to it; he made a rudder, too, with which to steer. And then he caulked the raft from end to end with willow withes, to guard against the water, and much material he used. Meanwhile, Calypso, the heavenly goddess, brought him cloth to make a sail, and well did he contrive this too. Braces and halyards and sheet-ropes he set up in her and then with levers heaved her into the sacred sea.

The fourth day came, and he had finished all. So on the fifth divine Calypso sent him from the island, putting upon him fragrant clothes and giving him a bath. A skin the goddess gave him, filled with dark wine, a second large one full of water, and provisions in a sack. She put upon the raft whatever delicacies pleased him and sent along his course a fair and gentle breeze. Joyfully to the breeze royal Odysseus spread his sail, and with his rudder skillfully he steered from where he sat. No sleep fell on his eyelids as he gazed upon the Pleiads, on Boötes which sets late, and on the Bear which men call Wagon too, which turns around one spot, watching Orion, and alone does not dip in the Ocean-stream; for Calypso, the heavenly goddess, bade him to cross the sea with the Bear upon his left. So seventeen days he sailed across the sea, on the eighteenth there came in sight the dim heights of Phaeacia, where nearest him it lay. It seemed a shield laid on the misty sea.

But now the mighty Earth-shaker, coming from Ethiopia, spied him afar from the mountains of the Solymi;* for Odysseus came in

---

*The region of eastern Asia.

sight as he sailed along the sea. And Poseidon grew more angered in spirit, and shaking his head he muttered to his heart:

"Aha! so then the gods have changed their plan about Odysseus, while I was with the Ethiopians! And here he is close to the land of the Phaeacians, where he is destined to escape from the ending of the woe that follows him. Yet still I hope to plunge him into sufficient ill."

So saying, he gathered clouds and stirred the deep, grasping the trident in his hands; he started tempests of wind from every side, and covered with his cloak both land and sea; night broke from heaven; forth rushed together Eurus and Notus, hard-blowing Zephyrus, and sky-born Boreas,* rolling up heavy waves. Then did Odysseus' knees grow feeble, and his very soul, and in dismay he said to his stout heart:

"Ah, woe is me! What will become of me at last? I fear that all the goddess told was true, when she declared that on the sea, before I reached my native land I should have my fill of sorrow. Now all is come to pass. Ah, with what clouds Zeus overcasts the outstretched sky! He stirred the deep, and tempests wind hurry from every side. Swift death is sure! Thrice, four times happy Danaäns who in the time gone by fell on the plain of Troy to please the sons of Atreus! Would I had died there too, and met my doom the day the Trojan host hurled at me bronze spears over the body of the son of Peleus! Then had I found a burial, and the Achaeans had borne my name afar. Now I must be cut off by an inglorious death."

As thus he spoke, a great wave broke on high and madly plunging whirled his raft about; far from the raft he fell and sent the rudder flying from his hand. The mast snapped in the middle under the fearful tempest of opposing winds that struck, and far in the sea canvas and sail-yard fell. The water held him long submerged; he could not rise at once after the crash of the great wave, for the clothing which divine Calypso gave him weighed him down. At

---

*Eurus is the east wind; Notus, south; Boreas, north; and Zephyrus, west.

The Raft of Odysseus—from a painting by N.C. Wyeth

length, however, he came up, spitting from his mouth the bitter brine which plentifully trickled also from his head. Yet even then, spent as he was, he did not forget his raft, but pushing on amid the waves laid hold of her, and in her middle got a seat and so escaped death's ending. But her the great wave drove along its current, up and down. As when in autumn Boreas drives thistleheads along the plain, and close they cling together, so the winds drove her up and down the deep. One moment Notus tossed her on for Boreas to drive; the next would Eurus give her up for Zephyrus to chase.

But the daughter of Cadmus saw him, fair-ankled Ino, that goddess pale who formerly was mortal and of human speech, but now in the water's depths shares the gods' honors.[23] She pitied Odysseus, cast away and meeting sorrow, and like a sea-bird on the wing she rose from the sea's trough, and lighting on his strong-built raft spoke to him thus:

"Unhappy man, why is earth-shaking Poseidon so furiously enraged that he makes many ills spring up around you? Destroy you shall he not, however furious he be! Only do this,—you seem to me not to lack understanding. Strip off these clothes, and leave your raft for winds to carry. Then strike out with your arms and seek a landing on the Phaeacian coast, where fate allows you safety. Here, spread this veil underneath your breast. It is immortal; have no fear of suffering or death. But when your hands shall touch the shore, untie and fling the veil into the wine-dark sea, well off the shore, yourself being turned away."

Saying this, the goddess gave the veil, and she herself plunged back into the surging sea, in likeness of a sea-bird. The dark wave closed around. Then hesitated long-tried royal Odysseus, and in dismay he said to his stout heart:

"Ah me! I fear that here again an immortal plots me harm in bidding me leave my raft. I will not yet obey; for in the distance I saw land, where it was said my safety lies. This I will do, for best it seems: so long as the beams hold in the fastenings, here I will stay and bide what I must bear; but when the surge shatters my raft, then I will swim. There is no better plan."

While he thus doubted in his mind and heart, earth-shaking Poseidon raised a great wave, gloomy and grievous, and with arching crest, and launched it on him. And as a gusty wind tosses a heap of grain when it is dry, and some it scatters one way, some another, so were the long beams scattered. But Odysseus mounting a beam, as if he rode a steed, stripped off the clothing which divine Calypso gave, spread quickly the veil underneath his breast, and plunged down headlong in the sea, with hands outstretched, ready to swim. The great Earth-shaker spied him, and shaking his head he muttered to his heart:

"Thus, after meeting many ills, be tossed about the sea until you join a people who are favorites of Zeus; but even then, I trust, you will not laugh at danger."

Saying this, he lashed his full-maned horses and came to Aegae, where his lordly dwelling stands.

And now Athene, daughter of Zeus, formed a fresh project. She barred the pathway of the other winds, bade them to cease and all be laid to rest; but she roused bustling Boreas and before it broke the waves, that safely among the oar-loving Phaeacians might come high-born Odysseus, freed from death and doom.

Then two nights and two days on the resistless waves he drifted; many a time his heart faced death. But when the fair-haired dawn brought the third day, then the wind ceased; there came a breathless calm; and close at hand he spied the coast, as he cast a keen glance forward, upborne on a great wave. As when the precious life is watched by children in a father, who lies in sickness, suffering great pain and slowly wasting,—for a hostile power assails him,—and then the one thus prized the gods set free from danger; so precious in Odysseus' eyes appeared the land and trees. Onward he swam, impatient for his feet to touch the ground. But when he was as far away as one can call, he heard a pounding of the ocean on the ledges; for the great waves roared as on the barren land they madly dashed, and all was whirled in spray. There was no harbor here to hold a ship, no open roadstead; only projecting bluffs, ledges, and reefs. At this Odysseus' knees grew feeble, and his very soul, and in dismay he said to his stout heart:

"Alas! when Zeus now lets me see unlooked-for land, and forcing my way along the gulf I finally reach its end, no landing anywhere appears out of the foaming sea. Outside are jagged reefs; around thunder the surging waves, and smooth and steep rises the rocky shore. To the edge the sea is deep, and impossible it is to get a footing with both feet and so escape from harm. If I should try to land, great sweeping waves might dash me on the solid rock; useless would the attempt be! But if I swim still farther, hoping to find a sloping shore and harbors off the sea, I fear a sweeping storm may bear me yet again along the swarming sea, loudly lamenting; or God may send upon me a monster of the deep,—and many such great Amphitrite breeds,—for I know how angry is the great Land-shaker."

While he thus doubted in his mind and heart, a huge wave bore him onward toward the rugged shore. There would his skin have been stripped off and his bones broken, had not the goddess, clear-eyed Athene, given him counsel. Struggling, he grasped the rock with both his hands and clung there, groaning, till the great wave passed. That one he thus escaped, but the back-flowing water struck him again, still struggling, and swept him out to sea. And just as, when a polyp is torn from out its bed, about its suckers clustering pebbles cling, so on the rocks pieces of skin were stripped from his strong hands. The great wave covered him. Then miserably, before his time, Odysseus would have died, if clear-eyed Athene had not given him ready thought. Rising beyond the waves which thundered on the coast, he swam along outside, eying the land, in hopes to find a sloping shore and harbors off the sea. But when, as he swam, he reached the mouth of a fair-flowing river, there the ground seemed most fit, clear of all stones and sheltered from the breeze. As he felt the river flowing forth, within his heart he prayed:

"Listen O lord, whoe'er thou art![24] Thee, long desired, I find, when flying from the sea and from Poseidon's threats. Respected even of immortal gods is he who comes a fugitive, as I here now come to thy current and thy knees through weary toil. Show pity, lord! I call myself thy suppliant."

He spoke, and the god straightway stayed the stream and checked the waves, before him made a calm, and brought him safely into the river's mouth. Both knees hung loose, and both his sturdy arms, for by the brine his power was broken. His body was all swollen, and water gushed in streams from mouth and nostrils. So, breathless and speechless, in a swoon he lay and dire fatigue engulfed him. But when he gained his breath, and in his breast the spirit rallied, then he unbound the veil of the goddess and dropped it in the river running out to sea; and back a great wave bore it down the stream, and Ino soon received it in her friendly hands. But he, retreating from the river, lay down among the rushes and kissed the bounteous earth, and in dismay he said to his stout heart:

"Ah me! What shall I do? What will become of me even now? If by the stream I watch throughout the weary night, may not the bitter frost and the fresh dew together after this swoon end my exhausted life? The breeze from off a river blows cool toward early morning. But if I climb the hill-side up to the dusky wood and sleep in the thick bushes,—supposing that the chill and weariness depart and pleasant sleep come on,—I am afraid I may become the wild beasts' prey and prize."

Yet on reflecting thus, this seemed the better way: he hastened therefore to the wood. This he found near the water, with open space around. He crept under a pair of shrubs sprung from a single spot; the one was wild, the other common, olive. These no force of wind with its chill breath could pierce, no sunbeams smite, nor rain pass through, they grew so thickly intertwined with one another. Under them crept Odysseus, and quickly with his hands he scraped a bed together, an ample one, for a thick fall of leaves was there, enough to shelter two or three men in winter-time, however severe the weather. This long-tried royal Odysseus saw with joy, and lay down in the midst, heaping the fallen leaves above. As a man hides a brand in a dark bed of ashes, at some outlying farm where neighbors are not near, hoarding a seed of fire not otherwise to be lighted, even so did Odysseus hide himself in leaves, and on his eyes Athene poured a sleep, quickly to ease him from the fatigue of toil, letting his eyelids close.

BOOK VI

The Landing in Phaeacia

Thus long-tried royal Odysseus slumbered here, heavy with sleep and toil; but Athene went to the land and town of the Phaeacians. This people once in ancient times lived in the open Highlands, near that rude folk the Cyclops, who often plundered them, being in strength more powerful than they. Moving them thence, godlike Nausithoüs, their leader, established them at Scheria, aloof from trading folk. He ran a wall around the town, built houses there, made temples for the gods, and laid out farms; but he long since had met his doom and gone to the house of Hades, and Alcinoüs now was reigning, trained in wisdom by the gods. To this man's dwelling came the goddess, clear-eyed Athene, planning a safe return for brave Odysseus. She hastened to a chamber, richly wrought, in which a maid was sleeping, of form and beauty like the immortals, Nausicaä, daughter of proud Alcinoüs. Near by two maidens, blessed with beauty by the Graces, slept by the threshold, one on either hand. The shining doors were shut; but Athene, like a breath of air, moved to the maid's couch, stood by her head, and thus addressed her,—taking the likeness of the daughter of Dymas, the famed seaman, a maiden just Nausicaä's age, dear to her heart. Taking her guise, thus spoke clear-eyed Athene:

"Nausicaä, how did your mother have a child so heedless? Your gay clothes lie uncared for, though the wedding time is near, when you must wear fine clothes yourself and furnish them to those that may attend you. From things like these a good repute arises, and father and honored mother are made glad. Then let us go to wash them at the dawn of day, and I will go to help, that you may soon be ready; for really not much longer will you be a maid. Already you have for suitors the chief ones of the land throughout Phaeacia, where you too were born. Come, then, beg your good father early in the morning to harness the mules and cart, so as to carry the men's clothes, gowns, and bright-hued rugs. Yes, and for you yourself it is more decent so than setting forth on foot; a long way from the city are the pools."

Saying this, clear-eyed Athene passed away, off to Olympus, where they say the dwelling of the gods stands fast forever. Never with winds is it disturbed, nor by the rain made wet, nor does the snow come near; but everywhere the upper air spreads cloudless, and a bright radiance plays over all; and there the blessed gods are happy all their days. There now came the clear-eyed one, when she had spoken with the maid.

Soon bright-throned morning came, and waked fair-robed Nausicaä. She marveled at the dream, and hastened through the house to tell it to her parents, her dear father and her mother. She found them still indoors: her mother sat by the hearth among the waiting-women, spinning sea-purple yarn; she met her father at the door, just going forth to join the famous princes at the council, to which the high Phaeacians summoned him. So standing close beside him, she said to her dear father:

"Papa dear, could you not have the wagon harnessed for me,— the high one, with good wheels,—to take my nice clothes to the river to be washed which now are lying dirty? Surely for you yourself it is but proper, when you are with the first men holding councils, that you should wear clean clothing. Five good sons too are here at home,—two married, and three merry young men still,—and they are always wanting to go to the dance wearing fresh clothes. And this is all a trouble on my mind."

Such were her words, for she was shy of mentioning the joy of marriage to her father; but he understood it all, and answered thus:

"I do not grudge the mules, my child, nor anything beside. Go! Quickly shall the servants harness the wagon for you, the high one, with good wheels, fitted with rack above."

Saying this, he called to the servants, who gave heed. Out in the court they made the easy mule-cart ready; they brought the mules, and yoked them to the wagon. The maid took from her room her pretty clothing, and stowed it in the polished wagon; her mother put in a chest food the maid liked, of every kind, put delicacies in, and poured some wine into a goat-skin bottle,—the maid, meanwhile, had got into the wagon,—and gave her in a golden flask some liquid oil, that she might bathe and anoint herself, she and the waiting-women. Nausicaä took the whip and the bright reins, and cracked the whip to start. There was a clatter of the mules, and steadily they pulled, drawing the clothing and the maid,—yet not alone; beside her went the waiting-women too.

When now they came to the fair river's current, where the pools were always full,—for in abundance clear water bubbles from beneath to cleanse the foulest stains,—they turned the mules loose from the wagon, and let them stray along the eddying stream, to crop the honeyed pasturage. Then from the wagon they took the clothing in their arms, carried it into the dark water, and stamped it in the pits with rivalry in speed. And after they had washed and cleansed it of all stains, they spread it carefully along the shore, just where the waves washed up the pebbles on the beach. Then bathing and anointing with the oil, they presently took dinner on the river bank and waited for the clothes to dry in the sunshine. And when they were refreshed with food, the maids and she, they then began to play at ball, throwing their veils off. White-armed Nausicaä led their sport; and as the huntress Artemis goes down a mountain, down long Taÿgetus or Erymanthus, exulting in the boars and the swift deer, while round her sport the woodland nymphs, daughters of aegis-bearing Zeus, and glad is Leto's* heart, for over all the rest her child towers by head and brow, and easily marked is she, though all are fair; so did this virgin pure excel her women.

But when Nausicaä thought to turn toward home once more, to

---

*Leto is the mother of Artemis and Apollo, but is otherwise a minor goddess.

yoke the mules and fold up the clean clothes, then a new plan the goddess formed, clear-eyed Athene; for she would have Odysseus wake and see the bright-eyed maid, who might to the Phaeacian city show the way. Just then the princess tossed the ball to one of her women, and missing her it fell in the deep eddy. Thereat they screamed aloud. Royal Odysseus woke, and sitting up debated in his mind and heart:

"Alas! To what men's land am I come now? Lawless and savage are they, with no regard for right, or are they kind to strangers and reverent toward the gods? It was as if there came to me the delicate voice of maids—nymphs, it may be, who haunt the craggy peaks of hills, the springs of streams and grassy marshes; or am I now, perhaps, near men of human speech? Suppose I make a trial for myself, and see."

So saying, royal Odysseus crept from the thicket, but with his strong hand broke a spray of leaves from the close wood, to be a covering round his body for his nakedness. He set off like a lion that is bred among the hills and trusts its strength; onward it goes, beaten with rain and wind; its two eyes glare; and now in search of oxen or of sheep it moves, or tracking the wild deer; its belly bids it make trial of the flocks, even by entering the guarded folds;[25] so was Odysseus about to meet those fair-haired maids, all naked though he was, for need constrained him. To them he seemed a loathsome sight, befouled with brine. They hurried off, one here, one there, over the stretching sands. Only the daughter of Alcinoüs stayed, for in her breast Athene had put courage and from her limbs took fear. Steadfast she stood to meet him. And now Odysseus doubted whether to make his suit by clasping the knees of the bright-eyed maid, or where he stood, aloof, in winning words to make that suit, and try if she would show the town and give him clothing. Reflecting thus, it seemed the better way to make his suit in winning words, aloof; for fear if he should clasp her knees, the maid might be offended. Forthwith he spoke, a winning and shrewd speech:

"I am your suppliant, princess. Are you some god or mortal? If one of the gods who hold the open sky, to Artemis, daughter of mighty Zeus, in beauty, height, and bearing I find you most resemble. But if you are a mortal, living on the earth, most happy are your father and your honored mother, most happy your brothers also. Surely their hearts ever grow warm with pleasure over you, when watching such a blossom moving in the dance. And then how happy he, beyond all others, who shall with gifts prevail and lead you home. For I never before saw such a being with these eyes—no man, no woman. I am amazed to see. At Delos once, by Apollo's altar, something like you I noticed, a young palm-shoot springing up; for there too I came, and a great troop was with me, upon a journey where I was to meet with bitter trials. And just as when I looked on that I marveled long within, since never before sprang such a stalk from earth; so, lady, I admire and marvel now at you, and greatly fear to touch your knees. Yet grievous woe is on me. Yesterday, after twenty days, I escaped the wine-dark sea, and all that time the waves and boisterous winds bore me from the island of Ogygia. Now some god cast me here, that probably here also I may meet with trouble; for I do not think trouble will cease, but much the gods will first accomplish. Then, princess, have compassion, for it is you to whom through many grievous toils I first am come; none else I know of all who own this city and this land. Show me the town, and give me a rag to throw around me, if you had perhaps on coming here some wrapper for your linen. And may the gods grant all that in your thoughts you long for: husband and home and true accord may they bestow; for a better and higher gift than this there cannot be, when with accordant aims man and wife have a home. Great grief it is to foes and joy to friends; but they themselves best know its meaning."

Then answered him white-armed Nausicaä: "Stranger, because you do not seem a common, senseless person,—and Olympian Zeus himself distributes fortune to mankind and gives to high and low even as he will to each; and this he gave to you, and you must bear it therefore,—now you have reached our city and our land, you shall not lack for clothes nor anything besides which it is fit a hard-pressed suppliant should find. I will point out the town and tell its people's name. The Phaeacians own this city and this land, and I am the daughter of proud Alcinoüs, on whom the might and power of the Phaeacians rests."

She spoke, and called her fair-haired waiting-women: "My women, stay! Why do you run because you saw a man? You surely do not think him evil-minded. The man is not alive, and never will be born, who can come and offer harm to the Phaeacian land: for we are very dear to the immortals; and then we live aloof, far on the surging sea, no other tribe of men has dealings with us. But this poor man is here through having lost his way, and we should give him aid; for in the charge of Zeus all strangers and beggars stand, and a small gift is welcome. Then give, my women, to the stranger food and drink, and bathe him in the river where there is shelter from the breeze."

She spoke; the others stopped and called to one another, and down they brought Odysseus to the place of shelter, even as Nausicaä, daughter of proud Alcinoüs, had ordered. They placed a robe and tunic there for clothing, they gave him in the golden flask the liquid oil, and bade him bathe in the stream's currents. Then to the waiting-women said royal Odysseus:

"Women, stand here aside, while by myself I wash the salt from off my back and with the oil anoint me, for it is long since ointment touched my skin. But before you I will not bathe; for I am ashamed to bare myself among you fair-haired maids."

So he spoke; the women went away, and told it to the maid. And now with water from the stream royal Odysseus washed his skin clean of the salt which clung about his back and his broad shoulders, and wiped from his head the foam brought by the barren sea; and when he had thoroughly bathed and oiled himself and had put on the clothing which the chaste maiden gave, Athene, daughter of Zeus, made him taller than before and stouter to behold, and she made the curling locks to fall around his head as on the hyacinth flower. As when a man lays gold on silver,—some skillful man whom Hephaestus and Pallas Athene have trained in every art, and he fashions graceful work; so did she cast a grace upon his head and shoulders. He walked apart along the shore, and there sat down, beaming with grace and beauty. The maid observed; then to her fair-haired waiting-women said:

"Listen, my white-armed women, while I speak. Not without purpose on the part of all the gods that hold Olympus is this man's meeting with the godlike Phaeacians. A while ago, he really seemed to me ill-looking, but now he is like the gods who hold the open sky. Ah, might a man like this be called my husband, having his home here, and content to stay! But give, my women, to the stranger food and drink."

She spoke, and very willingly they heeded and obeyed, and set beside Odysseus food and drink. Then long-tried royal Odysseus eagerly drank and ate, for he had long been fasting.

And now to other matters white-armed Nausicaä turned her thoughts. She folded the clothes and laid them in the beautiful wagon, she yoked the stout-hoofed mules, mounted herself, and calling to Odysseus thus she spoke and said:

"Arise now, stranger, and hasten to the town, that I may bring you on the way to my wise father's house, where you shall see. I promise you, the best of all Phaeacia. Only do this,—you seem to me not to lack understanding: while we are passing through the fields and farms, here with my women, behind the mules and cart, walk rapidly along, and I will lead the way. But as we near the town,—round which is a lofty rampart, a beautiful harbor on each side and a narrow road between,—there curved ships line the road; for every man has his own mooring-place. Beyond is the assembly near the beautiful grounds of Poseidon, constructed out of blocks of stone deeply imbedded. Further along, they make the black ships' tackling, cables and canvas, and shape out the oars; for the Phaeacians do not care for bow and quiver, only for masts and oars of ships and the trim ships themselves, with which it is their joy to cross the foaming sea. Now the rude talk of such as these I would avoid, that no one afterwards may give me blame. For very crude people are about the place, and some coarse man might say, if he should meet us: 'What tall and handsome stranger is following

Nausicaä? Where did she find him? A husband he will be, her very own. Some castaway, perhaps, she rescued from his vessel, some foreigner; for we have no neighbors here. Or at her prayer some long-entreated god has come straight down from heaven, and he will keep her his forever. So much the better, if she has gone herself and found a husband elsewhere! The people of our own land here, Phaeacians, she disdains, though she has many high-born suitors.' So they will talk, and for me it would prove a scandal. I should myself censure a girl who acted so, who, heedless of friends, while father and mother were alive, mingled with men before her public wedding. And, stranger, listen now to what I say, that you may soon obtain assistance and safe conduct from my father. Near our road you will see a stately grove of poplar trees, belonging to Athene; in it a fountain flows, and round it is a meadow. That is my father's park, his fruitful vineyard, as far from the town as one can call. There sit and wait a while, until we come to the town and reach my father's palace. But when you think we have already reached the palace, enter the city of the Phaeacians, and ask for the palace of my father, proud Alcinoüs. Easily is it known; a child, though young, could show the way; for the Phaeacians do not build their houses like the dwelling of Alcinoüs their prince. But when his house and court receive you, pass quickly through the hall until you find my mother. She sits in the firelight by the hearth, spinning sea-purple yarn, a marvel to behold, and resting against a pillar. Her handmaids sit behind her. Here too my father's chair rests on the selfsame pillar, and here he sits and sips his wine like an immortal. Passing him by, stretch out your hands to our mother's knees, if you would see the day of your return in gladness and with speed, although you come from far. If she regards you kindly in her heart, then there is hope that you may see your friends and reach your stately house and native land."

Saying this, with her bright whip she struck the mules, and fast they left the river's streams; and well they trotted, well they plied their feet, and skillfully she reined them that those on foot might follow,—the waiting-women and Odysseus,—and moderately she used the lash. The sun was setting when they reached the famous grove, Athene's sacred ground, where royal Odysseus sat down. And thereupon he prayed to the daughter of mighty Zeus:

"Listen, thou child of aegis-bearing Zeus, unwearied one! Oh hear me now, although before thou didst not hear me, when I was wrecked, what time the great Land-shaker wrecked me. Grant that I come among the Phaeacians welcomed and pitied by them."

So spoke he in his prayer, and Pallas Athene heard, but did not yet appear to him in open presence; for she regarded still her father's brother, who stoutly strove with godlike Odysseus till he reached his land.

BOOK VII

The Welcome of Alcinoüs

Here, then, long-tried royal Odysseus made his prayer; but to the town the strong mules bore the maid. And when she reached her father's famous palace, she stopped before the door-way, and round her stood her brothers, men like immortals, who from the cart unyoked the mules and carried the clothing in. The maid went to her chamber, where a fire was kindled for her by an old Apeiraean woman, the chamber-servant Eurymedousa, whom long ago curved ships brought from Apeira; her they had chosen from the rest to be the gift of honor for Alcinoüs, because he was the lord of all Phaeacians, and people listened to his voice as if he were a god. She was the nurse of white-armed Nausicaä at the palace, and she it was who kindled her the fire and in her room prepared her supper.

And now Odysseus rose to go to the city; but Athene kindly drew thick clouds around Odysseus, for fear some bold Phaeacian meeting him might trouble him with talk and ask him who he was. And just as he was entering the pleasant town, the goddess, clear-eyed Athene, came to meet him, disguised as a young girl bearing a water-jar. She paused as she drew near, and royal Odysseus asked:

"My child, could you not guide me to the house of one Alcinoüs, who is ruler of this people? For I am a toil-worn stranger newly come from a distant foreign shore. Therefore I know not one among the men who own this city and this land."

Then said to him the goddess, clear-eyed Athene: "Certainly, good old stranger, I will show the house for which you ask, for it is not far from my good father's. But follow in silence; I will lead the way. Cast not a glance at any man and ask no questions; for our people do not well endure a stranger, nor courteously receive a man who comes from elsewhere. They trust in their swift ships and traverse the great deep, as the Earth-shaker allows them. Swift are their ships as wing or thought."

Saying this, Pallas Athene led the way in haste, and he walked after in the footsteps of the goddess. So the Phaeacians, famed for shipping, did not observe him walking through the town among them, because Athene, the fair-haired powerful goddess, did not allow it, but in the kindness of her heart cast a magic mist about him. And now Odysseus admired the harbors, the trim ships, the meeting-places of the lords themselves, and the long walls that were so high, fitted with palisades, a marvel to behold. Then as they neared the famous palace of the king, the goddess, clear-eyed Athene, thus began:

"Here, good old stranger, is the house you bade me show. You will see heaven-descended kings sitting at table here. But enter, and have no misgivings in your heart; for the courageous man in all affairs better attains his end, come he from whence he may. First you shall find the Queen within the hall. Arete is her name; sprung from the self-same ancestry as King Alcinoüs. In early days earth-shaking Poseidon begot Nausithoüs by Periboea, the chief of womankind in beauty and youngest daughter of that bold Eurymedon who once was king of the presumptuous giants;[26] but he brought ruin on his impious tribe and on himself. By Periboea Poseidon had a son, sturdy Nausithoüs, who was king of the Phaeacians. Nausithoüs begot Rhexenor and Alcinoüs; but before Rhexenor had a son, Apollo of the silver bow smote him within his hall, soon after he was wed, and he left behind an only child, Arete. Alcinoüs took Arete for his wife, and he has honored her as no one else on earth is honored among the women who today keep houses for their husbands. Such heartfelt honor has she had, and has it still, from her own children, from Alcinoüs himself, and from the people also, who gaze on her as on a god and greet her with welcomes when she walks about the town. For of sound judgment, woman though she is, she has no lack; and those whom she regards, though men, find troubles clear away. If she regards you kindly in her heart, then there is hope that you may see your friends and reach your high-roofed house and native land."

Saying this, clear-eyed Athene passed away, over the barren sea. She turned from pleasant Scheria, and came to Marathon and wide-wayed Athens and entered there the strong house of Erechtheus.* Meanwhile Odysseus neared the lordly palace of Alcinoüs, and his heart was deeply stirred so that he paused before he crossed the brazen threshold; for a sheen as of the sun or moon played through the high-roofed house of proud Alcinoüs. On either hand ran walls of bronze from threshold to recess, and round about the ceiling was a cornice of dark metal. Doors made of gold closed in the solid building. The doorposts were of silver and stood on a bronze threshold, silver the lintel overhead, and gold the handle. On the two sides were gold and silver dogs; these had Hephaestus wrought with subtle craft to guard the house of proud Alcinoüs, creatures immortal, young forever. Within were seats planted against the wall on this side and on that, from threshold to recess, in long array; and over these were strewn light finespun robes, the work of women. Here the Phaeacian leaders used to sit, drinking and eating, holding constant cheer. And golden youths on massive pedestals stood and held flaming torches in their hands to light by night the palace for the feasters.

In the king's house are fifty serving maids, some grinding at the mill the yellow corn, some plying looms or twisting yarn, who as they sit are like the leaves of a tall poplar; and from their close-spun linen liquid oil will fall. And as Phaeacian men are skilled beyond all others in speeding a swift ship along the sea, so are their women practiced at the loom; for Athene has given them in large measure skill in fair works and noble minds.

Without the court and close beside its gate is a large garden,

---

*A legendary Athenian hero-king, worshiped in conjunction with Poseidon.

covering four acres; around it runs a hedge on either side. Here grow tall thriving trees—pears, pomegranates, apples with shining fruit, sweet figs and thriving olives. On them fruit never fails; it is not gone in winter or in summer, but lasts throughout the year; for constantly the west wind's breath brings some to bud and mellows others. Pear ripens upon pear, apple on apple, cluster on cluster, fig on fig. Here too a teeming vineyard has been planted, one part of which, the drying place, lying on level ground, is heating in the sun; elsewhere men gather grapes; and elsewhere still they tread them. In front, the grapes are green and shed their flower, but a second row are now just turning dark. And here trim garden-beds, along the outer line, spring up in every kind and all the year are gay. Near by, two fountains rise, one scattering its streams throughout the garden, one bounding by another course beneath the court-yard gate toward the high house; from this the townsfolk draw their water. Such at the palace of Alcinoüs were the gods' splendid gifts.

Here long-tried royal Odysseus stood and gazed. Then after he had gazed to his heart's fill on all, he quickly crossed the threshold and came within the house. He found the Phaeacian captains and councilors pouring libations from their cups to the clear-sighted killer of Argus, to whom they always offer a last cup when they prepare for bed. Along the hall went long-tried royal Odysseus, still clad in the thick cloud which Athene cast about him, until he came to Arete and to King Alcinoüs. About Arete's knees Odysseus threw his arms, and then the magic cloud retreated. Seeing the man, the people of the house were hushed and marveled as they gazed, and thus Odysseus made his supplication:

"Arete, daughter of divine Rhexenor, to your husband I am come, and to your knees, through many toils, and to these feasters too. The gods bestow upon them the blessing of long life, and to his children may each leave the wealth within his hall and every honor men have given. But quickly grant me aid to reach my native land; for long cut off from friends I have been meeting hardship."

When he had spoken thus, he sat down on the hearth among the ashes by the fire, while all were hushed to silence. At last the old lord Echeneüs spoke, the oldest man of the Phaeacian race, preëminent in speech and full of knowledge of the past. He with good will addressed them thus, and said:

"Alcinoüs, this is not quite honorable for you; it is unseemly that a stranger should be sitting on the hearth among the ashes. Awaiting words of yours, these men hold back. Come then, raise up the stranger, seat him on a silver-studded chair, and bid the pages mix more wine, that we may also pour to Zeus, the Thunderer, who waits on worthy suppliants. And let the housekeeper give supper to the stranger from what she has in store."

Now when revered Alcinoüs heard his word, he took by the hand Odysseus, keen and crafty, raised him from the hearth and placed him on a shining chair, making his son arise, manly Laodamas, who sat beside his father, for his father loved him best. And water for the hands a servant brought in a beautiful pitcher made of gold, and poured it out over a silver basin for their washing, and spread a polished table by their side. And the grave housekeeper brought bread and placed before them, setting out food of many a kind, freely giving of her store. So long-tried royal Odysseus drank and ate. And now to the page revered Alcinoüs said:

"Pontonoüs, mix a bowl and pass the wine to all within the hall, that we may also pour to Zeus, the Thunderer, who waits on worthy suppliants."

He spoke; Pontonoüs stirred the bracing wine and served to all, with a first pious portion for the cup. So after they had poured and drunk as their hearts would, then thus Alcinoüs addressed them, saying:

"Listen, Phaeacian captains and councilors, and let me tell you what the heart within me bids. After the feast is over, go to your homes and rest; and in the morning we will call more elders here, and entertain the stranger at the hall, and make fit offering to the gods. Then afterwards we will take thought about his going, so that the stranger, free from toil and trouble, may by our guidance reach his land in gladness and with speed, although he comes from far. So shall he, meanwhile, meet no ill or harm till he set foot in his own land; there, in the days to come, he shall receive whatever fate and the stern spinners wove in his birth-thread when his mother bore him. But if he be some deathless one come from above, then do the gods herein deal with us strangely; for heretofore the gods have always shown themselves without disguise, and when we offer splendid hecatombs they sit beside us at the feast, even like ourselves. And if a man, walking alone, meet them upon his way, they do not hide; for we are of their kin, as are the Cyclops and the wild tribes of Giants."

Then wise Odysseus answered him and said: "Alcinoüs, other thoughts of me be yours! I am not like the deathless ones who hold the open sky, either in form or bearing, but on the contrary I am like men that die; and whomsoever you have known bearing most grief among mankind, his sorrows I could equal. Yes, even more distresses still I might relate which first and last I bore at the gods' bidding. But let me now, though sick at heart, take food; for nothing is more brutal than an angry belly. Perforce it bids a man attend, sadly though he be worn, though grief be on his mind. Even so, I too have grief upon my mind, and yet this eternally calls me to eat and drink; all I have borne it makes me quite forget, and bids me take my fill. But do you hasten at the dawn of day to land unhappy me in my own country, much though I still must bear; and let life cease when once I have beheld my goods, my slaves, and my great high-roofed house."

He spoke, and all approved and bade send forth the stranger, for rightly had he spoken. Then after they had poured and drunk as their hearts would, desiring rest, they each departed homeward. So in the hall was royal Odysseus left behind; Arete, too, and godlike Alcinoüs sat beside him, while servants cleared away the dishes of the meal. Then thus began white-armed Arete; for when she saw Odysseus she knew his robe and tunic to be the beautiful clothing which she herself had made—she and her waiting-women; and speaking in winged words, she said:

"Stranger, I will myself first ask you this: Who are you? Of what

reached my halls and tarried long distressed for lack of aid. Come, let us launch into the sacred sea a black ship, freshly fitted, and let the two and fifty youths be chosen from the land who have at former times been found the best. Then after lashing carefully the oars upon the pins, all disembark and take a hasty meal, coming for this to me; I will make good provision for you all. That charge I give the youths. But for the rest of you, you sceptered kings, come to my goodly palace, that there within my hall we entertain the stranger; let none refuse; and call the sacred bard, Demodocus, for surely the gods have granted him exceeding skill in song, to cheer us in whatever way his soul is moved to sing."

So saying, he led the way, the sceptered princes followed, and a page went to seek the sacred bard, while two and fifty picked young men departed, as he ordered, to the shore of the barren sea. On coming to the ship and to the sea, they launched the black ship into deep water, put mast and sail in the black ship, fitted the oars into their leathern slings, all in due order, and up aloft spread the white sail. Out in the stream they moored her, then took their way to the great house of wise Alcinoüs. Filled were the porticoes, the courts, and rooms with those already come; many were there, both young and old. For them Alcinoüs sacrificed twelve sheep, eight white-toothed swine, two slow-paced oxen; these the men flayed and served, and made a merry feast.

Meanwhile the page drew near, leading the honored bard. The Muse had greatly loved him, and had given him good and ill: she took away his eyesight, but gave delightful song. Pontonoüs placed for him among the feasters a silver-studded chair, backed by a lofty pillar, and hung the tuneful lyre upon its peg above his head, and the page showed him how to reach it with his hand. By him he set a tray and a good table, and placed thereon a cup of wine to drink as need should bid. So on the food spread out before them they laid hands. Now after they had stayed desire for drink and food, the Muse impelled the bard to sing men's glorious deeds, a lay whose fame was then as wide as is the sky. He sang the strife of Odysseus with Pelian Achilles,—how they once quarreled at the gods' high feast with furious words, and Agamemnon, king of men, rejoiced in spirit when the bravest of the Achaeans quarreled;[27] for Phoebus Apollo had by oracle declared it so should be, at hallowed Pytho, when Agamemnon crossed its stony threshold to ask for a response. Then was the day the tide of woe began to roll on Trojans and on Danaäns by will of mighty Zeus.

So sang the famous bard. Meanwhile Odysseus clutched his great purple cloak in his stout hands and drew it round his head, hiding his beautiful face; for he felt shame before the Phaeacians as from beneath his brow he dropped the tears. But when the sacred bard paused in the song, Odysseus dried his tears, took from his head the cloak, and seizing his double cup poured offerings to the gods. Then as the other would begin again, cheered on to sing by the Phaeacian chiefs,—for they enjoyed the story,—again would Odysseus, covering his head, break into sobs. And yet he hid from all the rest the tears he shed; only Alcinoüs marked him and took heed, for he sat near and heard his deep-drawn sighs; and to the Phaeacians, who delight in oars, he straightway said:

"Listen, Phaeacian captains and councilors! Now have we satisfied desire for the shared feast and for the lyre, which is the fellow of the stately feast. Let us then come away and try all kinds of games, so that the stranger, going home, may tell his friends how greatly we surpass all other men in boxing, wrestling, long-jumping, speed of foot."

So saying, he led the way, the others followed after. The page hung on its peg the tuneful lyre, then took by the hand Demodocus and led him from the hall, guiding his steps along the selfsame road by which the rest of the Phaeacian chiefs went forth to view the games. Thus to the assembly-place they came, a great troop following after, thousands in number; and many a gallant youth stood waiting there. Forth stood Acroneüs, Ocyalus and Elatreus, Nauteus and Prymneus, Anchialus and Eretmeus, Ponteus and Proreus, Thoön, Anabasineüs and Amphialus the son of Polyneüs, son of the carpenter. Forth also stood a youth like murderous Ares,* Euryalus, the son of Naubolus, who was the first in beauty and in stature of all Phaeacians after brave Laodamas. Forth stood three sons of good Alcinoüs,—Laodamas, Halius, and matchless Clytoneüs. At first they tried each other in the foot-race. Straight from a mark their track was measured; and all flew swiftly off together, raising the dust along the plain. Best in the race was gallant Clytoneüs; and by such space as at the plough the mule-course runs, so far he shot ahead and reached the crowd; the rest were left behind. Next in the hardy wrestling-match they had a trial, and here Euryalus surpassed all champions. At long-jumping Amphialus was foremost, while at the discus the leader was Elatreus. In boxing it was Laodamas, the good son of Alcinoüs. So when all hearts were gladdened by the games, up spoke Laodamas, son of Alcinoüs:

"Come, friends, and let us ask the stranger if he knows games and has some skill in any. In build, at all events, he is no common man,—in thighs, and calves, and arms above, strong neck, and massive chest. Fit years he does not lack, only he has been broken down by many hardships; for nothing, I maintain, is worse to break a man than sea-life, however strong he be."

Then answered him Euryalus, and said: "Laodamas, what you say is rightly spoken. Go, challenge him yourself by word of mouth."

Now when the good son of Alcinoüs heard his words, he went and stood before them all and thus addressed Odysseus:

"Come, good old stranger, do you also try the games, if you have skill in any. Games you should know. There is no greater glory for a man in all his life than what he wins with his own feet and hands. Come then, and try! Drive trouble from your heart! Your journey hence shall not be long delayed. Already the ship is launched, the sailors ready."

Then wise Odysseus answered him and said: "Laodamas, why

---

*The god of war, son of Zeus and Here.

mock me with this challenge? Sorrow is on my heart far more than games; for in times past much have I borne and much have I toiled, and now I sit in your assembly longing for my home and supplicate your king and all this people."

Then answered back Euryalus, and mocked him to his face: "No, indeed, stranger, you do not look like one expert in games, much as these count with men; more like a person moving to and fro on ships of many oars, captain of trading seamen, one whose mind is on his cargo, watching freights and greedy gains. You are not like an athlete."

But looking sternly on him wise Odysseus said: "Stranger, your words are rude. You seem a heedless person. So true it is that not to all alike the gods grant what is pleasing, in stature, wisdom, and the power of speech. For one man is in form inferior, but a god crowns his words with beauty, and men behold him and rejoice; with sure effect he speaks and a sweet modesty; he shines where men are gathered, and as he walks the town men gaze as on some god. And one again in form is like the immortals, but his is not the crowning grace of words. So you, in form, are excellent,—better a god could not fashion,—but you are weak in judgment. You stirred the very soul within my breast by talking so discourteously. No! I am not unskilled in games, as you declare; I was among the foremost, I maintain, while I could trust my youth and these my arms. Now I am overwhelmed with pain and trouble; for much have I endured, cleaving my way through wars of men and through the boisterous seas. Still even so, all woe-worn as I am, I will attempt the games, because your words were galling; you provoked me, talking thus."

He spoke, and with his cloak still on he sprang and seized a discus larger than the rest and thick, heavier by not a little than those which the Phaeacians were using for themselves. This with a twist he sent from his stout hand. The stone hummed as it went; down to the ground crouched the Phaeacian oarsmen, notable men at sea, at the stone's cast. Past all the marks it flew, swift speeding from his hand. Athene marked the distances, taking a human form, and thus she spoke and cried aloud:

"A blind man, stranger, could pick out your piece by feeling merely, because it is not huddled in the crowd, but lies ahead of all. Have a good heart, this bout at least; for no Phaeacian will reach that or overpass it."

She spoke, and glad was long-tried royal Odysseus, pleased that he saw a true friend in the ring. And now with lighter heart he called to the Phaeacians:

"Come up to that, young men! Soon I will send another as far, I think, or farther. And if there is one among you all whose heart and spirit bids, come, let him try me—for you vexed me very deeply—in boxing, wrestling, or the foot-race even; it matters not to me; let any Phaeacian try, except Laodamas. He is my host, and who would quarrel with his entertainer? Witless the man must be, and altogether worthless, who challenges his host to games when in a foreign land; he hinders his own welfare. None of the rest I either dread or scorn, but I will gladly know you all and prove you face to face. Not at all weak am I in any games men practice. I understand full well handling the polished bow, and I should be the first to strike my man when sending an arrow in the throng of foes, however many comrades stood around and shot at their men too. None except Philoctetes excelled me with the bow at Troy, when we Achaeans tried the bow. All others I declare I far surpass, all that are living now and eating bread on earth. The men of former days I will not seek to rival,—Hercules, and Eurytus of Oechalia,—for these would rival with the bow immortals even. Wherefore great Eurytus died all too soon; no old age came upon him in his home, because in wrath Apollo slew him; for Eurytus had challenged him to try the bow. I send the spear farther than other men an arrow. Only I fear that in the foot-race some Phaeacian may outstrip me; for rudely battered have I been on many waters, having no ease at sea for any length of time; therefore my joints are weakened."

So he spoke, and all were hushed to silence; only Alcinoüs answering said: "Stranger, without discourtesy to us is all you say; you merely seek to prove the prowess that is yours, indignant that the man beside you in the ring insulted you, though surely no man would dispraise your prowess who knew within his heart what it was fit to say. But listen now to words of mine, that you may have a tale to tell to other heroes when, feasting in your hall with wife and children, you recollect our prowess and the feats Zeus has vouchsafed us from our fathers' days till now. We are not faultless boxers, no, nor wrestlers; but in the foot-race we run swiftly, and in our ships excel. Dear to us ever is the feast, the harp, the dance, changes of clothes, warm baths, and bed. Come then, Phaeacian dancers, the best among you make us sport, that so the stranger on returning home may tell his friends how we surpass all other men in sailing, running, in the dance and song. Go, one of you, forthwith, and fetch Demodocus the tuneful lyre that lies within our hall."

So spoke godlike Alcinoüs, and a page sprang to fetch from the king's house the hollow lyre. Then rose the appointed judges, nine in all, whose public work it was to order all things at the ring; they smoothed the dancing-ground and cleared a fair wide ring. Meanwhile the page drew near and brought his tuneful lyre to Demodocus, who thereupon stepped to the centre, and round him stood young men in the first bloom of years, skillful at dancing. They struck the splendid dance-ground with their feet; Odysseus watched their twinkling feet, and was astonished.

And now the bard, touching his lyre, began a beautiful song about the loves of Ares and crowned Aphrodite: how at the first they lay together in the palace of Hephaestus, privily; and many a gift he gave, and wronged the bed of lord Hephaestus. Soon to Hephaestus came the tell-tale Sun, who had observed their meeting. And when Hephaestus heard the galling tale, he hastened to his smithy meditating evil in his heart, there set upon its block the mighty anvil and forged him fetters none might break or loose, fetters to hold securely. So after he had wrought his snare, in anger against Ares, hastening to the chamber where his own dear bed was set, around its posts on every side he dropped his nets; and many too hung drooping from the rafter, like delicate spiderwebs which nobody could see, not even the blessed gods, so shrewdly were they fashioned. Then after he had spread the snare all round the bed, he made a show of going off to Lemnos, that stately citadel which in his sight is far the dearest of all spots on earth. Now Ares of the golden rein had kept no careless watch, and so espied craftsman Hephaestus setting forth. He hastened to the house of famed Hephaestus, keen for the love of fair-crowned Cytherea. She, just come home from visiting her sire, the powerful son of Kronos, was sitting down. He came within the door, and holding her by the hand he spoke and thus addressed her:

"Come, dear, to bed, and let us take our pleasure; for Hephaestus is no longer here at home, but gone at last to Lemnos, to the harsh-tongued Sintians."

He spoke, and pleasant it seemed to her to lie beside him. So the pair went and lay down in bed, and all about them dropped the nets fashioned by shrewd Hephaestus; it was not in their power to move or raise a limb. This they saw only then when there was no escape. But on them came the famous strong-armed god, who had turned back before he reached the land of Lemnos; for in his stead the Sun kept watch and told him all. He hastened to the house, with heavy heart, stood at the porch, wild rage upon him, and raised a fearful cry, calling to all the gods:

"O Father Zeus, and all you other blessed gods that live forever, come see a sight for laughter, deeds not to be endured! For I being lame, this Aphrodite, daughter of Zeus, ever dishonors me and gives her love to deadly Ares, since he is handsome and is sound of limb, while I was born a cripple. Yet nobody is to blame for that but my two parents,—would they had never given me birth! But you shall see where lie the loving pair who stole into my bed. I smart to see them! And yet I think they will not lie much longer thus, however great their love. Shortly they will not wish to sleep together; but still my snare and mesh shall hold them, till her father pays me back the many wedding gifts I gave to get the shameless girl, seeing his child was fair, though not true-hearted."

He spoke, and the gods gathered at the bronze threshold of his house. Poseidon came, who girds the land, the fortune-bringer Hermes came, and the far-working king Apollo. The goddesses for shame all stayed at home. So at the portal stood the gods, the givers of good things, and uncontrollable laughter broke from the blessed gods as they beheld the arts of shrewd Hephaestus; and glancing at his neighbor one would say:

"Wrong-doing brings no gain. Slow catches swift; as here Hephaestus, who is slow, caught Ares, who is swiftest of the gods that hold Olympus,—catching him by his craft, though lame himself. Now Ares owes the adulterer's fine."

So they conversed together. And now to Hermes spoke the king, the son of Zeus, Apollo: "O Hermes, son of Zeus, guide, giver of good things, would you not like, though loaded down with heavy bonds, to lie in bed by golden Aphrodite?"

Then answered him the guide, the killer of Argus: "Would it might be, far-shooting king Apollo, though thrice as many bonds, bonds numberless, should hold me fast, and all you gods and goddesses should come and see, I wish I might lie by golden Aphrodite!"

He spoke, and laughter rose among the immortal gods. But Poseidon did not laugh; he earnestly entreated Hephaestus, the great craftsman, to loosen Ares. And speaking in winged words he said:

"Loose him, and I engage, as you desire, that he shall pay all dues before the immortal gods."

Then said to him the famous strong-armed god: "Poseidon, encircler of the land, ask not for this. From triflers, even pledges in the hand are trifles. How could I hold you bound before the immortal gods, if Ares should evade both debt and bond and flee?"

Then said to him the earth-shaker, Poseidon: "Hephaestus, even if Ares does evade the debt and flee, still I myself will pay."

Then answered him the famous strong-armed god: "I cannot and I must not tell you no."

So saying, mighty Hephaestus raised the net, and the pair loosed from the net, so very strong, sprang up at once. He went to Thrace; but she, the laughter-loving Aphrodite, came to Cyprus, into the town of Paphos, where is her grove and fragrant shrine. There did the Graces bathe her and anoint her with imperishable oil, such as bedews the gods that live forever, and they arrayed her in a dainty robe, a marvel to behold.

So sang the famous bard. Odysseus joyed in heart to hear, as did the others also, the Phaeacian oarsmen, notable men at sea.

And now Alcinoüs called on Halius and Laodamas to dance alone, for none could rival them. So taking in hand a goodly purple ball which skillful Polybus had made them, one, bending backward, flung it toward the dusky clouds; the other, leaping upward from the earth, easily caught the ball before his feet touched ground again. Then after they had tried the ball straight in the air, they danced upon the bounteous earth with tossings to and fro. Other young men beat time for them, standing around the ring, and a loud sound of stamping rose. Then to Alcinoüs said royal Odysseus:

"Mighty Alcinoüs, renowned of all, you boasted that your dancers were the best, and now it is proved true. I am amazed to see."

He spoke; revered Alcinoüs was pleased, and to the Phaeacians who delight in oars he straightway said:

"Listen, Phaeacian captains and councilors! This stranger really seems a man of understanding. Come, then, and let us give such guest-gift as is fitting. Twelve honored kings bear sway throughout this land and are its rulers, and a thirteenth am I. Let each present a spotless robe and tunic and a talent of precious gold.* And let us speedily fetch all together, so that the stranger, having these in hand, may come to supper glad at heart. Let too Euryalus give satisfaction to the man, by word and gift; for his speech was unbecoming."

He spoke, and all approved and gave their orders, and for the bringing of the gifts each man sent forth his page. But Euryalus made answer to the king and said: "Mighty Alcinoüs, renowned of all, I will indeed give satisfaction to the stranger, as you bid; for I will give this bronze blade. Its hilt is silver, and a sheath of fresh-cut ivory encloses it. Of great worth he will find it."

So saying, he put into Odysseus' hands the silver-studded sword,

---

*A talent, equal to 60 minas, was a high denomination of gold.

and speaking in winged words he said: "Hail, good old stranger! If any word was uttered that was harsh, straight let the sweeping winds bear it away. But the gods grant that you may see your wife and reach your land; for long cut off from friends you have been meeting hardship."

Then wise Odysseus answered him and said: "You too, my friend, all hail! May the gods grant you fortune, and may you never miss the sword you give, making amends besides in what you say."

He spoke, and round his shoulders slung the silver-studded sword. As the sun set, the noble gifts were there; stately pages bore them to the palace of Alcinoüs, where the sons of good Alcinoüs, receiving them, laid the fair gifts before their honored mother. But for the princes revered Alcinoüs led the way, and entering the house they sat them down on the high seats. Then to Arete spoke revered Alcinoüs:

"Bring hither, wife, a serviceable chest, the best you have, and lay therein a spotless robe and tunic. Then heat upon the fire a caldron for the stranger and warm some water, that, having bathed and seen all gifts put safely by which the kind Phaeacians brought him, he may enjoy the feast and hear the singer's song. Moreover I will give him my goodly golden chalice, that as he pours libations at his hall to Zeus and to the other gods he may be mindful all his days of me."

He spoke, and Arete told the maids to set a great kettle on the fire as quickly as they could. They set the kettle which supplied the bath upon the blazing fire, they poured in water, put the wood beneath, and lighted. Around the belly of the kettle crept the flame, and so the water warmed. Meanwhile Arete brought the stranger a goodly chest from out the chamber; she put therein the beautiful gifts,—the clothing and the gold which the Phaeacians gave,—and she herself put in a robe and goodly tunic, and speaking in winged words she said:

"See to the lid yourself and deftly tie the cord, lest some one rob you on the way, when sailing by and by, on the black ship, you rest in pleasant sleep."

When long-tried royal Odysseus heard these words, he straight-way fitted on the lid and deftly tied the cunning knot which potent Circe once had taught him. Thereafter the housewife called him to come to the bath and bathe; and he was pleased to see the steaming water, for he was not used to care like this since he had left fair-haired Calypso's home; but there he had as constant care as if he were a god. Now when the maids had bathed him and anointed him with oil and put upon him a goodly coat and tunic, forth from the bath he came and went to join the drinkers, and Nausicaä, with beauty given her of the gods, stood by a column of the strong-built roof and marveled at Odysseus as she looked into his eyes, and speaking in winged words she said:

"Stranger, farewell! When you are once again in your own land, remember me, and how before all others it is to me you owe the saving of your life."

Then wise Odysseus answered her and said: "Nausicaä, daughter of proud Alcinoüs, Zeus grant it so—he the loud thunderer, hus-band of Here—that I go home and see my day of coming back. Then would I there too, as to any god, give thanks to you forever, all my days; for, maiden, it was you who gave me life."

He spoke, and took his seat by King Alcinoüs. Men were already serving food and mixing wine. The page drew near, leading the honored bard, Demodocus, beloved of all, and seated him among the feasters, backed by a lofty pillar. Then to the page said wise Odysseus, cutting a piece of chine, with plenty of meat upon it, off a white-toothed boar, the rich fat on its sides:

"Page, set before Demodocus this piece of meat, that he may eat and I may do him homage, sad though I be myself; for at the hands of all on earth bards meet respect and honor, because the Muse has taught them song and loves the race of bards."

He spoke, and the page bore the food and put it in the hands of lord Demodocus. He took it and was pleased, and on the food spread out before them they laid hands. But after they had stayed desire for drink and food, then to Demodocus said wise Odysseus:

"Demodocus, I praise you beyond all mortal men, whether your teacher was the Muse, the child of Zeus, or was Apollo. With perfect truth you sing the lot of the Achaeans, all that they did and bore, the whole Achaean struggle, as if yourself were there, or you had heard the tale from one who was. Pass on then now, and sing the building of the wooden horse, made by Epeius with Athene's aid, which royal Odysseus once conveyed into the citadel,—a thing of craft, filled full of men, who by its means sacked Ilios.* And if you now rightly relate the tale, forthwith I will declare to all mankind how bounteously God gave to you a wondrous power of song."

So he spoke. Then the other, stirred by the god, began and showed his skill in song: starting the story where some Argives boarding the well-benched ships were setting sail and spreading fire through the camp; while others still, under renowned Odysseus, lay in the assembly of the Trojans hidden in the horse; for the Trojans themselves had dragged it to their citadel. So there it stood, while long and uncertainly the people argued, seated around it. Three plans were finding favor: either to split the hollow trunk with ruthless axe; or else to drag it to the height and hurl it down the rocks; or still to spare the monstrous image, as a propitiation for the gods. And thus at last it was to end; for it was fated they should perish if their city should enclose the enormous wooden horse, where all the Argive chiefs were lying, bearing to the Trojans death and doom. He sang how they overthrew the town, these sons of the Achaeans, issuing from the horse, leaving their hollow ambush. Each for himself, he sang, pillaged the stately city; but Odysseus went like Ares to the palace of Deïphobus with godlike Menelaus; and there, he said, braving the fiercest fight, at last he won the day by aid of fierce Athene.

So sang the famous bard. Odysseus melted into tears, and all below his eyes his cheeks were wet. And as a woman wails and clings to her dear husband, who falls for town and people, seeking to shield his home and children from the ruthless day; seeing him dying,

---

*Troy.

gasping, she flings herself on him with a piercing cry; while men behind, smiting her with their spears on back and shoulder, force her along to bondage to suffer toil and trouble; with pain most pitiful her cheeks are thin; so pitifully fell the tears beneath Odysseus' brows. And yet he hid from all the rest the tears he shed; only Alcinoüs marked him and took heed, for he sat near and heard his deep-drawn sighs; and to the Phaeacians, who delight in oars, he straightway said:

"Listen, Phaeacian captains and councilors, and let Demodocus hush now the tuneful lyre, because not to the pleasure of us all he sings today; for since we supped and since the sacred bard began, this stranger has not ceased from bitter sighs. Surely some grief hovers about his heart. Let then the bard cease singing, that all alike be merry, stranger and entertainers, for that is better far; since for the worthy stranger's sake all things are ready now, escort and friendly gifts, which heartily we grant. Even as a brother is the stranger and the suppliant treated by any man who has a grain of understanding.

"And do not you, with wily purpose, longer hide what I shall ask; plain speech is better. Tell me the name by which at home your father and mother called you,—they and the other folk, your townsmen and your neighbors; for none of all mankind can lack a name, be he of low degree or high, when once he has been born; since in the very hour of birth parents give names to all. And tell me of your land, your home, and city, that there our ships may bear you with a discerning aim; for on Phaeacian ships there are no pilots, nor are there rudders such as other vessels carry, but the ships understand the will and mind of man. They know the cities and rich lands of every nation, and swiftly they cross the sea-gulf, shrouded in mist and cloud. On them there is no fear of being harmed or lost. Still, this is what I heard Nausithoüs, my father, tell: he said Poseidon was displeased because we were safe guides for all mankind; and he averred the god one day would wreck a staunch ship of the Phaeacians, returning home from pilotage upon the misty sea, and then would throw a lofty mound about our city. That was the old man's story, and this the god may fulfill, or else it may go unfulfilled, as pleases him. But now declare me this and plainly tell where you have wandered and what countries you have seen. About the men and stately towns, too, let me hear,—what ones were fierce and savage, with no regard for right, what ones were kind to strangers and reverent toward the gods. And tell me why you weep and grieve within your breast on hearing of the lot of Argive Danaäns and of Ilios. This the gods wrought; they spun the thread of death for some, that others in the time to come might have a song. Had you some relative who fell at Ilios? One who was dear? some daughter's husband or wife's father?—they who stand closest to us after our flesh and blood. Or was it possibly some friend who pleased you well, a gallant comrade? For a friend with an understanding heart is worth no less than a brother."

BOOK IX

The Story Told to Alcinoüs—the Cyclops

Then wise Odysseus answered him and said: "Mighty Alcinoüs, renowned of all, surely it is a pleasant thing to hear a bard like this, one who is even like the gods in voice. For happier occasion I think there cannot be than when good cheer possesses a whole people, and feasting through the houses they listen to a bard, seated in proper order, while beside them stand the tables supplied with bread and meat, and, dipping wine from the mixer,* the pourer bears it round and fills the cups. That is a sight most pleasing. But your heart bids you learn my grievous woes, and so to make me weep and sorrow more. What shall I tell you first, then, and what last? For many are the woes the gods of heaven have given me. First, I will tell my name, that you, like all, may know it; and I accordingly, seeking deliverance from my day of doom, may be your guest-friend, though my home is far away. I am Odysseus, son of Laërtes, who for all craft am noted among men, and my renown reaches to heaven. My home is Ithaca, a land far seen; for on it is the lofty height of Neriton, covered with waving woods. Around lie many islands, very close to one another,—Doulichion, Same, and woody Zacynthus. Ithaca itself lies low along the sea, far to the west,—the others stretching eastward, toward the dawn,—a rugged land, and yet a kindly nurse. A sweeter spot than my own land I shall not see. Calypso, a heavenly goddess, sought to keep me by her side within her hollow grotto, desiring me to be her husband; so too Aeaean Circe, full of craft, detained me in her palace, desiring

---

*A vessel for mixing wine, never drunk pure, with water.

me to be her husband; but they never beguiled the heart within my breast. Nothing more sweet than home and parents can there be, however rich one's dwelling far in a foreign land, cut off from parents. But let me tell you of the grievous journey home which Zeus ordained me on my setting forth from Troy.

"The wind took me from Ilios and bore me to the Ciconians, to Ismarus. There I destroyed the town and slew its men; but from the town we took the women and great stores of treasure, and parted all, that none might go lacking his proper share. This done, I warned our men swiftly to fly; but they, in utter folly, did not heed. Much wine was drunk, and they slaughtered on the shore a multitude of sheep and slow-paced, crook-horned oxen. Meanwhile, escaped Ciconians began to call for aid on those Ciconians who were their neighbors and more numerous and brave than they,—a people dwelling inland, skillful at fighting in chariot or on foot, as need might be. Accordingly at dawn they gathered, thick as leaves and flowers appear in spring. And now an evil fate from Zeus beset our luckless men, causing us many sorrows; for setting the battle in array by the swift ships, all fought and hurled their bronze spears at one another. While it was morning and the day grew stronger, we steadily kept them off and held our ground, though they were more than we; but as the sun declined, toward curfew-time, then the Ciconians turned our men and routed the Achaeans. Six of the crew of every ship fell in their harness there; the rest fled death and doom.

"Thence we sailed on with aching hearts, glad to be clear of death, though missing our dear comrades; yet the curved ships did not pass on till we had called three times to each poor comrade who died upon the plain, cut off by the Ciconians. But now cloud-gathering Zeus sent the north wind against our ships in a fierce tempest, and covered with his clouds both land and sea; night broke from heaven. The ships drove headlong onward, their sails torn into tatters by the furious wind. These sails we lowered, in terror for our lives, and rowed the ships themselves hurriedly toward the land. There for two nights and days continuously we lay, gnawing our hearts because of toil and trouble. But when the fair-haired dawn brought the third day, we set our masts, and hoisting the white sails we sat us down, while wind and helmsmen kept us steady. And now I should have come unharmed to my own land, but that the swell and current, in doubling Maleia, and northern winds turned me aside and drove me past Cythera.*

"Thence for nine days I drifted before the deadly blasts along the swarming sea; but on the tenth we touched the land of Lotus-eaters, men who make food of flowers. So here we went ashore and drew us water, and soon by the swift ships my men prepared their dinner. Then after we had tasted food and drink, I sent some sailors forth to go and learn what men who live by bread dwelt in the land,— selecting two, and joining with them a herald as a third. These straightway went and mingled with the Lotus-eaters. These Lotus-eaters had no thought of harm against our men; indeed, they gave them lotus to taste; but whosoever of them ate the lotus' honeyed fruit wished to bring tidings back no more and never to leave the place, but with the Lotus-eaters there desired to stay, to feed on lotus and forget his going home. These men I brought back weeping to the ships by very force, and dragging them under the benches of our hollow ships I bound them fast, and bade my other trusty men to hasten and embark on the swift ships, that none of them might eat the lotus and forget his going home. Quickly they came aboard, took places at the pins, and sitting in order smote the foaming water with their oars.

"Thence we sailed on with aching hearts, and came to the land of the Cyclops,[28] a rude and lawless folk, who, trusting to the immortal gods, plant with their hands no plant, nor ever plough, but all things spring unsown and without ploughing,—wheat, barley, and grape-vines with wine in their heavy clusters, for rain from Zeus makes the grape grow. Among this people no assemblies meet; they

---

*Maleia refers to the southern tip of the Greek mainland; Cythera is a nearby island.

have no stable laws. They live on the tops of lofty hills in hollow caves; each gives the law to his own wife and children, and cares for no one else.

"Now a rough island stretches along outside the harbor, not close to the Cyclops' coast nor yet far out, covered with trees. On it innumerable wild goats breed; no tread of man disturbs them; none comes here to follow hounds, to toil through woods and climb the crests of hills. The island is not held for flocks or tillage, but all unsown, untilled, it evermore is bare of men and feeds the bleating goats. Among the Cyclops are no red-cheeked ships, nor are there shipwrights who might build the well-benched ships to do them service, sailing to foreign towns, as men are wont to cross the sea in ships to one another. With ships they might have worked the well-placed island; for it is not at all a worthless spot, but would bear all things duly. For here are meadows on the banks of the gray sea, moist, with soft soil; here vines could never die; here is smooth ploughing-land; a very heavy crop, and always well in season, might be reaped, for the under soil is rich. Here is a quiet harbor, never needing moorings,—throwing out anchor-stones or fastening cables,—but merely to run in and wait awhile till sailor hearts are ready and the winds are blowing. Just at the harbor's head a spring of sparkling water flows from beneath a cave; around it poplars grow. Here we sailed in, some god our guide, through murky night; there was no light to see, for round the ships was a dense fog. No moon looked out from heaven; it was shut in with clouds. So no one saw the island; and the long waves rolling on the shore we did not see until we beached our well-benched ships. After the ships were beached, we lowered all our sails and forth we went ourselves upon the shore; where falling fast asleep we awaited sacred dawn.

"But when the early rosy-fingered dawn appeared, in wonder at the island we made a circuit round it, and nymphs, daughters of aegis-bearing Zeus, started the mountain goats, to give my men a meal. Immediately we took our bending bows and our long hunting spears from out the ships, and parted in three bands began to shoot; and soon God granted ample game. Twelve ships were in my train;

to each there fell nine goats, while ten they set apart for me alone. Then all throughout the day till setting sun we sat and feasted on abundant meat and pleasant wine. For the ruddy wine of our ships was not yet spent; some still was left, because our crews took a large store in jars the day we seized the sacred citadel of the Ciconians. And now we looked across to the land of the neighboring Cyclops, and marked the smoke, the sounds of men, the bleat of sheep and goats; but when the sun went down and darkness came, we laid us down to sleep upon the beach. Then as the early rosy-fingered dawn appeared, holding a council, I said to all my men:

" 'The rest of you, my trusty crews, stay for the present here; but I myself, with my own ship and my own crew, go to discover who these men may be,—if they are fierce and savage, with no regard for right, or kind to strangers and reverent toward the gods.'

"When I had spoken thus, I went on board my ship, and called my crew to come on board and loose the cables. Quickly they came, took places at the pins, and sitting in order smote the foaming water with their oars. But when we reached the neighboring shore, there at the outer point, close to the sea, we found a cave, high, overhung with laurel. Here many flocks of sheep and goats were nightly housed. Around was built a yard with a high wall of deep-embedded stone, tall pines, and crested oaks. Here a man-monster slept, who shepherded his flock alone and far apart; with others he did not mingle, but quite aloof followed his lawless ways. Thus had he grown to be a freakish monster; not like a man who lives by bread, but rather like a woody peak of the high hills, seen single, clear of others.

"Now to my other trusty men I gave command to stay there by the ship and guard the ship; but I myself chose the twelve best among my men and sallied forth. I had a goat-skin bottle of the dark sweet wine given me by Maron, son of Evanthes, priest of Apollo, who watches over Ismarus. He gave me this because we guarded him and his son and wife, through holy fear; for he dwelt within the shady grove of Phoebus Apollo. He brought me splendid gifts: of fine-wrought gold he gave me seven talents, gave me a mixing-bowl of solid silver, and afterwards filled me twelve jars with wine, sweet and unmixed, a drink for gods. None knew that wine among the slaves and hand-maids of his house, none but himself, his own dear wife, and one sole house-keeper. Whenever they drank the honeyed ruddy wine, he filled a cup and poured it into twenty parts of water, and still from the bowl came a sweet odor of a surprising strength; then to refrain had been no easy matter. I filled a large skin full of this and took it with me, and also took provision in a sack; for my stout heart suspected I soon should meet a man arrayed in mighty power, a savage, ignorant of rights and laws.

"Quickly we reached the cave, but did not find him there; for he was tending his fat flock afield. Entering the cave, we looked around. Here crates were standing, loaded down with cheese, and here pens thronged with lambs and kids. In separate pens each sort was folded: by themselves the older, by themselves the later born, and by themselves the younglings. Swimming with whey were all the vessels, the well-wrought pails and bowls in which he milked. Here my men pressed me strongly to take some cheeses and go back; then later, driving the kids and lambs to our swift ship out of the pens, to sail away over the briny water. But I refused,—far better had I yielded,—hoping that I might see him and he might offer gifts. But he was to prove, when seen, no pleasure to my men.

"Kindling a fire here, we made burnt offering and we ourselves took of the cheese and ate; and so we sat and waited in the cave until he came from pasture. He brought a ponderous burden of dry wood to use at supper time, and tossing it down inside the cave raised a great din. We hurried off in terror to a corner of the cave. But into the wide-mouthed cave he drove his sturdy flock, all that he milked; the males, both rams and goats, he left outside in the high yard. And now he set in place the huge door-stone, lifting it high in air, a ponderous thing; no two and twenty carts, staunch and four-wheeled, could start it from the ground; such was the rugged rock he set against the door. Then sitting down, he milked the ewes and bleating goats, all in due order, and underneath put each one's young. At once he curdled half of the white milk, and gathering it in wicker baskets, set it by; half he left standing in the pails, ready for him to take and drink, and have it for his supper. So after he had busily performed his tasks, he kindled a fire, noticed us, and asked:

" 'Ha, strangers, who are you? Where do you come from, sailing the watery ways? Are you upon some business? Or do you rove at random, as the pirates roam the seas, risking their lives and bringing ill to strangers?'

"As he thus spoke, our very souls were crushed within us, dismayed by the heavy voice and by the monster himself; nevertheless I answered thus and said:

" 'We are from Troy, Achaeans, driven by shifting winds out of our course across the great gulf of the sea; homeward we fared, but through strange ways and wanderings are come hither; so Zeus was pleased to purpose. Subjects of Agamemnon, son of Atreus, we boast ourselves to be, whose fame is now the widest under heaven; so great a town he sacked, so many people slew. But chancing here, we come before your knees to ask that you will offer hospitality, and in other ways as well will give the gift which is the stranger's due. O mighty one, respect the gods. We are your suppliants, and Zeus is the avenger of the suppliant and the stranger; he is the stranger's friend, attending the deserving.'

"So I spoke, and from a ruthless heart he at once answered: 'You are simple, stranger, or come from far away, to bid me dread the gods or shrink before them. The Cyclops pay no heed to aegis-bearing Zeus, nor to the blessed gods; because we are much stronger than themselves. To shun the wrath of Zeus, I would not spare you or your comrades, did my heart not bid. But tell me where you left your staunch ship at your coming. At the far shore, or near? Let me but know.'

"He thought to tempt me, but he could not cheat a knowing man like me; and I again replied with words of guile: 'The Earth-shaker, Poseidon, wrecked my ship and cast her on the rocks at the land's end, drifting her on a headland; the wind blew from the sea; and I with these men here escaped from utter ruin.'

"So I spoke, and from a ruthless heart he answered nothing, but starting up laid hands on my companions. He seized on two and dashed them to the ground as if they had been dogs. Their brains ran out upon the floor, and wet the earth. Tearing them limb from limb, he made his supper, and ate as does a mountain lion, leaving nothing, entrails, or flesh, or marrow bones. We in our tears held up our hands to Zeus, at sight of his cruel deeds; helplessness held our hearts. But when the Cyclops had filled his monstrous maw by eating human flesh and pouring down pure milk, he laid himself in the cave full length among his flock. And I then formed the plan within my daring heart of closing on him, drawing my sharp sword from my thigh, and stabbing him in the breast where the midriff holds the liver, feeling the place out with my hand. Yet second thoughts restrained me, for then we too had met with utter ruin; for we could never with our hands have pushed from the tall door the enormous stone which he had set against it. Thus then with sighs we awaited sacred dawn.

"But when the early rosy-fingered dawn appeared, he kindled a fire, milked his goodly flock, all in due order, and underneath put each one's young. Then after he had busily performed his tasks, seizing once more two men, he made his morning meal. And when the meal was ended, he drove from the cave his sturdy flock, and easily moved the huge door-stone; but afterwards put it back as one might put the lid upon a quiver. Then to the hills, with many a call, he steered his sturdy flock, while I was left behind brooding on evil and thinking how I might have vengeance, would but Athene grant my prayer. And to my mind this seemed the wisest way. There lay beside the pen a great club of the Cyclops, an olive stick still green, which he had cut to be his staff when dried. Inspecting it, we guessed its size, and thought it like the mast of a black ship of twenty oars,— some broad-built merchantman which sails the great gulf of the sea; so huge it looked in length and thickness. I went and cut away a fathom's length of this, laid it before my men, and bade them shape it down. They made it smooth. I then stood by to point the tip and, laying hold, I charred it briskly in the blazing fire. The piece I now put carefully away, hiding it in the dung which lay about the cave in great abundance; and then I bade my comrades fix by lot who the bold men should be to help me raise the stake and grind it in his eye, when pleasant sleep should come. Those drew the lot whom I myself would most gladly have chosen; four were they, for a fifth I counted in myself. He came toward evening, shepherding the fleecy flock, and forthwith drove his sturdy flock into the wide-mouthed cave, all with much care; he did not leave a sheep in the high yard outside, either through some suspicion, or God bade him so to do. Again he set in place the huge door-stone, lifting it high in air, and, sitting down, he milked the ewes and bleating goats, all in due order, and underneath put each one's young. Then after he had busily performed his tasks, he seized once more two men and made his supper. And now it was that drawing near the Cyclops I thus spoke, holding within my hands an ivy bowl filled with dark wine:

" 'Here, Cyclops, drink some wine after your meal of human flesh, and see what sort of liquor our ship held. I brought it as an offering, thinking that you might pity me and send me home. But you are mad past bearing. Reckless! How should a stranger come to you again from any people, when you do not act with decency?'

"So I spoke; he took the cup and drank it off, and mightily pleased he was with the taste of the sweet liquor, and thus he asked me for it yet again:

" 'Give me some more, kind sir, and at once tell your name, that I may give a stranger's gift with which you shall be pleased. Ah yes, the Cyclops' fruitful fields bear wine in their heavy clusters, for rain from Zeus makes the grape grow; but this is a bit of ambrosia and nectar.'

"So he spoke, and I again offered the sparkling wine. Three times I brought and gave; three times he drank it in his folly. Then as the wine began to dull the Cyclops' senses, in winning words I said to him:

" 'Cyclops, you asked my noble name, and I will tell it; but give the stranger's gift, just as you promised. My name is Noman. Noman I am called by mother, father, and by all my comrades.'

"So I spoke, and from a ruthless heart he at once answered: 'Noman I eat up last, after his comrades; all the rest first; and that shall be the stranger's gift for you.'

"He spoke, and sinking back fell flat; and there he lay, lolling his thick neck over, till sleep, that conquers all, took hold upon him. Out of his throat poured wine and scraps of human flesh; heavy with wine, he spewed it forth. And now it was I drove the stake under a heap of ashes, to bring it to a heat, and with my words emboldened all my men, that none might flinch through fear. Then when the olive stake, green though it was, was ready to take fire, and through and through was all aglow, I snatched it from the fire, while my men stood around and Heaven inspired us with great courage. Seizing the olive stake, sharp at the tip, they plunged it in his eye, and I, perched up above, whirled it around. As when a man bores ship-beams with a drill, and those below keep it in motion with a strap held by the ends, and steadily it runs; even so we seized the fire-pointed stake and whirled it in his eye. Blood bubbled round the heated thing. The vapor singed off all the lids around the eye, and even the brows, as the ball burned and its roots crackled in the flame. As when a smith dips a great axe or adze into cold water, hissing loud, to temper it,—for that is strength to steel,—so hissed his eye about the olive stake. A hideous roar he raised; the rock resounded; we hurried away in terror. He wrenched the stake out of his eye, all dabbled with the blood, and flung it off in frenzy. Then he called loudly on the Cyclops who dwelt about him in the caves, along the windy heights. They heard his cry, and ran from every side, and standing by the cave they asked what ailed him:

" 'What has come on you, Polyphemus, that you scream so in the immortal night, and so keep us from sleeping? Is a man driving off your flocks in spite of you? Is a man murdering you by craft or force?'

"Then in his turn from out the cave big Polyphemus answered: 'Friends, Noman is murdering me by craft. Force there is none.'

"But answering him in winged words they said: 'If no man harms you then and you are alone, illness which comes from mighty Zeus you cannot fly. Nay, make your prayer to your father, lord Poseidon.'

"This said, they went their way, and in my heart I laughed,—my name, that clever notion, so deceived them. But now the Cyclops, groaning and in agonies of anguish, by groping with his hands took the stone off the door, yet sat himself inside the door with hands outstretched, to catch whoever ventured forth among the sheep; for he probably hoped in his heart that I should be so silly. But I was planning how it all might best be ordered that I might win escape from death both for my men and me. So many a plot and scheme I framed, as for my life; great danger was at hand. Then to my mind this seemed the wisest way: some rams there were of a good breed, thick in the fleece, handsome and large, which bore a dark blue wool. These I quietly bound together with the twisted willow withes on which the giant Cyclops slept,—the brute,—taking three sheep together. One, in the middle, carried the man; the other two walked by the sides, keeping my comrades safe. Thus three sheep bore each man. Then for myself,—there was a ram, by far the best of all the flock, whose back I grasped, and curled beneath his shaggy belly there I lay, and with my hands twisted in that enormous fleece I steadily held on, with patient heart. Thus then with sighs we awaited sacred dawn.

"Soon as the early rosy-fingered dawn appeared, the rams hastened to pasture, but the ewes bleated unmilked about the pens, for their udders were well-nigh bursting. Their master, racked with grievous pains, felt over the backs of all the sheep as they stood up, but foolishly did not notice how under the breasts of the woolly sheep men had been fastened. Last of the flock, the ram stalked to the door, cramped by his fleece and me the crafty plotter; and feeling him over, big Polyphemus said:

" 'What, my pet ram! Why do you move across the cave hindmost of all the flock? Till now you never lagged behind, but with your long strides you were always first to crop the tender blooms of grass; you were the first to reach the running streams, and first to wish to turn to the stall at night: yet here you are the last. Ah, but you miss your master's eye, which a villain has put out,—he and his vile companions,—blunting my wits with wine. Noman it was,—not, I assure him, safe from destruction yet. If only you could sympathize and get the power of speech to say where he is skulking from my rage, then should that brain of his be knocked about the cave and dashed upon the ground. So might my heart recover from the ills which miserable Noman brought upon me.'

"So saying, from his hand he let the ram go forth, and after we were come a little distance from the cave and from the yard, first from beneath the ram I freed myself and then set free my comrades. So at quick pace we drove away those long-legged sheep, heavy with fat, many times turning round, until we reached the ship. A welcome sight we seemed to our dear friends, as men escaped from death. Yet for the others they began to weep and wail; but this I did not suffer; by my frowns I checked their tears. Instead, I bade them at once toss the many fleecy sheep into the ship, and sail away over the briny water. Quickly they came, took places at the pins, and sitting in order smote the foaming water with their oars. But when I was as far away as one can call, I shouted to the Cyclops in derision:

" 'Cyclops, no weakling's comrades you were destined to devour in the deep cave, with brutal might. But it was also destined your bad deeds should find you out, audacious wretch, who did not hesitate to eat the guests within your house! For this did Zeus chastise you, Zeus and the other gods.'

"So I spoke, and he was angered in his heart the more; and tearing off the top of a high hill, he flung it at us. It fell before the dark-bowed ship a little space, but failed to reach the rudder's tip. The sea surged underneath the stone as it came down, and swiftly toward the land the wash of water swept us, like a flood-tide from the deep, and forced us back to shore. I seized a setting-pole and shoved the vessel off; then inspiring my men, I bade them fall to their oars that we might flee from danger,—with my head making signs,—and bending forward, on they rowed. When we had traversed twice the distance on the sea, again to the Cyclops would I call; but my men, gathering round, sought with soft words to stay me, each in his separate way:

" 'O reckless man, why seek to vex this savage, who even now, hurling his missile in the deep, drove the ship back to shore? We verily thought that we were lost. And had he heard a man make but a sound or speak, he would have crushed our heads and our ships' beams, by hurling jagged granite; for he can throw so far.'

"So they spoke, but did not move my daring spirit; again I called aloud out of an angry heart: 'Cyclops, if ever mortal man asks you the story of the ugly blinding of your eye, say that Odysseus made you blind, the spoiler of cities, Laërtes' son, whose home is Ithaca.'

"So I spoke, and with a groan he answered: 'Ah, surely now the ancient oracles are come upon me! Here once a prophet lived, a prophet brave and tall, Telemus, son of Eurymus, who by his prophecies obtained renown and in prophetic works grew old among the Cyclops. He told me it should come to pass in aftertime that I should lose my sight by means of one Odysseus; but I was always watching for the coming of some tall and comely person, arrayed in mighty power; and now a little miserable feeble creature blinded me of my eye, overcoming me with wine. Nevertheless, come here, Odysseus, and let me give the stranger's gift, and beg the famous Land-shaker to aid you on your way. His son am I; he calls himself my father. He, if he will, shall heal me; none else can, whether among the blessed gods or mortal men.'

"So he spoke, and answering him said I: 'Ah, would I might as surely strip you of life and being and send you to the house of Hades, as it is sure the Earth-shaker will never heal your eye!'

"So I spoke, whereat he prayed to lord Poseidon, stretching his hands forth toward the starry sky: 'Hear me, thou girder of the land, dark-haired Poseidon! If I am truly thine, and thou art called my father, vouchsafe no coming home to this Odysseus, spoiler of cities, Laërtes' son, whose home is Ithaca. Yet if it be his lot to see his friends once more, and reach his stately house and native land, late let him come, in evil plight, with loss of all his crew, on the vessel of a stranger, and may he at his home find trouble.'

"So spoke he in his prayer, and the dark-haired god gave ear. Then once more picking up a stone much larger than before, the Cyclops swung and sent it, putting forth stupendous power. It fell behind the dark-bowed ship a little space, but failed to reach the rudder's tip. The sea surged underneath the stone as it came down, but the wave swept us forward and forced us to the shore.

"Now when we reached the island where our other well-benched ships waited together, while their crews sat round them sorrowing, watching continually for us, as we ran in we beached our ship among the sands, and forth we went ourselves upon the shore. Then taking the Cyclops' sheep out of the hollow ship, we parted all, that none might go lacking his proper share. The ram my armed companions gave to me alone, a mark of special honor in the division of the flock; and on the shore I offered him to Zeus of the dark cloud, the son of Kronos, who is the lord of all, burning the thighs. He did not heed the sacrifice. Instead, he purposed that my well-benched ships should all be lost, and all my trusty comrades. But all through-out that day till setting sun we sat and feasted on abundant meat and pleasant wine; and when the sun went down and darkness came, we laid us down to sleep upon the beach. Then as the early rosy-fingered dawn appeared, inspiring my men, I bade them come on board and loose the cables. Quickly they came, took places at the pins, and sitting in order smote the foaming water with their oars.

"Thence we sailed on, with aching hearts, glad to be clear of death, though missing our dear comrades."

BOOK X

Aeolus, the Laestrygonians, and Circe

Soon we drew near the island of Aeolia, where Aeolus, the son of Hippotas, dear to immortal gods, dwelt on a floating island. All round it is a wall of bronze, not to be broken through, and smooth and steep rises the rocky shore. Within the house of Aeolus, twelve children have been born, six daughters and six sturdy sons, and here he gave his daughters to his sons to be their wives. Here too with their loved father and honored mother they hold continual feast; before them countless viands lie. By day the steaming house resounds even to its court; by night they sleep by their chaste wives under the coverlets on well-bored bedsteads. Their city it was we reached, their goodly dwelling. For a full month here Aeolus made me welcome, and he questioned me of all, of Ilios, the Argive ships, and the return of the Achaeans. So I related all the tale in its due order. And when I furthermore asked him about my journey and entreated him for aid, he did not tell me no, but made provision for my going. He gave me a sack,—flaying therefor a nine-year ox,—and in it bound the courses of the blustering winds; for the son of Kronos made him steward of the winds, to stay or rouse which one he would. Upon my hollow ship he tied the sack with a bright cord of silver, that not a breath might stir, however little. Then for my aid he sent the west wind forth, to blow and bear along my ships and men. But it was not to be; by our folly we were lost.

"Nine days we sailed, as well by night as day. Upon the tenth our native fields appeared, so close at hand that we could see men tending fires. Then sweet sleep overcame me, wearied as I was; for I had all the time managed the vessel's sheet and yielded it to no one else among the crew, that so we might the sooner reach our native land. Meanwhile my men began to talk with one another, and to tell how I was bringing gold and silver home as gifts from Aeolus, the generous son of Hippotas; and glancing at his neighbor one would say:

" 'See how this man is welcomed and esteemed by all mankind, come to whose town and land he may! He brings a store of goodly treasure out of the spoils of Troy, while we, who toiled along the selfsame road, come home with empty hands. Now Aeolus gives him friendly gifts. Come, then, and let us quickly see what there is here, and how much gold and silver the sack holds.'

"Such was their talk, and the ill counsel of the crew prevailed; they loosed the sack, and out rushed all the winds. At once a sweeping storm bore off to sea my weeping comrades, far from their native land. And I, awaking, hesitated in my gallant heart whether to cast myself out of the ship into the sea and perish there, or saying nothing to endure and bide among the living. I forced myself to stay; covering my head, I lay down, while the ships were driven by the cruel storm of wind back to the island of Aeolia, my comrades sighing deeply.

"So here we went ashore and drew us water, and soon by the swift ships my men prepared a meal. Then after we had tasted food and drink, taking a herald and a comrade with me, I turned toward the lordly house of Aeolus. I found him at the feast, beside his wife and children. We entered the hall and on the threshold by the doorposts sat us down; and they all marveled in their hearts and questioned:

" 'How came you here, Odysseus? What hostile power assailed you? With care we sent you forth, to let you reach your land and home or anywhere you pleased.'

"So they spoke, and with an aching heart I answered: 'A wicked crew betrayed me—they and a cruel sleep. But heal my woes, my friends, for you have power.'

"So I spoke, addressing them in humble words. Then all the rest were silent, but the father answered thus: 'Out of the island instantly, vilest of all that live! I may not aid or send upon his way a man detested by the blessed gods. Begone! for you are here because detested by the immortals.'

"Therewith he turned me loud lamenting from his door. Thence we sailed on, with aching hearts. Worn was the spirit of my men under the heavy rowing, caused by our folly too; aid on our way appeared no more.

"Six days we sailed, as well by night as day, and on the seventh came to the steep citadel of Lamos, Telepylus in Laestrygonia,* where one shepherd leading home his flock calls to another, and the other answers as he leads his own flock forth. Here a man who never slept might earn a double wage: this, herding kine; that, tending silvery sheep; so close are the outgoings of the night and day. Now when we reached the splendid harbor,—round which the rock runs steep, continuous all the way, and the projecting cliffs, facing each other, stretch forward at the mouth, and narrow is the entrance,—into the basin all the rest steered their curved ships, and so the ships lay in the hollow harbor close-anchored, side by side; for no wave swelled within it, large or small, but a clear calm was all around. I alone posted my black ship without the harbor, there at the point, lashing my cables to the rock. Then climbing up, I took my stand on a rugged point of outlook. From it no work of man or beast was to be seen, only we saw some smoke ascending from the ground. So I sent sailors forth to go and learn what men who live by bread dwelt in the land,—selecting two, and joining with them a herald as a third. Leaving the ship, they took a beaten road where carts brought timber from the lofty hills down to the town below. Before the town they met a maiden drawing water, the stately daughter of the Laestrygonian Antiphates. She had come down to the clear-flowing fountain of Artacia, from which they used to fetch the water for the town. So my men, drawing near, addressed her and inquired who was the king of the folk here and whom he ruled; whereat she pointed to her father's high-roofed house. But when they entered

---

*Telepylus is the city, founded by Lamos.

the lordly hall, they found a woman there huge as a hilltop; at her they were aghast. Forthwith she called from the assembly noble Antiphates, her husband, who sought to bring upon my men a miserable end. Immediately seizing one, he made his meal of him; and the two others, dashing off, came flying to the ships. Then he raised a cry throughout the town, and hearing it, the mighty Laestrygonians gathered from here and there, seeming not men but giants. Then from the rocks they hurled down ponderous stones; and soon among the ships arose a dreadful din of dying men and crashing ships. As men spear fish, they gathered in their loathsome meal. But while they slaughtered these in the deep harbor, I drew my sharp sword from my thigh and cut the cables of my dark-bowed ship; and quickly inspiring my men, I bade them fall to their oars, that we might flee from danger. They all tossed up the water, in terror for their lives, and joyously to sea, away from the beetling cliff, my ship sped on; but all the other ships went down together there.

"Thence we sailed on with aching hearts, glad to be clear of death, though missing our dear comrades. And now we reached the island of Aeaea, where fair-haired Circe dwelt, a mighty goddess, human of speech. She was own sister of the sorcerer Aeëtes;[29] both were the children of the beaming Sun and of a mother Perse, the daughter of Oceanus. Here we bore landward with our ship and ran in silence into a sheltering harbor, God our guide. Landing, we lay two days and nights, gnawing our hearts because of toil and trouble; but when the fair-haired dawn brought the third day, I took my spear and my sharp sword, and from the ship walked briskly up to a place of distant view, hoping to see some work of man or catch some voice. So climbing up, I took my stand on a rugged point of outlook, and smoke appeared rising from open ground at Circe's dwelling, through some oak thickets and a wood. Then for a time I doubted in my mind and heart whether to go and search the matter while I saw the flaring smoke. Reflecting thus, it seemed the better way first to return to the swift ship and to the shore; there give my men their dinner, and send them forth to search.

"But on my way, as I drew near to the curved ship, some god took pity on me all forlorn, and sent a high-horned deer into my very path. From feeding in the wood he came to the stream to drink, for the sun's power oppressed him. As he stepped out, I struck him in the spine midway along the back; the bronze spear pierced him through; down in the dust he fell with a moan, and his life flew away. Setting my foot upon him, I drew from the wound the bronze spear and laid it on the ground; then I plucked twigs and osiers, and wove a rope a fathom long, twisted from end to end, with which I bound together the monstrous creature's legs. So with him upon my back I walked to the black ship leaning upon my spear, because it was not possible to hold him with my hand upon my shoulder; for the beast was very large. Before the ship I threw him down and then with cheering words aroused my men, standing by each in turn:

" 'We shall not, friends, however sad, go to the halls of Hades until our destined day. But while there still is food and drink in the swift ship, let us attend to eating, not waste away with hunger.'

"So I spoke, and my words they quickly heeded. Throwing their coverings off upon the shore beside the barren sea, they gazed upon the deer; for the beast was very large. Then after they had satisfied their eyes with gazing, they washed their hands and made a glorious feast. Thus all throughout the day till setting sun we sat and feasted on abundant meat and pleasant wine; and when the sun went down and darkness came, we laid us down to sleep upon the beach. Then as the early rosy-fingered dawn appeared, holding a council, I said to all my men:

" 'My suffering comrades, hearken to my words: for since, my friends, we do not know the place of dusk or dawn, the place at which the beaming sun goes under ground nor where he rises, let us at once consider if a wise course be left. I do not think there is; for I saw, on climbing to a rugged outlook, an island which the boundless deep encircles like a crown. Low in the sea it lies; midway across, I saw a smoke through some oak thickets and a wood.'

"As I thus spoke, their very souls were crushed within them, remembering the deeds of Laestrygonian Antiphates and the cruelty of the daring Cyclops, the devourer of men. They cried aloud and let the big tears fall; but no good came to them from their lamenting.

"Now the whole body of my armed companions I told off in two bands, and to each band assigned a leader: the one I led, godlike Eurylochus the other. Straightway we shook the lots in a bronze helmet, and the lot of bold Eurylochus leapt out the first. So he departed, two and twenty comrades following, all in tears; and us they left in sorrow too behind. Within the glades they found the house of Circe, built of smooth stone upon commanding ground. All round about were mountain wolves and lions, which Circe had charmed by giving them evil drugs. These creatures did not spring upon my men, but stood erect, wagging their long tails, fawning. As hounds fawn round their master when he comes from meat, because he always brings them delicacies that they like, so round these men the strong-clawed wolves and lions fawned. Still my men trembled at the sight of the strange beasts. They stood before the door of the fair-haired goddess, and in the house heard Circe singing with sweet voice, while tending her great imperishable loom and weaving webs, fine, beautiful, and lustrous as are the works of gods. Polites was the first to speak, one ever foremost, and one to me the nearest and the dearest of my comrades:

" 'Ah, friends, somebody in the house is tending a great loom and singing sweetly; all the pavement rings. A god it is or woman. Then let us quickly call.'

"He spoke, the others lifted up their voice and called; and suddenly coming forth, she opened the shining doors and invited them in. The rest all followed, heedless. Only Eurylochus remained behind, suspicious of a snare. She led them in and seated them on couches and on chairs, and made a potion for them,—cheese, barley, and yellow honey, stirred into Pramnian wine,—but mingled with the food pernicious drugs, to make them quite forget their native land. Now after she had given the cup and they had drunk it off, straight with a wand she smote them and penned them up in sties; and they took on the heads of swine, the voice, the bristles, and even the shape, yet was their reason as sound as it had been before. Thus, weeping, they were penned; and Circe flung them acorns, chestnuts, and cornel-fruit to eat, such things as swine that wallow in the mire are wont to eat.

"Eurylochus, meanwhile, came to the swift black ship to bring me tidings of my men and tell their bitter fate. Strive as he might, he could not speak a word, so stricken was he to the soul with sore distress; his eyes were filled with tears, his heart felt anguish. But when we all in great amazement questioned him, then he described the loss of all his men:

" 'We went, as you commanded, noble Odysseus, through the thicket and found within the glades a beautiful house, built of smooth stone upon commanding ground. There somebody was tending a great loom and loudly singing, some god or woman. The others lifted up their voice and called; and suddenly coming forth, she opened the shining doors and invited them in. The rest all followed, heedless; but I remained behind, suspicious of a snare. They vanished, one and all; not one appeared again, though long I sat and watched.'

"So he spoke; I slung my silver-studded sword about my shoulders,—large it was and made of bronze,—and my bow with it, and bade him lead me back the selfsame way. But he, clasping my knees with both his hands, entreated me, and sorrowfully said in winged words:

" 'O heaven-descended man, bring me not there against my will, but leave me here; for well I know you never will return, nor will you bring another of your comrades. Rather, with these now here, let us speed on; for we might even yet escape the evil day.'

"So he spoke, and answering him said I: 'Eurylochus, remain then here yourself, eating and drinking by the black hollow ship; but I will go, for strong necessity is on me.'

"Saying this, I passed up from the ship and from the sea. But when, in walking up the solemn glades, I was about to reach the great house of the sorceress Circe, there I was met, as I approached the house, by Hermes of the golden wand, in likeness of a youth, the first down on his lip,—a time of life most pleasing. He held my hand and spoke, and thus addressed me:

" 'Where are you going, hapless man, along the hills alone, ignorant of the land? Your comrades yonder, at the house of Circe, are penned like swine and kept in fast-closed sties. You come to free them? No, I am sure you will return no more, but there, like all the rest, you too will stay. Still, I can keep you clear of harm and give you safety. Here, take this potent herb and go to Circe's house; this shall protect your life against the evil day. And I will tell you all the magic arts of Circe: she will prepare for you a potion and cast drugs into your food; but even so, she cannot charm you, because the potent herb which I shall give will not permit it. And let me tell you more: when Circe turns against you her long wand, then drawing the sharp sword from your thigh spring upon Circe as if you meant to slay her. In terror she will bid you to her bower. And do not you refuse the goddess's bower, that so she may release your men and care for you. But bid her swear the blessed ones' great oath that she is not meaning now to plot you a fresh woe and when you are defenceless make you feeble and unmanned.'

"As he thus spoke, the killer of Argus gave the herb, drawing it from the ground, and pointed out its nature. Black at the root it is, like milk its blossom, and the gods call it moly. Hard is it for a mortal man to dig; with gods all things may be.

"Hermes departed now to high Olympus, along the woody island. I made my way to Circe's house, and as I went my heart grew very dark. But I stood at the gate of the fair-haired goddess, stood there and called, and the goddess heard my voice. Suddenly coming forth, she opened the shining doors and bade me in; I followed her with aching heart. She led me in and placed me on a silver-studded chair, beautiful, richly wrought, with a footstool for the feet, and she prepared a potion in a golden cup for me to drink, but put therein a drug, with wicked purpose in her heart. Now after she had given the drink and I had drunk it off, and yet it had not charmed me, smiting me with her wand, she spoke these words and cried: 'Off to the sty, and lie there with your fellows!'

"She spoke; I drew the sharp blade from my thigh and sprang upon Circe as if I meant to slay her. With a loud cry, she cowered and clasped my knees, and sorrowfully said in winged words:

" 'Who are you? Of what people? Where is your town and kindred? I marvel much that drinking of these drugs you were not charmed. None, no man else, ever withstood these drugs who tasted them, so soon as they had passed the barrier of his teeth; but in your breast there is a mind which cannot be beguiled. Surely you are adventurous Odysseus, who the god of the golden wand, the killer of Argus, always declared would come upon his way from Troy,— he and his swift black ship. Nay, then, put up your blade within its sheath, and let us now turn to my bower, that there we two may know our love and learn to trust each other.'

"So she spoke, and answering her said I: 'Circe, why ask me to be gentle toward you when you have turned my comrades into swine within your halls, and here detain me and with treacherous purpose invite me to your bower and to approach your side that when I am defenceless you may make me feeble and unmanned? But I will never willingly approach your bower till you consent, goddess, to swear a solemn oath that you are not meaning now to plot me a new woe.'

"So I spoke, and she then took the oath which I required. So after she had sworn and ended all that oath, then I approached the beauteous bower of Circe.

"Meanwhile attendants plied their work about the halls,—four maids, who were the serving-women of the palace. They are the children of the springs and groves and of the sacred streams that run into the sea. One threw upon the chairs beautiful cloths; purple she spread above, linen below. The next placed silver tables by the chairs and set forth golden baskets. A third stirred in a bowl the cheering wine—sweet wine in silver—and filled the golden cups. A fourth brought water and kindled a large fire under a great kettle, and let the water warm. Then when the water in the glittering copper boiled, she seated me in the bath and bathed me from the kettle about the head and shoulders, tempering the water well, till from my joints she drew the sore fatigue. And after she had bathed me and anointed me with oil and put upon me a goodly coat and tunic, she led me in and placed me on a silver-studded chair, beautiful, richly wrought, with a footstool for the feet, and water for the hands a servant brought me in a beautiful pitcher made of gold, and poured it out over a silver basin for my washing, and spread a polished table by my side. Then the grave housekeeper brought bread and placed before me, setting out food of many a kind, freely giving of her store, and bade me eat. But that pleased not my heart; I sat with other thoughts; my heart foreboded evil.

"When Circe marked me sitting thus, not laying hands upon my food but cherishing sore sorrow, approaching me she said in winged words: 'Why do you sit, Odysseus, thus, like one struck dumb, gnawing your heart, and touch no food nor drink? Do you suspect some further guile? You have no cause for fear, for even now I swore to you a solemn oath.'

"So she spoke, and answering her said I: 'Ah, Circe, what upright man could bring himself to taste of food or drink before he had released his friends and seen them with his eyes? But if you in sincerity will bid me drink and eat, then set them free; that I with my own eyes may see my trusty comrades.'

"So I spoke, and from the hall went Circe, wand in hand. She opened the sty doors, and forth she drove what seemed like nine-year swine. A while they stood before her, and, passing along the line, Circe anointed each one with a counter-charm. So from their limbs fell the hair which at the first the accursed drug which potent Circe gave had made to grow; and once more they were men, men younger than before, much fairer too and taller to behold. They knew me, and each grasped my hand, and from them all passionate sobs burst forth, and all the house gave a sad echo. The goddess pitied us, even she, and standing by my side the heavenly goddess said:

" 'High-born son of Laërtes, ready Odysseus, go now to your swift ship and to the shore, and first of all draw up your ship upon the land, and store within the caves your goods and all your gear, and then come back yourself and bring your trusty comrades.'

"So she spoke, and my high heart assented. I went to the swift ship and to the shore, and found by the swift ship my trusty comrades in bitter lamentation, letting the big tears fall. As the stalled calves skip round a drove of cows returning to the barn-yard when satisfied with grazing; with one accord they all bound forth, the folds no longer hold them, but with continual bleat they frisk about their mothers; so did these men, when they caught sight of me, press weeping round. To them it seemed as if they had already reached their land, their very town of rugged Ithaca where they were bred and born; and through their sobs they said in winged words:

" 'Now you have come, O heaven-descended man, we are as glad as if we were approaching Ithaca, our native land. But tell about the loss of all our other comrades.'

"So they spoke; I in soft words made answer: 'Let us now first of all draw up our ship upon the land and store within the caves our goods and all our gear; then hasten all of you to follow me, and see your comrades in the magic house of Circe drinking and eating, holding constant cheer.'

"So I spoke, and my words they quickly heeded. Eurylochus alone tried to hold back my comrades, and speaking in winged words he said: 'Poor fools, where are we going? Why are you so in love with ill that you will go to Circe's hall and let her turn us all to swine and wolves and lions, that we may then keep watch at her great house, against our wills? Such deeds the Cyclops did when to his lair our comrades came, and with them went this reckless man, Odysseus; for through his folly those men also perished.'

"As he thus spoke, I hesitated in my heart whether to draw my keen-edged blade from my stout thigh and by a blow bring down his head into the dust, near as he was by tie of marriage; but with soft words my comrades stayed me, each in his separate way:

" 'High-born Odysseus, we will leave him, if you like, here by the ship to guard the ship; but lead us to the magic house of Circe.'

"Saying this, they passed up from the ship and from the sea. Yet did Eurylochus not tarry by the hollow ship; he followed, for he feared my stern rebuke.

"But in the meanwhile to my other comrades at the palace Circe had given a pleasant bath, anointed them with oil, and put upon them fleecy coats and tunics; merrily feasting in her halls we found them all. When the men saw and recognized each other, they wept aloud and the house rang around; and standing by my side the heavenly goddess said:

" 'High-born son of Laërtes, ready Odysseus, let not this swelling grief rise further now. I myself know what hardships you have borne upon the swarming sea and how fierce men harassed you on the land. Come, then, eat food, drink wine, until you find once more that spirit in the breast which once was yours when you first left your native land of rugged Ithaca. Now, worn and spiritless, your thoughts still dwell upon your weary wandering. This many a day your heart has not been glad, for sorely have you suffered.'

"So she spoke, and our high hearts assented. Here, then, day after day, for a full year, we sat and feasted on abundant meat and pleasant wine. But when the year was gone and the round of the seasons rolled, as the months waned and the long days were done, then calling me aside my trusty comrades said:

" 'Ah, sir, consider now your native land, if you are destined ever to be saved and reach your stately house and native land.'

"So they spoke, and my high heart assented. Yet all throughout that day till setting sun we sat and feasted on abundant meat and pleasant wine; and when the sun went down and darkness came, my men lay down to sleep throughout the dusky halls. But I, on coming to the beauteous bower of Circe, made supplication to her by her knees, and to my voice the goddess hearkened; and speaking in winged words, I said:

" 'Circe, fulfill the promise made to send me home; for now my spirit stirs, with that of all my men, who vex my heart with their complaints when you are gone away.'

"So I spoke, and straight the heavenly goddess answered: 'High-born son of Laërtes, ready Odysseus, stay no longer at my home against your will. But you must first perform a different journey, and go to the halls of Hades and of dread Persephone, there to consult the spirit of Teiresias of Thebes,—the prophet blind, whose mind is steadfast still.[30] To him, though dead, Persephone has granted reason, to him alone sound understanding; the rest are flitting shadows.'

"As she thus spoke, my very soul was crushed within me, and sitting on the bed I fell to weeping; my heart no longer cared to live and see the sun. But when of weeping and of writhing I had had my fill, then thus I answered her and said: 'But, Circe, who will be my pilot on this journey? None by black ship has ever reached the land of Hades.'

"So I spoke, and straight the heavenly goddess answered: 'Highborn son of Laërtes, ready Odysseus, let not the lack of pilot for your ship disturb you, but set the mast, spread the white sail aloft, and sit down; the breath of Boreas shall bear her onward. When you have crossed by ship the Ocean-stream to where the shore is rough and the grove of Persephone stands,—tall poplars and seed-shedding willows,—there beach your ship by the deep eddies of the Ocean-stream, but go yourself to the charnel-house of Hades. There is a spot where into Acheron run Pyriphlegethon and Cocytus, a stream which is an off-shoot of the waters of the Styx; a rock here forms the meeting-point of the two roaring rivers. To this spot then, hero, draw near, even as I bid; and dig a pit, about a cubit either way, and round its edges pour an offering to all the dead,—first honey mixture, next sweet wine, and thirdly water, and over all strew the white barley-meal. Make many supplications also to the strengthless dead, vowing when you return to Ithaca to take the barren cow that is your best and offer it in your hall, heaping the pyre with treasure; and to Teiresias separately to sacrifice a sheep, for him alone, one wholly black, the very choicest of your flock. So when with vows you have implored the illustrious peoples of the dead, offer a ram and a black ewe, bending their heads toward Erebus, but turn yourself away facing the river's stream; to you shall gather many spirits of those now dead and gone. Then forthwith call your men, and bid them take the sheep now lying there slain by the ruthless sword, and flay and burn them, and call upon the gods,—on powerful Hades and on dread Persephone,—while you yourself, drawing your sharp sword from your thigh, sit still and do not let the strengthless dead approach the blood till you have made inquiry of Teiresias. Thither the seer will quickly come, O chief of men, and he will tell your course, the stages of your journey, and of your homeward way, how you may pass along the swarming sea.'

"Even as she spoke, the gold-throned morning came. On me she put a coat and tunic for my raiment; and the nymph dressed herself in a long silvery robe, fine spun and graceful; she bound a beautiful golden girdle round her waist, and put a veil upon her head. Then through the house I passed and roused my men with cheering words, standing by each in turn:

" 'Sleep no more now, nor drowse in pleasant slumber, but let us go, for potent Circe has at last made known the way.'

"So I spoke, and their high hearts assented. Yet even from there I did not bring away my men in safety. There was a certain Elpenor, the youngest of them all, a man not very firm in fight nor sound of understanding, who, parted from his mates, lay down to sleep upon the magic house of Circe, seeking for coolness when overcome with wine. As his companions stirred, hearing the noise and tumult, he suddenly sprang up and quite forgot how to come down again by the long ladder, but fell headlong from the roof; his neck was broken in its socket, and his soul went down to the house of Hades.

"As my men mustered there, I said to them: 'You think, perhaps, that you are going home to your own native land; but Circe has marked out for us a different journey, even to the halls of Hades and of dread Persephone, there to consult the spirit of Teiresias of Thebes.'

"As I thus spoke, their very souls were crushed within them, and sitting down where each one was they moaned and tore their hair; but no good came to them from their lamenting.

"Now while we walked to the swift ship and to the shore, in sadness, letting the big tears fall, Circe went on before, and there by the black ship tied a black ewe and ram, passing us lightly by. When a god does not will, what man can spy him moving to and fro?"

BOOK XI

The Land of the Dead

Now when we came down to the ship and to the sea, we in the first place launched our ship into the sacred sea, put mast and sail in the black ship, then took the sheep and drove them in, and we ourselves embarked in sadness, letting the big tears fall. And for our aid behind our dark-bowed ship came a fair wind to fill our sail, a welcome comrade, sent us by fair-haired Circe, the mighty goddess, human of speech. So when we had done our work at the several ropes about the ship we sat down, while wind and helmsman kept her steady; and all day long the sail of the running ship was stretched. Then the sun sank, and all the ways grew dark.

"And now she reached earth's limits, the deep stream of the Ocean, where the Cimmerian people's* land and city lie, wrapt in a fog and cloud. Never on them does the shining sun look down with his beams, as he goes up the starry sky or as again toward earth he turns back from the sky, but deadly night is spread abroad over these hapless men. On coming here, we beached our ship and set the sheep ashore, then walked along the Ocean-stream until we reached the spot foretold by Circe.

"Here Perimedes and Eurylochus held fast the victims, while drawing my sharp blade from my thigh, I dug a pit, about a cubit either way, and round its edges poured an offering to all the dead,— first honey-mixture, next sweet wine, and thirdly water, and over all I strewed white barley-meal; and I made many supplications to the

---

*A legendary people at the western extremity of the world.

strengthless dead, vowing when I returned to Ithaca to take the barren cow that was my best and offer it in my hall, heaping the pyre with treasure; and to Teiresias separately to sacrifice a sheep, for him alone, one wholly black, the choicest of my flock. So when with prayers and vows I had implored the peoples of the dead, I took the sheep and cut their throats over the pit, and forth the dark blood flowed. Then gathered there spirits from out of Erebus of those now dead and gone,—brides, and unwedded youths, and worn old men, delicate maids with hearts but new to sorrow, and many pierced with brazen spears, men slain in fight, wearing their blood-stained armor. In crowds around the pit they flocked from every side, with awful wail. Pale terror seized me. Nevertheless, inspiring my men, I bade them take the sheep now lying there slain by the ruthless sword, and flay and burn them, and call upon the gods,—on powerful Hades and on dread Persephone,—while I myself, drawing my sharp sword from my thigh, sat still and did not let the strengthless dead approach the blood till I had made inquiry of Teiresias.

"First came the spirit of my man, Elpenor. He had not yet been buried under the broad earth; for we left his body at the hall of Circe, unwept, unburied, since another task then pressed. I wept to see him and pitied him from my heart, and speaking in winged words I said:

" 'Elpenor, how came you in this murky gloom? Faster you came on foot than I in my black ship.'

"So I spoke, and with a groan he answered: 'Highborn son of Laërtes, ready Odysseus, Heaven's cruel doom destroyed me, and excess of wine. After I went to sleep on Circe's house, I did not notice how to go down again by the long ladder, but fell headlong from the roof; my neck was broken in its socket, and my soul came down to the house of Hades. Now I entreat you by those left behind, not present here, by your wife, and by the father who cared for you when little, and by Telemachus whom you left at home alone,—for I know, as you go hence out of the house of Hades, you will touch with your staunch ship the island of Aeaea,—there then, my master, people? Who gave this clothing to you? Did you not say you came to us when lost at sea?"

Then wise Odysseus answered her and said: "Hard it were, Queen, fully to tell my woes, because the gods of heaven have given me many; still, what you ask and seek to know I will declare. Ogygia is an island lying far out at sea, where the daughter of Atlas dwells, crafty Calypso, a fair-haired, powerful goddess. Her no one visits, neither god nor mortal man; but hapless me some heavenly power brought to her hearth, and all alone, for Zeus with a gleaming bolt smote my swift ship and wrecked it in the middle of the wine-dark sea. There all the rest of my good comrades perished, but I myself caught in my arms the keel of my curved ship and drifted for nine days. Upon the tenth, in the dark night, gods brought me to the island of Ogygia, where dwells Calypso, the fair-haired, powerful goddess. Receiving me, she loved and cherished me, and often said that she would make me an immortal, young forever; but she never beguiled the heart within my breast. Here for seven years I lingered, and often with my tears bedewed the immortal robes Calypso gave. But when the eighth revolving year was come, she bade me, even urged me, to depart, whether through message sent from Zeus or that her own mind changed. Upon a strong-built raft she sent me forth, giving abundant food, bread and sweet wine; she clad me in immortal robes and sent along my course a fair and gentle breeze. For seventeen days I sailed across the sea; on the eighteenth there came in sight the dim heights of your coast, and I was glad at heart—ill-fated I, who yet must meet the sore distress which earth-shaking Poseidon sent on me. For he awoke the winds and barred my progress, stirred marvelously the waters, and the waves did not suffer me, despite my many groans, to ride my raft. This soon the tempest shattered, but I by swimming forced my way through the flood, till at your coast the wind and water brought me in. Here, as I tried to land, the waves upon the shore might well have overcome me, casting me on great rocks and on forbidding ground; but I turned back and swam until I reached a stream where the ground seemed most fit, all clear of stones and sheltered from the breeze. Gathering my strength, I staggered out, and the immortal night drew near. Off to a distance from the heaven-descended stream I walked, and fell asleep among the bushes, heaping the leaves around; and here God poured upon me a slumber without end. For lying among the leaves and sad at heart, I slept all night till morning, then till noon; the sun was going down as the sweet slumber left me. And now upon the shore I saw your daughter's maids, playing a game, and she among them seemed a goddess. To her I made entreaty, and she did not lack sound judgment, such as you could not think that a young person meeting you would show; for usually the young are giddy. She gave me bread enough and sparkling wine, she bathed me in the river and gave to me these clothes. Thus, though in trouble, I have told you all the truth."

Then answered him Alcinoüs and said: "Stranger, in this my child behaved not rightly, in that she did not bring you hither with her maids. Yet it was she from whom you first sought aid."

Then wise Odysseus answered him and said: "Sir, do not for this reproach the blameless girl. For she instructed me to follow with the maids; but I would not, for fear and very shame, lest possibly your heart might be offended at the sight. Suspicious creatures are we sons of men on earth."

Then answered him Alcinoüs and said: "Stranger, the heart within my breast is not one lightly troubled. Better, good sense in all things. O father Zeus, Athene, and Apollo, that such a man as you, so like in mind to me, might take my child, be called my son-in-law, and here abide! For I would give you house and goods if you would like to stay. Against your wish, shall no Phaeacian hold you. That, father Zeus forbid! Nay, I will fix your setting forth, and you may rest secure; tomorrow shall it be. And you shall be lying all the time wrapt in a sleep, while my men speed you onward over calm seas until you reach your land and home or anywhere you please— yes, though it were beyond Euboea, which is called the farthest shore by those among our people who once saw it when they carried light-haired Rhadamanthus to visit Tityus, the son of Gaia.* So far they went, without fatigue performing all, and on the selfsame day finished the journey home. But you yourself shall judge how excellent my ships and young men are in tossing up the water with the oar."

He spoke, and glad was long-tried royal Odysseus, who, making his prayer, uttered these words and said:

"O father Zeus, all that Alcinoüs has said may he fulfill. Then on the fruitful earth his name shall never die, and I shall reach my home."

So they conversed together. Meantime white-armed Arete bade her maids to set a bed beneath the portico, to lay upon it beautiful purple rugs, spread blankets over these, and then place woolen mantles on the outside for a covering. So the maids left the hall, with torches in their hands. And after they had spread the comfortable bed with busy speed, they summoned Odysseus, drawing near and saying: "Up, stranger, come to sleep. Your bed is ready." So did they speak, and to him rest seemed delightful. Thus long-tried royal Odysseus lay down to sleep upon the well-bored bedstead beneath the echoing portico. But Alcinoüs slept in the recess of his high hall; his wife, the queen, making her bed beside him.

---

*Tityus was sent to Hades for raping Leto.

BOOK VIII

The Stay in Phaeacta

Soon as the early rosy-fingered dawn appeared, revered Alcinoüs rose from bed, and up rose also high-born Odysseus, spoiler of cities. And now revered Alcinoüs led the way to the assembly-place of the Phaeacians, which lay beside the ships. When they were come, they took their seats on polished stones, set side by side; while Pallas Athene went throughout the town in likeness of the page of shrewd Alcinoüs, planning a safe return for brave Odysseus; and approaching one and another man, she gave the word:

"Come here, Phaeacian captains and councilors, come, hasten to the assembly to hear about the stranger who came but lately to the house of wise Alcinoüs, when cast away at sea. In form he is like the immortals."

With words like these she stirred in each a zeal and a desire, and speedily the assembly-place and all its seats were filled with those who came. Then many marveled when they saw the wise son of Laërtes; for Athene cast a wondrous grace about his head and shoulders, and made him taller than before and stouter to behold, that so he might find favor in all Phaeacian eyes as one of power and worth, and that he might win too the many games in which the Phaeacians tried Odysseus. So when they were assembled and all had come together, Alcinoüs thus addressed them, saying:

"Listen, Phaeacian captains and councilors, and let me tell you what the heart within me bids. This stranger—who he is I do not know—came here as a wanderer from peoples east or west. He begs us for assistance and prays it be assured. Then let us, even as heretofore, furnish assistance promptly; for never has a stranger

I charge you, think of me. Do not, in going, leave me behind, un-wept, unburied, deserting me, lest I become a cause of anger to the gods against you; but burn me in the armor that was mine, and on the shore of the foaming sea erect the mound of an unhappy man, that future times may know. Do this for me, and fix upon my grave the oar with which in life I rowed among my comrades.'

"So he spoke, and answering him said I: 'Unhappy man, this will I carry out and do for you.'

"In such sad words talking with one another, there we sat,—I on the one side, holding my blade over the blood, while the specter of my comrade, on the other, told of his many woes.

"Now came the spirit of my dead mother, Anticleia, daughter of brave Autolycus, whom I had left alive on setting forth for sacred Ilios. I wept to see her and pitied her from my heart; but even so, I did not let her—deeply though it grieved me—approach the blood till I had made inquiry of Teiresias.

"Now came the spirit of Teiresias of Thebes, holding his golden sceptre. He knew me, and said to me: 'High-born son of Laërtes, ready Odysseus, why now, unhappy man, leaving the sunshine, have you come here to see the dead and this forbidding place? Yet, draw back from the pit and turn your sharp blade from the blood, that I may drink and speak what will not fail.'

"So he spoke, and drawing back I thrust my silver-studded sword into its sheath. And after he had drunk of the dark blood, then thus the blameless seer addressed me:

" 'You are looking for a joyous journey home, glorious Odysseus, but a god will make it hard; for I do not think you will elude the Land-shaker, who bears a grudge against you in his heart, angry because you blinded his dear son. Yet even so, by meeting hardship you may still reach home, if you will curb the passions of yourself and crew when once you bring your staunch ship to the Thrinacian island,* safe from the dark blue sea, and find the pasturing cattle

---

*An island sacred to the sun god, Helios.

and sturdy sheep of the Sun, who all things oversees, all overhears. If you leave these unharmed and heed your homeward way, you still may come to Ithaca, though you shall meet with hardship. But if you harm them, then I predict the loss of ship and crew; and even if you yourself escape, late shall you come, in evil plight, with loss of all your crew, on the vessel of a stranger. At home you shall find trouble,—bold men devouring your living, wooing your matchless wife, and offering bridal gifts. Nevertheless, on your return, you surely shall avenge their crimes. But after you have slain the suitors in your halls, whether by stratagem or by the sharp sword boldly, then journey on, bearing a shapely oar, until you reach the men who know no sea and do not eat food mixed with salt. These therefore have no knowledge of the red-cheeked ships, nor of the shapely oars which are the wings of ships. And I will name a sign easy to be observed, which shall not fail you: when another traveler, meeting you, shall say you have a winnowing fan on your white shoulder, there fix in the ground your shapely oar, and make fit offerings to lord Poseidon—a ram, a bull, and the sow's mate, a boar,—and turning homeward offer sacred hecatombs to the immortal gods who hold the open sky, all in the order due. Upon yourself death from the sea shall very gently come and cut you off bowed down with hale old age. Round you shall be a prosperous people. I speak what shall not fail.'

"So he spoke, and answering him said I: 'Teiresias, these are the threads of destiny the gods themselves have spun. Nevertheless, declare me this, and plainly tell: I see the spirit of my dead mother here; silent she sits beside the blood and has not, although I am her son, deigned to look in my face or speak to me. Tell me, my master, how may she know that it is I?'

"So I spoke, and at once answering me said he: 'A simple saying I will tell and fix it in your mind: whomever among these dead and gone you let approach the blood, he shall declare the truth. But whomsoever you refuse, he shall turn back again.'

"So saying, into the house of Hades passed the spirit of the great Teiresias, after telling heaven's decrees; but I still held my place until my mother came and drank of the dark blood. She knew me instantly, and sorrowfully said in winged words:

" 'My child, how came you in this murky gloom, while still alive? Awful to the living are these sights. Great rivers are between, and fearful floods,—mightiest of all, the Ocean-stream, not to be crossed on foot, but only on a strong-built ship. Are you but now come here, upon your way from Troy, wandering a long time with your ship and crew? Have you not been in Ithaca, nor seen your wife at home?'

"So she spoke, and answering her said I: 'My mother, need brought me to the house of Hades, here to consult the spirit of Teiresias of Thebes. I have not yet been near Achaea nor once set foot upon my land, but have been always wandering and meeting sorrow since the first day I followed royal Agamemnon to Ilios, famed for horses, to fight the Trojans there. But now declare me this and plainly tell: what doom of death that lays men low overwhelmed you? Some long disease? Or did the huntress Artemis attack and slay you with her gentle arrows? And tell me of my father and the son I left; still in their keeping are my honors? Or does at last an alien hold them, while people say that I shall come no more? Tell me, moreover, of my wedded wife, her purposes and thoughts. Is she abiding by her child and keeping all in safety? Or was she finally married by some chief of the Achaeans?'

"So I spoke, and straight my honored mother answered: 'Indeed she stays with patient heart within your hall, and wearily the nights and days are wasted with her tears. Nobody yet holds your fair honors; in peace Telemachus farms your estate, and sits at equal feasts where it befits the lawgiver to be a guest; for all give him a welcome. Your father stays among the fields, and comes to town no more. Bed has he none, bedstead, nor robes, nor bright-hued rugs; but through the winter he sleeps in the house where servants sleep, in the dust beside the fire, and wears upon his body sorry clothes. Then when the summer comes and fruitful autumn, wherever he may be about his slope of vineyard-ground a bed is piled of leaves fallen on the earth. There lies he in distress, woe waxing strong within, longing for your return; and hard old age comes on. Even so I also died and met my doom: not that at home the sure-eyed huntress attacked and slew me with her gentle arrows; nor did a sickness come, which oftentimes by sad decay steals from the limbs the life; but longing for you—your wise ways, glorious Odysseus, and your tenderness,— took joyous life away.'

"As she thus spoke, I yearned, though my mind hesitated, to clasp the spirit of my mother, even though dead. Three times the impulse came; my heart urged me to clasp her. Three times out of my arms like a shadow or a dream she flitted, and the sharp pain about my heart grew only more; and speaking in winged words, I said:

" 'My mother, why not stay for me who long to clasp you, so that in the very house of Hades, throwing our arms round one another, we two may take our fill of piercing grief? Or is it a phantom high Persephone has sent, to make me weep and sorrow more?'

"So I spoke, and straight my honored mother answered: 'Ah, my own child, beyond all men ill-fated! In no manner is Persephone, daughter of Zeus, beguiling you, but this is the way with mortals when they die: the sinews then no longer hold the flesh and bones together; for these the strong force of the blazing fire destroys, when once the life leaves the white bones, and like a dream the spirit flies away. But now, press quickly on into the light, and of all this take heed, to tell your wife hereafter.'

"So we held converse there; but now the women came—for high Persephone had sent them—who were great men's wives and daughters.[31] Round the dark blood in throngs they gathered and I considered how to question each. Then to my mind this seemed the wisest way: I drew my keen-edged blade from my stout thigh and did not let them all at once drink the dark blood, but one by one they came, and each declared her lineage, and I questioned all.

"There I saw Tyro first, of noble ancestry, who told of being sprung from gentle Salmoneus; told how she was the wife of Cretheus, son of Aeolus. She loved a river-god, divine, Enipeus, who flows the fairest of all streams on earth. So she would walk by the fair currents of Enipeus, and in his guise the Land-shaker, who girds the land, met her at the outpouring of the eddying stream. The heaving water compassed them, high as a hill and arching, and hid the god and mortal woman. He touched the maiden and she fell asleep. Then on departing he took her hand and spoke and thus addressed her:

" 'Be happy, lady, in my love. In the revolving year you shall bear noble children; for the love of the immortals is not barren. Rear them yourself and cherish them. And now go home. Hold fast and speak it not. I am Poseidon, the shaker of the land.'

"So saying, he plunged into the surging sea. She then bore Pelias and Neleus, who both became strong ministers of mighty Zeus. Pelias dwelt in the open country of Iolcas, rich in flocks, the other at sandy Pylos. And sons to Cretheus also this queen of women bore—Aeson, and Pheres, and Amythaon, the charioteer.

"And after her I saw Antiope, Asopus' daughter, who boasted she had been the spouse of Zeus himself. To him she bore two sons, Amphion and Zethus, who first laid the foundations of seven-gated Thebes and fortified it; because, unfortified, they could not dwell in open Thebes, for all their power.

"And after her I saw Alcmene, wife of Amphitryon, her who bore dauntless Hercules, the lion-hearted, as spouse of mighty Zeus; and Megara, harsh Creon's daughter, whom the tireless son of Amphitryon took to wife.

"The mother of Oedipus I saw, fair Epicaste, who did a monstrous deed through ignorance of heart, in marrying her son. He, having slain his father, married her; and soon the gods made the thing known to men. In pain at pleasant Thebes he governed the Cadmeians, through the gods' destroying purpose; and she went down to Hades, the strong jailer, fastening a fatal noose to the high rafter, abandoned to her grief. To him she left the many woes which the avengers of a mother bring.

"Beautiful Chloris, too, I saw, whom Neleus once married for her beauty after making countless gifts, the youngest daughter of that Amphion, son of Iasus, who once held sway at Minyan Orchomenus. She was the queen of Pylos and bore Neleus famous children, Nestor and Chromius and Periclymenus the headstrong.

And beside these she bore that stately Pero, the marvel of mankind, whom all her neighbors wooed. But to none would Neleus give her save to him who should drive from Phylace the crook-horned, broad-browed cattle of haughty Iphiclus, and dangerous cattle were they. A blameless seer alone would undertake to drive them; but cruel doom of God prevented, harsh bonds and clownish herdsmen. Yet after days and months were spent, as the year rolled and other seasons came, then haughty Iphiclus released him on his telling all the oracles. The will of Zeus was done.

"Leda I saw, the wife of Tyndareus, who bore to Tyndareus two stalwart sons: Castor, the horseman, and Polydeuces, good at boxing. These in a kind of life the nourishing earth now holds, and even beneath the ground they have from Zeus the boon that today they be alive, tomorrow dead; and they are allotted honors like the gods.

"Iphimedeia I saw, wife of Aloëus, who said she had been once loved by Poseidon. She bore two children, but short-lived they proved,—Otus, the godlike, and the far-famed Ephialtes,—whom the fruitful earth made grow to be the tallest and most beautiful of men, after renowned Orion; for at nine years they were nine cubits broad, and in height they reached nine fathoms. Therefore they even threatened the immortals with raising on Olympus the din of furious war. Ossa they strove to set upon Olympus, and upon Ossa leafy Pelion, that so the heavens might be scaled. And this they would have done, had they but reached their period of full vigor; but the son of Zeus whom fair-haired Leto bore destroyed them both before below their temples the downy hair had sprung and covered their chins with the fresh beard.

"Phaedra and Procris, too, I saw, and beautiful Ariadne, daughter of wizard Minos, whom Theseus tried to bring from Crete to the slopes of sacred Athens. But he gained naught thereby; before she came, Artemis slew her in sea-encircled Dia,—prompted by the report of Dionysus.

"Maera and Clymene I saw, and odious Eriphyle who took a bribe of gold as the price of her own husband. But all I cannot tell, nor even name the many heroes' wives and daughters whom I saw; before that, the immortal night would wear away. Already it is time to sleep, at the swift ship among the crew or here. My journey hence rests with the gods and you."

As thus he ended, all were hushed to silence, held by the spell throughout the dusky hall. White-armed Arete was the first to speak: "Phaeacians, how seems to you this man in beauty, height, and balanced mind within? My guest indeed he is, but each one shares the honor. Be not in haste then to dismiss him, nor stint your gifts to one so much in need. By favor of the gods great wealth is in your houses."

Then also spoke the old lord Echeneüs, who was the oldest of Phaeacian men: "My friends, not wide of the mark, nor of her reputation, speaks the wise queen; therefore give heed. Yet word and work rest with Alcinoüs here."

Then answered him Alcinoüs and said: "Even as she speaks that word shall be, if I be now the living lord of oar-loving Phaeacians! But let our guest, however much he longs for home, consent to stay at all events until tomorrow, till I shall make our gift complete. To send him hence shall be the charge of all, especially of me; for power within this land rests here."

Then wise Odysseus answered him and said: "Mighty Alcinoüs, renowned of all, if you should bid me stay a year and then should send me forth, giving me splendid gifts, that is what I would choose; for much more to my profit would it be with fuller hands to reach my native land. Then should I be regarded more and welcomed more by all who saw me coming home to Ithaca."

Then answered him Alcinoüs and said: "Odysseus, we judge you by your looks to be no cheat or thief; though many are the men the dark earth breeds, and scatters far and wide, who fashion falsehoods out of what no man can see. But you have a grace of word and a noble mind within, and you told your tale as skillfully as if you were a bard, relating all the Argives' and your own sore troubles. But now declare me this and plainly tell: did you see any of the godlike comrades who went with you to Ilios and there met doom? The night is very long; yes, vastly long. The hour for sleeping at the hall is not yet come. Tell me the wondrous story. I could be well content till sacred dawn, if you were willing in the hall to tell us of your woes."

Then wise Odysseus answered him and said: "Lord Alcinoüs, renowned of all, there is a time for stories and a time for sleep; yet if you wish to listen longer, I would not shrink from telling tales more pitiful than these, the woes of my companions who died in after-time, men who escaped the grievous war-cry of the Trojans to die on their return through a wicked woman's will.

"When, then, chaste Persephone had scattered here and there those spirits of tender women, there came the spirit of Agamemnon, son of Atreus, sorrowing. Around thronged other spirits of men who by his side had died in the house of Aegisthus and there had met their doom. He knew me as soon as he had drunk of the dark blood; and then he cried aloud and let the big tears fall, and stretched his hands forth eagerly to grasp me. But no, there was no strength or vigor left, such as was once within his supple limbs. I wept to see him, and pitied him from my heart, and speaking in winged words I said:

" 'Great son of Atreus, Agamemnon, lord of men, what doom of death that lays men low overtook you? Was it on shipboard that Poseidon smote you, raising unwelcome blasts of cruel wind? Or did fierce men destroy you on the land, while you were cutting off their cattle or their fair flocks of sheep, or while you fought to win their town and carry off their women?'

"So I spoke, and straightway answering me said he: 'No, high-born son of Laërtes, ready Odysseus, on shipboard Poseidon did not smite me, raising unwelcome blasts of cruel wind, nor did fierce men destroy me on the land; it was Aegisthus, plotting death and doom, who slew me, aided by my accursed wife, when he had bidden me home and had me at the feast, even as one cuts the ox down at his stall. So thus I died a lamentable death, and all my men, with no escape, were slain around me; like white-toothed swine at some rich, powerful man's wedding, or banquet, or gay festival. You have yourself been present at the death of many men,—men slain in single combat and in the press of war; yet here you would have felt your heart most touched with pity, to see how round the mixing-bowl and by the loaded tables we lay about the hall, and all the pavement ran with blood. Saddest of all, I heard the cry of Priam's daughter, Cassandra, whom crafty Clytaemnestra slew beside me; and I, on the ground, lifted my hands and clutched my sword in dying. But she, the brutal woman, turned away and did not deign, though I was going to the house of Hades, to draw with her I and my eyelids down and press my lips together. Ah, what can be more horrible and brutish than a woman when she admits into her thoughts such deeds as these! And what a shameless deed she plotted, to bring about the murder of the husband of her youth! I used to think how glad my coming home would be, even to my children and my slaves; but she, intent on such extremity of crime, brought shame upon herself and all of womankind who shall be born hereafter, even on well-doers too.'

"So he spoke, and answering him said I: 'Alas! The house of Atreus far-seeing Zeus has sorely plagued with women's arts, from the beginning: for Helen's sake how many of us died; and Clytaemnestra plotted for you while absent.'

"So I spoke, and at once answering me said he: 'Never be you, then, gentle to your wife, nor speak out all you really mean; but tell a part and let a part be hid. And yet on you, Odysseus, no violent death shall ever fall from your wife's hand; for truly wise and of an understanding heart is the daughter of Icarius, heedful Penelope. As a young bride we left her, on going to the war. A child was at her breast, an infant then, who now perhaps sits in the ranks of men, and happy too; for his dear father, coming home, will see him, and he will meet his father with embrace, as children should. But my wife did not let me feast my eyes upon my son; before he came, she slew me. Nay, this I will say further: mark it well. By stealth, not openly, bring in your ship to shore, for there is no more faith in woman. But now declare me this and plainly tell if you hear my son is living still—at Orchomenus, perhaps, or sandy Pylos, or at the home of Menelaus in broad Sparta; for surely nowhere on earth has royal Orestes died.'

"So he spoke, and answering him said I: 'O son of Atreus, why question me of this? Whether he be alive or dead I do not know. To speak vain words is ill.'

"In such sad words talking with one another mournfully we stood, letting the big tears fall. And now there came the spirit of Achilles, son of Peleus, and of Patroclus too, of gallant Antilochus, and of Ajax who was first in beauty and in stature of all the Danaäns after the gallant son of Peleus. But the spirit of swift-footed Aeacides* knew me, and sorrowfully said in winged words:

" 'High-born son of Laërtes, ready Odysseus, rash as you are, what will you undertake more desperate than this! How dared you come down here to the house of Hades, where dwell the senseless dead, specters of toil-worn men?'

"So he spoke, and answering him said I: 'Achilles, son of Peleus, foremost of the Achaeans, I came for consultation with Teiresias, hoping that he might give advice for reaching rugged Ithaca. I have not yet been near Achaea nor once set foot upon my land, but have had constant trouble; while as for you, Achilles, no man was in the past more fortunate, nor in the future shall be; for formerly, during your life, we Argives gave you equal honor with the gods, and now you are a mighty lord among the dead when here. Then do not grieve at having died, Achilles.'

"So I spoke, and straightway answering me said he: 'Mock not at death, glorious Odysseus. Better to be the hireling of a stranger, and serve a man of mean estate whose living is but small, than be the ruler over all these dead and gone. No, tell me tales of my proud son, whether or not he followed to the war to be a leader; tell what you know of gallant Peleus, whether he still has honor in the cities of the Myrmidons; or do they slight him now in Hellas and in

---

*Descendant of Aeacus.

Phthia,* because old age has touched his hands and feet? I am myself no longer in the sunlight to defend him, nor like what I once was when on the Trojan plain I routed a brave troop in rescuing the Argives. If once like that I could but come, even for a little space, into my father's house, frightful should be my might and my resistless hands to any who are troubling him and keeping him from honor.'

"So he spoke, and answering him said I: 'Indeed, of gallant Peleus I know nothing. But about your dear son Neoptolemus, I will tell you all the truth, as you desire; for it was I, in my trim hollow ship, who brought him from Scyros to the armed Achaeans. And when encamped at Troy we held a council, he always was the first to speak, and no word missed its mark; godlike Nestor and I alone surpassed him. Moreover, on the Trojan plain, when we Achaeans battled, he never tarried in the throng nor at the rallying-place, but pressed before us all, yielding to none in courage. Many a man he slew in mortal combat. Fully I cannot tell, nor even name the host he slew in fighting for the Argives; but how he vanquished with his sword the son of Telephus, Eurypylus the hero. Many of that Ceteian band fell with their leader, destroyed by woman's bribes. So goodly a man as he I never saw, save kingly Memnon.

" 'Then when we entered the horse Epeius made,—we chieftains of the Argives,—and it lay all with me to shut or open our close ambush, other captains and councilors of the Danaäns would wipe away a tear, and their limbs shook beneath them; but watching him, at no time did I see his fair skin pale, nor from his cheeks did he wipe tears away. Often he begged to leave the horse; he fingered his sword-hilt and his bronze-tipped spear, longing to vex the Trojans. Yet after we overthrew the lofty town of Priam, he took his share of spoil and an honorable prize, and went on board unharmed, not hit by bronze point nor wounded in close combat, as for the most part happens in war; random Ares rages.'

---

*A region of central Greece.

"So I spoke, and the spirit of swift-footed Aeacides departed with long strides across the field of asphodel, pleased that I said his son was famous.

"But the other spirits of those dead and gone stood sadly there; each asked for what he loved. Only the spirit of Ajax, son of Telamon, held aloof, still angry at the victory I gained in the contest at the ships for the armor of Achilles. The goddess mother of Achilles offered the prize, and the sons of the Trojans were the judges,— they and Pallas Athene. Would I had never won in such a strife, since thus the earth closed round the head of Ajax, who in beauty and achievement surpassed all other Danaäns save the gallant son of Peleus. To him I spoke in gentle words and said:

" 'Ajax, son of gallant Telamon, will you not, even in death, forget your wrath about the accursed armor? To plague the Argives the gods gave it, since such a tower as you were lost thereby. For you as for Achilles, son of Peleus, do we Achaeans mourn unceasingly. None was to blame but Zeus, who, fiercely hating all the host of Danaän spearmen, brought upon you this doom. Nay, king, draw near, that you may listen to our voice and hear our words. Abate your pride and haughty spirit.'

"I spoke; he did not answer, but went his way after the other spirits of those dead and gone, on into Erebus. Yet then, despite his wrath,[32] he should have spoken, or I had spoken to him, but that the heart within my breast wished to see other spirits of the dead.

"There I saw Minos, the illustrious son of Zeus, a golden scepter in his hand, administering justice to the dead from where he sat, while all around men called for judgment from the king, sitting and standing in the wide-doored hall of Hades.

"Next I marked huge Orion drive through the field of asphodel the game that in his life he slew on the lonely hills. He held a club of solid bronze that never can be broken.

"And Tityus, I saw, the son of far-famed Gaia, stretched on the plain; across nine hundred feet he stretched. Two vultures sat beside him, one upon either hand, and tore his liver, piercing the organ within. Yet with his hands he did not keep them off; for he did violence to Leto, the honored wife of Zeus, as she was going to Pytho through pleasant Panopeus.

"Tantalus, too, I saw in grievous torment and standing in a pool. It touched his chin. He strained for thirst, but could not take and drink; for as the old man bent, eager to drink, the water always was absorbed and disappeared, and at his feet the dark earth showed. A god made it dry. Then leafy-crested trees drooped down their fruit,—pears, pomegranates, apples with shining fruit, sweet figs, and thriving olives. But when the old man stretched his hand to take, a breeze would toss them toward the dusky clouds.

"And Sisyphus I saw in bitter pains, forcing a monstrous stone along with both his hands. Tugging with hand and foot, he pushed the stone upward along a hill. But when he thought to heave it on clean to the summit, a mighty power would turn it back, and so once more down to the ground the wicked stone would tumble. Again he strained to push it back; sweat ran from off his limbs, and from his head a dust cloud rose.

"And next I marked the might of Hercules,—his phantom form; for he himself is with the immortal gods reveling at their feasts, wed to fair-ankled Hebe, child of great Zeus and golden-sandaled Here. Around him rose a clamor of the dead, like that of birds, fleeing all ways in terror; while he, like gloomy night, with his bare bow and arrow on the string, glared fearfully, as if forever shooting. Terrible was the baldric round about his breast, a golden belt where marvelous devices had been wrought, bears and wild boars and fierce-eyed lions, struggles and fights, murders and blood-sheddings. Let the artificer design no more who once achieved that sword-belt by his art. Soon as he saw, he knew me, and sorrowfully said in winged words:

" 'High-born son of Laërtes, ready Odysseus, so you, poor man, work out a cruel task such as I once endured when in the sunlight. I was the son of Kronian Zeus, yet I had pains unnumbered; for to one very far beneath me I was bound, and he imposed hard labors. He even sent me here to carry off the dog, for nothing he supposed could be a harder labor. I brought the dog up hence, and dragged him forth from Hades. Hermes was my guide, he and clear-eyed Athene.'

"So saying, back he went into the house of Hades, while I still held my place, hoping there yet might come some other heroes who died long ago. And more of the men of old I might have seen, as I desired,—Theseus and Peirithoüs, famous children of the gods;— but ere they came, myriads of the people of the dead gathered with awful cry. Pale terror seized me; I thought perhaps the Gorgon head of some deadly monster high Persephone might send out of the house of Hades. So, turning to my ship, I called my crew to come on board and loose the cables. Quickly they came, took places at the pins, and down the Ocean-stream the flowing current bore us, with oarage first and then a pleasant breeze."

BOOK XII

The Sirens, Scylla, Charybdis, and the Cattle of the Sun

After our ship had left the current of the Ocean-stream and come into the waters of the open sea and to the island of Aeaea, where is the dwelling of the early dawn, its dancing-ground and place of rising, as we ran in we beached our ship among the sands, and forth we went ourselves upon the shore; where, falling fast asleep, we awaited sacred dawn.

"But when the early rosy-fingered dawn appeared, I sent men forward to the house of Circe to fetch the body of the dead Elpenor. Then hastily cutting logs, where the coast stood out most boldly we buried him, in sadness, letting the big tears fall. After the dead was burned and the armor of the dead man, we raised a mound, and dragged a stone upon it, and fixed on the mound's highest point his shapely oar.

"With all this we were busied; nevertheless, our coming from the house of Hades was not concealed from Circe, but quickly she arrayed herself and came to meet us. Her maids bore bread and stores of meat and ruddy sparkling wine; and standing in the midst of all, the heavenly goddess said:

" 'Madman! who have gone down alive into the house of Hades, thus twice to meet with death while others die but once, come, eat this food and drink this wine here for today, and when tomorrow comes you shall set sail. I will myself point out the way and fully show you all; lest by unhappy lack of skill you be distressed on sea or land and suffer harm.'

"So she spoke, and our high hearts assented. Thus all throughout the day till setting sun we sat and feasted on abundant meat and pleasant wine; and when the sun had set and darkness came, my men lay down to sleep by the ship's cables; but leading me by the hand apart from my good comrades, the goddess bade me sit, herself reclined beside me, and asked me for my story. So I related all the tale in its due order. Then thus spoke potent Circe:

" 'All this is ended now; but listen to what I say, and God himself shall help you to remember. First you will meet the Sirens, who cast a spell on every man who goes their way. Whoso draws near unwarned and hears the Sirens' voices, by him no wife nor little child shall ever stand, glad at his coming home; for the Sirens cast a spell of penetrating song, sitting within a meadow. Near by is a great heap of rotting human bones; fragments of skin are shriveling on them. Therefore sail on, and stop your comrades' ears with sweet wax kneaded soft, that none of the rest may hear. If you yourself will listen, see that they bind you hand and foot on the swift ship, upright against the mast-block,—round it let the rope be wound,—that so with pleasure you may hear the Sirens' song. But if you should entreat your men and bid them set you free, let them with still more fetters bind you fast.

" 'After your men have brought the ship past these, what is to be your course I will not fully say; do you yourself ponder it in your heart. I will describe both ways. Along one route stand beetling cliffs, and on them roar the mighty waves of dark-eyed Amphitrite; the blessed gods call them the Wanderers. This way not even winged things can pass,—no, not the gentle doves which bear ambrosia to father Zeus; but one of them the smooth rock always draws away, though the father puts another in to fill the number. No ship of man ever escapes when once come here, but in one common ruin planks of ships and sailors' bodies are swept by the sea-waves and storms of deadly flame. The only coursing ship that ever passed this way was Argo, famed of all, when voyaging from Aeëtes; and her the waves would soon have dashed on the great rocks, but Here brought her through from love of Jason.[33]

" 'By the other way there are two crags, one reaching up to the broad heavens with its sharp peak. Clouds gather about it darkly

and never float away; light strikes its peak neither in heat nor harvest. No mortal man could clamber up or down it, though twenty hands and feet were his; for the rock is smooth, as though it were polished. About the middle of the crag is a dim cave, facing the west and Erebus, the very way where you must steer your rounded ship, glorious Odysseus; and from that rounded ship no lusty youth could with a bow-shot reach the hollow cave. Here Scylla dwells and utters hideous cries; her voice like that of a young dog, and she herself an evil monster. None can behold her and be glad, be it a god who meets her. Twelve feet she has, and all misshapen; six necks, extremely long; on each a frightful head; in these three rows of teeth, stout and close-set, fraught with dark death. As far as the waist she is drawn down within the hollow cave; but she holds forth her heads outside the awful chasm and fishes there, spying around the crag for dolphins, dogfish, or whatever larger creature she may catch, such things as great-voiced Amphitrite breeds by thousands. Never could sailors boast of passing her in safety; for with each head she takes a man, snatching him from the dark-bowed ship.

" 'The second crag is lower, you will see, Odysseus, and close beside the first; you well might shoot across. On it a fig-tree stands, tall and in leafy bloom, underneath which divine Charybdis sucks the dark water down. For thrice a day she sends it up, and thrice she sucks it down,—a fearful sight! May you not happen to be there when it goes down, for nobody could save you then from ill, not even the Earth-shaker. But swiftly turn your course toward Scylla's crag, and speed the ship along; for surely it is better to miss six comrades from your ship than all together.'

"So she spoke, and answering her, said I: 'Yet, goddess, tell me this in very truth: might I not possibly escape from deadly Charybdis, and then beat off that other when she assails my crew?'

"So I spoke, and straight the heavenly goddess answered: 'Foolhardy man! Still bent on strife and struggle! Will you not yield even to immortal gods? This is no mortal being, but an immortal woe,—dire, hard, and fierce, and not to be fought down. Courage is nothing; flight is best. For if you arm and linger by the rock, I fear that,

issuing forth once more, she may attack you with her many heads and carry off as many men. Therefore with zeal speed on; and call on Force, the mother of this Scylla, who bore her for a bane to humankind; she will restrain her from a second onset.

" 'Next, you will reach the island of Thrinacia, where in great numbers feed the cattle and the sturdy flocks of the Sun,—seven droves of cattle and just as many beautiful flocks of sheep, fifty in each. Of them, no young are born, nor do they ever die. Goddesses are their shepherds, nymphs of fair hair, Phaëthousa and Lampetia, whom to the exalted Sun divine Neaera bore. These their potent mother bore and reared, and sent them to the island of Thrinacia to dwell afar and keep their father's flocks and crook-horned cattle. If you leave these unharmed and heed your homeward way, you still may come to Ithaca, though you shall meet with hardship. But if you harm them, then I predict the loss of ship and crew; and even if you yourself escape, late shall you come, in evil plight, with loss of all your crew.'

"Even as she spoke, the gold-throned morning came, and up the island the heavenly goddess went her way; I turned toward my ship, and called my crew to come on board and loose the cables. Quickly they came, took places at the pins, and sitting in order smote the foaming water with their oars. And for our aid behind our dark-bowed ship came a fair wind to fill our sail, a welcome comrade, sent us by fair-haired Circe, the mighty goddess, human of speech. When we had done our work at the several ropes about the ship, we sat us down, while wind and helmsman kept her steady.

"Now to my men, with aching heart, I said: 'My friends, it is not right for only one or two to know the oracles which Circe told, that heavenly goddess. Therefore I speak, that, knowing all, we so may die, or fleeing death and doom, we may escape. She warns us first against the marvelous Sirens, and bids us flee their voice and flowery meadow. Only myself she bade to hear their song; but bind me with galling cords, to hold me firm, upright against the mast-block,— round it let the rope be wound. And if I should entreat you, and bid you set me free, then with still more fetters bind me fast.'

"Thus I, relating all my tale, talked with my comrades. Meanwhile our staunch ship swiftly neared the Sirens' island; a fair wind swept her on. On a sudden the wind ceased; there came a breathless calm; Heaven hushed the waves. My comrades, rising, furled the sail, stowed it on board the hollow ship, then sitting at their oars whitened the water with the polished blades. But I with my sharp sword cut a great cake of wax into small bits, which I then kneaded in my sturdy hands. Soon the wax warmed, forced by the powerful pressure and by the rays of the exalted Sun, the lord of all. Then one by one I stopped the ears of all my crew; and on the deck they bound me hand and foot, upright against the mast-block, round which they wound the rope; and sitting down they smote the foaming water with their oars. But when we were as far away as one can call and driving swiftly onward, our speeding ship, as it drew near, did not escape the Sirens, and thus they lifted up their penetrating voice:

" 'Come here, come, Odysseus, whom all praise, great glory of the Achaeans! Bring in your ship, and listen to our song. For none has ever passed us in a black-hulled ship till from our lips he heard ecstatic song, then went his way rejoicing and with larger knowledge. For we know all that on the plain of Troy Argives and Trojans suffered at the gods' behest; we know whatever happens on the bounteous earth.'

"So spoke they, sending forth their glorious song, and my heart longed to listen. Knitting my brows, I signed my men to set me free; but bending forward, on they rowed. And straightway Perimedes and Eurylochus arose and laid upon me still more cords and drew them tighter. Then, after passing by, when we could hear no more the Sirens' voice nor any singing, quickly my trusty crew removed the wax with which I stopped their ears, and set me free from bondage.

"Soon after we left the island, I observed a smoke, I saw high waves and heard a plunging sound. From the hands of my frightened men down fell the oars, and splashed against the current. There the ship stayed, for they worked the tapering oars no more. Along the ship I passed, inspiring my men with cheering words, standing by each in turn:

" 'Friends, hitherto we have not been untried in danger. Here is no greater danger than when the Cyclops penned us with brutal might in the deep cave. Yet out of that, through energy of mine, through will and wisdom, we escaped. These dangers, too, I think some day we shall remember. Come then, and what I say let us all follow. You with your oars strike the deep breakers of the sea, while sitting at the pins, and see if Zeus will set us free from present death and let us pass in safety. And, helmsman, these are my commands for you; lay them to heart, for you control the rudders of our hollow ship: keep the ship off that smoke and surf and hug the crags, or else, before you know it, she may veer off that way, and you will bring us into danger.'

"So I spoke, and my words they quickly heeded. But Scylla I did not name,—that hopeless horror,—for fear through fright my men might cease to row, and huddle all together in the hold. I disregarded too the hard command of Circe, when she had said I must by no means arm. Putting on my glittering armor and taking in my hands my two long spears, I went upon the ship's fore-deck, for thence I looked for the first sight of Scylla of the rock, who brought my men disaster. Nowhere could I detect her; I tired my eyes with searching up and down the dusky cliff.

"So up the strait we sailed in sadness; for here lay Scylla, and there divine Charybdis fearfully sucked the salt sea-water down. Whenever she belched it forth, like a kettle in fierce flame all would foam swirling up, and overhead spray fell upon the tops of both the crags. But when she gulped the salt sea-water down, then all within seemed in a whirl; the rock around roared fearfully, and down below the bottom showed, dark with the sand. Pale terror seized my men; on her we looked and feared to die.

"And now it was that Scylla snatched from the hollow ship six of my comrades who were best in skill and strength. Turning my eyes toward my swift ship to seek my men, I saw their feet and hands already in the air as they were carried up. They screamed

aloud and called my name for the last time, in agony of heart. As when a fisher, on a jutting rock, with long rod throws a bait to lure the little fishes, casting into the deep the horn of stall-fed ox; then, catching a fish, flings it ashore writhing; even so were these drawn writhing up the rocks. There at her door she ate them, loudly shrieking and stretching forth their hands in mortal pangs toward me. That was the saddest sight my eyes have ever seen, in all my toils, searching the ocean pathways.

"Now after we had passed the rocks of dire Charybdis and of Scylla, straight we drew near the pleasant island of the god. Here were the goodly broad-browed cattle and the many sturdy flocks of the exalted Sun. While still at sea, on the black ship, I heard the lowing of stalled cattle and the bleat of sheep; and on my mind fell words of the blind prophet, Teiresias of Thebes, and of Aeaean Circe, who very strictly charged me to shun the island of the Sun, the cheerer of mankind. So to my men with aching heart I said:

" 'My suffering comrades, hearken to my words, that I may tell you of the warnings of Teiresias, and of Aeaean Circe, who very strictly charged me to shun the island of the Sun, the cheerer of mankind; for there our deadliest danger lay, she said. Then past the island speed the black ship on her way.'

"As I spoke thus, their very souls were crushed within them, and instantly Eurylochus, with surly words, made answer: 'Headstrong are you, Odysseus; more than man's is your mettle, and your limbs never tire; and yet you must be made of nothing less than iron not to allow your comrades, worn with fatigue and sleep, to land, though on this sea-encircled island we might make once more a savory supper. Instead, just as we are, night falling fast, you bid us journey on and wander from the island over the misty deep. But in the night rough winds arise, fatal to vessels; and how could any one escape from utter ruin if by some chance a sudden storm of wind should come, the south wind or the blustering west, which wreck ships often, heedless of sovereign gods? No, let us now obey the dark night's bidding, let us prepare our supper and rest by the black ship; tomorrow morning we will embark and sail the open sea.'

"So spoke Eurylochus, the rest assented, and then I knew some god intended ill; and speaking in winged words I said:

" 'Eurylochus, plainly you force me, since I am only one. But come, all swear me now a solemn oath that if we find a herd of cattle or great flock of sheep, none in mad willfulness will slay a cow or sheep; but be content, and eat the food immortal Circe gave.'

"So I spoke, and they then took the oath which I required. And after they had sworn and ended all their oath, we moored our staunch ship in the rounded harbor, near a fresh stream, and my companions left the ship and busily got supper. But after they had stayed desire for drink and food, then calling to remembrance their dear comrades, they wept for those whom Scylla ate, those whom she snatched out of the hollow ship; and as they wept, on them there came a pleasant sleep. Now when it was the third watch of the night and the stars crossed the zenith, cloud-gathering Zeus sent forth a furious wind in a fierce tempest, and covered with his clouds both land and sea; night broke from heaven. And when the early rosy-fingered dawn appeared, we beached our ship, hauling her up into a hollow cave where there were pretty dancing-grounds and haunts for nymphs. Then holding a council, I said to all my men:

" 'Friends, there is food and drink enough on the swift ship; let us then spare the cattle, for fear we come to harm, for these are the herds and sturdy flocks of a dread god, the Sun, who all things oversees, all overhears.'

"So I spoke, and their high hearts assented. But all that month incessant south winds blew; there came no wind except from east and south. So long as they had bread and ruddy wine, they spared the cattle because they loved their lives. But when the vessel's stores were now all spent, and roaming by necessity they sought for game,—for fish, for fowl, for what might come to hand, caught by their crooked hooks,—and hunger pinched their bellies, then I departed by myself far up the island, to beg the gods to show my homeward way. And when by a walk across the island I had escaped my crew, I washed my hands where there was shelter from the breeze, and offered prayer to all the gods that hold Olympus. But they poured down sweet sleep upon my eyelids, while Eurylochus began his evil counsel to my crew:

" 'My suffering comrades, hearken to my words. Hateful is every form of death to wretched mortals; and yet to die by hunger, and so to meet one's doom, is the most pitiful of all. Come then, and let us drive away the best of the Sun's cattle, and sacrifice them to the immortals who hold the open sky. And if we ever come to Ithaca, our native land, we will at once build a rich temple to the exalted Sun, and put therein many fair offerings. If then the Sun, wroth for his high-horned cattle, seeks to destroy our ship, and other gods consent, for my part I would rather, open-mouthed in the sea, give up my life at once than slowly let it wear away here in this desert island.'

"So spoke Eurylochus; the rest assented. Forthwith they drove away the best of the Sun's cattle out of the field close by; for not far from the dark-bowed ship the cattle were grazing, crook-horned and beautiful and broad of brow. Round them they stood and prayed the gods, stripping the tender leaves from off a lofty oak; for they had no white barley on the well-benched ship. Then after prayer, when they had cut the throats and flayed the cattle, they cut away the thighs, wrapped them in fat in double layers, and placed raw flesh thereon. They had no wine to pour upon the blazing victims, but using water for libation they roasted all the entrails. So after the thighs were burned and the inward parts were tasted, they sliced the rest and stuck it upon spits.

"And now the pleasant sleep fled from my eyelids; I hastened to the swift ship and the shore. But on my way, as I drew near to the curved ship, around me came the savory smell of fat. I groaned and called aloud to the immortal gods:

" 'O father Zeus, and all you other blessed gods that live forever, truly to my ruin you laid me in ruthless sleep, while my men left behind plotted a monstrous deed.'

"Soon to the exalted Sun came long-robed Lampetia,* bearing him word that we had slain his cattle; and straightway with an angry heart he thus invoked the immortals:

" 'O father Zeus, and all you other blessed gods that live forever, avenge me on the comrades of Laërtes' son, Odysseus, who insolently slew the cattle in which I joy as I go forth into the starry sky, or as again toward earth I turn back from the sky. But if they do not make me fit atonement for the herd, I will go down to Hades and shine among the dead.'

"Then answered him cloud-gathering Zeus, and said: 'O Sun, do you shine on among the immortals and on the fruitful fields of mortal men. Soon I will smite their swift ship with a gleaming bolt, and cleave it in pieces in the middle of the wine-dark sea.'

"All this I heard from fair-haired Calypso, who said she heard it from the Guide-god Hermes.

"Now when I came to the ship and to the sea, I rebuked my men, confronting each in turn. But no help could we find; the cattle were dead already. Soon too the gods made prodigies appear: the skins would crawl; the spitted flesh, both roast and raw, would moan; and sounds came forth like those of cows.

"For six days afterwards my trusty comrades feasted, for they had driven away the best of the Sun's cattle; but when Zeus, the son of Kronos, brought the seventh day round, then the wind ceased to blow a gale, and we in haste embarking put forth on the open sea, setting our mast and hoisting the white sail.

"Nevertheless when we had left the island and no other land appeared, but only sky and sea, the son of Kronos set a dark cloud over the hollow ship and the deep gloomed below. The ship ran on for no long time; for soon a shrill west wind arose, blowing a heavy gale. The storm of wind snapped both the forestays of the mast. Back the mast fell, and all its gear lay scattered in the hold. At the ship's stern it struck the helmsman on the head and crushed his

---

*A daughter of the sun god.

skull, all in an instant; like a diver from the deck he dropped, and from his frame the strong life fled. Zeus at the same time thundered, hurling his bolt against the ship. She quivered in every part, struck by the bolt of Zeus, and filled with sulphur smoke. Out of the ship my comrades fell and then like sea-fowl were borne by the side of the black ship along the waves; God cut them off from coming home.

"I myself paced the ship until the surge tore her ribs off the keel, which the waves then carried along dismantled. The mast broke at the keel; but to it clung the backstay, made of ox-hide. With this I bound the two together, keel and mast, and getting a seat on these, I drifted before the deadly winds.

"And now the west wind ceased to blow a gale; but soon the south wind came and brought me anguish that I must measure back my way to fell Charybdis. All night I drifted on, and with the sunrise I came to Scylla's crag and dire Charybdis. She at that moment sucked the salt sea-water down; and when to the tall fig-tree I was upward borne, I clutched and clung as a bat clings. Yet could I nowhere set my feet firmly down or climb the tree; for its roots were far away and out of reach its branches, and these were long and large, and overspread Charybdis. But steadily I clung, until she should disgorge my mast and keel; and as I hoped they came, though it was late. But at the hour one rises from the assembly for his supper, after deciding many quarrels of contentious men, then was it that the timbers came to light out of Charybdis. I let go feet and hands, and down I dropped by the long timbers, and getting a seat on these rowed onward with my hands. But the father of men and gods gave me no further sight of Scylla, or else I should not have escaped from utter ruin.

"Thence for nine days I drifted; on the tenth, at night, gods brought me to the island of Ogygia, where dwells Calypso, a fair-haired powerful goddess, human of speech. She welcomed me and gave me care. Why tell the tale? It was but yesterday I told it in the hall to you and your good wife; and it is irksome to tell a plain-told tale a second time."

BOOK XIII

From Phaeacia to Ithaca

As he thus ended, all were hushed to silence, held by the spell throughout the dusky hall. At length, Alcinoüs answering said: "Odysseus, having crossed the bronze threshold of my high-roofed house, you shall be aided home with no more wanderings, be sure, long as you now have suffered. And this I say insistently to everybody here, to you who in my hall drink of the elders' sparkling wine and listen to the bard: you know that in a polished chest lie garments for the stranger, with rich-wrought gold and all the other gifts which the Phaeacian councilors have brought him here. But let us also, each man here, give a caldron and large tripod; then gathering the cost among the people, we will repay ourselves. For one to give outright were hard indeed."

So said Alcinoüs, and his saying pleased them; and now desiring rest, they each departed homeward. But when the early rosy-fingered dawn appeared, they hastened to the ship and brought the gladdening bronze. Revered Alcinoüs, going himself aboard the vessel, stowed it all carefully beneath the benches, so that it might not incommode the crew upon the passage while they labored at the oars. Then to Alcinoüs' house they went and turned to feasting.

In their behalf revered Alcinoüs offered an ox to Zeus of the dark cloud, the son of Kronos, who is the lord of all; and having burned the thighs, they held a glorious feast and made them merry. Among them sang the sacred bard, Demodocus, beloved of all. Nevertheless Odysseus would often turn his face toward the still shining sun, eager to see its setting, because he was impatient to be gone. As a man longs for supper whose pair of tawny oxen all day long have dragged the jointed plough through the fresh field; gladly for him the sunlight sinks and sends him home to supper; stiff are his knees for walking; so gladly for Odysseus sank the sun. Straightway he turned to the oar-loving Phaeacians, and speaking to Alcinoüs especially he said:

"Mighty Alcinoüs, renowned of all, pour a libation and send me safely forth. Fare you all well! All that my heart desired is ready— escort and friendly gifts—and may the gods of heaven make them a blessing! My true wife may I find on coming home, and dear ones safe! And you who stay, may you make glad your wedded wives and children! The gods bestow all happiness, and may no ill inhabit here!"

He spoke, and all approved and bade send forth the stranger, for rightly had he spoken. Then said revered Alcinoüs to the page: "Pontonoüs, mix a bowl and pass the wine to all within the hall, that with a prayer to father Zeus we may send forth the stranger to his native land."

He spoke; Pontonoüs stirred the cheering wine and served to all in turn; then to the blessed gods who hold the open sky they poured libations where they sat. But royal Odysseus rose, placed in Arete's hand the double cup, and speaking in winged words he said:

"Fare you well, queen, for all the years until old age and death, which visit all, shall come. I go my way; may you within this home enjoy your children, people, and Alcinoüs the king!"

So saying, royal Odysseus crossed the threshold. With him revered Alcinoüs sent a page, to show the way to the swift ship and to the shore. Arete too sent slave-maids after: one with the spotless robe and tunic, one to accompany the close-packed chest, and one bore bread and ruddy wine.

Now when they came to the ship and to the sea, straight the tall seamen took the stores and laid them by within the hollow ship, even all the food and drink. Then for Odysseus they spread a rug and linen sheet on the hollow vessel's deck, so that he might sleep soundly, there at the stern; and he himself embarked and laid him down in silence. The other men took places at the pins, each one in order, and loosed the cable from the perforated stone. But now when bending to their work they tossed the water with their oars, upon Odysseus' lids deep slumber fell, sound and most pleasant, very like to death. And as upon a plain four harnessed stallions spring forward all together at the crack of whip, and lifting high their feet speed swiftly on their way; even so the ship's stern lifted, while in her wake followed a huge upheaving wave of the resounding sea. Safely and steadily she ran; no circling hawk, swiftest of winged things, could keep beside her. Running thus rapidly she cut the ocean waves, bearing a man of godlike wisdom, a man who had before met many griefs of heart, cleaving his way through wars of men and through the boisterous seas, yet here slept undisturbed, heedless of all he suffered.

As that most brilliant star arose which comes the surest herald of the light of early dawn, the sea-borne ship drew near the island.

Now in the land of Ithaca there is a certain harbor sacred to Phorcys,* the old man of the sea. Here two projecting jagged cliffs slope inward toward the harbor and break the heavy waves raised by wild winds without. Inside, without a cable, ride the well benched ships when once they reach the roadstead. Just at the harbor's head a leafy olive stands, and near it a pleasant darksome cave sacred to nymphs, called Naiads. Within the cave are bowls and jars of stone, and here bees hive their honey. Long looms of stone are here, where nymphs weave purple robes, a marvel to behold. Here are ever-flowing springs. The cave has double doors: one to the north, accessible to men; one to the south, for gods. By this, men do not pass; it is the immortals' entrance.

Here they rowed in, knowing the place of old. The ship ran up the shore full half her length, by reason of her speed; so was she driven by her rowers' arms. The men then left the timbered ship and came ashore, and straightway took Odysseus from the hollow ship—him and his linen sheet and bright-hued rug—and set him

---

*A minor sea god, not to be confused with the shape-shifting Proteus.

on the sands, still sunk in sleep. They also brought the treasure out which the Phaeacian chiefs gave him at his departure, prompted by kind Athene, and laid it all together by an olive trunk a little off the road; for fear, before Odysseus woke, some passer-by might harm it. Then they departed homeward. Nevertheless the Earth-shaker did not forget the threats with which at first he threatened great Odysseus, but thus he asked the purposes of Zeus:

"O father Zeus, no more shall I be honored among immortal gods if mortal men, the people of Phaeacia, honor me not, though men of my own kin. For I had meant that through much hardship Odysseus should return; I never tried to cut him off from coming altogether, because you gave him once a promise and confirmed it with a nod. Yet these Phaeacians have borne him through the sea on their swift ship asleep, and set him down in Ithaca, and given him glorious gifts—such stores of bronze and gold and woven stuffs as Odysseus never would have won from Troy itself, had he returned unharmed with his due share of spoil."

Then answered him cloud-gathering Zeus and said: "For shame, wide-ruling Land-shaker! What are you saying? The gods do not refuse you honor. Hard would it be to cast dishonor on our oldest and our best. And as to men, if any, led by pride and power, dishonors you, vengeance is yours and shall be ever. Do what you will, even all your heart's desire!"

Then earth-shaking Poseidon answered: "Soon would I do, dark-clouded one, all that you say, but that I ever dread and would avoid your wrath. Even now this shapely ship of the Phaeacians, returning home from pilotage upon the misty sea, I would destroy,—that they henceforth may hold aloof and cease to give men aid,—and I would throw a lofty mound about their city."

Then answered him cloud-gathering Zeus and said: "Friend, this appears to me the better way. When all the people of the town look off and see her sailing, then turn her into stone close to the shore,—yet like a swift ship still,—that all the folk may marvel, and throw a lofty mound about their city."

On hearing this, earth-shaking Poseidon hastened to Scheria, where the Phaeacians live, and waited there. Then as the sea-borne ship drew near, running full swiftly, the Earth-shaker drew near her too, turned her to stone and rooted her to the bottom, forcing her under with his outspread hand, and went his way; but in winged words to one another talked the Phaeacian oarsmen, notable men at sea. And glancing at his neighbor a Phaeacian man would say:

"Hah! Who stopped the swift ship on the sea as she was running in? In full sight too she was."

So they would say, but knew not how things were. And now Alcinoüs addressed them thus: "Ah, surely then the ancient oracles are come to pass, told by my father, who said Poseidon was displeased because we were safe guides for all mankind; and he averred the god one day would wreck a shapely ship of the Phaeacians, returning home from pilotage upon the misty sea, and so would throw a lofty mound about our city. That was the old man's tale, and now it all comes true. However, what I say let us all follow: stop piloting the men who come from time to time here to our city; and to Poseidon let us offer twelve choice bulls, that he may have compassion and so not throw a lofty mound about our city."

He spoke, and all the people feared and brought the bulls. And then to lord Poseidon, standing around his altar, the captains and councilors of the Phaeacians offered prayer.

Meanwhile within his native land royal Odysseus woke from sleep, and did not know the land from which he had been gone so long; for a goddess spread a cloud around, even Pallas Athene, daughter of Zeus, that she might render him unknown and herself tell him all; and that his wife, his townsfolk, and his friends might never know him until the suitors paid the price of all their lawless deeds. Thus to its master all the land looked strange,—the footpaths stretching far away, the sheltered coves, steep rocks, and spreading trees. Rising, he stood and gazed upon his land, then groaned and smote his thighs with outspread hands, saying in anguish:

"Alas! To what men's land am I come now? Lawless and savage are they, with no regard for right, or are they kind to strangers and reverent toward the gods? Where shall I leave my many goods, and to where shall I turn? Would these had stayed with the Phaeacians where they were, and I myself had found some other powerful prince who might have entertained me and sent me on my way! Now, where to store my goods I do not know; yet here I must not leave them, to fall a prey to strangers. Not at all wise and just were the Phaeacian captains and councilors in bringing me to this strange shore. They promised they would carry me to far-seen Ithaca, but that they did not do. May Zeus, the god of suppliants, reward them! For over all men watches Zeus, chastising those who sin. However, let me count my goods, and see that the Phaeacians took none away upon their hollow ship."

So saying, he counted the beautiful tripods, the caldrons, gold, and goodly woven stuffs, and none was lacking. Then sighing for his native land he paced the shore of the resounding sea in sadness. Near him Athene drew, in form of a young shepherd, yet delicate as are the sons of kings. Doubled about her shoulders she wore a fine-wrought mantle; under her shining feet her sandals, and in her hand a spear. To see her made Odysseus glad. He went to meet her, and speaking in winged words he said:

"Friend, since you are the first I find within this land, I bid you welcome, and hope you come with no ill-will. Then, save these goods and save me too! I supplicate you as a god, and I approach your knees. And tell me truly this, that I may know full well, what land is this? What people? What sort of men dwell here? Is it a far-seen island, or a tongue of fertile mainland that stretches out to sea?"

Then said to him the goddess, clear-eyed Athene: "You are simple, stranger, or come from far away, to ask about this land. It is not quite so nameless. Many men know it well, men dwelling toward the east and rising sun, and those behind us also toward the twilit west. It is a rugged land, not fit for driving horses, yet not so very poor though lacking plains. Grain grows abundantly and wine as well; the showers are frequent and the dews refreshing; here is good pasturage for goats and cattle; trees of all kinds are here, and never-failing springs. So, stranger, the name of Ithaca has gone as far as Troy, which is, they say, a long way from Achaea."

She spoke, and glad was long-tried royal Odysseus, filled with delight over his native land through what was said by Pallas Athene, daughter of aegis-bearing Zeus; and speaking in winged words he said,—yet uttered not the truth, but turned his words awry, ever revolving in his breast some gainful purpose:

"In lowland Crete, I heard of Ithaca far off beyond the sea, and now I reach it—I and these goods of mine. I left an equal portion to my children and fled away from home; for I had killed the dear son of Idomeneus,* Orsilochus, the runner, who on the plains of Crete beat all us toiling men in speed of foot. The cause was this: he sought to cut me off from all the Trojan spoil to gain which I bore grief of heart, cleaving my way through wars of men and through the boisterous seas; and all because I did not, as he wished, serve with his father in the land of Troy, but led my separate men. With a bronze spear I struck him as he was coming from his farm and I was lying with a comrade near the road. A very dark night screened the sky; no man observed us; secretly I took his life. So after I had slain him with my bronze pointed spear, I straightway sought a ship, asked aid of the proud Phoenicians, and gave them from my booty what they wished. I bade them take me on their ship and set me down at Pylos, or else at sacred Elis where the Epeians rule. But strength of wind turned them aside, though much against their will; they meant no wrong; and missing our course, here we arrived last night. With much ado we rowed into the port, and gave no thought to supper, hungry although we were, but simply disembarking from the ship, we all lay down. Then, weary as I was, sweet sleep came on me; and the Phoenicians, taking my treasure from the hollow ship, laid it upon the sands where I was lying, and they embarked and sailed away to stately Sidon. So I was left behind with aching heart."

As he thus spoke, the goddess, clear-eyed Athene, smiled and patted him with her hand. Her form grew like a woman's,—one fair

---

*King of Crete and a hero of the Trojan War.

and tall and skilled in fine work,—and speaking in winged words she said:

"Prudent and wily must one be to overreach you in craft of any kind, even though it be a god who strives to match you. Bold, shifty, and insatiate of wiles, will you not now within your land cease from the false misleading tales which from the bottom of your heart you love? But let us talk no longer thus, both being versed in lies; for you are far the best of men in plots and tales, and I of all the gods am famed for craft and wiles. And yet you did not know me, Pallas Athene, daughter of Zeus, me who am ever near to guard you in all toil, me who have made you welcome to all Phaeacian folk! Now I am come to frame with you a scheme to hide the treasure which the Phaeacian chiefs, through my advice and prompting, gave you at setting forth; and I will tell you too what griefs you must endure within your stately house. Bear them, because you must. Do not report to man or woman of them all that you are come from wandering; but silently receive all pains and bear men's blows."

Then wise Odysseus answered her and said: "Hard is it, goddess, for a man, however wise he be, to know when you are near. You take all forms. I very well remember how kind to me you were when all we young Achaeans were in the war at Troy. But since we overthrew the lofty town of Priam, since we went away in ships and God dispersed the Achaeans, I never once have seen you, daughter of Zeus, nor known you to draw near my ship protecting me from harm. Yet bearing ever in my breast a stricken heart, I wandered till the gods delivered me from ill, when in the rich land of the Phaeacians you cheered me by your words and led me to the city. Now I entreat you by your father's name, for I cannot think that I am come to far-seen Ithaca. No, I have strayed to some strange shore, and you in mockery, I think, have told this tale to cheat me. But tell me, have I really reached my own dear land?"

Then answered him the goddess, clear-eyed Athene: "Such thoughts as these are ever in your breast; therefore I cannot leave you even in misfortune, because you are discreet, wary, and steadfast. For any other man on coming back from wanderings would eagerly have hastened home to see his wife and children; but you have no desire to know or hear of them till you have proved your wife, who as of old sits in your hall and wearily the nights and days are wasted with her tears. But I for my part never doubted. I knew within my heart that you would come, though with the loss of all your men. But I did not wish to quarrel with Poseidon, my father's brother, who bore a grudge against you in his heart, angry because you blinded his dear son. Come then, and let me point you out the parts of Ithaca, that so you may believe. Here is the port of Phorcys, the old man of the sea; here at the harbor's head the leafy olive; and near at hand the pleasant dim-lit cave, sacred to nymphs called Naiads; here is the arching cavern too, where oftentimes you made due sacrifices to the nymphs; and this is the wood-clad hill of Neriton."

The goddess, speaking thus, scattered the cloud, and plain the land appeared. Then glad was long-tried royal Odysseus, and he exulted in his land and kissed the bounteous earth, and straightway prayed the nymphs with outstretched hands:

"O Naiad Nymphs, daughters of Zeus, I said I should not see you any more, yet now with loving prayers I give you greeting. Gifts will we also give, even as of old, if the daughter of Zeus, our captain, graciously grants me life and prospers my dear son."

Then said to him the goddess, clear-eyed Athene: "Be of good courage! Let not these things disturb your mind! But in a corner of the wondrous cave let us lay by the goods, instantly, now, here to remain in safety; then let us plan how all may turn out well."

So saying, the goddess entered the dim-lit cave, and searched about the cave for hiding-places. Odysseus too brought here all he had, gold and enduring bronze and fair-wrought clothing, things given by the Phaeacians. All these were laid away with care, and at the entrance a stone was set by Pallas Athene, daughter of aegis-bearing Zeus. Then sitting down at the foot of the sacred olive, they planned the death of the audacious suitors; and thus began the goddess, clear-eyed Athene:

"High-born son of Laërtes, ready Odysseus, consider how to lay hands on the shameless suitors, who for three years have held dominion in your hall, wooing your matchless wife and offering bridal gifts; while she, continually mourning at heart over your coming, gives hopes to all, has promises for each, and sends each messages; but her mind has a different purpose."

Then wise Odysseus answered her and said: "Certainly here at home I too had met the evil fate of Agamemnon, son of Atreus, had you not, goddess, duly told me all. Come then, and frame a plot for me to win revenge. And do you stand beside me, inspiring hardy courage, even so as when we tore the shining crown from Troy. If you would stand as stoutly by me, clear-eyed one, then I would face three hundred men, mated with you, dread goddess, with you for my strong aid."

Then answered him the goddess, clear-eyed Athene: "I surely will be with you; you shall never be forgot when we begin the work. Some too, I think, shall spatter with their blood and brains the spacious floor, some of these suitors who devour your living. But let me make you strange to all men's view. I will shrivel the fair flesh on your supple limbs, pluck from your head the yellow locks, and clothe you in such rags that they who see shall loathe the wearer. And I will cloud your eyes, so beautiful before, that you may seem repulsive to all the suitors here, and even to your wife and the son you left at home. But first seek out the swineherd, the keeper of your swine; for he is loyal, loving your son and steadfast Penelope. You will find him sitting by his swine. They feed along the Raven Crag by the spring of Arethusa,* eating the pleasant acorns and drinking the shaded water, a food which breeds abundant fat in swine. There wait, and sitting by his side question him fully; while I go on to Sparta, the land of lovely women, to summon thence Telemachus, your son, Odysseus. He went to spacious Lacedaemon to visit Menelaus, hoping to learn if you were still alive."

---

*A spring named for the nymph transformed into it.

Then wise Odysseus answered her and said: "Why, knowing all, did you yourself not tell him? Must he too meet with sorrow, roaming the barren sea, while others eat his substance?"

Then answered him the goddess, clear-eyed Athene: "Nay, let him not too much oppress your heart. I was myself his guide, and helped him win a noble name by going thither. He meets no hardship there, but sits at ease within the palace of the son of Atreus, with plenty all around. Young men, indeed, now lie in wait on their black ship and seek to cut him off before he gains his native land. Yet this I think shall never be; rather the earth shall cover some of the suitors who devour your living."

So having said, Athene touched him with her wand, shriveled the fair flesh on his supple limbs, plucked from his head the yellow locks, and made the skin of all his limbs the skin of an old man. Likewise she clouded his eyes, so beautiful before, and gave him for his clothing a wretched robe and tunic, tattered and foul and grimed with filthy smoke. Then over all she threw a swift deer's ample hide, stripped of its hair; and gave him a staff and miserable wallet, full of holes, which hung upon a cord.

So having formed their plans, they parted; and thereupon the goddess went to sacred Lacedaemon, seeking Odysseus' son.

BOOK XIV

The Stay with Eumaeus

B ut from the harbor, up the rocky path, along the woody country on the hills, Odysseus went to where Athene bade him seek the noble swineherd, who guarded his estate more carefully than any man royal Odysseus owned.

He found him sitting in his porch, by which was built a high-walled yard upon commanding ground, a handsome yard and large, with space around. With his own hands the swineherd built it for the swine after his lord was gone, without assistance from the queen or old Laërtes, constructing it with blocks of stone and coping it with thorn. Outside the yard he drove down stakes the whole way round, stout and close-set, of split black oak. Inside the yard he made twelve sties alongside one another, as bedding places for the swine; and fifty swine that wallow in the mire were penned in each, all of them sows for breeding; the boars, much fewer, lay outside. On these the gallant suitors feasted and kept their number small; for daily the swineherd sent away the best fat hog he had. Three hundred and sixty they were now. Hard by, four dogs, like wild beasts, always lay, dogs which the swineherd bred, the overseer. He was himself now fitting sandals to his feet, cutting for them a well-tanned hide. The other men were gone their several ways: three with the swine to pasture; a fourth sent to the town to take to the audacious suitors, as was ordered, a hog to slay and satisfy their souls with meat.

But now the ever-barking dogs suddenly spied Odysseus, and baying rushed upon him; at which Odysseus calmly sat down and from his hand let fall his staff. Yet here at his own farm he would have come to cruel grief, had not the swineherd, springing swiftly after, dashed from the door and from his hand let fall the leather. Scolding the dogs, he drove them off this way and that with showers of stones, and thus addressed his master:

"Old man, my dogs had nearly torn you to pieces here, all of a sudden, and so you would have brought reproach on me. Ah well! The gods have given me other griefs and sorrows; for over my matchless master I sit and sigh and groan, and tend fat hogs for other men to eat; while he, perhaps longing for food, wanders about the lands and towns of men of alien speech,—if he still lives and sees the sunshine. But follow me, old man, into the lodge; so that you too, when satisfied with food and drink, may tell where you are come from and what troubles you have borne."

So saying, to the lodge the noble swineherd led the way, and bringing Odysseus in made him a seat. Beneath, he laid thick brushwood, and on the top he spread a shaggy wild goat's great soft skin, his usual bed. Odysseus was pleased that he received him so, and spoke and thus addressed him:

"Stranger, may Zeus and the other deathless gods grant all you most desire for treating me so kindly!"

And, swineherd Eumaeus, you answered him and said: "Stranger, it is not right for me to slight a stranger, not even one in poorer plight than you; for in the charge of Zeus all strangers and beggars stand, and our small gift is welcome. But so it is with servants, continually afraid when new men are their masters! Surely the gods kept him from coming who would have loved me well and given me for my own the things a generous master always allows his man—a house, a plot of ground, and a fair wife—at least when one has labored long, and God has made his work to prosper, as he makes prosper all the work I undertake. So would my master have well rewarded me, had he but grown old here. But he is gone! Would all the tribe of Helen had gone too, down on their knees! for she has made the knees of many men grow weak. Yes, he too went for Agamemnon's honor to Ilios, famed for horses, to fight the Trojans there."

So saying, he hurriedly girt his tunic with his belt, and went to the sties where droves of pigs were penned. Selecting two, he brought them in and killed them both, singed them and sliced them and stuck them upon spits, and roasting all the meat offered it to Odysseus, hot on the spits themselves. He sprinkled it with white barley. Then in an ivy bowl he mixed some honeyed wine, and taking a seat over against Odysseus thus cheerily began:

"Now, stranger, eat what servants have, this young pig's flesh. The fatted hogs are eaten by the suitors, who have no reverence in their hearts nor any pity. Yet reckless deeds the blessed gods love not; they honor justice and men's upright deeds. Why, evil-minded cruel men who land on a foreign shore, and Zeus allows them plunder so that they sail back home with well-filled ships,—even on the hearts of such falls a great fear of heavenly wrath. But these men know of something, having heard the utterance of some god about his mournful end, and therefore they are minded to court his wife so lawlessly, never departing to their homes, but at their ease wasting this wealth with recklessness and sparing nothing. For every day and night sent us by Zeus, they slay their victims, no mere one or two; and wine they also waste with reckless draughts. My master's means were vast. No noble has so much on the dark mainland or in Ithaca itself. No twenty men together have such revenues as he. I will reckon up the sum. Twelve herds upon the mainland; as many flocks of sheep; as many droves of swine; as many roving bands of goats; all shepherded by foreigners and herdsmen of his own. Then here in Ithaca graze roving bands of goats, eleven in all, along the farther shore, and trusty herdsmen watch them. Of these the herdsman every day drives up the fatted goat that seems the best. My task it is to guard and keep these swine, and picking carefully the best to send it to the suitors."

So spoke the swineherd, while his companion hungrily ate his meat and drank with eagerness his wine in silence, sowing seeds of evil for the suitors. But after he had dined and stayed his heart with food, Eumaeus, filling for his guest the cup from which he drank, gave it brimful of wine. Odysseus took it and was glad at heart, and speaking in winged words he said:

"My friend, who was the man that bought you with his wealth

and was so very rich and powerful as you say? You said he died for Agamemnon's honor. Tell me. I may have known some such as he. Zeus and the other deathless gods must know if I have seen him and can give you news. For I have traveled far."

Then said to him the swineherd, the overseer: "Old man, no traveler coming here to tell of him could win his wife or son to trust the story. Lightly do vagrants seeking hospitality tell lies, and never care to speak the truth. So when a vagabond reaches the land of Ithaca, he comes and chatters cheating stories to my queen. And she receives him well and, giving entertainment, questions him closely, while from her weeping eyelids trickle tears; for that is the way with wives when husbands die afar. You too, old man, would soon be patching up a tale if somebody would give you clothes, a coat and tunic. But probably already dogs and swift birds have plucked the flesh from off his bones and life has left him; or fishes devoured him in the deep, and on the land his bones are lying, wrapped in a heap of sand. So he died, far away, and for his friends sorrow is left behind—for all of them, and most of all for me; for never another such kind master shall I find, go where I may, not even if I return to my father's and mother's house, where I was born and where my parents reared me. Yet nowadays for them I do not greatly grieve, much as I wish to see them and to be in my own land; but longing possesses me for lost Odysseus. Why, stranger, though he is not here I speak his name with awe; for he was very kind and loved me from his heart, and worshipful I call him even when far away."

Then long-tried royal Odysseus answered thus: "Friend, though you stoutly contradict and say he will not come, and ever unbelieving is your heart, yet I declare, not with mere words but with an oath, Odysseus will return. Give me the fee for welcome news when he arrives at home. Then clothe me in a coat and tunic, goodly garments. Before that time, however great my need, I will take nothing; for hateful as the gates of hell is he who pressed by poverty tells cheating tales. First then of all the gods be witness Zeus, and let this hospitable table and the hearth of good Odysseus whereto I come be witness: all this shall be accomplished exactly as I say. This very year Odysseus comes. As this moon wanes and as the next appears, he shall return and punish all who wrong his wife and gallant son."

And, swineherd Eumaeus, you answered him and said: "Old man, I never then shall give that fee for welcome news, nor will Odysseus reach his home. Nay, drink in peace. Let us turn to other thoughts, and do not bring such matters to remembrance. Ah, my heart aches within when one recalls my honored master! As for the oath, why let it be; yet may Odysseus come, as I desire!—I and Penelope, Laërtes the old man, and prince Telemachus. But now I have unceasing grief about Odysseus' child, Telemachus; whom when the gods had made to grow like a young sapling, and I would often say that he would stand in men's esteem not an inch behind his father, glorious in form and beauty, some god or man upset the balanced mind within, and off he went for tidings of his father to hallowed Pylos. And now the lordly suitors watch for his coming home, hoping to have the race of prince Arceisius* blotted from Ithaca and left without a name. However, let us leave him too, whether he falls or flies, or whether the son of Kronos holds over him his arm. But come, old man, relate to me your troubles; and tell me truly this, that I may know full well: Who are you? Of what people? Where is your town and kindred? On what ship did you come? And how did sailors bring you to Ithaca? Whom did they call themselves? For I am sure you did not come on foot."

Then wise Odysseus answered him and said: "Well, I will very plainly tell you this. But had we in the lodge food and sweet wine for long, and should we feast in quiet, letting others do our work, then might I easily not finish in a year the tale of all the toils I bore by the gods' bidding.

"Of a family in lowland Crete I boast that I was born, a rich man's son. There were many sons besides, born and brought up within that hall, sons of a lawful wife. Me a slave-mother bore, a

---

*Founder of the Ithacan royal line.

concubine; yet he gave me equal honor with his true-begotten sons, this Castor, son of Hylax, whose child I say I am. Among the Cretans he was honored through the land as if he were a god, because of his prosperity, his wealth, and famous sons; but death's doom bore him to the house of Hades, and his disdainful sons divided up his living, casting lots. Me they assigned a very meager share, besides my dwelling. Nevertheless, I took to wife the daughter of a wealthy house, winning her by my merit; because I was no weakling and not afraid of war. Now all is gone. Yet still, when you see stubble I think you know the grain; hardships innumerable have pressed me sore. In those days Ares and Athene gave me courage, and strength to break the line; and when I picked our bravest for an ambush, sowing the seeds of evil for our foes, my swelling heart cast not a look on death; but charging ever foremost, I would catch upon my spear whatever foeman showed less speed than I. Such was I once in war; labor I never liked, nor household duty, which breeds good children. But ships equipped with oars were ever my delight, battles and polished javelins and arrows—appalling things, which are to others hateful. Whatever God put in my heart I liked; for different men delight in different deeds. Before the young Achaeans went to Troy, nine times I led forth men and sea-bound ships to plunder foreign tribes; and much I gained. Out of the spoil I picked what pleased me and then obtained much afterwards by lot. Thus rapidly my household grew, and I became a man of weight and honor with the Cretans. But when far-seeing Zeus ordained the unhappy voyage which made the knees of many men grow weak, they called on me and famed Idomeneus to lead the ships to Ilios. We could not tell them no; the people's voice was stern. There for nine years we young Achaeans battled, and in the tenth, destroying the town of Priam, turned homewards with our ships. But God dispersed the Achaeans; especially for hapless me wise Zeus intended ill. Only a month I stayed at home, glad in my children, in my wedded wife and in my goods; and then my heart impelled me to make a voyage to Egypt with gallant comrades and with ships well fitted. Nine ships I fitted, and my force was gathered soon.

"For six days afterwards my trusty comrades feasted, and I provided many victims to offer to the gods and make my men their feast. Embarking on the seventh, we sailed from lowland Crete, the north wind fresh and fair, and moved off easily as if down stream. No ship met harm; but safe and sound we sat, while wind and helmsmen kept us steady. In five days we arrived at Egypt's flowing stream, and in the Egyptian river I anchored my curved ships. Then to my trusty men I gave command to stay there by the ships and guard the ships, while I sent scouts to points of observation; but giving way to lawlessness and following their own bent, they presently began to pillage the fair fields of the Egyptians, carrying off wives and infant children and slaughtering the men. Soon the din reached the city. The people there, hearing the shouts, came forth at early dawn, and all the plain was filled with footmen and with horsemen and with the gleam of bronze. Then Zeus, the thunderer, brought on my men a cruel panic, and none dared stand and face the foe. Danger encountered us on every side. So the Egyptians slew many of our men with the sharp sword, and carried others off alive to work for them in bondage. But Zeus himself put in my heart this plan. Would I had rather died, and met my doom there by the stream of Egypt! For since that day sorrow has held me fast. At once I took the well-made helmet from my head and shield from off my shoulders, and flinging away my spear, I ran to meet the horses of the king. I clasped and kissed his knees; he spared and pitied me, and seating me in his chariot bore me weeping home. A multitude with spears rushed after, intent on killing me, for they were much enraged. He held them back, dreading the wrath of Zeus, the stranger's friend, who ever visits evil deeds with his displeasure. Here I stayed seven years, and I amassed much wealth among the Egyptians; for they all gave me gifts. But when the eighth revolving year was come, a certain Phoenician came, full of deceiving arts, a greedy sailor, one who had wrought much harm to men already. He now prevailed upon me by his lies, and took me with him till we reached Phoenicia, where was his home and wealth. Here at his house I stayed throughout the year. But after days and months were spent, as the year rolled and other seasons came, he set me on a sea-bound ship sailing for Libya, falsely professing I should share his gains; but purposing to sell me there and reap a large reward. I followed him on board, suspecting him, but helpless. And now the ship sped on, with north wind fresh and fair, through the mid sea past Crete, Zeus purposing our ruin.

"For when we had left Crete and no other land appeared, but only sky and sea, the son of Kronos set a dark cloud over the hollow ship, and the deep gloomed below. Zeus at the same time thundered, hurling his bolt against the ship. She quivered in every part, struck by the bolt of Zeus, and filled with sulphur smoke. Out of the ship my comrades fell, and then like sea-fowl were borne by the side of the black ship along the waves; God cut them off from coming home. But helping me, whose heart was filled with anguish, Zeus put the long mast of the dark-bowed ship into my hands, so that I might once more escape from death. To this I clung and drifted before deadly winds. Nine days I drifted; on the tenth, in the dark night, the vast and rolling waters cast me on the coast of the Thesprotians.* Here the king of the Thesprotians, lord Pheidon, entertained me, and freely too; it was his son who found me, overcome with cold and toil, and took me home, with his own hand supporting me until we reached his father's palace. He gave me also a coat and tunic for my clothing.

"Here, then, I heard about Odysseus; for Pheidon said he had him as his guest and friend upon his homeward voyage. He showed me all the treasure that Odysseus had obtained, the bronze and gold and well-wrought iron; and really it would support man after man ten generations long, so large a stock was stored in the king's palace. Odysseus himself, he said, was gone at that time to Dodona,† to learn from the sacred lofty oak the will of Zeus, and how he might return, whether openly or by stealth, to the rich land of Ithaca, when now so long away. Moreover, in my presence, as he offered a libation

---

*Residents of a region of the west coast of Greece.
†Site of an oracle in northwestern Greece.

in his house, he swore the ship was launched and sailors waiting to bring him home to his own native land. But he sent me off before, for a ship of the Thesprotians happened to be starting for the Doulichian* grain-fields. He bade her men conduct me carefully to king Acastus; but in their hearts a wicked scheme found favor, to bring me yet once more into the depths of woe. For when the sea-bound ship was far from shore, they planned a life of slavery for me. They stripped me of my clothes, my coat and tunic, and gave instead the wretched frock and the tunic full of holes which you yourself now see. Toward night they reached the fields of far-seen Ithaca. Here with a twisted rope they bound me fast upon the well-benched ship, and disembarking they hastily took supper on the shore. Meanwhile the gods themselves lightly untied my cords; and I, wrapping my robe about my head and sliding down the slippery rudder, brought my breast into the sea, where swimming hard I oared my way with my two hands, and very soon was out of the water, clear of them. Climbing the bank where there were clumps of leafy trees, I lay down and hid. With loud cries ran the others here and there; but when there seemed no profit in any further search, they entered their hollow ship once more. So the gods with ease concealed me and brought me to this farm of a sagacious man. It was my lot to live still longer."

Then, swineherd Eumaeus, you answered him and said: "Alas, poor stranger! You have deeply stirred my heart by telling me this tale of all your woes and wanderings. Yet here I think you err: you never can persuade me with talk about Odysseus. Why should a man like you tell lies for nothing? I understand about my master's coming; he has been hated utterly by all the gods, who did not let him die among the Trojans nor in the arms of friends when the skein of war was wound. Then would the whole Achaean host have made his grave, and for his son in after days a great name had been gained. Now, silently the robber winds have swept him off. I, mean-

---

*As in Doulichion, an island near Ithaca.

while, dwell aloof among the swine. To the town I never go, unless sometimes heedful Penelope commands my going, when any tidings come. Ah, then the people sit around and closely question, some grieving for their long-gone master, some glad to eat his substance and make him no amends. But as for me, I have no mind to search and question since an Aetolian fellow cheated me with his tale. He killed a man, and wandering far and wide came to my farmstead here, and I received him kindly. He told me how in Crete he saw Odysseus with Idomeneus, mending the ships which storms had shattered. He said he would be here by summer or by harvest, bringing a store of wealth and all his gallant crew. You too, old woe-worn man, now Heaven has brought you here, do not by lying tales attempt to please or win me; since out of no such cause I show respect and kindness, but out of reverence for Zeus the stranger's friend, and pity too for you."

Then wise Odysseus answered him and said: "Surely in you there is a heart so unbelieving that by an oath I did not move it nor win you to believe. But let us make a promise now, and for us both hereafter our witnesses shall be the gods who hold Olympus: if ever to this house your master comes, clothe me in coat and tunic and send me to Doulichion, where I desire to be. But if your master does not come, as I declare he will, send out your men and throw me down the lofty cliff, that other beggars may beware of telling lying tales."

Then answering said the noble swineherd: "Stranger, fine fame and fortune would be mine among mankind, both now and evermore, if after I had brought you to the lodge and given you welcome I turned about and slew you and took away your life! With a clear heart thereafter I should pray to Zeus, the son of Kronos! Well, it is supper-time; and may my comrades soon be here to get at the lodge a savory supper!"

So they conversed together. Presently came the swine and those who kept them. They shut them up to sleep in their accustomed sties, and a prodigious noise arose from the penned swine. Then to his comrades called the noble swineherd:

"Fetch me the best hog hither, to slaughter for the stranger who comes from far away. We too will have some cheer, who for a long time now have plagued ourselves over the white-toothed swine. Others devour our labor and make us no amends."

So saying, with the ruthless axe he cleft some wood. The others brought a boar, well fatted, five years old, and stood him on the hearth; and now the swineherd, being of upright heart, did not forget the immortal gods. At the beginning he cast into the fire hairs from the head of the white-toothed boar, and prayed to all the gods that wise Odysseus might return to his own home. Next raising high a bludgeon of oak, saved when he split the wood, he dealt a blow and the boar's life departed. The others cut the throat and singed the boar, and quickly laid him open. The swineherd then laid the raw meat, selected from each joint, into rich fat. Some parts of this, sprinkled with barley meal, they cast into the fire; the rest they sliced and stuck on spits, roasted with care, drew it all off, and tossed it all together on the plates. And now the swineherd rose to carve,— for well he knew his duties,—and as he carved divided all in seven portions. The first for the Nymphs and Hermes, Maia's son, he set aside with prayer, passing the rest to each. Odysseus he honored with the whole length of the chine, cut from the white-toothed boar, and so rejoiced his master. Addressing him, said wise Odysseus:

"Eumaeus, may you be as dear to father Zeus as now to me, for honoring with kindness such as I."

And, swineherd Eumaeus, you answered him and said: "Good stranger, eat; enjoy what lies before you! A god gives and withholds, as is his pleasure. His power is over all."

He spoke and burned the consecrated pieces to the ever-living gods; then pouring sparkling wine, he put the cup into the hands of city-sacking Odysseus, and sat him down by his own portion. Mesaulius passed them bread, a man the swineherd had acquired after his lord was gone, without assistance from the queen or lord Laërtes; with his own means he bought him of the Taphians. So on the food spread out before them they laid hands. Then after they had stayed desire for drink and food, Mesaulius took away the bread; and so to sleep, sated with bread and meat, they hastened.

And now the night came on, moonless and foul. Zeus rained all night; and strong the west wind blew, a wet wind always. To his companions spoke Odysseus, making trial of the swineherd to see if he would pull his own coat off and offer him, or order one of the men to give a coat, through love of him.

"Listen, Eumaeus, and all you other men, and I will boast a bit and tell a story; for intoxicating wine so bids, which sets a man, even if wise, to singing loud and laughing lightly, and makes him dance and brings out stories really better left untold. But since I have begun to chatter, I'll not be silent. Would I were in my prime, my vigor firm, as in the days when we went under Troy and set an ambush. Odysseus was our captain, and Atreides Menelaus, and with them I was third; for so they ordered. Now when we reached the city and the lofty wall, in the thick bushes by the citadel, among some reeds and marsh-grass, curled up beneath our armor, we lay down to sleep. An ugly night came on, although the north wind fell, and bleak it was. From overhead came snow, like hoarfrost, cold; and ice formed on the edges of our shields. Then all the other men had coats and tunics, and slept in comfort with their shields snug round their shoulders. But I at starting foolishly left my coat with my companions, because I did not think I should be cold at all; so off I came with nothing but my shield and colored doublet. But when it was the third watch of the night and the stars crossed the zenith, I spoke to Odysseus who was near, nudging him with my elbow, and readily he listened:

" 'High-born son of Laërtes, ready Odysseus, I shall not be among the living long. This cold is killing me, because I have no coat. Some god beguiled me into wearing nothing but my tunic. Now there is no escape.'

"So said I, and he at once had an idea in mind,—so ready was he both to plan and fight,—and speaking in an undertone he said: 'Keep quiet for the present, lest some other Achaean hear.'

"Then raising his head and resting on his elbow, thus he spoke:

'Hark, friends! A dream from heaven came to me in my sleep. Yes, we have come a long way from the ships. Would there were some one here to tell Atreides Agamemnon, the shepherd of the people, to send us more men hither from the fleet.'

"As he thus spoke, up Thoas sprung, Andraemon's son, who, quickly casting off his purple coat, went running to the ships. I, in his garment, lay comfortably down till gold-throned morning dawned.

"So would I now were in my prime, my vigor firm; then one of the swineherds of the farm might give a coat, through kindness and respect for a deserving man. Now they despise me for the sorry clothes I wear."

Then, swineherd Eumaeus, you answered him and said: "Old man, the boastings you have uttered are not ill. You have not spoken an improper or a silly word. Therefore you shall not lack for clothes nor anything besides which it is fit a hard-pressed suppliant should find,—at least for now; tomorrow you shall wrap yourself in your own rags. There are not many coats and extra tunics here to wear, but simply one apiece. But when Odysseus' son returns, he will give a coat and tunic for your clothing and send you where your heart and soul may bid you go."

So saying, he rose and placed a bed beside the fire, and threw upon it skins of sheep and goats. On this Odysseus lay down, and over him Eumaeus threw a great shaggy coat which lay at hand as extra clothing, to put on when there came a bitter storm.

So here Odysseus slept, and by his side the young men slept, but not the swineherd. A bed here pleased him not, thus parted from his swine, but he prepared to venture forth. Glad was Odysseus that Eumaeus took such care of his estate while he was gone. And first Eumaeus slung a sharp-edged sword about his sturdy shoulders, put on his storm-proof shaggy coat, picked up the fleece of a large full-grown goat, took a sharp spear to keep off dogs and men, and went away to rest where lay the white-toothed swine under a hollow rock, sheltered from Boreas.

BOOK XV

Telemachus and Eumaeus

Now to spacious Lacedaemon went Pallas Athene to seek the noble son of resolute Odysseus, wishing to call his home to mind and bid him hasten. She found Telemachus and the worthy son of Nestor lying within the porch of famous Menelaus. The son of Nestor was still wrapped in gentle sleep; but to Telemachus came no welcome sleep, for through the immortal night thoughts in his heart about his father kept him waking. So clear-eyed Athene, drawing near, addressed him thus:

"Telemachus, it is not well to wander longer far from home, leaving your wealth behind and persons in your house so insolent as these; for they may swallow all your wealth, sharing with one another, while you are gone a fruitless journey. Nay, with all haste urge Menelaus, good at the war-cry, to send you forth, that you may find your blameless mother still at home. Already her father and her brothers press her to wed Eurymachus; for he excels all suitors in his gifts and overtops their dowry. But let her not against your will take treasure from your home. You know a woman's way: she strives to enrich his house who marries her, while of her former children and the husband of her youth when he is dead she thinks not, and she talks of him no more. Go then and put your household in the charge of her among the maids who seems the best, until the gods grant you an honored wife. And let me tell you more; lay it to heart; by a deliberate plan the leaders of the suitors now guard the strait between Ithaca and rugged Samos, and seek to cut you off before you gain your native land. Yet this I think shall never be; rather the earth shall cover some of the suitors who devour your living. Still, keep your staunch ship off the islands and sail both night and day; and one of the immortals who guards and keeps you safe shall send a favoring breeze. When then you reach the nearest shore of Ithaca, send forward to the city your ship and all her crew, and go yourself before all else straight to the swineherd, who is the keeper of your swine and ever loyal. There rest a night, but send the swineherd to the city to bear the news to heedful Penelope how you are safe and how you have returned from Pylos."

So saying, Athene passed away to high Olympus. But from sweet sleep Telemachus waked Nestor's son, touching him with his heel, and thus addressed him: "Wake, Nestor's son, Peisistratus! Bring out the strong-hoofed horses and yoke them to the car, that we may make our journey."

Then Nestor's son, Peisistratus, made answer: "Telemachus, we cannot, eager for the journey though we are, drive in the dusky night. It will be morning soon. Wait then awhile until the royal son of Atreus, the spearman Menelaus, brings his gifts, places them in the chariot, and sends us forth with cheering words upon our way. For a guest remembers all his days the hospitable man who showed him kindness."

He spoke, and soon the gold-throned morning came; and Menelaus, good at the war-cry, now drew near, just risen from bed by fair-haired Helen. When the son of Odysseus spied him, in haste he girt his glossy tunic round his body, and threw a great cloak round his sturdy shoulders. So forth he went and drawing near thus spoke Telemachus, the son of princely Odysseus:

"O son of Atreus, heaven-descended Menelaus, leader of hosts, now at last let me go to my own native land; for my heart longs for home."

Then answered Menelaus, good at the war-cry: "Telemachus, I will not keep you longer if you desire to go. I blame a host if over-kind, or over-rude. Better, good sense in all things. It is an equal fault to thrust away the guest who does not care to go, and to detain the impatient. Best make the stranger welcome while he stays, and speed him when he wishes. But wait until I bring you gifts and place them in your chariot, beautiful gifts, as you yourself shall see. And let me bid the maids prepare a meal here in the hall from our abundant stores. It brings dignity and honor and benefit besides to feast before you travel along the boundless earth. Then if you choose to make a tour through Hellas and mid-Argos, so far I will attend you; for I will yoke my horses and guide you through the towns. No one will send us empty off, but each will give some single thing to bear away, a brazen tripod, caldron, pair of mules or golden goblet."

Then again answered him discreet Telemachus: "O son of Atreus, heaven-descended Menelaus, leader of hosts, at present I had rather go to my own home, for I left behind at starting no guardian of my goods; so while I seek my godlike father, I may myself be lost, or else may lose out of my house some valued treasure."

When Menelaus, good at the war-cry, heard his words, he at once bade his wife and maids prepare a meal there in the hall from his abundant stores. And now the son of Boëthoüs, Eteoneus, entered, just risen from his bed; for he lived not far away. Menelaus, good at the war-cry, told him to light the fire and roast the meat; and when he heard, he did not disobey. Menelaus himself, meanwhile, went down to a fragrant chamber; yet not alone, for Helen went and Megapenthes. And when they came where lay his treasure, the son of Atreus took a double cup and ordered Megapenthes to bring a silver bowl, while Helen lingered by the chests where were the embroidered robes which she herself had wrought. Out of these robes the royal lady, Helen, drew forth one to bear away, one handsomest in work and largest, which sparkled like a star; it lay beneath the others. Then forth they hastened through the palace till they found Telemachus, whom light-haired Menelaus thus addressed:

"Telemachus, as your heart hopes, may Zeus, the thunderer, husband of Here, grant you a safe return! And out of all the gifts stored in my house as treasures, I will give you that which is most beautiful and precious: I will give a well-wrought bowl. It is of solid silver, its rim finished with gold, the work of Hephaestus. Lord Phaedimus, the king of the Sidonians, gave it, when his house sheltered me on my way homeward. And now to you I gladly give it."

So saying, the lordly son of Atreus put in his hands the double cup. Then the bright silver bowl strong Megapenthes brought and set before him, while at his side stood fair-cheeked Helen, holding the robe, and thus she spoke and said:

"I too, dear child, will give a gift, this keepsake from the hands of Helen against the wished-for wedding time, for your wife then to wear. Meanwhile, in your good mother's charge lay it away at home: and may you with rejoicing reach your stately house and native land."

So saying, she laid it in his hands; he took it and was glad. Then lord Peisistratus put in the chariot-box the gifts as he received them, viewing them all with wonder. Light-haired Menelaus led them to the house, where they took seats on benches and on chairs. Now water for the hands a servant brought in a beautiful pitcher, made of gold, and poured it out over a silver basin for their washing, and spread a polished table by their side. And the grave house-keeper brought bread and placed before them, setting out food of many a kind, freely giving of her store. The son of Boëthoüs, too, carved meat and passed them portions, and the son of famous Menelaus poured their wine: and on the food spread out before them they laid hands. Then after they had stayed desire for drink and food, Telemachus and Nestor's gallant son harnessed the horses, mounted the gay chariot, and off they drove from porch and echoing portico. After them came the son of Atreus, light-haired Menelaus, in his right hand a golden cup of bracing wine, for them to pour at starting. He stopped before the horses and pledging them he said:

"A health to you, young men! And say the same to Nestor, the shepherd of the people; for he was kind to me as any father those days we young Achaeans were in the war at Troy."

Then answered him discreet Telemachus: "Even as you say, O heaven-descended prince, when we arrive we will report all these your words. And would that coming home to Ithaca, I there might find Odysseus in my home, and so might say how after meeting every kindness here with you I went my way and carried many precious treasures with me!"

On his right, as he was speaking, flew an eagle, bearing within his claws a large white goose, a tame fowl from the yard. People ran shouting after, men and women. But as the bird drew near, he darted to the right before the horses. All saw it and were glad, and in their breasts their hearts grew warm. And thus began Peisistratus, the son of Nestor:

"Think, heaven-descended Menelaus, leader of hosts! Is it we to whom a god shows this sign, or is it you?"

He spoke and valiant Menelaus pondered, doubting what he should think and rightly answer. But long-robed Helen, taking up the word, spoke thus: "Hearken and I will prophesy such things as the immortals bring to mind, things which I think will happen. As the eagle caught the goose,—she, fattened in the house; he, coming from the hills where he was born and bred,—so shall Odysseus, through many woes and wanderings, come home and take revenge. Even now, perhaps, he is at home, sowing the seeds of ill for all the suitors."

Then answered her discreet Telemachus: "Zeus grant it so, he the loud thunderer, husband of Here! Then would I there too, as to any god, give thanks to you."

He spoke and laid the lash upon the horses, and very quickly they started toward the plain, hastening through the city; and all day long they shook the yoke they bore between them.

Now the sun sank and all the ways grew dark; and the men arrived at Pherae, before the house of Diocles, the son of Orsilochus, whose father was Alpheius. There for the night they rested; he gave them entertainment. Then as the early rosy-fingered dawn appeared, they harnessed the horses, mounted the gay chariot, and off they drove from porch and echoing portico. Telemachus cracked the whip to start, and not unwillingly the pair flew off, and by and by they came to the steep citadel of Pylos. Then said Telemachus to Nestor's son:

"O son of Nestor, could you give and carry out a promise I shall ask? Friends of old we call ourselves, through parents' friendship. Besides, we are alike in years, and this our journey makes the tie more close. Do not then, heaven-descended prince, take me beyond my ship, but leave me there; for fear old Nestor, meaning kindness, detain me at his house against my will, when I should hasten on."

So he spoke, and the son of Nestor doubted within his heart if he could rightly give and carry out that promise. Yet on reflecting thus, it seemed the better way. He turned his horses toward the swift ship and the shore, took out and set by the ship's stern the goodly gifts,—the clothing and the gold which Menelaus gave,—and hastening Telemachus, spoke thus in winged words:

"Quickly embark and summon all your crew before I reach my home and tell old Nestor ; for in my mind and heart full well I know how stern his temper is. He will not let you go; he will himself come here and call you. I tell you, too, go back he will not empty-handed; for he will be very angry, notwithstanding what you say."

So saying, he drove his full-maned horses to the town of Pylos, and quickly reached the palace. But Telemachus, inspiring his crew, called to them thus: "Put all the gear in order, friends, on the black ship; and come aboard yourselves and let us make our journey."

So he spoke, and willingly they heeded and obeyed; quickly they came on board and took their places at the pins.

With these things he was busied, and now by the ship's stern was making prayers and offerings to Athene, when up there came a wanderer, exiled from Argos through having killed a man. He was a seer, and of the lineage of Melampus.[34] In former times Melampus lived at Pylos, the mother-land of flocks, and had a very wealthy home among the Pylians. Then he went to a land of strangers and departed from his country, flying from high-souled Neleus, lordliest of living men, who for a full year held by force his great possessions. He meanwhile in the halls of Phylacus was kept in bitter bondage and suffered great distress, because of the daughter of Neleus and the delusion deep which the divine sharp-scourging fury brought his mind. But he escaped his doom and drove the bellowing oxen from Phylace to Pylos; and punishing matchless Neleus for his disgraceful deed, he brought the maiden home to be his brother's wife. So he came to a land of strangers, grazing Argos, where afterwards he was to live, sovereign of many Argives. And here he took a wife and built a high-roofed house, and he begot two sturdy sons, Antiphates and Mantius. Antiphates again begot brave Oicles, and Oicles Amphiaraüs, the summoner of hosts, whom Zeus the aegis-bearer and Apollo tenderly loved, and showed him every favor; and yet he did not reach the threshold of old age, but died at Thebes, destroyed by woman's bribes. To him were born two sons, Alcmaeon and Amphilochus. Now Mantius begot Cleitus and Polypheides; but gold-throned dawn took Cleitus, by reason of his beauty, to dwell with the immortals. Of eager Polypheides Apollo made a seer, the best among mankind when Amphiaraüs died. Quarrelling with his father, he withdrew to Hyperesia; and there he dwelt and prophesied for all men.

It was his son drew near, named Theoclymenus, and stood before Telemachus. He found him making offerings and prayers beside the swift black ship: and speaking in winged words he said:

"Friend, since I find you offering burnt-offerings here, by these offerings and the god I will entreat you, and by your own life too, and that of those who follow: tell truly all I ask. Hold nothing back. Who are you? Of what people? Where is your town and kindred?"

Then answered him discreet Telemachus: "Well, stranger, I will plainly tell you all. By birth I am of Ithaca. My father is Odysseus—if ever such there were! But long ago he died, a mournful death; so I, with men and a black ship, am come to gather news of my long-absent father."

Then answered godlike Theoclymenus: "Like you, I too am far from home, because I killed a kinsman. He has many relatives and friends in grazing Argos, and with the Achaeans their influence is large. To shun the death and the dark doom which they would deal, I flee; for I must be a wanderer now from tribe to tribe. Set me upon your ship, a fugitive and suppliant. Let them not kill me; for I know they will pursue."

Then answered him discreet Telemachus: "I shall not thrust you forth from the trim ship against your will. Then follow! In our land you shall receive what we can give."

So saying he took the bronze spear from Theoclymenus and laid it on the deck of the curved ship. Telemachus himself came on the sea-bound ship and sat him in the stern, while by his side sat Theoclymenus. The others loosed the cables. And now Telemachus, inspiring his men, bade them lay hold upon the tackling, and they busily obeyed. Raising the pine-wood mast, they set it in the hollow socket, binding it firm with forestays, and tightened the white sail with twisted ox-hide thongs. And a favorable wind clear-eyed Athene sent, which swept with violence along the sky, so that the scudding ship might swiftly make her way through the salt ocean water. Thus on they ran, past Crouni and the pleasant streams of Chalcis. The sun was setting and the ways were growing dark as the ship drew near to Pherae, driven by the breeze of Zeus; then on past sacred Elis where the Epeians rule. From here Telemachus steered for the Pointed Isles, uncertain if he should escape from death or fall a prey.

Meanwhile at the lodge Odysseus and the noble swineherd were eating supper, and with them supped the others. And after they had stayed desire for drink and food, thus spoke Odysseus,—making trial of the swineherd, to see if he would longer give a hearty welcome and urge his staying at the farm, or if he would send him straightway to the town:

"Listen, Eumaeus and all you other men! I want to go tomorrow to beg about the town, for fear I burden you and these your men. Only direct me well, and give me a trusty guide to show the way. Once in the city, I must wander by myself, and hope some man will give a cup and crust. And if I come to the house of princely Odysseus, there I will tell my tale to heedful Penelope and join the audacious suitors, who might perhaps give me a meal, since they have plenty. Soon I could serve them well in all they want. For let me tell you this, and do you mark and listen: by favor of the Guide-god, Hermes, who lends the grace and dignity to all the deeds of men, in servants' work I have no equal,—in laying a fire well, splitting dry wood, carving and roasting meat, and pouring wine,—indeed, in all the ways that poor men serve their betters."

Then deeply moved said you, swineherd Eumaeus: "Why,

stranger, how came such notions in your mind? You certainly must long to die that very instant when you consent to plunge into the throng of suitors, whose arrogance and outrage reach to the iron heavens. Their servants are not such as you; but younger men, well dressed in coats and tunics, ever with glossy heads and handsome faces, are they who do them service. Their polished tables are laden with bread and meat and wine. No, stay with us! Nobody is disturbed that you are here, not I myself, nor any one of these my men. And when Odysseus' son returns, he will give a coat and tunic for your clothing and send you where your heart and soul may bid you go.

Then answered him long-tried royal Odysseus: "May you, Eumaeus, be as dear to father Zeus as now to me, for having stopped my wandering and saved me bitter woe. Nothing is harder for a man than restless roaming. It's for the cursed belly's sake that men meet cruel ills when wandering, misfortune, and distresses come. Yet while you keep me here, bidding me wait your master, pray tell me of the mother of princely Odysseus, and of his father, whom when he went away he left behind on the threshold of old age. Are they still living in the sunshine, or are they now already dead and in the house of Hades?"

Then said to him the swineherd, the overseer: "Well, stranger, I will plainly tell you all. Laërtes is still living, but ever prays to Zeus to let life leave his limbs here at his home; for he mourns exceedingly his absent son and the early-wedded trusty wife whose death distressed him sorely and brought him into premature old age. In sorrow for her famous son, she pined away—a piteous death! May none die so who dwells with me, who is my friend and does me kindness. While she still lived, much as she suffered, pleasant it was to ask for her and make inquiries; for it was she who brought me up with long-robed Ctimene, her stately daughter, the youngest child she bore. With her I was brought up and I was honored little less. Then when we reached together the longed-for days of youth, they sent Ctimene to Same and obtained large wedding gifts, while me my lady dressed in coat and tunic, goodly garments, and giving sandals for my feet she sent me to the farm; yet in her heart she loved me more and more. Now all that love I lack, though the good gods bless all I undertake. By work I get my meat and drink, and give to the deserving, but from the queen I cannot win one cheering word or deed; trouble has fallen on the house through overbearing men. Yet servants long to speak with their mistress face to face, from her to learn of all, with her to eat and drink, and then take something also to the fields. Such things warm servants' hearts."

Then answering said wise Odysseus: "Swineherd Eumaeus, certainly when you were small you must have wandered far from home and kindred. Tell me about it; tell me plainly too. Was the wide-wayed city of your people sacked, the city where your father and honored mother dwelt? Or when you were alone among your sheep and cattle, did enemies take you on their ships and bring you over seas to the palace of a man who paid a proper price?"

Then said to him the swineherd, the overseer: "Stranger, since now you ask of this and question me, quietly listen; take your ease, and sit and drink your wine. These nights are vastly long. There is time enough to sleep, and time to cheer ourselves with hearing stories. You must not go to bed till bed-time; too much sleeping harms. As for the others here, if anybody's heart and liking bids, let him go off and sleep; then early in the morning after eating, let him attend his master's swine. But let us drink and feast within the lodge and please ourselves with telling one another tales of piteous ill; for afterwards a man finds pleasure in his pains, when he has suffered long and wandered long. So I will tell you what you ask and seek to know.

"There is an island, Syria it is called,—you may have heard its name,—above Ortygia,* where the sun's course turns; not very thickly settled, good however, with excellent flocks and herds and full of corn and wine. Into this land dearth never comes, nor any foul disease attacks unhappy men; but when the families throughout

---

*The identities of Syria (not the modern nation) and Ortygia remain unknown.

the town grow old, Apollo and Artemis come with silver bow and slay them with their gentle arrows. Here are two towns and all the land is shared between them. Over them both my father ruled, Ctesius, son of Ormenus, a man like the immortals.

"There Phoenicians came, notable men at sea, but greedy rogues, with countless trinkets in their black-hulled ship. Now in my father's house lived a Phoenician woman, handsome and tall and skilled in fine work; and her the wily Phoenicians led astray. In the first days, when she was washing clothes beside the hollow ship, a man seduced her by love and kindness; for these things turn the heads of womankind, even the upright too. Then he asked her who she was and whence she came; whereat she pointed straightway to my father's high-roofed house.

" 'I boast of being born in Sidon,* rich in bronze, and am the daughter of Arybas, a man of abounding wealth. But Taphian pirates seized me as I wandered through the fields, and brought me here across the sea to the palace of a man who paid a proper price.'

"Then said the man who secretly seduced her: 'Return then home again with us, to see your father's and your mother's high-roofed house, and see them too; for they are living still and still accounted rich.'

"Then answered him the woman thus and said: 'It may be, if you sailors pledge yourselves by oath to take me home unharmed.'

"So she spoke, and they all took the oath which she required. Then after they had sworn and ended all their oath, once more the woman answered them and said: 'Be quiet for the present! Let none among your crew utter a word to me, in meetings on the street or at the well, or some one coming to the old king's house may tell; and he, if he understands, will bind me in bitter bonds and plot your ruin. So bear in mind my words, and press the purchase of your cargo; then when the ship is filled with freight, let a messenger come quickly to the palace, and I will bring whatever gold I find at hand.

---

*A prosperous Phoenician (that is, Canaanite) trading city, on the coast of modern Lebanon.

Another kind of passage-money I would gladly give. At home I tend a child,—so bright a boy!—who runs beside me out of doors. Him I might bring on board, and he would fetch a mighty sum from any foreign folk you visit.'

"So saying, she departed to the stately palace. And they continued with us all the year, and by their trading gathered in their hollow ship large stores. But when the hollow ship was freighted to set sail, they sent a messenger to tell the woman. This crafty man came to my father's house, bringing a golden necklace strung with amber beads. The maids about the house and my good mother kept fingering the chain, and eyeing it, and offering a price. The man meanwhile signed to the woman silently, and having given his sign departed to the hollow ship. The woman, then, taking me by the hand, led me off out of doors. In the fore part of the house she found some cups and tables, where people had been feasting who waited on my father. They were now gone to a public gathering and debate. Quickly she hid three goblets in her breast and bore them off. I innocently followed. The sun was setting and the roads were growing dark; but we walked swiftly on and came to the well-known harbor where the Phoenicians' sea-bound ship was lying. Embarking there, the men set sail upon their watery way, making us too embark. Zeus sent us wind. Six days we sailed, as well by night as day; but when Zeus, the son of Kronos, brought the seventh day round, the huntress Artemis struck down the woman, and, like a sea-bird, in the hold she dropped. They threw her overboard, a prey to seals and fishes, and I was left behind with aching heart. But wind and water bore us thence and brought us here to Ithaca, and here Laërtes bought me with his wealth. This is the way I came to see this land."

Then thus replied high-born Odysseus: "Eumaeus, you have deeply stirred the heart within my breast, telling these tales of all the troubles you have borne. Yet side by side with evil Zeus surely gave you good, since at the end of all your toils you reached the house of a kind man who furnishes you food and drink in plenty. A comfortable life you lead; but I come here a wanderer through many cities."

So they conversed together, then lay and slept a little while, not long; for soon came bright-throned dawn.

Meantime, approaching shore, the comrades of Telemachus slackened their sail, hastily lowered the mast, and with their oars rowed the vessel to her moorings. Here they cast anchor and made fast the cables; and going forth themselves upon the shore, prepared their dinner and mixed the sparkling wine. Then after they had stayed desire for food and drink, discreet Telemachus was first to speak:

"Sail the black-hulled ship, my men, straight to the town; I go to the fields and herdsmen. At evening, after looking at the farm, I too will come to town. Tomorrow I will make you payment for your voyage by a bounteous feast of meat and pleasant wine."

Then up spoke godlike Theoclymenus: "Where shall I go, my child? To whose house come, of all the men who rule in rocky Ithaca? Or shall I go directly to your mother's house and yours?"

Then answered him discreet Telemachus: "At any other time I would bid you come to us, because we have no lack of means of welcome. But for yourself it would be somewhat dreary now. I shall be gone, and my mother will not see you; for she is not often in the same room with the suitors, but in an upper chamber far away she tends her loom. But I will name another man to whom you well might go: Eurymachus, the illustrious son of skillful Polybus, whom nowadays the men of Ithaca look upon as a god; for he is certainly the chief man here. He much desires to wed my mother and obtain the honors of Odysseus. Nevertheless, Olympian Zeus, who dwells in the clear sky, knows whether before the wedding he will meet a day of ill."

Even as he spoke, upon his right there flew a bird, a hawk, Apollo's speedy messenger. With his claws he tore the dove he held and scattered down its feathers to the ground, midway between the ship and Telemachus himself. Then Theoclymenus, calling Telemachus aside from his companions, held fast his hand and spoke and thus addressed him:

"Telemachus, not without God's warrant flew this bird upon our right. I knew him at a glance to be a bird of omen. There is no house in Ithaca more kingly than your own; and you shall always be the rulers here."

Then answered him discreet Telemachus: "Ah stranger, would these words of yours might be fulfilled! Soon should you know my kindness and many a gift from me, and every man you met would call you blessed."

Then turning to Peiraeus, his good comrade: "Peiraeus, son of Clytius, you always do my bidding best of all the men who followed me to Pylos; so take this stranger to your home and treat him kindly, and show him honor till the time that I shall come."

Then answered him Peiraeus, the famous spearman: "Telemachus, though you stay long, I still will entertain him; no lack of welcome shall there be."

So saying, Peiraeus went aboard the ship and called the crew to come on board and loose the cables. Quickly they came and took their places at the pins. Telemachus, however, bound to his feet his beautiful sandals and took his heavy spear, tipped with sharp bronze, from the ship's deck. The sailors loosed the cables and thrusting off the ship sailed to the town, as they were ordered by Telemachus, son of princely Odysseus. But him, meanwhile, his feet bore swiftly onward until he reached the yard where were the countless swine with whom the trusty swineherd lodged, still faithful to his master.

BOOK XVI

The Recognition by Telemachus

Now at the lodge Odysseus and the noble swineherd prepared their breakfast in the early dawn, before the lighted fire, having already sent the herdsmen with the droves of swine forth to the fields. As Telemachus drew near, the dogs that love to bark began to wag their tails, but did not bark. Royal Odysseus noticed the dogs wagging their tails, and the sound of footsteps reached him; and straightway to Eumaeus he spoke these winged words:

"Eumaeus, certainly a friend is coming, at least a man you know; for the dogs do not bark, but wag their tails, and I hear the tramp of feet."

The words were hardly uttered when his son stood in the doorway. In surprise up sprang the swineherd, and from his hands the vessels fell with which he had been busied, mixing sparkling wine. He went to meet his master, and kissed his face, each of his beautiful eyes, and both his hands, letting the big tears fall. And as a loving father greets the son who comes from foreign lands, ten years away, his only child, now grown a man, for whom he long has sorrowed; even so the noble swineherd took princely Telemachus in his arms and kissed him again and again, as one escaped from death, and sobbing said to him in winged words:

"So you are here, Telemachus, dearer than light to me! I said I should not see you any more after you went away by ship to Pylos. Come in then, child, and let me cheer my heart with looking at you, just come from far away. You do not often visit the farm and herdsmen. You tarry in the town; for nowadays you need to watch the wasteful throng of suitors."

Then answered him discreet Telemachus: "So be it, father! It's for your sake I am here, to see you with my eyes, and hear you tell if my mother still is staying at the hall, or if at last some stranger won her, and so Odysseus' bed, empty of occupants, stands covered with foul cobwebs."

Then answered him the swineherd, the overseer: "Indeed she stays with patient heart within your hall, and wearily the nights and days are wasted with her tears."

So saying, Eumaeus took Telemachus' bronze spear, and Telemachus went in and over the stone threshold. As he drew near, his father, Odysseus, yielded him his seat; but Telemachus on his part checked him, saying:

"Be seated, stranger. Elsewhere we shall find a seat at this our farm. Here is a man will give one."

He spoke, and his father turned and sat once more; but the swineherd threw green brushwood down and on its top a fleece, on which the dear son of Odysseus sat down. And now the swineherd brought platters of roasted meat, which those who ate the day before had left. Bustling about he heaped bread in the baskets, and in an ivy bowl mixed honeyed wine, then took a seat himself over against princely Odysseus, and on the food spread out before them they laid hands. So after they had stayed desire for drink and food, to the noble swineherd said Telemachus:

"Father, whence came this stranger? How did his sailors bring him to Ithaca? Whom did they call themselves? For I am sure he did not come on foot."

Then, swineherd Eumaeus, you answered him and said: "Well, I will tell you all the truth, my child. He calls himself by birth of lowland Crete, but says he has passed through many cities in his wanderings; so Heaven ordained his lot. Lately he ran away from a ship of the Thesprotians and came to my farm here. I place him in your charge. Do what you will. He calls himself your suppliant."

Then answered him discreet Telemachus: "Eumaeus, truly these are bitter words which you have said. How can I take a stranger home? I am myself but young and cannot trust my arm to right me with the man who wrongs me first. Moreover my mother's feeling wavers, whether to bide beside me here and keep the house, and thus revere her husband's bed and heed the public voice, or finally to follow some chief of the Achaeans who courts her in the hall with largest gifts. However, since the stranger has reached your lodging here, I will clothe him in a coat and tunic, goodly garments, give him a two-edged sword and sandals for his feet, and I will send him where his heart and soul may bid him go. Or, if you like, serve him yourself and keep him at the farm; and I will send him clothing and all his food to eat, so that he may not burden you and yours. Down there among the suitors I would not have him go; for they are full of wanton pride. So they might mock him,—a cruel grief to me. Hard is it even for a powerful man to act against a crowd; because together they are far too strong."

Then said to him long-tried royal Odysseus: "Friend,—for surely I too have a right to answer,—my heart is sore at hearing what you say, that suitors work abomination at the palace against a man like you. But tell me, do you willingly submit, or are the people of your land adverse to you, led by some voice of a god? Or have you any cause to blame your brothers, on whom a man relies for aid when bitter strifes arise? Would that, to match my spirit, I were young as you, and were the son of good Odysseus, or even Odysseus' self come from his wanderings, as there still is room for hope; then quickly should my foe strike off my head, or I would prove the bane of all these suitors when I should cross the hall of Laërtes' son Odysseus. And should they by their number crush me, all single and alone, far rather would I die, cut down within my hall, than constantly behold disgraceful deeds, strangers abused, and slave-maids dragged to shame through the fair palace, wine running waste, men eating up my bread, all idly, uselessly, to win what cannot be!"

Then answered him discreet Telemachus: "Well, stranger, I will plainly tell you all. My people as a whole bear me no grudge or hate;

nor yet can I blame brothers, on whom a man relies for aid when bitter strifes arise; for the son of Kronos made our race run in a single line. Arceisius begot a single son Laërtes; and he, the single son Odysseus; Odysseus left me here at home, the single son of his begetting, and of me had no joy. But bands of evil-minded men now fill my house; for all the nobles who bear sway among the islands— Doulichion, Same, and woody Zacynthus—and they who have the power in rocky Ithaca, all court my mother and despoil my home. She neither declines the hated suit nor has she power to end it, while they with feasting impoverish my home and soon will bring me also to destruction. However, in the lap of the gods these matters lie. But, father, quickly go and say to steadfast Penelope that I am safe and have returned from Pylos. I will stay here; do you come hither too; and tell your tidings to her only. Let none of the rest of the Achaeans hear; for many are they that plot against me."

Then, swineherd Eumaeus, you answered him and said: "I see, I understand; you speak to one who knows. But now declare me this and plainly say, shall I go tell Laërtes on my way, wretched Laërtes, who for a time, though grieving greatly for Odysseus, still oversaw his fields and with his men at home would drink and eat as appetite inclined; but from the day you went by ship to Pylos did never eat nor drink the same, they say, nor oversaw his fields, but full of moans and sighs sits sorrowing, while the flesh wastes upon his bones."

Then answered him discreet Telemachus: "It's hard, but though it grieves us, we will let him be; if all that men desire were in their power, the first thing we should choose would be the coming of my father. No, give your message and return, and do not wander through the fields to find Laërtes. But tell my mother to send forthwith her housemaid there, yet privately; for to the old man she might bear the news."

So saying, he dispatched the swineherd, who took his sandals, bound them to his feet, and went to town. Yet not unnoticed by Athene swineherd Eumaeus left the farm; but she herself drew near in likeness of a woman, one fair and tall and skilled in fine work. By the lodge door she stood, visible to Odysseus. Telemachus did not glance her way nor notice her; for not to every one do gods appear. Odysseus saw her, and the dogs; yet the dogs did not bark, but whining slunk away across the place. With her brows she made a sign; royal Odysseus understood, came forth from the hall past the great courtyard wall, and stood before her, and Athene said:

"High-born son of Laërtes, ready Odysseus, tell now your story to your son. Hide it no longer. Then having planned the suitors' death and doom, go forward both of you into the famous city. And I myself will not be far away, for I am eager for the combat."

She spoke and with a golden wand Athene touched Odysseus. And first she laid a spotless robe and tunic on his body, and then increased his bulk and bloom. Again he grew dark-hued; his cheeks were rounded, and dark the beard became about his chin. This done, she went away; and now Odysseus entered the lodge. His son was awe-struck and reverently turned his eyes aside, fearing it was a god. Then speaking in winged words he said:

"Stranger, you seem a different person now and a while ago. Your clothes are different and your flesh is not the same. You surely are one of the gods who hold the open sky. Nay, then, be gracious! So will we give you grateful offerings and fine-wrought gifts of gold. Have mercy on us!"

Then long-tried royal Odysseus answered: "I am no god. Why liken me to the immortals? I am your father, him for whom you sighed and suffered long, enduring outrage at the hands of men."

So saying, he kissed his son and down his cheeks upon the ground let fall a tear, which always hitherto he sternly had suppressed. But Telemachus—for he did not yet believe it was his father—finding his words once more made answer thus:

"No, you are not Odysseus, not my father! Some god beguiles me, to make me weep and sorrow more. No mortal man by his own wit could work such wonders, unless a god came to his aid and by his will made him with ease a young man or an old. For lately you were old and meanly clad; now you are like the gods who hold the open sky."

Then wise Odysseus answered him and said: "Telemachus, it is not right when here your father stands, to marvel overmuch and to be so amazed. Be sure no other Odysseus ever will appear; but as you see me, it is I, I who have suffered long and wandered long, and now in the twentieth year come to my native land. This is the work of our captain, Athene, who makes me what she will,—for she has power,—now like a beggar, now again a youth in fair attire. Easily can the gods who hold the open sky give glory to a mortal man, or give him shame."

So saying, down he sat; at which Telemachus, throwing his arms round his good father, began to sob and pour forth tears, and in them both arose a longing of lament. Loud were their cries and more unceasing than those of birds, ospreys or crook-clawed vultures, when farmers take away their young before the wings are grown: so pitifully fell the tears beneath their brows. And daylight had gone down upon their weeping, had not Telemachus suddenly addressed his father thus:

"Why, father, by what ship did sailors bring you to Ithaca? Whom did they call themselves? For I am sure you did not come on foot."

Then said to him long-tried royal Odysseus: "Well, I will tell you, child, the very truth. The Phaeacians brought me here, notable men at sea, who pilot others too who come their way. They brought me across the sea on a swift ship asleep, landed me here in Ithaca and gave me glorious gifts, much bronze and gold and woven stuff; which treasures by the gods' command are laid away in caves. Here I now am by bidding of Athene, that we may plan together the slaughter of our foes. Come tell me then the number of the suitors, that I may know how many and what sort of men they are; and so, weighing the matter in my gallant heart, I may decide if we can meet them quite alone, without allies, or whether we shall seek the aid of others."

Then answered him discreet Telemachus: "Truly, father, I have ever heard your great renown, what a warrior you are in arm and what a sage in council. But now you speak of something far too vast; I am astonished. Two could not fight a troop of valiant men. The suitors number no mere ten, nor twice ten either; many more. You shall soon learn their number. From Doulichion, two and fifty chosen youths and six attendants; four and twenty men from Same; from Zacynthus twenty young Achaeans; twelve out of Ithaca itself, all men of mark, with whom are also the page Medon and the sacred bard, besides two followers skilled in table service. If we confront all these within the hall, bitter and grievous may the vengeance be over your coming. So if you possibly can think of aid, consider who will aid us now whole-heartedly."

Then said to him long-tried royal Odysseus: "Yet, let me speak, and you mark and listen. Consider if Athene, joined with father Zeus, suffice for us, or shall I seek for other aid?"

Then answered him discreet Telemachus: "Excellent helpers are the two you name, who sit among the clouds on high. All else they govern, all mankind and the immortal gods."

Then said to him long-tried royal Odysseus: "Not long will they be absent from the mighty fray when in my hall between the suitors and ourselves the test of war is tried. But go at early morning at once home, and join the audacious suitors. Thereafter the swineherd shall bring me to the city, like an old and wretched beggar. And if they treat me rudely in my home, let the faithful heart within your breast endure what I must bear; yes, though they drag me through the palace by the heels and out of door, or hurl their missiles at me, see and be patient still. Bid them, however, cease their folly, and with gentle words dissuade. They will not heed you, for their day of doom draws near. But this I will say further; mark it well. When wise Athene puts it in my mind, then I will nod my head, and you take note. And all the fighting gear that lies about the hall collect and lay in a corner of the lofty chamber, carefully, every piece. Then with soft words beguile the suitors when they, because they miss it, question you: 'I put it by out of the smoke, for it looks no longer like the armor which Odysseus left behind when he went away to Troy; it is all tarnished, where the scent of fire has come near. Besides, the son of Kronos brought this graver fear to mind. You might when full of wine begin a quarrel and give each other wounds, making a scandal of the feast and of your wooing. Steel itself draws men on.' Yet privily reserve two swords, two spears, two leathern shields, for us to seize—to rush and seize. And thereupon shall Pallas Athene and all-wise Zeus confound the suitors. And this I will say further; mark it well. If you are truly mine, my very blood, then that Odysseus now is here let no man know; let not Laërtes learn it, let not the swineherd, let none of the household, nor Penelope herself. But you and I alone will test the temper of the women. And we might also try the serving-men, and see who honors and respects us in his heart, and who neglects and scorns a man like you."

Then answered him his noble son and said: "My father, you shall know my heart, believe me, by and by. No hesitant thoughts are mine; and yet I think your plan will prove for neither of us gain, and so I say: Consider! Long will you vainly go, trying the different men among the farms; while undisturbed within the hall these waste your wealth with recklessness and do not spare. But I advise your finding out the women, and learning who dishonor you and who are guiltless. As to the men about the place, I would not prove them. Let that at any rate be thought of later, when you are really sure of signs from aegis-bearing Zeus."

So they conversed together. But in the meanwhile on to Ithaca ran the staunch ship which brought Telemachus and all his crew from Pylos. When they had entered the deep harbor, they hauled the black-hulled ship ashore, and stately footmen carried their armor and straightway bore the goodly gifts to Clytius' house. And now they sent a page to the palace of Odysseus, to tell the news to heedful Penelope,—how Telemachus was at the farm, but had ordered that the ship sail to the city,—lest the stately queen should be alarmed and shed a swelling tear. So the two met, the herald and the noble swineherd, upon the selfsame errand, bearing tidings to the queen. And when they reached the palace of the noble king, the page said to Penelope in hearing of her maids: "O queen, your son has come from Pylos." But the swineherd stood beside Penelope and so reported all that her dear son had bade him say. Then when he had delivered all his charge, he departed to his swine, and left the court and hall.

But the suitors grew dismayed and downcast in their hearts, and came forth from the hall past the great courtyard wall and there before the gate sat down to council; and first Eurymachus, the son of Polybus, addressed them:

"Friends, here is a monstrous action impudently brought to pass, this journey of Telemachus. We said it should not be. Come, then, and let us launch the best black ship we have, and get together fishermen for rowers, quickly to carry tidings to our friends, and bid them sail for home with all the speed they may."

The words were hardly uttered when Amphinomus, turning in his place, sighted the ship in the deep harbor, some of her crew furling the sail and some with oars in hand. Then lightly laughing, thus he called to his companions:

"No need to send a message now, for here they are. Some god has told our plot; or our men saw the vessel pass and could not catch her."

He spoke, and all arose and hastened to the shore. Swiftly the black-hulled ship was hauled ashore, and stately footmen carried their armor. The men themselves went in a body to the assembly and suffered no one, either young or old, to join them there; and thus Antinoüs, Eupeithes' son, addressed them:

"Strange, how the gods help this man out of danger! By day our sentries sat upon the windy heights, posted in close succession; and after sunset, we did not pass the night ashore, but sailed our swift ship on the sea, awaiting sacred dawn, lying in wait to seize and slay Telemachus. Meantime some god has brought him home. Then let us here contrive a miserable ending for Telemachus, not letting him escape; for while he lives, nothing, be sure, will prosper. He is himself shrewd in his thoughts and plans, and people here proffer us no more aid. Come then, before he gathers the Achaeans in a council. Backward he will not be, I think. He will be full of wrath, and rising he will tell to all how we contrived his sudden death but could not catch him. And when men hear our evil deeds, they will not praise them; but they may cause us trouble and drive us from our country, and we may have to go away into the land of strangers. Let us be quick, then, and seize him in the fields far from the city, or on the road at least; and let us take possession of his substance and his wealth, sharing all suitably among ourselves; the house, however, we might let his mother keep, or him who marries her. If this plan does not please you, and you will let him live to hold his father's fortune, then let us not devour his store of pleasant things by gathering here; but from his own abode let each man make his wooing, and press his suit with gifts. So may Penelope marry the man who gives her most and comes with fate to favor."

As he thus spoke, the rest were hushed to silence. But Amphinomus addressed them now and said—Amphinomus, the illustrious son of noble Nisus and grandson of Aretias, who from Doulichion, rich in wheat and grass, had led a band of suitors, and more than all the rest found favor with Penelope through what he said, because his heart was upright—he with good will addressed them thus and said:

"No, friends, I would not like to kill Telemachus, it is a fearful thing to kill one of a royal line. Let us at least first ask the gods for counsel; and if the oracles of mighty Zeus approve, I will myself share in the killing and urge the others too; but if the gods turn from us, I warn you to forbear."

So said Amphinomus, and his saying pleased them. Soon they arose and entered the hall of Odysseus, and went and took their seats on polished chairs.

Heedful Penelope, meanwhile, had planned anew to show herself among the suitors, overbearing in their pride. Within the palace she learned of the intended murder of her son, for the page Medon told her, who overheard the plot; so to the hall she went with her attendant women. And when the royal lady reached the suitors, she stood beside a column of the strong-built roof, holding before her face her delicate veil; and she rebuked Antinoüs and spoke to him and said:

"Antinoüs, full of all insolence and wicked guile, in Ithaca they say you are the foremost person of your years in judgment and in speech. But such you never were. Madman! Why do you seek the death and ruin of Telemachus, and pay no heed to suppliants, though Zeus be witness for them? It is impious plotting crimes against one's fellow men. Do you not know your father once took refuge here, in terror of the people? For they were very angry because he joined with Taphian pirates and troubled the Thesprotians, men who were our allies. So the people would destroy him,—would snatch his life away, and swallow all his large and pleasant living; but Odysseus held them back and stayed their madness. Yet you insultingly devour his house; you woo his wife, murder his child, and make me wholly wretched. Forbear, I charge you, and bid the rest forbear!"

Then answered her Eurymachus, the son of Polybus: "Daughter of Icarius, heedful Penelope; be of good courage! Let not these things disturb your mind! The man is not alive, and never will be born, who shall lay hands upon your son, Telemachus, so long as I have life and sight on earth. For this I tell you, and it shall be done: soon the dark blood of such a man shall flow around my spear. Many a time the spoiler of towns, Odysseus, has set me on his knee, put roasted meat into my hands and given me ruddy wine. Therefore I hold Telemachus dearest of all mankind. I bid him have no fear of death, at least not from the suitors. Death from the gods can no man shun."

So he spoke, cheering her, yet was himself plotting the murder. But she, going to her bright upper chamber, bewailed Odysseus, her dear husband, till on her lids clear-eyed Athene caused a sweet sleep to fall.

At evening the noble swineherd joined Odysseus and his son. Busily they prepared their supper, having killed a yearling pig. And Athene, drawing near, touched with her wand Laërtes' son, Odysseus, and made him old once more and clad him in mean clothes; for fear the swineherd looking in his face might know, and go and tell the tale to steadfast Penelope, not holding fast the secret in his heart.

Now Telemachus first addressed the swineherd, saying: "So you are come, noble Eumaeus. What news then in the town? Are the haughty suitors at home again after their ambush, or are they watching still for me to pass?"

Then, swineherd Eumaeus, you answered him and said: "I had no mind to search and question while stumbling through the town. My inclination bade me to tell my message with all speed and hasten home. There overtook me, though, an eager herald of your crew, a page, who told his story to your mother first. Moreover, this I know, because I saw it: I was already on the road above the town, where stands the hill of Hermes, when I saw a swift ship entering our harbor. A crowd of men were on her. Heavy she was with shields and double-pointed spears. It was they, I thought, and yet I do not know."

As he thus spoke, revered Telemachus smiled, and glancing at his father shunned the swineherd's eye.

Now ceasing from their labor of laying out the meal, they fell to feasting. There was no lack of appetite for the shared feast. And after they had stayed desire for drink and food, they turned toward bed and took the gift of sleep.

BOOK XVII

The Return of Telemachus to Ithaca

Soon as the early rosy-fingered dawn appeared, Telemachus, the son of princely Odysseus, bound to his feet his goodly sandals, took the heavy spear which fitted well his hand, and setting off to town, addressed his swineherd thus:

"Father, I go to the city to let my mother see me; for I know she will not cease from gloomy grief and crying until she sees me myself. This charge I lay on you: bring the poor stranger to the city, to beg his living there; and whosoever will shall give a cup and crust. I cannot put up all; my heart is full of trouble. And if the stranger chafes at this, so much the worse for him. I like to speak the truth."

But wise Odysseus answered him and said: "Friend, I do not care to tarry here. Better a beggar should beg his living in the town than in the fields; and he who will may give; for I am now too old to stay about a farm and answer all the orders of an overseer. Go then your way; this man shall be my guide, even as you bid, when I have warmed me at the fire and when the sunshine comes. The clothes I wear are miserably bad, and the early frost may harm me; the town is far, they say."

He spoke, and through the farm-stead passed Telemachus, moving with rapid stride and sowing seeds of evil for the suitors. And when he reached his stately dwelling, he took his spear and set it up by a tall pillar, while he himself went farther in and over the stone threshold.

His nurse was first to see him, Eurycleia, now busy spreading fleeces on the carven chairs. With a burst of tears she came straight forward; and other slave-maids of hardy Odysseus gathered round and fondly kissed his face and neck. Then from her chamber came heedful Penelope, like Artemis or golden Aphrodite. Round her dear son, weeping, she threw her arms, and kissed his face and both his beauteous eyes, and sobbing said to him in winged words:

"So you are come, Telemachus, dearer than light to me! I said I should not see you any more after you went away by ship to Pylos, so secretly, without consent of mine, to hear about your father. Come then and tell me all you chanced to see."

But wise Telemachus made answer: "My mother, do not stir my tears nor move my heart within, for I am only now escaped from utter ruin. But bathe, and putting on fresh garments, go to your upper chamber with your maids, and vow to pay full hecatombs to all the gods if Zeus some day will grant us deeds of vengeance. But I will go to the market-place to find a stranger who joined me on my journey here from Pylos. I sent him forward with my gallant crew and bade Peiraeus take him home and entertain him well and give him honor till the time that I should come."

Such were his words; unwinged, they rested with her. Bathing, and putting on fresh garments, she vowed to all the gods to pay full hecatombs if Zeus some day would grant her deeds of vengeance.

Presently through the hall forth went Telemachus, his spear in hand, two swift dogs following after; and marvelous was the grace Athene cast about him, that all the people gazed as he drew near. And round him flocked the haughty suitors, kind in their talk but in their hearts brooding on evil. He turned aside from the great company of these and off where Mentor sat with Antiphus and Halitherses, who were of old his father's friends, he went and sat him down; and much they questioned. Peiraeus, the famous spearman, now drew near, leading the stranger through the city to the market-place. Not long then from his guest delayed Telemachus, but came to meet him; though Peiraeus was the first to speak and say:

"Telemachus, quickly send women to my house, and let me send to you what Menelaus gave."

Then answered him discreet Telemachus: "Peiraeus, as yet we do not know how matters here will be. Suppose the haughty suitors at the palace should slay me privily and share my father's goods, I had rather you yourself should keep and enjoy the gifts than any one of these. But if I sow for these men death and doom, when I am gladdened merrily fetch all here."

So saying, he led the way-worn stranger home. And entering the stately buildings, they threw their coats upon the couches and the chairs, and went to the polished baths and bathed. And when the maids had bathed them and anointed them with oil, and put upon them fleecy coats and tunics, out of the baths they came and sat upon the couches. And water for the hands a slave-maid brought in a beautiful pitcher made of gold, and poured it out over a silver basin for their washing, and spread a polished table by their side. Then the grave housekeeper brought bread and placed before them, setting out food of many a kind, freely giving of her store. The mother of Telemachus sat on the farther side, by a column of the hall, resting upon a couch, spinning fine threads of yarn. So on the food spread out before them they laid hands. And after they had stayed desire for drink and food, then thus began heedful Penelope:

"Telemachus, I go to my upper chamber and lie on my bed,— which has become for me a bed of sorrows, ever watered with my tears since Odysseus went away to Ilios with the Atreidae,—because you did not deign before the haughty suitors entered, plainly to tell what tidings you have heard about your father's coming."

Then answered her discreet Telemachus: "No, mother, I will tell you all the truth. We went to Pylos, to Nestor, the shepherd of the people. And he, receiving me within his lofty palace, gave me such hearty welcome as a father gives his child when lately come from far, after long time away; so heartily he entertained me, he and his noble sons. Of hardy Odysseus, he said he had not heard from any man on earth, if he were alive or dead. But with horses and a strong-built chariot he sent me to the son of Atreus, to the spearman Menelaus. There I saw Argive Helen, her in behalf of whom Argives and Trojans bore so much at the gods' bidding. And Menelaus, good at the war-cry, soon asked me on what errand I came to royal Lacedaemon. I told him all the truth. And then he answered thus and said to me: 'Heavens! In a very brave man's bed they sought to lie, the weaklings! As when in the den of a strong lion a hind has laid asleep her new-born sucking fawns, then roams the slopes and grassy hollows seeking food, and by and by into his lair the lion comes and on both hind and fawns brings ghastly doom; so shall Odysseus bring a ghastly doom on these. Ah father Zeus, Athene, and Apollo! if with the power he showed one day in stately Lesbos, when he rose and wrestled in a match with Philomeleides, and down he threw him heavily while the Achaeans all rejoiced,—if as he was that day Odysseus now might meet the suitors, they all would find quick turns of fate and bitter rites of marriage. But as to what you ask thus urgently, I will not turn to talk of other things and so deceive you; but what the unerring old man of the sea told me, in not a word will I disguise or hide from you. He said he saw Odysseus on an island, in great distress, at the hall of the nymph Calypso, who holds him there by force. No power has he to reach his native land, for he has no ships fitted with oars, nor crews to bear him over the broad ocean-ridges.' So said the son of Atreus, the spearman Menelaus. And this accomplished, back I sailed; the gods gave breezes and brought me swiftly to my native land."

So he spoke, and stirred the heart within her breast. But godlike Theoclymenus addressed them thus: "O honored wife of Laërtes' son Odysseus, certainly Menelaus did not know the truth. Listen instead to words of mine; for I will plainly prophesy and not conceal. First then of all the gods be witness Zeus, and let this hospitable table and the hearth of good Odysseus whereto I come be witness; Odysseus is already within his native land,—biding his time or moving,—and, understanding all these wicked deeds, is sowing seeds of ill for all the suitors. As proof, while on the well-benched ship I marked a bird of omen, and I announced it to Telemachus."

Then said to him heedful Penelope: "Ah stranger, would these words of yours might be fulfilled! Soon should you know my kindness and many a gift from me, and every man you met would call you blessed."

So they conversed together. Meanwhile before the palace of Odysseus the suitors were making merry, throwing the discus and the hunting-spear upon the level pavement, holding riot as of old. But now when it was dinner-time, and from the fields around the flocks returned,—the shepherds leading who were wont to lead,— then Medon spoke; a man most loved of all the pages, one who was ever present at their feasts:

"Now, lads, since all your hearts are cheered with sports, come to the house and let us lay the table. One's dinner at the proper time is no bad thing."

He spoke, and up they sprang and went to heed his words. And entering the stately buildings, they threw their coats upon the couches and the chairs, and they began to kill great sheep and fatted goats, to kill sleek pigs and the heifer of the herd, and so to make their meal.

Meanwhile at the farm Odysseus and the noble swineherd were making ready to depart to town. And thus began the swineherd, the overseer: "Stranger, so you desire to go to town today, just as my master ordered, though I myself would rather leave you as a watch-man for the farm; but of him I stand in fear and awe, lest he hereafter chide me. Hard is a master's censure. Come then and let us go. The day is passing. It will be colder by and by toward night."

Then wise Odysseus answered him and said: "I see, I understand; you speak to one who knows. Let us go on, and all the way be my guide. But give me a stick, if you have one cut, to lean upon; for you said the road was rough."

He spoke, and round his shoulders slung his miserable wallet, full of holes, which hung upon a cord. Eumaeus gave the staff desired, and so the two set forth; but dogs and herdsmen stayed behind to keep the farm. On to the town Eumaeus led his lord, like an old and wretched beggar, leaning upon a staff. Upon his back were mis-erable clothes.

Now as they walked along the rugged road, nearing the city, they reached a stone-built fountain, running clear, from which the towns-folk draw their water, a fountain made by Ithacus, by Neritus and

Polyctor. There was a grove of stream-fed poplars, encircling it, and from the rock above ran the cool water, while at the top was built an altar to the nymphs, where all who passed made offerings. Here the son of Dolius, Melanthius, met them, driving the goats that were the best of all the flock, to make the suitors' dinner. Two herdsmen followed after. Seeing Eumaeus and Odysseus, he broke into abuse; and speaking to them, used rude and indecent words, which stirred Odysseus' blood:

"Now sure enough the vile man leads the vile! As ever, the god brings like and like together! Where are you carrying that glutton, you good-for-nothing swineherd, that nasty beggar to make mischief at our feasts? A man to stand and rub his back on many doors and tease for scraps of food, but not for swords and caldrons. If you would let me have him for a watchman at my farm, to be a stable-cleaner and fetch fodder to the kids, he might by drinking whey grow a big thigh. But no! For he has learned bad ways and will not turn to work. He will prefer to beg about the town, grubbing for stuff to feed his greedy maw. But this I tell you, and it shall be done: if he comes near the house of princely Odysseus, many a footstool from men's hands flying around his head his ribs shall thump, as he is knocked about the house."

He spoke and as he passed recklessly kicked Odysseus on the hip, but did not force him from the pathway. Fixed he stood. Odysseus doubted whether to spring and with his cudgel take his life, or to lift him in the air and dash his head upon the ground. But he was patient, and by thought restrained himself. And now the swineherd, looking him in the face, rebuked the man and stretching forth his hands prayed thus aloud:

"Nymphs of the fountain, daughters of Zeus, if ever Odysseus burned on thy altars thighs of lambs and kids, and wrapped them in rich fat, grant this my prayer! May he return and Heaven be his guide! Then would he scatter all the pride you now recklessly assume, roaming continually around the town, while careless herdsmen let the flock decay."

Then answered him Melanthius the goatherd: "So, so! How the

cur talks, as if he knew some magic arts! Some day I'll take him on a black and well-benched ship far off from Ithaca, and get me a great fortune. Oh that Apollo of the silver bow would smite Telemachus at home today, or let him fall before the suitors, as certainly as for Odysseus, far in foreign lands, the day of coming home is lost!"

So saying, he left them slowly plodding on, and off he went and soon he came to the king's palace. Entering at once, he took his seat among the suitors over against Eurymachus, for he liked him best of all. Then those who served passed him a portion of the meat, while the grave housekeeper brought bread and set before him, for him to eat. Meantime Odysseus and the noble swineherd halted as they drew near, while round them came notes of the hollow lyre; for Phemius lifted up his voice to sing before the suitors. And taking the swineherd by the hand, Odysseus said:

"Surely, Eumaeus, this is the goodly palace of Odysseus, easy to notice even among many. Building joins building here. The court is built with wall and cornice, and a double gate protects. No man may scorn it. I notice too that a great company are banqueting within; for the savory steam mounts up, and in the house resounds the lyre, made by the gods the fellow of the feast."

And, swineherd Eumaeus, you answered him and said: "You notice quickly, dull of thought in nothing. Come then and let us plan what we must do. You enter the stately buildings first and mingle with the suitors, while I stay here behind; or if you like, wait you, and I will go. But do not linger long, or somebody may spy you at the door and throw a stone or strike you. Take care, I say!"

Then long-tried royal Odysseus answered: "I see, I understand; you speak to one who knows. But go you on before, I will stay here behind: for I am not unused to blows and missiles. Staunch is my soul; for many dangers have I borne from waves and war. To those let this be added. Yet I cannot disregard a gnawing belly, the pest which brings so many ills to men. To ease it, timbered ships are fitted and carry woe to foemen over barren seas."

So they conversed together. But a dog lying near lifted his head and ears. Argos it was, the dog of hardy Odysseus, whom long ago he reared but never used. Before the dog was grown, Odysseus went to sacred Ilios. In the times past young men would take him on the chase, for wild goats, deer, and hares; but now he lay neglected, his master gone away, upon a pile of dung which had been dropped before the door by mules and oxen, and which lay there in a heap for slaves to carry off and fertilize the broad lands of Odysseus. Here lay the dog, this Argos, full of fleas. Yet even now, seeing Odysseus near, he wagged his tail and dropped both ears, but toward his master he had not strength to move. Odysseus turned aside and wiped away a tear, swiftly concealing from Eumaeus what he did; then at once thus he questioned:

"Eumaeus, it is strange this dog lies on the dung-hill. His form is good; but I am not sure if he has speed of foot to match his beauty, or if he is merely what the table-dogs become which masters keep for show."

And, swineherd Eumaeus, you answered him and said: "Aye truly, that is the dog of one who died afar. If he were as good in form and action as when Odysseus left him and went away to Troy, you would be much surprised to see his speed and strength. For nothing could escape him in the forest-depths, no creature that he started; he was keen upon the scent. Now he has come to ill. In a strange land his master perished, and the indifferent women give him no more care; for slaves, when masters lose control, will not attend to duties. Ah, half the value of a man far-seeing Zeus destroys when the slave's lot befalls him!"

So saying, he entered the stately house and went straight down the hall among the lordly suitors. But upon Argos fell the doom of darksome death when he beheld Odysseus, twenty years away.

By far the first to see the swineherd as he walked along the hall was princely Telemachus, and he quickly gave a nod to call him to his side. Glancing around, Eumaeus took a stool which stood at hand, where the carver sat at feasts within the hall when carving for the suitors the many joints of meat; carrying the stool to the table of Telemachus, he placed it on the farther side and there sat down.

And then a page took up a dish of meat and passed it, and from the basket gave him also bread.

Close following after, Odysseus entered the palace, like an old and wretched beggar leaning upon a staff. Upon his back were miserable clothes. He sat down on the ash-wood threshold just within the door, leaning against the cypress post which long ago the carpenter had smoothed with skill and leveled to the line. But to the swineherd said Telemachus, calling him to his side and taking a whole loaf from the goodly basket and also all the meat his hands stretched wide would hold:

"Take this and give the stranger, and bid him move about and beg of all the suitors. Shyness is no good comrade for a needy man."

He spoke, and the swineherd went as soon as he heard the order, and standing by Odysseus said in winged words: "Stranger, Telemachus gives this, and bids you move about and beg of all the suitors. Shyness, he says, is no good comrade for a beggar man."

Then answering him, said wise Odysseus: "O Zeus above, may Telemachus be blessed among mankind, and may he get whatever in his heart he longs for!"

He spoke, and took the food with both his hands and laid it down before his feet on his mean wallet, and so ate, the while within the hall the bard was singing. But when the meal was ended and the sacred bard had ceased, the suitors raised an uproar in the hall. And now Athene, drawing near Laërtes' son, Odysseus, urged him to gather crusts among the suitors, and learn who were the righteous ones and who the lawless; though not even thus would she preserve a man of them from ruin. So off he went to beg of all from left to right, stretching his hand around as if he had been long a beggar. They pitied him and gave, and wondering at the man asked one another who he was and whence he came; and Melanthius, the goatherd, said:

"Hear from me, suitors of the illustrious queen, something about the stranger. I saw him a while ago; and certainly it was the swineherd brought him here. The man himself I do not really know, nor of what tribe he boasts himself to be."

When he had spoken, Antinoüs rebuked the swineherd thus: "Infamous swineherd, why bring this man to town? Have we not here already plenty of vagabonds and nasty beggars to make mischief at our feasts? Do you not mind that men devour the living of their lord by gathering here? And do you ask this fellow too to come?"

Then, swineherd Eumaeus, you answered him and said: "Antinoüs, you speak but ill, noble although you are. Who ever goes and calls a stranger from abroad? Unless indeed the stranger is a master of some craft, a prophet, healer of disease, or builder, or else a wondrous bard who pleases by his song; for these are welcomed by mankind the wide world through. A beggar, who would ask to be a torment to himself? But you are always harsh—more than the other suitors—to the servants of Odysseus, especially to me. And yet I do not care, so long as heedful Penelope is living in the palace, Penelope and prince Telemachus."

Then said discreet Telemachus: "Hush! Do not make him a long answer. It is Antinoüs' way ever to insult with ugly talk. He stirs up others too."

He spoke, and to Antinoüs in winged words he said: "Antinoüs, finely you care for me, as a father for his son, bidding me drive this stranger forth by a commanding word! The gods let that never be! Take of the food and give him. I do not grudge it; indeed I bid you give. Be not disquieted about my mother or any servant of the house of great Odysseus. But in your breast there is no thought of giving. Far better you like to eat than give to others."

Then answering said Antinoüs: "Telemachus, of the lofty tongue and the unbridled temper, what do you mean? If every suitor gave as much as I, for three months' space at least the house would miss him."

So saying, he seized his stool and drew it out from under the table where it lay. On it he used to set his dainty feet while feasting. Now all the rest had given food and filled with bread and meat the beggar's wallet. A moment and Odysseus would go back to the threshold to taste the Achaeans' bounty. Before Antinoüs he paused, and said:

"Give me some food, kind sir! You do not seem the poorest of the Achaeans; rather, the chief; for you are like a king. So you shall give me bread more generously than others, and I will sing your praise the wide world through. For once I lived in luxury among my mates, in a rich house, and often gave to wanderers, careless who they might be or with what needs they came. Servants I had in plenty, and everything besides by which men live at ease and are reputed rich. But Zeus, the son of Kronos, brought me low. His will it was. He sent me with a roving band of plunderers to Egypt, a long voyage, to my ruin. In Egypt's stream I anchored my curved ships; then to my trusty men I gave command to stay there by the ships and guard the ships, while I sent scouts to points of observation. But giving way to lawlessness and following their own bent, they presently began to pillage the fair fields of the Egyptians, carrying off wives and infant children and slaughtering the men. Soon the din reached the city. The people there, hearing the shouts, came forth at early dawn, and all the plain was filled with footmen and with horsemen and with the gleam of bronze. Then Zeus, the Thunderer, brought on my men a cruel panic, and none dared stand and face the foe. Danger encountered us on every side. So the Egyptians slew many of our men with the sharp sword, and carried others off alive to work for them in bondage. They gave me to a friend who chanced to meet them, upon his way to Cyprus, to Dmetor son of Iasus, who ruled with power in Cyprus. Thence I am now come hither, sore distressed."

Then answered him Antinoüs and said: "What god has brought us this pest to spoil our feast here? Stand off there in the middle, back from my table, or you shall find a bitter Egypt and a bitter Cyprus too, brazen and shameless beggar that you are! You go to all in turn, and they give lavishly. No scruple or compunction do they feel at being generous with others' goods, while there remains abundance for themselves."

Then stepping back said wise Odysseus: "Indeed! In you then wisdom does not go with beauty. From your own house you would not give a suppliant salt, if sitting at another's table you will not take and give me bread. Yet here there is abundance."

As he thus spoke, Antinoüs was angered in his heart the more, and looking sternly on him said in winged words: "Now you shall never leave the hall in peace, I think, now you have taunted me."

So saying, he seized his footstool, flung it and struck Odysseus on the back of the right shoulder, near the spine. Firm as a rock he stood; the missile of Antinoüs did not move him. Silent he shook his head, brooding on evil. Then once more walking toward the threshold, down he sat, laid down his well-filled wallet, and thus addressed the suitors:

"Hearken, you suitors of the illustrious queen, and let me tell you what the heart within me bids. One feels no smart or indignation in his mind if struck while fighting for his own possessions, his oxen, say, or white-wooled sheep; but Antinoüs gave this blow because of my poor belly, that wretched part which brings to men such ills. If then for beggars there be gods and furies, may death's doom seize Antinoüs before his marriage."

Then said Antinoüs, Eupeithes' son: "Stranger, sit still and eat, or go off elsewhere; or for such talk as this young men will drag you through the house by hand and foot, and strip off all your skin."

At these his words all were exceeding wroth, and a rude youth would say: "Antinoüs, it was not well done to assault the wretched wanderer. A doomed man you, if he should be a god come down from heaven. And gods in guise of strangers from afar in every form do roam our cities, marking the sin and righteousness of men."

So said the suitors; Antinoüs did not heed their words. But Telemachus nursed in his heart great indignation at the blow, yet let no tear fall from his eyelids to the ground. Silent he shook his head, brooding on evil.

When heedful Penelope heard how in the hall a man was struck, she said to her slave-maids: "May the archer-god Apollo strike you even so!" Whereat Eurynome the house-keeper made answer: "If only prayers of ours might be fulfilled, no one of them should see another bright-throned dawn."

And heedful Penelope replied: "Nurse, hateful are they all; their ways are evil; but Antinoüs is like dark doom itself. Into the house strays some poor stranger, and begs for bread, as need compels; then while all others gave and filled his wallet, Antinoüs struck him with a footstool on the back of the right shoulder."

So talked Penelope with her maids as she sat within her chamber, while royal Odysseus was busied with his meal. Then calling the noble swineherd, thus she spoke: "Go, noble Eumaeus, go bid the stranger come to me. I wish to greet him and to ask if he has heard of hardy Odysseus or with his own eyes seen him. He looks a traveled man."

Then, swineherd Eumaeus, you answered her and said: "Would, queen, the Achaeans would be still! What he can tell would charm your very soul. Three nights I had him; three days I kept him at the lodge; he came to me at once on escaping from his vessel. Yet all that time he never ended telling me his troubles. And just as when men gaze upon a bard who has been taught by gods to sing them moving lays, and they long to listen endlessly so long as the bard will sing; even so he held me spell-bound as he sat within my room. He calls Odysseus his ancestral friend, and says his home is Crete, where the race of Minos dwell. Thence he is now come here, deeply distressed and onward driven ever. He declares he has heard that Odysseus is at hand, in the rich land of the Thesprotians, a living man, and that he brings a mass of treasure home."

Then said to him heedful Penelope: "Go call him here, to tell his story here before my face. Let men make merry, sitting before the door, or here within the house. Their hearts are gay. Untouched at home their goods are lying, their bread and their sweet wine. On these their servants feed. But haunting this house of ours day after day, killing our oxen, sheep and fatted goats, these suitors hold high revel, drinking sparkling wine with little heed. Much goes to waste; for there is no man here fit, like Odysseus, to keep damage from our doors. But if Odysseus should return, home to his native land, soon with his son's help he would punish these men's crimes."

As she spoke thus, Telemachus loudly sneezed, and all the hall gave a great echo. Penelope laughed, and to Eumaeus straightway said in winged words: "Pray go and call the stranger before me, as I bade. Do you not notice how my son sneezed at my words? Therefore no partial death shall strike the suitors. On all it falls; none shall escape from death and doom. Nay, this I will say farther; mark it well: if I shall find that all the stranger tells is true, I will clothe him in a coat and tunic, goodly garments."

She spoke, and the swineherd went as soon as he heard the order, and standing near the stranger said in winged words: "Here, good old stranger, heedful Penelope is calling, the mother of Telemachus. Her heart inclines her to ask for tidings of her husband, so full of grief is she. And if she finds that all you tell is true, she will clothe you in a coat and tunic, things that you greatly need. Moreover, you shall beg your bread about the land and fill your belly. Whoever will shall give."

Then said to him long-tried royal Odysseus: "Eumaeus, I would straightway tell my whole true story to the daughter of Icarius, heedful Penelope; for well I know about Odysseus. We have borne the self-same sorrows. But I have fears about this crowd of cruel suitors, whose arrogance and outrage reaches the iron heavens; for even now when, as I walked along the hall doing no harm, this person struck and hurt me, neither Telemachus nor others interfered. Bid then Penelope, however eager, wait in the hall till sunset; then let her ask about her husband's coming, after giving me a seat beside the fire; for the clothes I wear are poor. That, you yourself well know; because it was of you I first sought aid."

He spoke, and the swineherd went as soon as he heard the order. But as he crossed the threshold, thus spoke Penelope: "Are you not bringing him, Eumaeus? What does the wanderer mean? Is he afraid of some bad man, or simply shy at being in the palace? To be a homeless man and shy is bad."

Then, swineherd Eumaeus, you answered her and said: "Rightly he speaks, as any man must think, if he would shun the violence of these audacious men. He bids you wait till sunset. And it is better too for you, my queen, to speak to the stranger privately and listen to his tale."

Then said to him heedful Penelope: "Not without wisdom thinks the stranger thus, whoever he may be; for mortal men have never yet so wantonly wrought outrage."

She spoke, and the noble swineherd entered the throng of suitors, when he had told her all; and at once to Telemachus he spoke these winged words,—his head bent close, that others might not hear:

"My dear, I go to guard the swine and matters there, your live-lihood and mine; do you mind all things here. Above all else, keep yourself safe and see that nothing happens. Many of the Achaeans are forming wicked plans, whom Zeus confound before harm falls on us!"

Then answered him discreet Telemachus: "So be it, father! Go when you have supped; and in the morning come and bring us goodly victims. To me and the immortal gods leave all things here."

He spoke, and once more down Eumaeus sat upon a polished bench. Then, after having satisfied desire for food and drink, he departed to his swine, leaving the courts and hall crowded with feasters, who with dance and song were making merry; for evening now drew near.

BOOK XVIII

The Fight of Odysseus and Irus

There came into the hall a common beggar, who used to beg about the town of Ithaca, and everywhere was noted for his greedy belly, eating and drinking without end. He had no strength nor sinew, but in bulk was large to see. Arnaeus was his name, the name his honored mother gave at his birth; but Irus* all the young men called him, because he used to run on errands at anybody's bidding. Coming in now, he tried to drive Odysseus from the house, and jeeringly he spoke these winged words:

"Get up, old man, and leave the door-way, or you will soon be dragged off by the leg. Do you not see how everybody gives the wink and bids me drag you forth? I still hold back. Up, then! Or soon our quarrel comes to blows."

But looking sternly on him wise Odysseus said: "Sir, I am doing you no harm by deed or word, nor do I grudge it when men take and give you much. This door will hold us both. Surely you should not grudge the goods of others. You seem a wanderer, like myself; but the gods may grant us fortune. Yet do not challenge me too far with show of fist, or you may rouse my rage; and old as I am, I still might stain your breast and lips with blood. Then I should have more peace tomorrow than today; for a second time, I think, you would not seek the hall of Laërtes' son, Odysseus."

Then angrily replied the beggar Irus: "Pah! How glibly the glutton talks, like an old oven-woman! But I will do him an ugly turn, knocking him right and left, and scattering all the teeth out of his

*The nickname "Irus" is a pun on Iris, the rainbow, a messenger goddess.

223

jaws upon the ground, as if he were a pig spoiling the corn. Gird yourself then, that all these men may watch our fighting. Yet how could you defend yourself against a younger man?"

Thus on the well-worn threshold before the lofty door they fiercely wrangled. Revered Antinoüs observed them, and gaily laughing he thus addressed the suitors:

"Friends, nothing so good as this has ever happened. What sport some god sends this house! The stranger here and Irus are goading one another on to blows. Let us quickly set them on!"

He spoke, and laughing all sprang up and flocked around the tattered beggars, and Antinoüs, Eupeithes' son, called out: "Hearken, you haughty suitors, while I speak. Here are goat-paunches lying by the fire, set there for supper, full of fat and blood. Whichever wins and proves the better man, let him step forth and take what one of these he will; and that man shall hereafter always attend our feasts and we will allow no other beggar to come here asking alms."

So said Antinoüs, and his saying pleased them. But in his subtlety said wise Odysseus: "It is not fair, my friends, a younger man should fight an old one, one broken too by trouble. Yet a reckless belly forces me to bear his blows. Come then, all swear a solemn oath that nobody helping Irus will strike with heavy hand an unfair blow, and put me down before the man by surprise."

He spoke, and all then took the oath which he required. And after they had sworn and ended all their oath, once more revered Telemachus spoke out among them: "Stranger, if heart and daring spirit tempt you to meet the man, be not afraid of any of the Achaeans; for he shall fight the crowd who strikes at you. I am the host. The princes too assent, Antinoüs and Eurymachus, both honest-minded men."

He spoke, and all approved. Meanwhile Odysseus gathered his rags around his waist and showed his thighs, so fair and large, and his broad shoulders came in sight, his breast and sinewy arms. Athene, drawing nigh, filled out the limbs of the shepherd of the people, that all the suitors greatly wondered. And glancing at his neighbor one would say:

"Irus will soon be no more Irus, but catch a plague of his own bringing; so big a thigh the old man shows under his rags."

So they spoke, and Irus' heart was sorely shaken; nevertheless, the serving-men girt him and led him out, forcing him on in spite of fears. The muscles quivered on his limbs. But Antinoüs rebuked him and spoke to him and said:

"Better you were not living, loud-mouthed bully, and never had been born, if you quake and are so mightily afraid at meeting this old man, one broken by the troubles he has had. Nay, this I tell you and it shall be done: if he shall win and prove the better man, I will toss you into a black ship and send you to the mainland, off to king Echetus, the bane of all mankind; and he will cut your nose and ears off with his ruthless sword, and tearing out your bowels give them raw to dogs to eat."

So he spoke, and a trembling greater still fell on the limbs of Irus. But into the ring they led him, and both men raised their fists. Then long-tried royal Odysseus doubted whether to strike him so that life might leave him as he fell, or to strike lightly and but stretch him on the ground. Reflecting thus, it seemed the better way lightly to strike, for fear the Achaeans might discover it was he. So when they raised their fists, Irus struck the right shoulder of Odysseus; but he struck Irus on the neck below the ear and crushed the bones within. Forthwith from out his mouth the red blood ran, and down in the dust he fell with a moan, gnashing his teeth and kicking on the ground. The lordly suitors raised their hands and almost died with laughter. But Odysseus caught Irus by the foot and dragged him through the door-way, until he reached the courtyard and the opening of the porch. Against the courtyard wall he set him up aslant, then thrust a staff into his hand, and speaking in winged words he said:

"Sit there awhile, and scare off dogs and swine; and do not try to be the lord of strangers and of beggars, while pitiful yourself, or perhaps some worse fate may fall upon you."

He spoke, and round his shoulder slung his miserable wallet, full of holes, which hung upon a cord, then once more walking to the threshold he sat down; meanwhile the others pressed indoors with merry laughter and thus accosted him:

"Stranger, may Zeus and the other immortal gods grant all you wish for most, even all your heart's desire, for stopping this insatiate fellow's begging through the land. Soon we will take him to the mainland, off to king Echetus, the bane of all mankind."

So they spoke, and royal Odysseus was happy in the omen. Antinoüs too set a great paunch before him, full of fat and blood, and Amphinomus took two loaves out of the basket and offered them, and pledged him in a golden cup and said: "Hail, aged stranger! May happiness be yours in time to come, though you are tried by many troubles now!"

Then wise Odysseus answered him and said: "Indeed, Amphinomus, you seem a man of understanding. Such was your father too; for I have heard a good report of Nisus of Doulichion, how he was brave and rich. They say you are his son. You appear kind. So I will speak and do you mark and listen. Earth breeds no creature frailer than a man, of all that breathe and move upon the earth. For he says he never more will meet with trouble, so long as the gods give vigor and make his knees be strong. Then when the blessed gods send sorrow, this too he bears with patient heart, though much against his will. Ever the mood of man while on the earth is as the day which the father of men and gods bestows. Once among men I too was counted prosperous; but many wrongs I wrought, led on by pride and sense of power, confident in my father's and my brothers' aid. Wherefore let none in any wise be reckless, but calmly take whatever gifts the gods provide. Yet I behold you suitors working wrong, wasting the wealth and worrying the wife of one who, I can tell you, will not be absent long from friends and native land; for he is very near. May then some heavenly power conduct you to your homes! And may you not encounter him whenever he returns to his own native land! Surely not bloodless will the parting be between the suitors and himself when underneath this roof he comes once more."

He spoke, and pouring a libation drank the honeyed wine, then back in the hands of the guardian of the people placed the cup. Amphinomus walked down the hall heavy at heart, shaking his head; his soul foreboded ill. Yet even so he did not escape his doom; for Athene bound him fast, beneath the hand and spear of Telemachus to be by fate laid low. So back he turned and took the seat from which he first arose.

And now the goddess, clear-eyed Athene, put in the mind of Icarius' daughter, heedful Penelope, to show herself among the suitors; that she might thus open the suitors' hearts most largely, and so become more highly prized by husband and by son than heretofore. Idly she laughed and thus she spoke and said:

"Eurynome, my heart is longing as it never longed before to show myself among the suitors, hateful although they be. I would say to my son a word that may be useful; tell him to mingle not at all with the audacious suitors, for they speak kindly but have evil thoughts behind."

And in her turn Eurynome, the housewife, answered: "Truly, my child, in all this you speak rightly. Go then and tell this saying to your son and do not hide it; only first wash your body and anoint your cheeks. Go not with such a tear-stained face. To grieve incessantly makes matters worse. And now your son is what you often prayed the immortals you might see him, a bearded man already."

Then said to her heedful Penelope: "Eurynome, urge me not, out of kindness, to wash my body and anoint me with the oil. All charm of mine the gods who hold Olympus took away when he departed in the hollow ships. But tell Autonoë and Hippodameia to come hither, to attend me in the hall. Among the men I will not go alone, for very shame."

So she spoke, and through the hall forth the old woman went to give the message to the maids and bid them come with speed.

Then a new plan the goddess formed, clear-eyed Athene. She

poured sweet slumber on the daughter of Icarius; and lying back she slept and every joint relaxed, there on her couch. Meanwhile the heavenly goddess gave her immortal gifts, to make the Achaeans marvel. And first she bathed her lovely cheeks with an immortal bloom, like that with which crowned Cytherea* anoints herself when going to the joyous dance among the Graces. She made her also taller and larger to behold, and made her whiter than the new-cut ivory. So having done, the heavenly goddess went her way; and out of the hall the white-armed slave-maids came, entering the room with noise. Sweet slumber left Penelope. She drew her hands across her cheeks and thus she spoke:

"Ah, utterly wretched as I am, soft slumber wrapped me round. Would that chaste Artemis would send a death so soft,—instantly, now,—that, sad at heart no more, I might not waste my days mourning the many-sided worth of him, my husband, the best of all Achaeans!"

So saying, down she went from her bright upper chamber, yet not alone; two slave-maids followed her. And when the royal lady reached the suitors, she stood beside a column of the strong-built roof, holding before her face her delicate veil, the while a faithful slave-maid stood upon either hand. The suitors' knees grew weak; with love their hearts were entranced. Each prayed to be her spouse. But she addressed Telemachus, her own dear son:

"Telemachus, your mind and judgment are no longer sound. While still a boy you managed more discreetly. But now when you are grown and come to man's estate, and any stranger would call you the son of a man of worth, if he observed your height and beauty,—now mind and judgment are not trusty any more. For only see what happened in the hall: you let this stranger be maltreated there. And what will be thought if a stranger, seated within our house, should meet with harm through brutal handling? Shame and disgrace would come on you from all men."

---

*Aphrodite.

Then answered her discreet Telemachus: "Mother, I do not blame you for your anger. Yet in my heart I know and fully understand the right and wrong. Before, I was a child, and I am not always able now to see what wise ways are; for the suitors disconcert me, coming on every side with wicked plans, while I have none to help. However, the quarrel of Irus and the stranger turned out in no way to the suitors' mind. In strength the stranger proved the better man. Ah father Zeus, Athene, and Apollo, would that the suitors in our halls might beaten hang their heads,—some in the yard, some in the house,—and so their limbs be loosed, as that same Irus at the courtyard gate now sits and hangs his head, like a man drunk, and cannot stand straight on his feet nor go off home, wherever that may be, because his limbs are loose."

So they conversed together. But now Eurymachus addressed Penelope: "Daughter of Icarius, heedful Penelope, if all Achaeans in Iasian Argos could behold you now, more suitors would be feasting in your halls tomorrow; for you excel all womankind in beauty, height, and balanced mind within."

Then answered him heedful Penelope: "Eurymachus, all excellence of mine in face or form the immortals took away the day the Argive host took ship for Ilios, and with them went my lord Odysseus. If he would come and tend this life of mine, greater would be my fame and fairer then. Now I am in distress, such woes some god thrusts upon me. Ah, when he went and left his native land, holding my hand,—my right hand, by the wrist,—he said: 'Wife, I do not think the armed Achaeans will all come back from Troy safe and unharmed; for they say the Trojans are good fighters,—hurlers of spears, drawers of bows, and riders on swift horses,—such men as soon decide the struggle of uncertain war. Therefore I do not know if a god will bring me back, or if I shall be captured there in Troy. On you must rest the care of all things here. Be mindful of my father and my mother here at home, as you are now, and even more when I am gone. And when you see our son a bearded man, then marry whom you will, and leave the house now yours.' Such were his words, and all now nears its end. The night will come when a detested marriage falls on doomed me, whom Zeus has stripped of fortune. One bitter vexation, too, touches my heart and soul: this never was the way with suitors heretofore; they who will court a lady of rank, a rich man's daughter, rivaling one another, bring oxen and sturdy sheep to feast the maiden's friends and give rich gifts besides. They do not, making no amends, devour another's substance."

She spoke, and glad was long-tried royal Odysseus to see her winning gifts and charming the suitors' hearts with pleasing words, while her mind had a different purpose.

Then said Antinoüs, Eupeithes' son: "Daughter of Icarius, heedful Penelope, if any Achaean cares to bring gifts here, accept them; for it is not gracious to refuse a gift. But we will never go to our estates, nor elsewhere either, till you are married to the best Achaean here."

So said Antinoüs, and his saying pleased them; and for the bringing of the gifts each man sent forth his page. The page of Antinoüs brought a fair large robe of many colors; on it were golden brooches, twelve in all, mounted with twisted clasps. To Eurymachus his page presently brought a chain, wrought curiously in gold and set with amber, bright as the sun. His servants brought Eurydamus a pair of earrings, each brilliant with three drops; from them great beauty sparkled. Out of the house of lord Peisander, son of Polyctor, his servant brought a necklace, a jewel exceptionally fine. And other servants brought still other fitting gifts from the Achaeans.

Then went the royal lady to her upper chamber, her slave-maids carrying the handsome gifts. Meanwhile the suitors to dancing and the joyous song turned merrily, and waited for the evening to come on. And on their merriment dark evening came. Straightway they set three braziers in the hall, to give them light, and piled upon them sapless logs,—long seasoned, very dry, and freshly split,—with which they mingled brands. By turns the maids of hardy Odysseus fed the fire; and he, the high-born wise Odysseus, thus addressed them:

"You slave-maids of Odysseus, a master long away, go to the room where your honored mistress stays. There twirl your spindles by her side and furnish her good cheer, as you sit within her hall, and card with your hands the wool. I will supply the light for all these here. Yes, if they wish to stay till bright-throned dawn, they will not weary me; I am practiced to endure."

At these his words the slave-maids laughed and glanced at one another, and Melantho* rudely mocked Odysseus—Melantho the fair-faced girl, daughter of Dolius, whom Penelope had reared and treated as her child, granting her every whim. But for all this, she entertained no sorrow for Penelope, but loved Eurymachus and was his mistress. She now reviled Odysseus in these abusive words:

"Why, silly stranger, you are certainly some imbecile, unwilling to go to the coppersmith's to sleep, or to the common lodge; but here you prate continually, braving these many lords and unabashed at heart. Surely the wine has touched your wits; or else it is your constant way to chatter idly. Are you beside yourself because you beat that drifter Irus? A better man than Irus may by and by arise, to box your skull with doughty blows and pack you out of doors all dabbled with your blood."

But looking sternly on her, wise Odysseus said: "You bitch, I go, and at once tell Telemachus what words you use; and he shall rend you limb from limb upon the spot."

So saying, by his words he frightened off the women. They hurried along the hall. The knees of each grew weak with terror, for they thought he spoke in earnest. He, meanwhile, keeping up the fire, stood by the blazing braziers observing all the men. But other thoughts his heart debated, thoughts not to fail of issue.

Yet Athene allowed the haughty suitors not altogether yet to cease from biting scorn. She wished more pain to pierce the heart of Laërtes' son, Odysseus. So Eurymachus the son of Polybus began to speak, and jeering Odysseus raised a laugh among his mates: "Listen, you suitors of the illustrious queen, and let me tell you what the heart within me bids. Not without guidance of a god this fellow

*Melantho and Melanthius are siblings.

comes to the household of Odysseus. At any rate, a torchlight seems to rise from his very head; for hair upon it there is none, no not the least."

With that he called to the spoiler of towns, Odysseus: "Stranger, if I would take you, would you like to work for hire on the outskirts of my farm,—there will be pay enough,—gathering stones for walls and setting out tall trees? There for a year I would provide you food, furnish you clothing and put sandals on your feet. Still, now that you have learned bad ways you will not care to work, but will prefer to beg about the town, so long as you can find wherewith to stuff your greedy maw."

Then wise Odysseus answered him and said: "Eurymachus, I wish that we might have a match at work, in spring-time when the days are long, upon the grass; and I would take a well-curved scythe and you another like it to test our power of work, fasting right up till dark, with grass still plenty. Or if again the match were driving oxen,—choice, tawny, large ones, both well fed with grass, equal in years and pulling well together, tireless in strength,—and here were a field four acres large, whose soil would take the plow; then you should see if I could cut a straight and even furrow. Or, once more, if the son of Kronos by some means stirred up war, this very day, and I had a shield and pair of spears and a bronze helmet fitted to my brow, then would you see me join the foremost in the fight, and you would no longer jest and talk about my belly. No, you are very proud and your temper is disdainful; no doubt you seem a great man and a mighty, because you mix with few and they of little worth. But should Odysseus come and reach his native land, soon would these doors, however wide, prove all too narrow, as you hurried through the porch."

As he spoke thus, Eurymachus grew angrier still at heart, and looking sternly on Odysseus, he spoke these winged words: "Wretch, I shall do you mischief soon for babbling so, braving these many lords and unabashed at heart. Surely the wine has touched your wits; or else it is your constant way to chatter idly. Are you beside yourself because you beat that drifter Irus?"

So saying, he seized a footstool; Odysseus crouched by the knees of Amphinomus of Doulichion, fearing Eurymachus, who hit the right hand of the wine-pourer. Down went his beaker clattering to the ground, and he himself fell moaning in the dust. But the suitors broke into uproar up and down the dusky hall, and glancing at his neighbor one would say:

"Would that the vagabond had perished elsewhere before he came in here! He would not then have caused this din. Here we are brawling over beggars. No more delight in jolly feasts; now worse things have their way!"

Then said to them revered Telemachus: "Sirs, you are mad, and do not hide what you have drunk and eaten. Some god excites you. But now that you have feasted well, go home to bed as quickly as you please. Yet I drive none away."

He spoke, and all with teeth set in their lips marveled because Telemachus had spoken boldly. And then Amphinomus, the illustrious son of noble Nisus, and grandson of Aretias, addressed them saying: "Friends, in answering what is fairly said, none should be angry and retort with spiteful words. Let none abuse the stranger nor any of the servants in great Odysseus' hall. Come then and let the wine-pourer give pious portions to our cups, that after a libation we each go home to bed. And let us leave the stranger here within Odysseus' hall, to be cared for by Telemachus; for to his house he came."

He spoke, and to them all his words were pleasing. So a bowl was brewed by the lord Moulius, a Doulichian page and follower of Amphinomus. To all in turn he served; and they, with a libation to the blessed gods, drank of the honeyed wine. Then after they had poured and drunk as their hearts would, desiring rest, they each departed homeward.

BOOK XIX

The Meeting with Penelope and the Recognition by Eurycleia

So in the hall was royal Odysseus left behind, plotting to slay the suitors with Athene's aid, and at once to Telemachus he spoke these winged words:

"Telemachus, this fighting gear must all be laid away, and with soft words you must beguile the suitors when they because they miss it question you: 'I put it by out of the smoke, for it looks no longer like the armor which Odysseus left behind when he went away to Troy; it is all tarnished, where the scent of fire has come nigh. Besides, this graver fear some god put in my mind. You might when full of wine begin a quarrel and give each other wounds, making a scandal of the feast and of your wooing. Steel itself draws men on.'"

He spoke, and Telemachus heeded his dear father, and calling aside his nurse Eurycleia, said: "Nurse, go and keep the women in their rooms while I place in the chamber my father's goodly armor, which as it lies uncared for round the house smoke stains, while he is gone. I have been foolish. Now I will place it where no scent of fire shall come near."

Then said to him his dear nurse Eurycleia: "Ah! Would, my child, you might incline to heedful ways, and mind the house and guard its treasures! But who shall go and bear the light? You will not let the women stir who might have lighted you."

Then answered her discreet Telemachus: "This stranger here; for I will allow no idle man to touch my bread, come he from whence he may."

Such were his words; unwinged, they rested with her. She locked

234

the doors of the stately hall. And now arose Odysseus and his gallant son and bore away the helmets, bulging shields and pointed spears. Before them Pallas Athene, holding a golden lamp, made beauteous light. Then Telemachus said to his father quickly:

"Father, my eyes behold a mighty marvel. The palace walls and the fair spaces, the pine-wood beams and the uprising pillars are all aglow as from a blazing fire. Surely a god is in this house, even such as they who hold the open sky."

But wise Odysseus answered him and said: "Hush, check your thoughts and ask no question. It is indeed a signal from the gods who hold Olympus. Go you to rest. I will continue here, to try these slave-maids and your mother more; and she shall weep and question me of all."

So he spoke, and through the hall forth went Telemachus with blazing torch, to rest within that chamber where he always lay when pleasant sleep drew near. Here then he laid him down, awaiting sacred dawn; while in the hall royal Odysseus stayed behind, plotting to slay the suitors with Athene's aid.

Now from her room came heedful Penelope, like Artemis or golden Aphrodite. Beside the fire where she was wont to sit, they placed a chair fashioned with spiral work of ivory and silver; which Icmalius, the carpenter, had made long time ago, setting upon the lower part a rest for feet, fixed to the chair itself. Over the whole a large fleece had been thrown. Here heedful Penelope now sat down. Soon came the white-armed slave-maids from their hall, and cleared away the abundant food, the tables, and the cups from which the proud lords had been drinking. The embers from the braziers they threw upon the floor, and in the braziers piled fresh heaps of wood to furnish light and warmth. Then thus Melantho once more mocked Odysseus:

"Stranger, are you still here, to plague us all night long, prowling about the house, watching the women? Be off, pervert, and be content with eating, or you will soon be hit with a brand and go."

But looking sternly on her, wise Odysseus said: "Twisted woman, why rail at me with such an angry heart? Is it that I am foul and wear mean clothes and beg about the land? Necessity constrains me. This is what beggars and what homeless people are. Yet once I lived in luxury among my mates, in a rich house, and often gave to wanderers, careless who they might be or with what need they came. Servants I had in plenty and everything besides by which men live at ease and are reputed rich. But Zeus, the son of Kronos, brought me low. His will it was. And you too, woman, some day yet may lose those charms in which you now excel the other slave-maids. Your mistress may become provoked to anger with you. Odysseus may return; there still is room for hope. But if he is dead, as you suppose, and to return no more, yet by Apollo's grace he has a worthy son, Telemachus, whose eye no woman in the hall escapes in her misdeeds; because he is no longer now the child he was."

Heedful Penelope heard what he was saying, and she rebuked her maid and spoke to her and said: "Not in the least, you bold and shameless creature, have you escaped my eye in doing guilty deeds. Your head shall answer for them. Full well you knew—you heard it from myself—that I intended to ask tidings of this stranger here in my hall about my husband; for I am deeply distressed."

She spoke, and to the house-keeper Eurynome she said: "Eurynome, pray bring a bench and a fleece on it, and let the stranger sit and tell his tale, and listen too to me; I wish to question him."

She spoke; the other with all speed brought her a polished bench and placed it there, and on it laid a fleece. Then long-tried royal Odysseus sat down, and thus began heedful Penelope:

"Stranger, I will myself first ask you this: who are you? Of what people? Where is your town and kindred?"

Then wise Odysseus answered her and said: "Lady, no man upon the boundless earth may speak dispraise of you, because your fame is wide as is the sky. Such is the glory of a blameless king who reverences the gods and rules a people numerous and mighty, upholding justice. For him the dark-soiled earth produces wheat and barley, trees bend low with fruit, the flock has constant issue, and the sea yields fish, under his righteous sway.[35] Because of him his people prosper. Question me, then, of all things else while I am here; but do not ask my lineage and home, nor fill my heart with still more pains by recollection. I am a man of sorrows; yet must I not in a strange house sit down to weep and wail. To grieve incessantly makes matters worse. One of these maids, or you yourself, might take it ill, and say my flood of tears came with a weight of wine."

Then answered him heedful Penelope: "Stranger, all excellence of mine in face or form the immortals took away the day the Argive host took ship for Ilios, and with them went my lord Odysseus. If he would come and tend this life of mine, greater would be my fame and fairer then. Now I am in distress, such woes God thrusts upon me. For all the nobles who bear sway among the islands—Doulichion, Same, and woody Zacynthus—and they who here in farseen Ithaca dwell round about, sue for unwilling me and waste my house. Wherefore I pay no heed to strangers or to suppliants, nor even to heralds who ply a public trade; but, longing for Odysseus, I waste my heart away. These men urge on my marriage: I wind my skein of guile. First, Heaven inspired my mind to set up a great loom within the hall and weave a robe, fine and exceeding large; and to the men said I, 'Young men who are my suitors, though royal Odysseus now is dead, forbear to urge my marriage till I complete this robe,—its threads must not be wasted,—a shroud for lord Laërtes, against the time when the fell doom of death that lays men low shall overtake him. Achaean wives about the land I fear might give me blame if he should lie without a shroud, he who had great possessions.' Such were my words, and their high hearts assented. Then in the daytime would I weave at the great web, but in the night unravel, after my torch was set. Thus for three years I hid my craft and cheated the Achaeans. But when the fourth year came, as time rolled on, when the months waned and the long days were done, then through the means of slave-maids—the thankless creatures—they came and caught me and upbraided me; so then I finished it, against my will, by force. Now I can neither shun the match nor find a fresh device. My parents too press me to marry, and my son chafes at the men who swallow up his living; noting it now, for now he is a man and fully able to heed his house, and Zeus guarantees him honor. Yet what of this! Tell me the lineage of which you come. You are not born of immemorial oak or rock."

Then wise Odysseus answered her and said: "O honored wife of Laërtes' son, Odysseus, will you not cease to question of my lineage? Well, I will tell the tale, though you deliver me to sorrows more than I now bear. But so it ever is when one is absent from his land as long as I, wandering from town to town, he meets with hardship! Still, I will tell you what you ask and seek to know.

"There is a country, Crete, in the midst of the wine-dark sea, a fair land and a rich, begirt with water. The people there are many, innumerable indeed, and they have ninety cities. Their speech is mixed; one language joins another. Here are Achaeans, here brave native Cretans, here Cydonians, crested Dorians, and noble Pelasgians. Of all their towns the capital is Cnosus, where Minos* became king when nine years old—Minos, the friend of mighty Zeus and father of my father, bold Deucalion. Deucalion begot me and the prince Idomeneus. Idomeneus, however, went in beaked ships to Ilios, in train of the Atreidae. My own proud name is Aethon,† and I am the younger born; he was the older and the better man. Here was it that I saw Odysseus and gave him entertainment; for into Crete a strong wind bore him, and while he steered toward Troy it forced him past Maleia. He anchored at Amnisus, where is Elithyia's cave, in a harbor hard to win, and he scarcely cleared the storm. At once he came to town, inquiring for Idomeneus; for he said he was his friend, beloved and honored. But it was now the tenth dawn, or the eleventh, since Idomeneus had gone with the beaked ships to Ilios. And so it happened it was I who brought him to the palace, where I entertained him well and gave him generous welcome from the abundance of my house. To him and all the men who followed I furnished barley-meal and sparkling wine from out the public store, with oxen enough for sacrifice to fill their hearts' desire. Here

---

*Legendary king of Crete, during whose rule the labyrinth was built.
†The name means "shining" or "bright."

for twelve days the noble Achaeans tarried; the strong wind Boreas constrained them and even near the shore let them not lie at anchor. Some baffling power aroused it. But on the thirteenth day the wind went down, and so they put to sea."

He made the many falsehoods of his tale seem like the truth. So as she listened, drops ran down; she melted into tears. And as the snow melts on the lofty mountains, when Eurus melts what Zephyrus has scattered, and at its melting flowing rivers fill; so did her fair cheeks melt with flowing tears, as she bewailed her husband who was seated by her side. Odysseus in his heart pitied his sobbing wife; but his eyes stood fixed as horn or iron, motionless in their sockets. Through craft he checked his tears. But when she had had her fill of tears and sighs, finding her words once more she said to him:

"Now, stranger, I shall put you to the test, I think, and see if at your hall you really entertained my husband and his gallant comrades, as you say. Tell me what sort of clothes he wore; what the man himself was like, and the comrades who were with him."

Then wise Odysseus answered her and said: "O lady, it is hard, with so long a time between, to tell you that; for twenty years are gone since he set forth and left my land. Still, I will tell you how my mind makes him appear. A cloak of purple wool Odysseus wore, made with a double fold. A brooch of gold upon it was fashioned with twin buckles, the front part ornamented. In his forepaws a dog held down a spotted fawn and clutched it as it writhed. This all admired and marveled how, though things of gold, the dog would clutch and choke the fawn, and how the fawn that struggled to escape would twitch its feet. His tunic too I noticed, gleaming across the flesh, just like the skin stripped down from a dried onion; so smooth it was, and glistening like the sun. And truly many a woman gazed on the man with wonder. But this I will say further; mark it well. I do not know if Odysseus wore this dress at home, or if a comrade gave it when he entered the swift ship, or yet perhaps some host. Odysseus was beloved by many men; few of the Achaeans equally. I gave him gifts myself,—a sword of bronze, a beautiful purple doublet and a bordered tunic; and I sent him off with honor on his well-benched ship. A herald a little older than himself attended him. I will describe what manner of man this herald was: bent in the shoulders, swarthy, curly-haired, and named Eurybates. Odysseus honored him beyond his other comrades, because he had a mind that suited well his own."

So he spoke, and stirred still more her yearning after tears, as she recognized the tokens which Odysseus exactly told. But when she had had her fill of tears and sighs finding her words once more she said to him:

"From this time forth, stranger, you who before were pitied shall in my halls be one beloved and honored. For I it was who gave the clothes which you describe. I folded them in the chamber and fixed the glittering brooch to be his pride. But I shall nevermore receive him homeward returning to his native land. Wherefore through evil fate Odysseus went by hollow ship to see accursed Ilios, name never to be named."

Then wise Odysseus answered her and said: "O honored wife of Laërtes' son, Odysseus, mar your fair face no more, nor waste your heart with sorrowing for your husband. And yet I do not blame you; for any woman weeps to lose the husband of her youth, whose children she has borne, whose love she tasted, though he were other than Odysseus, who they say is like the gods. Still, cease your grief and mark my word; for I will speak unerringly and nothing will I hide of what I lately heard about the coming of Odysseus,—how he is near, in the rich country of the Thesprotians, a living man, and bringing with him much good treasure which he has begged throughout the land. His trusty crew and hollow ship he lost on the wine-dark sea, when coming from the island of Thrinacia; for Zeus and the Sun were angry with him, because his crew killed the Sun's cattle. So they all perished in the surging sea; but he on his ship's keel was cast by a wave ashore on the coast of the Phaeacians, who are kinsmen of the gods. They honored him exceedingly, as if he were a god, and gave him many gifts and themselves wished to bring him home unharmed. And here in Ithaca Odysseus would have been long time ago, only it seemed a thing of greater profit to gather wealth by roaming far and wide,—so many gainful ways, beyond all mortal men, Odysseus understands; no living man can match him.

This is the story which the king of the Thesprotians, Pheidon, told me. Moreover in my presence, as he offered a libation in his house, he swore the ship was launched and sailors waiting to bring him home to his own native land. But he sent me off before, for a ship of the Thesprotians happened to be starting for the Doulichian grainfields. He showed me all the treasure that Odysseus had obtained; and really it would support man after man ten generations long, so large a stock was stored in the king's palace. Odysseus himself, he said, was gone at that time to Dodona, to learn from the sacred lofty oak the will of Zeus, and how he might return, whether openly or by stealth, to his dear native land when now so long away. So he is safe, and soon will come, and now is near at hand, and parted from friends and native land he will not tarry long. Lo, I will add an oath. First then of all the gods be witness Zeus, highest of gods and noblest, and let the hearth of good Odysseus whereto I come be witness; all this shall be accomplished exactly as I say. This very year Odysseus comes, as this moon wanes and as the next appears."

Then said to him heedful Penelope: "Ah, stranger, would these words of yours might be fulfilled! Soon should you know my kindness and many a gift from me, and every man you met would call you blessed. But yet the thought is in my heart how it will really be. Odysseus will return no more, nor you get passage hence; for there are no more masters in the house, able, as once Odysseus was—if ever he was here—to speed the worthy stranger forth or kindly to receive. Still, wash the stranger's feet, my women, and prepare his bed, bedstead and robes and bright-hued rugs, that well and warmly he may spend the time till gold-throned dawn; and early in the morning bathe and anoint him well, so that indoors beside Telemachus he may await his meal, seated within the hall. And woe to him who persecutes or annoys the man. Henceforth he shall get nothing here, though he be sorely vexed. For how could you think me, stranger, better than other women in will and careful wisdom, if you should sit at table in my hall unkempt and meanly clad? Men are short-lived. And if a man is harsh and thinks harsh thoughts, on him all call down curses while he lives, and when he dies revile him; but he who is gentle and thinks gentle thoughts, his praises strangers carry far and wide to all mankind, and many speak him well."

Then wise Odysseus answered her and said: "O honored wife of Laërtes' son, Odysseus, hateful to me are robes and bright-hued rugs, since first I left the snowy hills of Crete on board the long-oared ship. Here I would rest just as I used to lie through sleepless nights; for many a night I spent on a rough bed, awaiting sacred bright-throned dawn. Baths for the feet give me no pleasure, and foot of mine shall not be touched by any of these maids who serve the palace,—unless indeed there be some aged woman, sober-minded, one who has borne as many sorrows as myself. It would not trouble me that such a one should touch my feet."

Then said to him heedful Penelope: "Dear stranger,—and none discreet as you among the traveling strangers has been more welcome at my house, so suitably discreet is all you say,—I have an aged woman of an understanding heart, who gently nursed and tended that unfortunate and took him in her arms the day his mother bore him. She, feeble as she is, shall wash your feet. Come, rise up, heedful Eurycleia, and wash a man old as your master! Perhaps Odysseus is already such as he, in feet and hands; for soon in times of trouble men grow old."

As she spoke thus, the old woman hid her face in her hands and shed hot tears and uttered wailing words:

"Alas for you, my child! Helpless am I. Zeus surely hated you beyond all humankind, godfearing though you were. For no man ever burned to Zeus, the Thunderer, fat thighs so good or such choice hecatombs as you have offered when you prayed to reach a hale old age and rear your gallant son. And yet from you alone he utterly cut off the day of coming home. Even so perhaps women reviled him too at foreign tables, when he reached some lordly house, just as these brutes are all reviling you. To shun their insults and their many taunts, you do not let them wash you; and I, not loath, am bidden to it by the daughter of Icarius, heedful Penelope. So I will wash your feet, both for Penelope's own sake and for your own, because my heart within is stirred by sorrow. Yet mark the words I say! Many a way-worn stranger has come here; but one so like Odysseus I declare I never saw, as you are like him, form, and voice and feet."

Then wise Odysseus answered her and said: "Yes, woman, so says every one who sees us two, that we are like each other, even as you shrewdly say."

As he spoke thus, the old woman took the glittering basin which she used for washing feet and poured in much cold water, afterwards adding warm. Now Odysseus was sitting by the hearth, but soon turned toward the darkness; for suddenly into his mind there came the thought that in touching him she might detect the scar and thus the facts be known. So she drew near him and began to wash her master; and presently she found the scar which a boar inflicted long ago with his white tusk, when to Parnassus came Odysseus to see Autolycus and his sons. Good Autolycus was the father of the mother of Odysseus, and was famous among men for thievery and oaths. Hermes, the god, had given him skill, because to him Autolycus had burned well-pleasing things of lambs and kids; so Hermes gladly served him. Now Autolycus, visiting the fertile land of Ithaca, found there his daughter's son, a child new-born; and after supper Eurycleia laid the child upon his knees, and speaking thus she said:

"Autolycus, choose now a name to give your child's own child. He has been wished for long."

Then answered her Autolycus and said: "My son-in-law and daughter, give him the name I say. Since I come here odious to many men and women on the bounteous earth, therefore Odysseus be his name.* And I, when he is grown and visits the great palace of his mother's kin upon Parnassus, where my possessions lie, will give thereof to him and send him home rejoicing."

On this account Odysseus came to get the glorious gifts. And Autolycus and his sons gave him a welcome with friendly hands and courteous words; and Amphithea, his mother's mother, took Odysseus in her arms and kissed his face and both his beauteous eyes. Then Autolycus bade his famous sons to lay the dinner ready, and they hearkened to his call. They quickly brought an ox, five years old, and flayed and dressed it, laid it asunder, sliced it with skill, stuck it on spits, and roasting it with care served out the portions. Thus all throughout the day till setting sun they held their feast. There was no lack of appetite for the shared feast. But when the sun had set and darkness came, they lay down and took the gift of sleep.

When now the early rosy-fingered dawn appeared, they started on the hunt; the dogs went forth, the men themselves,—the sons of Autolycus,—and with them went royal Odysseus too. They climbed the steep and wood-clad mountain of Parnassus and soon they reached its windy ridges. Just then the sun began to touch the fields as he ascended from the calm and brimming stream of Ocean. And now to a glen the beaters came. Before them, following the tracks, the hounds ran on, the sons of Autolycus hastening after. With the sons went royal Odysseus, close on the hounds, wielding his outstretched spear. In a dense thicket there a huge boar lay. It was a spot no force of wind with its chill breath could pierce, no sunbeams smite, nor rain pass through, so dense it was, and a thick fall of leaves was in it. Here round the boar there came the tramp of men and dogs, as the beaters pushed along. Facing them from his lair, with bristling back, fire flashing in his eyes, the boar stood close at bay. Odysseus first sprang forward, raising the long spear in his sinewy hand, eager to give the blow; but the boar was quick and

---

*"Odysseus," related to "odious," approximately translates as "victim of hatred."

struck him on the knee, and by a side-thrust of his tusk tore the flesh deep, but reached no bone. And now Odysseus, by a downward blow, struck the right shoulder of the boar; clean through it the bright spear-point passed. Down in the dust he fell with a moan, and his life flew away. Then the good sons of Autolycus looked to the boar; and the wound of gallant princely Odysseus they bound up skillfully, and with a spell staunched the black blood, and soon they reached their father's house. So Autolycus and his sons when they had fully healed Odysseus and given him glorious gifts,—pleasing by kindness him who pleased them too,—sent him with speed to Ithaca, where his father and honored mother rejoiced at his return and questioned much how he had got the scar. He told them how, while he was hunting, a boar inflicted it with his white tusk when he had gone to Parnassus with Autolycus' sons.

This was the scar the woman felt with her flat hand. She knew it by the touch and dropped the foot. The leg fell in the basin; the copper rang, and tilting sidewise let all the water run upon the ground. Then joy and grief together seized her breast; her two eyes filled with tears, her full voice stayed; and laying her hand upon Odysseus' chin she said:

"You really are Odysseus, my dear child, and I never knew you till I handled my master over and over!"

She spoke and cast her eyes upon Penelope, meaning to let her know her lord was there. But Penelope could not catch the glance nor understand, because Athene drew away her notice; and Odysseus, feeling for Eurycleia's throat, clutched it with his right hand, then drew her closer toward him with his left and said:

"Why, mother, will you kill me? It was yourself who nursed me at the breast; and now through many hardships I come in the twentieth year to my own native land. Though you have found me out and a god inspired your heart, be silent, lest some other person in the hall may know. Or else,—I tell you, and certainly it shall be done,—if God by me subdues the lordly suitors, I will not spare even you, nurse though you are, when I shall slay the other serving-women in my halls."

Then answered heedful Eurycleia: "My child, what word has passed the barrier of your teeth? You know how steadfast, how inflexible my spirit is. I shall hold fast like stubborn rock or iron. And this I will say further: mark it well. If God by you subdues the lordly suitors, then I will name the women of the hall and tell you who dishonor you and who are guiltless."

But wise Odysseus answered her and said: "Mother, why talk of them? You have no need. I will myself observe them well and find out each. Be quiet with your story! Leave the matter to the gods!"

So he spoke, and through the hall forth went the aged woman to fetch water for his feet; for all the first was spilled. Now when she had washed him and anointed him with oil, again Odysseus drew his bench closer beside the fire, to warm himself,—but with his tatters hid the scar,—and thus began heedful Penelope:

"Stranger, there is but little more that I will ask; because the season of sweet rest will soon be here, for those to whom kind sleep will come when they are sad. But upon me God sends incessant sorrow. Day after day my joys are tears and sighs, as I watch my household tasks and watch my women. Then when night comes and slumber visits all, I lie in bed, and crowding on my heavy heart sharp cares sting me to weeping. As when Pandareos' daughter, the russet nightingale, sings sweetly at the coming in of spring, perched in the thick-leaved trees, and to and fro pours out her thrilling voice, in lamentation for her dear child, Itylus, whom with the sword she one day blindly slew, her son by royal Zethus;[36] so does my doubtful heart toss to and fro whether to bide beside my son and keep all here in safety,—my goods, my maids, and my great high-roofed house,—and thus revere my husband's bed and heed the public voice, or finally to follow some chief of the Achaeans who woos me in my hall with countless gifts. My son, while but a child and slack of understanding, did not permit my marrying and departing from my husband's house; but now that he is grown and come to man's estate, he prays me to go home again and leave the hall, so troubled is he for that wealth which the Achaeans waste. But come, interpret now and hear this dream of mine. I have twenty geese about the place who pick up corn out of the water, and I amuse myself with watching them. But from the mountain came a great hook-beaked eagle and broke the necks of all and killed my geese. In heaps they lay, scattered about the buildings, while he was borne aloft into the sacred sky. So I began to weep and wail,—still in my dream,—and fair-haired Achaean women gathered round and found me sadly sobbing that the eagle killed my geese. Then down again he came, lit on a jutting rafter, and with a human voice he checked my tears and said: 'Courage, O daughter of renowned Icarius! This is no dream, but true reality, which yet shall come to pass. The geese are suitors; and I, the eagle, was at the first a bird, but now, this second time, am come your husband to bring a ghastly doom on all the suitors.' At these his words sweet slumber left me, and opening my eyes I saw the geese about the buildings devouring corn beside the trough just as they used to do."

Then wise Odysseus answered her and said: "Lady, the dream cannot be understood by wresting it to other meanings; Odysseus surely has himself revealed what yet shall be. The suitors' overthrow is plain: on all it falls; none shall escape from death and doom."

But heedful Penelope said to him once more: "Stranger, in truth dreams do arise perplexed and hard to tell, dreams which come not, in men's experience, to their full issue. Two gates there are for unsubstantial dreams, one made of horn and one of ivory. The dreams that pass through the carved ivory delude and bring us tales that turn to naught; those that come forth through polished horn accomplish real things, whenever seen. Yet through this gate came not I think my own strange dream. Ah, welcome, were it so, to me and to my child! But this I will say further; mark it well. This is the fatal dawn which parts me from Odysseus' home; for now I shall propose a contest with the axes which when at home he used to set in line, like trestles, twelve in all; then he would stand a great way off and send an arrow through. This contest I shall now propose to all the suitors. And whoever with his hands shall lightliest bend the bow and shoot through all twelve axes, him I will follow and forsake this home, this bridal home, so very beautiful and full of wealth, a place I think I ever shall remember even in my dreams."

Then wise Odysseus answered her and said: "O honored wife of Laërtes' son, Odysseus, delay no longer this contest at the hall; for wise Odysseus will be here before the suitors, handling the polished bow, can stretch the string and shoot an arrow through the iron."

Then said to him heedful Penelope: "Stranger, if you were willing to sit beside me here and entertain me, no sleep should ever fall upon my eyes. And yet one cannot be forever without sleep; for to each thing the immortals fix a season, to be ordained for men upon the fruitful earth. So I will go to my upper chamber and lie on my bed, which has become for me a bed of sorrows, ever watered with my tears since Odysseus went away to see accursed Ilios,—name never to be named. There I must lie. You lie in the hall. Make a bed upon the floor, or the maids shall bring you bedding."

So saying, she went to her bright upper chamber, yet not alone; beside her went her waiting-women too. And coming to the chamber with the maids, she there bewailed Odysseus, her dear husband, till on her lids clear-eyed Athene caused a sweet sleep to fall.

BOOK XX

Before the Slaughter

Royal Odysseus made his bed within the porch. Upon the floor he spread an untanned hide, and on it many fleeces of the sheep which the Achaeans had been slaying; and when he had laid him down, Eurynome threw over him a cloak. So, meditating in his heart how he might harm the suitors, here lay Odysseus sleepless. Forth from the hall came women who had long been mistresses of the suitors, now making jests and merriment among themselves. The heart of Odysseus stirred within, and in his mind and heart he doubted much whether to hasten after and deal out death to each, or to allow to the audacious suitors one last and latest night. Within him growled his spirit. Even as a dog walks round her tender young, growling at any man she does not know and resolute to fight him; so within growled his spirit, incensed at these evil deeds. But he smote upon his breast and thus reproved his heart:

"Bear up, my heart! A thing more hideous than this you once endured with patience, that day the Cyclops, unrestrained in fury, devoured your sturdy comrades. Then you bore up till crafty planning brought from the cave you who had thought to die."

So he spoke, chiding the very spirit in his breast; and therefore in obedience his heart held firm and steadfast, yet he himself kept tossing to and fro. As when a man near a great glowing fire turns to and fro a sausage, full of fat and blood, anxious to have it quickly roast; so to and fro Odysseus tossed, and pondered how to lay hands upon the shameless suitors,—he being alone, and they so many. Near him Athene drew, descending out of heaven. In a woman's form she stood beside his head, and thus addressed him:

"Why wakeful still, unhappiest of men? This is your home, and in this home your wife and child, even such a son as others pray for."

But wise Odysseus answered her and said: "In all this, goddess, you speak rightly; and yet my heart within is pondering how to lay hands upon the shameless suitors,—I being alone, while they are always here together. A graver fear besides I ponder in my mind; suppose I slay them, by the aid of Zeus and you, where shall I flee then? Tell me this, I pray."

Then said to him the goddess, clear-eyed Athene: "O doubter! Men trust weaker friends, friends who are mortal and not wise as I. I am a god and will protect you to the end, through all your toils. And let me tell you plainly: should fifty troops of mortal men stand round about us, eager in the fight to slay, you still might drive away from them their oxen and sturdy sheep. No! No! Let slumber come! Evil it is to watch and wake all the night long. You shall come forth from peril yet."

So spoke she, and poured sleep upon his eyelids; and then the heavenly goddess departed to Olympus. But as the slumber seized him, freeing his heart from care, easing his limbs, his faithful wife awoke, and sitting up in her soft bed began to weep. When she had satisfied her heart with weeping, the royal lady prayed, and first to Artemis:

"O honored goddess Artemis, daughter of Zeus, strike now I pray an arrow in my breast and take away my life this very instant; or let a sweeping storm bear me its windy way and cast me in the streams of restless Ocean! As when storms seized Pandareos' daughters, whose parents gods had slain and they were left at home as orphans, then goddess Aphrodite brought them cheese, sweet honey and pleasant wine; Here endowed them, beyond all other women, with beauty and understanding; chaste Artemis gave stature; Athene taught them skill in honorable work. But while heavenly Aphrodite went to high Olympus, to win the maids the final boon of happy marriage,—a gift from Zeus, the Thunderer, who understands all well, all fortunes good or ill of mortal men,—the Harpies swept away the maids and gave them over to be servants to the dread Furies. Even so may those who have their dwellings on Olympus blot out me, or else may I receive a shaft from fair-haired Artemis, that I may go to my dread grave seeing Odysseus still, and never gladden heart of meaner husband! Yet ills like these are bearable if, with a burdened heart, one weeps by day and then by night has sleep. For such a one forgets all good and ill when once the eyelids close. But as for me, Heaven sends me cruel dreams. Again tonight there lay beside me one like him, such as he was when he departed with the army. My heart was glad. I said it was no dream, but truth at last."

While she was speaking, gold-throned morning came. And as she wept, royal Odysseus heard her voice and mused awhile. In his heart she seemed to know him and to stand beside his head. Gathering up the cloak and fleece in which he slept, he laid them in the hall upon a chair, carried the ox-hide out of doors and spread it down, and with uplifted hands prayed thus to Zeus:

"O father Zeus, if of good will the gods have led me over field and flood to my own land,—though ill ye brought me also,—let some one now awake speak a good word indoors, and another sign from Zeus be given outside the house!"

So spoke he in his prayer, and wise Zeus heard him and straightway thundered out of bright Olympus, out of the clouds above. Royal Odysseus was made glad. Moreover a woman grinding corn sent forth an ominous cry out of the house nearby, where stood the mills of the shepherd of the people. Twelve women in all worked here, preparing barley-meal and corn, men's marrow. The rest were sleeping, having ground their wheat; one only had not ended, for she was very weak. She, stopping at last her mill, uttered these words, an omen for her master:

"O father Zeus, who rulest over gods and men, loud hast thou thundered from the starry sky, and no cloud anywhere. Surely in this thou givest man a sign. Then bring to pass for miserable me the words I speak. May the suitors today for the last and latest time hold their glad feast within Odysseus' hall! They who with galling labor made my knees grow weak, while I prepared them meal, may they now feast their last!"

She spoke, and royal Odysseus was gladdened by her cry and by the thunder of Zeus. He said that woe was come upon the guilty.

And now the other handmaids of the goodly palace of Odysseus came together and kindled on the hearth a steady fire. Telemachus also, a mortal like a god, rose from his bed, put on his clothes, slung his sharp sword about his shoulder, under his shining feet bound his fair sandals, then took his ponderous spear, tipped with sharp bronze, and went and stood upon the threshold, saying to Eurycleia:

"Good nurse, have you provided for the stranger in the house comfort in bed and food? Or does he lie neglected? That is my mother's way, wise though she is. Blindly she honors one of the meaner sort, and sends the better man away unhonored."

Then heedful Eurycleia answered: "Now do not blame a blameless person, child! He sat and drank his wine as long as he inclined, and he said he wanted no more bread; she asked him that. And as soon as he began to think of rest and sleep, she bade her slave-maids spread his bed. Then he, like a man quite mean and miserable, refused to sleep upon a bed and under blankets, but on an undressed hide and fleecy sheepskins lay down within the porch. We put a cloak upon him."

So she spoke; and through the hall forth went Telemachus, his spear in hand, two swift dogs following after. He hastened to the assembly to join the armed Achaeans. But noble Eurycleia, daughter of Ops, Peisenor's son, called to the women:

"Come, stir about and sweep the house and sprinkle it, and beat the purple coverings on the shapely chairs. And others, take your sponges and wipe off all the tables, and clean the mixing-bowls and well-wrought double cups. And others still, go to the well for water, and fetch it quickly here. It is not long the suitors will be absent from the hall. They will be here very early. Today is for them all a holiday."

She spoke, and very willingly they heeded and obeyed. Twenty went to the dark well; the others plied their tasks with skill about the house. Soon came the Achaeans' laboring men, who neatly and skillfully split logs of wood; there came the women also, returning from the well. After them came the swineherd, driving three fat hogs, the best of all his herd. He let them feed about the pleasant yard, and said to Odysseus kindly:

"Stranger, do the Achaeans look after you any better, or do they still insult you in the hall, as at the first?"

Then wise Odysseus answered him and said: "Eumaeus, may the gods requite the wrongs which these in their abominable pride work in a house not theirs! They have no touch of shame."

So they conversed together. Melanthius now drew near, the goatherd, driving the goats that were the best of all his flock, to make the suitors' dinner. Two shepherds followed after. He tied his goats under the echoing portico and said to Odysseus rudely:

"Stranger, will you still be a nuisance in the house and beg of people? Will you not quit our doors? We never shall quite settle things, I think, until you taste my fists. Beyond all decency you keep on begging. Surely there are Achaean feasts elsewhere."

He spoke, but not a word did wise Odysseus answer. Silent he shook his head, brooding on evil.

A third now joined them, Philoetius, ever foremost, and brought the suitors a barren cow and fatted goats. The ferrymen brought them over, they who bring people too, whenever anybody comes their way. He tied the cattle carefully under the echoing portico and drawing near the swineherd asked:

"Who is the stranger, swineherd, lately come, and staying at the hall? Out of what tribe does he profess to be? Where are his kinsman and his native fields? Poor man! He seems in bearing like a lordly king. The gods may well send homeless people troubles when even for kings they weave a web of grief."

He spoke, and turning to Odysseus gave his right hand in welcome, and speaking in winged words he said: "Hail, good old stranger! May happiness be yours in time to come! Now you are bound by many ills. O father Zeus, none of the gods is crueler than thou! Thou carest not that men, when thou hast given them birth, be plunged in misery and sharp distress. A sweat came over me in looking at the man; my eyes were filled with tears for memory of Odysseus; for he too, I suppose, in just such tatters, is a wanderer among men,—if he indeed yet lives and sees the sunshine. But if he is already dead and in the house of Hades, then woe is me for good Odysseus, who gave me charge of cattle when I was but a boy in the land of the Cephallenians. And now the herds have grown enormously. No breed of broad-browed cattle ever pastured better. But strangers bid me drive these now for them to eat. For the son of the house they do not care, nor do they tremble at the wrath of gods; but they are bent on parting out their long-gone master's goods. And as for me, around one point my heart within keeps turning: it's very bad while the son lives to go to the land of strangers, cattle and all, to foreigners; worse still to stay with strangers' herds and sit about and suffer. Certainly long ago I would have fled and found some other mighty king,—life here cannot be borne,—but still I think of that unfortunate, how he may come from somewhere, and make a scattering of the suitors up and down the house."

Then wise Odysseus answered him and said: "Herdsman, because you do not seem a common, senseless person, but I perceive wisdom is in your heart, I will speak out and swear a solemn oath on what I say: so first of all the gods be witness Zeus, and let this hospitable table and the hearth of good Odysseus whereto I come be witness; while you are here Odysseus shall return, and you with your own eyes shall see him, if you will, slaying the suitors who now lord it here."

Then answered him the herdsman of the cattle: "Ah stranger, may the son of Kronos fulfill these words of yours! Then shall you know what might is mine and how my hands obey."

So also did Eumaeus pray to all the gods that wise Odysseus might return to his own house. So they conversed together.

Now for Telemachus the suitors had been plotting death and doom. But toward them, on the left, a bird came flying, a soaring eagle, clutching a timid dove; whereat Amphinomus called to them thus and said:

"Ah, friends, this plan of ours will not run well, this murder of Telemachus. Let us rather turn to feasting."

So said Amphinomus, and his saying pleased them. Entering the house of princely Odysseus, they threw their coats upon the couches and the chairs, and they began to kill great sheep and fatted goats, to kill sleek pigs and the heifer of the herd. They roasted the inward parts and passed them round, and mixed wine in the mixers. The swineherd passed the cups; Philoetius, ever foremost, handed them bread in goodly baskets; Melanthius poured the wine. So on the food spread out before them they laid hands.

And now Telemachus, with crafty purpose, seated Odysseus within the stately hall by the stone threshold, providing him a common bench and little table. He gave him portions of the inward parts and, pouring him wine into a golden cup, he thus addressed him:

"Sit here among the men and sip your wine, and I will keep you from the taunts and blows of all the suitors. This is no public house. It is Odysseus' own, acquired for me. Therefore you suitors check your taste for insult and abuse, or else there may be strife and quarrel here."

He spoke, and all with teeth set in their lips marveled because Telemachus had spoken boldly. Then said Antinoüs, Eupeithes' son: "Harsh as it is, Achaeans, let us take the bidding of Telemachus. He speaks with lofty threatening. Zeus, son of Kronos, hindered, or long ago we in the hall had stopped him, shrill talker though he be."

So said Antinoüs; Telemachus did not heed his words. For pages came, leading along the town a hecatomb of cattle sacred to the gods. Long-haired Achaeans, too, assembled in the shady grove of the archer-king Apollo.

But when the rest had roasted the outer flesh and drawn it off, dividing up the portions they held a famous feast. And those who served set for Odysseus a portion quite as large as that they took themselves; for this was the bidding of Telemachus, the son of princely Odysseus.

Yet Athene allowed the haughty suitors not altogether yet to cease from biting scorn. She wished more pain to pierce the heart of Laërtes' son, Odysseus. There was among the suitors a man of lawless life; Ctesippus was his name; he lived in Same. Proud of vast wealth, he courted the wife of Odysseus, long away. He it was now who thus addressed the audacious suitors:

"Listen, you haughty suitors, while I speak. This stranger here a while ago received a portion, and, as was proper, one as large as ours; for it is neither honorable nor fitting to worry strangers who may reach this palace of Telemachus. Come then and let me also give a hospitable gift, and he shall have wherewith to give a present to the bath-keeper or to some servant of the house of great Odysseus."

So saying, he flung with his strong hand an ox-hoof which lay near, taking it from the basket. Odysseus with quick turning of the head avoided it, and in his heart smiled grimly. It struck the massive wall. But Telemachus rebuked Ctesippus thus:

"Surely, Ctesippus, that was lucky for your life. You missed our guest. He shunned your missile. Else I had run you through the middle with my pointed spear, and in the place of wedding-feast your father had been busied with a funeral here. Let no man in this house henceforth show rudeness; for I now mark and understand each deed, good deeds as well as bad. Before, I was a child. And even yet we bear what nevertheless we see,—sheep slain, wine drunk, bread wasted,—for hard it is for one to cope with many. Well, then, do me no more deliberate wrong. But if you seek to slay me with the sword, that I would choose; and better far were death than constantly to behold disgraceful deeds, strangers abused, and slave-maids dragged to shame through the fair palace."

So he spoke and all were hushed to silence; but by and by said Agelaüs, son of Damastor: "Friends, in answering what is fairly said, none should be angry and retort with spiteful words. Let none abuse the stranger nor any of the servants in great Odysseus' hall. But to Telemachus and his mother I would say one friendly word; perhaps it may find favor in the mind of each. So long as your hearts hoped wise Odysseus would return to his own home, it was no harm to wait and hold the suitors at the palace. That was the better way, if but Odysseus had returned and reached his home once more. Now it is plain that he will never come. Go then, sit down beside your mother and plainly tell her this, to marry the man who is the best and offers most. So shall you keep in peace all that your father left, to eat and drink your fill, and she shall guide the household of another."

Then answered him discreet Telemachus: "Nay, Agelaüs, by Zeus I swear and by the sufferings of my father, who far away from Ithaca is dead or lost, it is not I delay my mother's marriage; indeed I urge her to marry whom she will, I will give countless gifts. But I hesitate to drive her forth, against her will, by a compulsive word. The gods let that never be!"

So spoke Telemachus, but Pallas Athene woke uncontrollable laughter in the suitors. She turned their wits awry. Now they would laugh as if with others' faces, and blood-bedabbled was the flesh they ate. Their eyes were filled with tears, their heart felt anguish; and godlike Theoclymenus addressed them thus:

"Ah, wretched men, what woe befalls you? Night shrouds your heads, your faces, and lower still, your knees. Wild cries are kindled; cheeks are wet with tears; walls and the fair mid-spaces drip with blood. The porch is full, the court is full, of shapes that haste to Erebus, down into darkness. The sun is blotted from the heavens; a foul fog covers all."

He spoke, and all burst into merry laughter; and thus began Eurymachus, the son of Polybus: "A crazy stranger this, new come from foreign lands! Quick then, young men, and guide him out of doors, off to the market, since he finds it here like night!"

Then godlike Theoclymenus made answer: "Eurymachus, I do not ask a guide; I have my eyes and ears, and my two feet, and in my breast a steadfast mind of no mean sort. By their aid I go forth, for I perceive evil approaching you which none shall shun or flee,— no, not a man among these suitors who in the house of great Odysseus work wantonly abominations to mankind."

So saying, forth he went out of the stately palace and found Pei-raeus, who received him kindly. Then all the suitors, glancing at one another, began to tease Telemachus by laughing at his guests, and a rude youth would say:

"Telemachus, no man is more unfortunate in guests than you. For instance, what a filthy vagabond is this you keep, one always wanting bread and wine, incapable of work or deeds of strength, simply a clutterer of the ground! And now this other fellow stands up and plays the prophet. But if you would heed me, the better way were this; to toss your guests into a ship of many oars and pack them off to Sicily, where they would fetch their price."

So said the suitors; Telemachus did not heed their words. Silent he watched his father, waiting ever till he should lay hands on the shameless suitors.

Now having set her goodly seat just opposite the door, the daughter of Icarius, heedful Penelope, attended to the talk of all within the hall. With laughter they prepared their dinner,—a pleasant meal, such as they liked,—and many a beast was slaughtered. But how could a feast be more unwelcome than the supper which a goddess and a valiant man were soon to serve them? For from the first they had wrought deeds of shame.

BOOK XXI

The Trial of the Bow

And now the goddess, clear-eyed Athene, put in the mind of Icarius' daughter, heedful Penelope, to offer to the suitors in the hall the bow and the gray steel, as means of sport and harbingers of death. She mounted the long stairway of her house, holding a crooked key in her firm hand,—a goodly key of bronze, having an ivory handle,—and hastened with her slave-maids to a far-off room where her lord's treasure lay, bronze, gold, and well-wrought steel. Here also lay his curved bow and the quiver for his arrows,—and many grievous shafts were in it still,—gifts which a friend had given Odysseus when he met him once in Lacedaemon,—Iphitus, son of Eurytus, a man like the immortals. At Messene the two met, in the house of wise Orsilochus. Odysseus had come hither to claim a debt which the whole district owed him; for upon ships of many oars Messenians carried off from Ithaca three hundred sheep together with their herdsmen. In the long quest for these, Odysseus took the journey when he was but a youth; for his father and the other elders sent him forth. Iphitus, on the other hand, was seeking horses; for twelve mares had been lost, which had as foals twelve hardy mules. These afterwards became the death and doom of Iphitus when he met the stalwart son of Zeus, the hero Hercules, who well knew deeds of daring; for Hercules slew Iphitus in his own house, although his guest, and recklessly did not regard the anger of the gods nor yet the proffered table, but slew the man and kept at his own hall the strong-hoofed mares. It was when seeking these that Iphitus had met Odysseus and given the bow which in old days great Eurytus was wont to bear, and which on dying in his lofty hall he left his son. To Iphitus, Odysseus gave a sharp-edged sword and a stout spear, as the beginning of a loving friendship. They never sat, however, at one another's table; ere that could be, the son of Zeus slew godlike Iphitus, the son of Eurytus, who gave the bow. Royal Odysseus when going off to war in the black ships would never take this bow. It always stood in its own place at home, as a memorial of his honored friend. In his own land he bore it.

Now when the royal lady reached this room and stood on the oaken threshold,—which long ago the carpenter had smoothed with skill and leveled to the line, fitting the posts thereto and setting the shining doors,—then quickly from its ring she loosed the strap, thrust in the key, and with a careful aim shot back the door-bolts. As a bull roars when feeding in the field, so roared the goodly door touched by the key and open flew before her. She stepped to a raised dais where stood some chests in which lay fragrant garments. Thence reaching up, she took from its peg the bow in the glittering case which held it. And now she sat down and laid the case upon her lap and loudly weeping drew her lord's bow forth. But when she had had her fill of tears and sighs, she hastened to the hall to meet the lordly suitors, bearing in hand the curved bow and the quiver for the arrows, and many grievous shafts were in it still. Beside her, slave-maids bore a box in which lay many a piece of steel and bronze, implements of her lord's for games like these. And when the royal lady reached the suitors, she stood beside a column of the strong-built roof, holding before her face her delicate veil, the while a faithful slave-maid stood upon either hand. And straightway she addressed the suitors, speaking thus:

"Listen, you haughty suitors who beset this house, eating and drinking ever, now my husband is long gone; no word of excuse can you suggest except your wish to marry me and win me for your wife. Well then, my suitors,—since before you stands your prize,—I offer you the mighty bow of prince Odysseus; and whoever with his hands shall lightliest bend the bow and shoot through all twelve axes, him I will follow and forsake this home, this bridal home, so very beautiful and full of wealth, a place I think I ever shall remember, even in my dreams."[37]

So saying, she bade Eumaeus, the noble swineherd, deliver to the suitors the bow and the gray steel. With tears Eumaeus took the arms and laid them down before them. Near by, the cowherd also wept to see his master's bow. But Antinoüs rebuked them, and spoke to them and said:

"You stupid boors, who only mind the passing minute, wretched pair, what do you mean by shedding tears, troubling this lady's heart, when already her heart is prostrated with grief at losing her dear husband? Sit down and eat in silence, or else go forth and weep, but leave the bow behind, a dread ordeal for the suitors; for I am sure this polished bow will not be bent with ease. There is not a man of all now here so powerful as Odysseus. I saw him once myself and well recall him, though I was then a child."

He spoke, but in his breast his heart was hoping to draw the string and send an arrow through the steel; yet he was to be the first to taste the shaft of good Odysseus, whom he now wronged though seated in his hall, while to like outrage he encouraged all his comrades. To these now spoke revered Telemachus:

"Ha! Zeus the son of Kronos has made me play the fool! My mother,—and wise she is,—says she will follow some strange man and quit this house; and I but laugh and in my silly soul am glad. Come then, you suitors, since before you stands your prize, a lady whose like cannot be found throughout Achaean land, in sacred Pylos, Argos, or Mycenae, in Ithaca itself, or the dark mainland, as you yourselves well know,—what needs my mother praise?—come then, delay not with excuse nor longer hesitate to bend the bow, but let us learn what is to be. I too might try the bow. And if I stretch it and send an arrow through the steel, then with no shame to me my honored mother may forsake this house and follow some one else, leaving me here behind; for I shall then be able to wield my father's arms."

He spoke, and flung his red cloak from his neck, rising full height, and put away the sharp sword also from his shoulder. First then he set the axes, marking one long furrow for them all, aligned by cord. The earth on the two sides he stamped down flat. Surprise filled all beholders to see how properly he set them, though he had never seen the game before. Then he went and stood upon the threshold and began to try the bow. Three times he made it tremble as he sought to make it bend. Three times he slacked his strain, still hoping in his heart to draw the string and send an arrow through the steel. And now he might have drawn it by force of a fourth tug, had not Odysseus shook his head and stopped the eager boy. So to the suitors once more spoke revered Telemachus:

"Ah! Shall I ever be a coward and a weakling, or am I still but young and cannot trust my arm to right me with the man who wrongs me first? But come, you who are stronger men than I, come try the bow and end the contest."

So saying, he laid by the bow and stood it on the ground, leaning it on the firm-set polished door. The swift shaft, too, he likewise leaned against the bow's fair knob, and once more took the seat from which he first arose. Then said to them Antinoüs, Eupeithes' son:

"Rise up in order all, from left to right, beginning where the cupbearer begins to pour the wine."

So said Antinoüs, and his saying pleased them. Then first arose Leiodes, son of Oenops, who was their soothsayer and had his place beside the goodly mixer, farthest along the hall. To him alone their lawlessness was hateful; he abhorred the suitor crowd. He it was now who first took up the bow and the swift shaft; and going to the threshold, he stood and tried the bow. He could not bend it. Tugging the string made sore his hands, his soft, unhorny hands; and to the suitors thus he spoke:

"No, friends, I cannot bend it. Let some other take the bow. Ah, many chiefs this bow shall rob of life and breath! Yet better far to die than live and still to fail in that for which we constantly are gathered, waiting expectantly from day to day! Now each man hopes and purposes at heart to win Penelope, Odysseus' wife. But when he shall have tried the bow and seen his failure, then to some other fair-robed woman of Achaea let each go, and offer her his suit and court her with his gifts. So may Penelope marry the man who gives her most and comes with fate to favor!"

When he had spoken, he laid by the bow, leaning it on the firm-set polished door. The swift shaft, too, he likewise leaned against the bow's fair knob, and once more took the seat from which he first arose. But Antinoüs rebuked him, and spoke to him, and said:

"Leiodes, what words have passed the barrier of your teeth? Strange words and harsh! Disturbing words to hear! As if this bow must rob our chiefs of life and breath because you cannot bend it! Why, your good mother did not bear you for a brandisher of bows and arrows. But others among the lordly suitors will bend it by and by."

So saying, he gave an order to Melanthius, the goatherd: "Hasten, Melanthius, and light a fire in the hall and set a long bench near, with fleeces on it; then bring me the large cake of fat which lies inside the door, that after we have warmed the bow and greased it well, we young men try it and so end the contest."

He spoke, and straightway Melanthius kindled a steady fire, and set a bench beside it with a fleece thereon, and brought out the large cake of fat which lay inside the door, and so the young men warmed the bow and made their trial. But yet they could not bend it; they fell far short of power. Antinoüs, however, still held back, and prince Eurymachus, who were the suitors' leaders; for they in manly excellence were quite the best of all.

Meanwhile out of the house at the same moment came two men, princely Odysseus' herdsmen of the oxen and the swine; and after them came royal Odysseus also. And when they were outside the gate, beyond the yard, speaking in gentle words Odysseus said:

"Cowherd, and you too, swineherd, may I tell a certain tale, or shall I hide it still? My heart bids speak. How ready would you be to aid Odysseus if he should come from somewhere, thus, on a sudden, and a god should bring him home? Would you support the suitors or Odysseus? Speak freely, as your heart and spirit bid you speak."

Then said to him the herdsman of the cattle: "O father Zeus, grant this my prayer! May he return and Heaven be his guide! Then shall you know what might is mine and how my hands obey."

So prayed Eumaeus too to all the gods, that wise Odysseus might return to his own home. So when he knew with certainty the heart of each, finding his words once more Odysseus said:

"Lo, it is I, through many grievous toils now in the twentieth year come to my native land! And yet I know that of my servants none but you desires my coming. From all the rest I have not heard one prayer that I return. To you then I will truly tell what shall hereafter be. If God by me subdues the lordly suitors, I will obtain you wives and give you wealth and homes established near my own; and henceforth in my eyes you shall be friends and brethren of Telemachus. Come then and I will show you too a very trusty sign,— that you may know me certainly and be assured in heart,—the scar the boar dealt long ago with his white tusk, when I once journeyed to Parnassus with Autolycus' sons."

So saying, he drew aside his rags from the great scar. And when the two beheld and understood it all, their tears burst forth; they threw their arms round wise Odysseus and passionately kissed his face and neck. So likewise did Odysseus kiss their heads and hands. And daylight had gone down upon their weeping had not Odysseus stayed their tears and said:

"Have done with grief and wailing, or someone coming from the hall may see, and tell the tale indoors. So, go in one by one, not all together. I will go first, you after. And let this be agreed: the rest within, the lordly suitors, will not allow me to receive the bow and quiver. But, noble Eumaeus, bring the bow along the room and lay it in my hands. Then tell the women to lock the hall's close-fitting doors; and if from their inner room they hear a moaning or a strife within our walls, let no one venture forth, but stay in silence at her work. And, noble Philoetius, in your care I put the court-yard gates. Bolt with the bar and quickly lash the fastening."

So saying, Odysseus made his way into the stately house, and went and took the seat from which he first arose. And soon the serving-men of princely Odysseus entered too.

Now Eurymachus held the bow and turned it up and down, trying to heat it at the glowing fire. But still, with all his pains, he could not bend it; his proud soul groaned aloud. Then bitterly he spoke; these were the words he said:

"Ah! here is woe for me and woe for all! Not that I so much mourn missing the marriage, though vexed I am at that. Still, there are enough more women of Achaea, both here in sea-encircled Ithaca and in the other cities. But if in strength we fall so short of princely Odysseus that we cannot bend his bow—oh, the disgrace for future times to hear!"

Then said Antinoüs, Eupeithes' son: "Not so, Eurymachus, and you yourself know better. Today throughout the land is the archer-god's high feast. Who then could bend a bow? No, quietly lay it by; and for the axes, what if we leave them standing? Nobody, I am sure, will carry one away and trespass on the house of Laërtes' son, Odysseus. Come then, and let the wine-pourer give pious portions to our cups, that after a libation we may lay aside curved bows. Tomorrow morning tell Melanthius, the goatherd, to drive us here the choicest goats of all his flock; and we will set the thighs before the archer-god, Apollo, then try the bow and end the contest."

So said Antinoüs, and his saying pleased them. Pages poured water on their hands; young men brimmed bowls with drink and served to all, with a first pious portion for the cups. And after they had poured and drunk as their hearts would, then in his subtlety said wise Odysseus:

"Listen, you suitors of the illustrious queen, and let me tell you what the heart within me bids. I beg a special favor of Eurymachus, and great Antinoüs too; for his advice was wise, that you now drop the bow and leave the matter with the gods, and in the morning some god shall grant the power to whom he may. But give me now the polished bow, and let me in your presence prove my skill and power and see if I have yet such vigor left as once there was within my supple limbs, or whether wanderings and neglect have ruined all."

At these his words all were outraged, fearing that he might bend the polished bow. So Antinoüs rebuked him, and spoke to him and said: "You scurvy stranger, with not a whit of sense, are you not satisfied to eat in peace with us, your betters, unstinted in your food and hearing all we say? Nobody else, stranger or beggar, hears our talk. It's wine that goads you, honeyed wine, a thing that has brought others trouble, when taken greedily and drunk without due measure. Wine crazed the Centaur, famed Eurytion, at the house of bold Peirithoüs, on his visit to the Lapithae.[38] And when his wits were crazed with wine, he madly wrought foul outrage on the household of Peirithoüs. So indignation seized the heroes. Through the porch and out of doors they rushed, dragging Eurytion forth, shorn by the pitiless sword of ears and nose. Crazed in his wits, he went his way, bearing in his bewildered heart the burden of his guilt. And hence arose a feud between the Centaurs and mankind; but the beginning of the woe he himself caused by wine. Even so I prophesy great harm to you, if you shall bend the bow. No kindness will you meet from any in our land, but we will send you by black ship straight to king Echetus, the bane of all mankind, out of whose hands you never shall come clear. Be quiet, then, and take your drink! Do not presume to vie with younger men!"

Then said to him heedful Penelope: "Antinoüs, it is neither honorable nor fitting to worry strangers who may reach this palace of Telemachus. Do you suppose the stranger, if he bends the great bow of Odysseus, confident in his skill and strength of arm, will lead me home and take me for his wife? He in his inmost soul imagines no such thing. Let none of you sit at the table disturbed by such a thought; for that could never, never, be!"

Then answered her Eurymachus, the son of Polybus: "Daughter of Icarius, heedful Penelope, we do not think the man will marry you. Of course that could not be. And yet we dread the talk of men and women, and fear lest one of the baser sort of the Achaeans say: 'Men far inferior sue for a good man's wife, and cannot bend his polished bow. But someone else,—a wandering beggar,—came, and easily bent the bow and sent an arrow through the steel. This they will say, to us a shame indeed."

Then said to him heedful Penelope: "Eurymachus, men cannot be in honor in the land and rudely rob the household of their prince. Why then count this a shame? The stranger is truly tall, and well-knit too, and calls himself the son of a good father. Give him the polished bow, and let us see. For this I tell you, and it shall be done; if he shall bend it and Apollo grants his prayer, I will clothe him in a coat and tunic, goodly garments, give him a pointed spear to keep off dogs and men, a two-edged sword, and sandals for his feet, and I will send him where his heart and soul may bid him go."

Then answered her discreet Telemachus: "My mother, no Achaean has better right than I to give or to refuse the bow to any as I will. And out of all who rule in rocky Ithaca, or in the islands off toward grazing Elis, none may oppose my will, even though I wished to put these bows into the stranger's hands and let him take them once for all away. Then seek your chamber and attend to matters of your own,—the loom, the distaff,—and bid the women ply their tasks. Bows are for men, for all, especially for me; for power within this house rests here."

Amazed, she turned to her own room again, for the wise saying of her son she laid to heart. And coming to the upper chamber with her maids, she there bewailed Odysseus, her dear husband, till on her lids clear-eyed Athene caused a sweet sleep to fall.

Meanwhile the noble swineherd, taking the curved bow, was bearing it away. But the suitors all broke into uproar in the hall, and a rude youth would say: "Where are you carrying the curved bow forth, you miserable swineherd? Crazy fool! Soon out among the swine, away from men, swift dogs shall eat you,—dogs you yourself have bred,—will but Apollo and the other deathless gods be gracious!"

At these their words the bearer of the bow laid it down where he stood, frightened because the crowd within the hall cried out upon him. But from the other side Telemachus called threateningly aloud:

"Nay, father! Carry on the bow! You cannot well heed all. Take care, or I, a nimbler man than you, will drive you to the fields with pelting stones. Superior in strength I am to you. Ah, would I were as much beyond the others in the house, beyond these suitors, in my skill and strength of arm! Then would I soon send somebody away in sorrow from my house; for men work evil here."

He spoke, and all burst into merry laughter and laid aside their bitter anger with Telemachus. And so the swineherd, bearing the bow along the hall, drew near to wise Odysseus and put it in his hands; then calling aside nurse Eurycleia, thus he said:

"Telemachus bids you, heedful Eurycleia, to lock the hall's close-fitting doors; and if a woman from the inner room hears moaning or a strife within our walls, let her not venture forth, but stay in silence at her work."

Such were his words; unwinged, they rested with her. She locked the doors of the stately hall. Then silently from the house Philoetius stole forth and at once barred the gates of the fenced court. Beneath the portico there lay a curved ship's cable, made of byblus plant.*
With this he lashed the gates, then passed indoors himself, and went and took the seat from which he first arose, eyeing Odysseus. Now Odysseus already held the bow and turned it round and round, trying it here and there to see if worms had gnawed the horn while its lord was far away. And glancing at his neighbor one would say:

"A sort of expert or con-man with the bow this fellow is. No doubt at home he has himself a bow like that, or means to make one like it. See how he turns it in his hands this way and that, ready for mischief,—rascal!"

Then would another rude youth answer thus: "Oh may he always meet such luck as when he is unable now to bend the bow!"

So talked the suitors. Meantime wise Odysseus, when he had handled the great bow and scanned it closely,—even as one well-skilled to play the lyre and sing stretches with ease round its new

---

*The plant from which papyrus also comes.

The Trial of the Bow—from a painting by N.C. Wyeth

peg a cord, securing at each end the twisted sheep-gut; so without effort did Odysseus string the mighty bow. Holding it now with his right hand, he tried its cord; and clear to the touch it sang, voiced like the swallow. Great consternation came upon the suitors. All faces then changed color. Zeus thundered loud for signal. And glad was long-tried royal Odysseus to think the son of crafty Kronos sent an omen. He picked up a swift shaft which lay beside him on the table, drawn. Within the hollow quiver still remained the rest, which the Achaeans soon should prove. Then laying the arrow on the arch, he drew the string and arrow notches, and forth from the bench on which he sat let fly the shaft, with careful aim, and did not miss an axe's ring from first to last, but clean through all sped on the bronze-tipped arrow; and to Telemachus he said:

"Telemachus, the guest now sitting in your hall brings you no shame. I did not miss my mark, nor in the bending of the bow make a long labor. My strength is sound as ever, not what the mocking suitors here despised. But it is time for the Achaeans to make supper ready, while it is daylight still; and then for us in other ways to make them sport,—with dance and lyre; for these attend a feast."

He spoke and frowned the sign. His sharp sword then Telemachus girt on, the son of princely Odysseus; clasped his right hand around his spear, and close beside his father's seat he took his stand, armed with the gleaming bronze.

BOOK XXII

The Slaughter of the Suitors

Then wise Odysseus threw off his rags and sprang to the broad threshold, bow in hand and quiver full of arrows. Out he poured the swift shafts at his feet, and thus addressed the suitors:

"So the dread ordeal ends! Now to another mark I turn, to hit what no man ever hit before, will but Apollo grant my prayer."

He spoke, and aimed a pointed arrow at Antinoüs. The man was in the act to raise his goodly goblet,—gold it was and double-eared,—and even now guided it in his hands to drink the wine. Death gave his heart no notice. For who could think that in this company of feasters one of the crowd, however strong, could bring upon him cruel death and dismal doom? But Odysseus aimed an arrow and hit him in the throat; right through his tender neck the sharp point passed. He sank down sideways; from his hand the goblet fell when he was hit, and at once from his nose ran a thick stream of human blood. Roughly he pushed his table back, kicking it with his foot, and scattered off the food upon the floor. The bread and roasted meat were thrown away. Into a tumult broke the suitors round about the hall when they saw the fallen man. They sprang from their seats and, hurrying through the hall, peered at the massive walls on every side. But nowhere was there shield or heavy spear to seize. Then they assailed Odysseus with indignant words:

"Stranger, to your sorrow you turn your bow on men! You never shall take part in games again. Swift death awaits you; for you have killed the leader of the noble youths of Ithaca. To pay for this, vultures shall eat you here!"

So each one spoke; they thought he had not meant to kill the man. They foolishly did not see that for them one and all destruction's cords were knotted. But looking sternly on them wise Odysseus said:

"Dogs! You have been saying all the time I never should return out of the land of Troy; and therefore you destroyed my home, outraged my slave-maids, and,—I alive,—covertly wooed my wife, fearing no gods that hold the open sky, nor that the indignation of mankind would fall on you hereafter. Now for you one and all destruction's cords are knotted!"

As he spoke thus, pale fear took hold on all. Each peered about to flee from instant death. Only Eurymachus made answer, saying:

"If you indeed be Ithacan Odysseus, now returned, justly have you described what the Achaeans have been doing,—full many crimes here at the hall and many in the field. But there at last lies he who was the cause of all, Antinoüs; for it was he who set us on these deeds, not so much needing and desiring marriage, but with this other purpose,—which the son of Kronos never granted,—that in the settled land of Ithaca he might himself be king, when he should treacherously have slain your son. Now he is justly slain. But spare your people, and we hereafter, making you public recompense for all we drank and ate here at the hall, will pay a fine of twenty oxen each and give you bronze and gold enough to warm your heart. Till this is done, we cannot blame your wrath."

But looking sternly on him, wise Odysseus said: "Eurymachus, if you would give me all your father's goods, and all your own, and all that you might gather elsewhere, I would not stay my hands from slaying until the suitors paid the price of all their lawless deeds. It lies before you then to fight or flee, if any man will save himself from death and doom. But some here will not flee, I think, from instant death."

As he spoke thus, their knees grew feeble and their very souls; but Eurymachus called out a second time: "Come, friends, the man will not hold back his ruthless hands; but having got possession of a polished bow and quiver, he will shoot from the smooth threshold until he kills us all. Let us then turn to fighting. Draw swords, and hold the tables up against his deadly arrows! Have at him all together! Perhaps we may dislodge him from the threshold and the door, then reach the town and quickly raise the alarm. So would the fellow soon have shot his last."

So saying, he drew his sharp two-edged bronze sword and sprang upon Odysseus with a fearful cry. But on the instant royal Odysseus shot an arrow and hit him in the breast beside the nipple, fixing the swift bolt in his liver. Out of his hand his sword dropped to the ground, and he himself, sprawling across the table, bent and fell, spilling the food and double cup upon the floor. With his brow he beat the pavement in his agony of heart, and with his kicking shook the chair. Upon his eyes gathered the mists of death.

Then Amphinomus assaulted glorious Odysseus, and dashing headlong forward drew his sharp sword, hoping to make Odysseus yield the door. But Telemachus was quick and struck him with his bronze spear upon the back, between the shoulders, and drove the spear-point through his chest. He fell with a thud and struck the ground flat with his forehead. Telemachus sprang back and left the long spear sticking in Amphinomus; for he feared if he should draw the long spear out, an Achaean might attack him, rushing on him with his sword, and as he stooped might stab him. So off he ran and hastily went back to his dear father; and standing close beside him, he said in winged words:

"Now, father, I will fetch a shield and pair of spears, and a bronze helmet also, fitted to your brow. And I will go and arm myself, and give some armor to the swineherd and to the cowherd too; for to be armed is better."

Then wise Odysseus answered him and said: "Run! Bring the arms while I have arrows to defend me, or they will drive me from the door when I am left alone."

He spoke, and Telemachus heeded his dear father, and hastened to the chamber where the glittering armor lay. Out of the store he chose four shields, eight spears, and four bronze helmets having horse hair plumes. These he bore off and hastily went back to his dear father. Telemachus first girt his body with the bronze, then the two herdsmen likewise girt themselves in worthy armor, and so all took their stand by Odysseus, keen and crafty.

He, just as long as he had arrows to defend him, shot down a suitor in the hall with every aim, and side by side they fell. Then when his arrows failed the princely bowman, he leaned the bow against the door-post of the stately room, letting it stand beside the bright face-wall, and he too slung a fourfold shield* about his shoulders, put on his sturdy head a shapely helmet, horsehair-plumed,—grimly the crest above it nodded,—and took in hand two ponderous spears pointed with bronze.

Now in the solid wall there was a postern-door; and level with the upper threshold of the stately hall, an opening to a passage, closed with jointed boards. Odysseus ordered the noble swineherd to guard this postern-door and in its neighborhood to take his stand, since this was the only exit. But to the suitors said Agelaüs, speaking his words to all:

"Friends, could not one of you climb by the postern-door and tell our people, and quickly raise the alarm? So would the fellow soon have shot his last."

Then said to him Melanthius the goatherd: "No, heaven-descended Agelaüs, that may in no way be; for the good court-yard door is terribly near at hand, and the mouth of the passage-way is narrow. One person there, if resolute, could bar the way for all. Yet I will fetch you from the chamber arms to wear; for there, I think, and nowhere else, Odysseus stored the armor,—he and his gallant son."

So having said, Melanthius, the goatherd, climbed to the chambers of Odysseus through the vent-holes of the hall. Out of the store he chose twelve shields, as many spears, and just as many bronze helmets having horsehair plumes; then turning back, he brought them very quickly and gave them to the suitors. And now did Odys-

---

*A shield made of four layers of ox hide.

seus' knees grow feeble and his very soul, when he saw them donning arms and waving in their hands long spears. Large seemed his task; and straightway to Telemachus he spoke these winged words:

"Surely, Telemachus, a woman of the house aids the hard fight against us; or else it is Melanthius."

Then answered him discreet Telemachus: "Father, the fault is mine; no other is to blame; for I it was who opened the chamber's tight-shut door and left it open. Their watchman was too good. But, noble Eumaeus, go and close the chamber-door, and see if any woman has a hand in this, or if,—as I suspect,—it is the son of Dolius, Melanthius."

So they conversed together. And now Melanthius, the goatherd, went to the room again to fetch more goodly armor. The noble swineherd spied him, and quickly to Odysseus, standing near, he said:

"High-born son of Laërtes, ready Odysseus, there is the knave whom we suspected, just going to the chamber. Speak plainly; shall I kill him if I prove the better man, or shall I bring him here to pay for all the crimes he plotted in your house?"

Then wise Odysseus answered him and said: "Here in the hall Telemachus and I will hold the lordly suitors, rage they as they may. You two tie the man's feet and hands and drag him within the chamber; there fasten boards upon his back, and lashing a twisted rope around him hoist him aloft, up the tall pillar, and bring him to the beams, that he may keep alive there long and suffer grievous torment."

So he spoke, and willingly they heeded and obeyed. They hastened to the chamber, unseen of him within. He was engaged in searching after armor in a corner of the room, while the pair stood beside the door-posts, one on either hand, and waited. Soon as Melanthius the goatherd crossed the threshold, in one hand bearing a goodly helmet and in the other a broad old shield coated in mold,— the shield of lord Laërtes, which he carried in his youth, now laid away, its strap-seams parted,—then on him sprang the two and dragged him by the hair within the door, threw him all horror-stricken to the ground, bound hands and feet together with a galling cord, which tight and fast they tied, as they were ordered by Laërtes' son, long-tried royal Odysseus; then they lashed a twisted rope around and hoisted him aloft, up the tall pillar, and brought him to the beams; and mocking him said you, swineherd Eumaeus:

"Now then, Melanthius, you shall watch the whole night long, stretched out on such a comfortable bed as suits you well. The early dawn out of the Ocean-stream shall not in golden splendor slip unheeded by, when you should drive goats for the suitors at the hall to make their meal."

Thus was he left there, fast in deadly bonds. The pair put on their armor, closed the shining door and went to join Odysseus, keen and crafty. Here they stood, breathing fury, four of them on the threshold, although within the hall were many men of might. But near them came Athene, the daughter of Zeus, likened to Mentor in her form and voice. To see her made Odysseus glad, and thus he spoke:

"Mentor, save us from ruin! Remember the good comrade who often aided you. You are of my own years."

He said this, though he understood it was Athene, the summoner of hosts. But the suitors shouted from the other side, down in the hall; and foremost in abuse was Agelaüs, son of Damastor:

"Mentor, do not let Odysseus lure you by his words to fight the suitors and to lend him aid; for I am sure even then we still shall work our will. And after we have slain these men, father and son, you too shall die beside them for deeds you thought to do within the hall. Here with your head you shall make due amends. And when with the sword we have cut short your power, whatever goods you have, within doors and without, we will combine with the possessions of Odysseus. We will not let your sons and daughters live at home, nor let your true wife linger in the town of Ithaca."

As he spoke thus, Athene grew more enraged in spirit and mocked Odysseus with these angry words: "Odysseus, you have no longer such firm power and spirit as when for the sake of white-armed high-born Helen you fought the Trojans nine years long unflinchingly, and vanquished many men in mortal combat, and by your wisdom Priam's wide-wayed city fell. Why, now returned to home and wealth and here confronted with the suitors, do you shrink from being brave? No, no, good friend, stand by my side, watch what I do, and see how, in the presence of the foe, Mentor, the son of Alcimus, repays a kindness."

She spoke, but gave him not quite yet the victory in full. Still she made trial of the strength and spirit both of Odysseus and his valiant son. Up to the roof-beam of the smoky hall she darted like a swallow, resting there.

Now the suitors were led by Agelaüs, son of Damastor, by Eurynomus, Amphimedon, and Demoptolemus; by Peisander, son of Polyctor, and wise Polybus; for these in manly excellence were quite the best of all who still were living, fighting for their lives. The rest the bow and storm of arrows had laid low. So to these men said Agelaüs, speaking his words to all:

"Now, friends, at last the man shall hold his ruthless hands; for Mentor has departed after uttering idle boasts, and the men at the front door are left alone. So hurl your long spears, but not all together! Now then, six let fly first; and see if Zeus allows Odysseus to be hit and us to win an honor. No trouble about the rest when he is down!"

He said, and all to whom he spoke let fly their spears with power. Athene made all vain. One struck the door-post of the stately hall; one the tight-fitting door; another's ashen shaft, heavy with bronze, crashed on the wall. And when the men were safe from the suitors' spears, then thus began long-tried royal Odysseus:

"Friends, let me give the word at last to our side too. Let fly your spears into the crowd of suitors, men who seek to slay and strip us, adding this to former wrongs!"

He spoke, and all with careful aim let fly their pointed spears. Odysseus struck down Demoptolemus; Telemachus, Euryades; the swineherd, Elatus; and the herdsman of the cattle, Peisander. All these together bit the dust of the broad floor, the other suitors falling back from hall to deep recess. Odysseus' men sprang forward and from the bodies of the dead pulled out the spears.

And now the suitors again let fly their pointed spears with power. Athene made them for the most part vain. One struck the door-post of the stately hall; one the tight-fitting door; another's ashen shaft, heavy with bronze, crashed on the wall. But Amphimedon wounded Telemachus on the wrist of the right hand, though slightly; the metal tore the outer skin. And Ctesippus with his long spear grazed Eumaeus on the shoulder which showed above his shield; the spear flew past and fell upon the ground.

Once more the men beside Odysseus, keen and crafty, let fly their sharp spears on the crowd of suitors. And now by Odysseus, the spoiler of cities, Eurydamas was hit; by Telamachus, Amphimedon; by the swineherd, Polybus; and afterwards the herdsman of the cattle hit Ctesippus in the breast and cried in triumph:

"Ha, son of Polytherses, ready mocker, never again give way to folly and big words! Leave boasting to the gods; they are stronger far than you. This gift off-sets the hoof you gave to great Odysseus a little while ago, when in his house he played the beggar man."

So spoke the herdsman of the crook-horned cattle. Then Odysseus wounded Damastor's son with his long spear, when fighting hand to hand. Telemachus wounded Evenor's son, Leiocritus, with a spear-thrust in the middle of the waist, and drove the point clean through. He fell on his face and struck the ground flat with his forehead. And now Athene from the roof above stretched forth her murderous aegis. Their souls were panic-stricken. They scurried through the hall like herded cows, on whom the glancing gadfly falls and maddens them, in springtime when the days are long. And as the crook-clawed hook-beaked vultures, descending from the hills, dart at the birds which fly the clouds and skim the plain, while the vultures pounce and kill them; defense they have not and have no escape, and men are merry at their capture; so the four chased the suitors down the hall and smote them right and left. There went up moans, a dismal sound, as skulls were crushed and all the pavement ran with blood.

But Leiodes, rushing forward, clasped Odysseus by the knees, and spoke imploringly these winged words: "I clasp your knees, Odysseus! Oh, respect and spare me! For I protest I never harmed a woman of the house by wicked word or act. No! and I used to try to stop the rest,—the suitors,—when one of them would do such deeds. But they were never ready to hold their hands from wrong. So through their own perversity they met a dismal doom; and I, their soothsayer, although I did no ill, must also fall. There is no gratitude for good deeds done!"

Then looking sternly on him wise Odysseus said: "If you avow yourself their soothsayer, many a time you must have prayed within the hall that the issue of a glad return might be delayed for me, while my dear wife should follow you and bear you children. Therefore you shall not now avoid a shameful death."

So saying, he seized in his sturdy hand a sword that lay near by, a sword which Agelaüs had dropped upon the ground when he was slain, and drove it through the middle of Leiodes' neck. While he yet spoke, his head rolled in the dust.

But the bard, the son of Terpes, still had escaped dark doom,— Phemius, who sang against his will among the suitors. He stood, holding the tuneful lyre in his hands, close to the postern-door; and in his heart he doubted whether to hasten from the hall to the massive altar of great Zeus, guardian of courts, and take his seat where oftentimes Laërtes and Odysseus had burned the thighs of beeves; or whether he should run and clasp Odysseus by the knees. Reflecting thus, it seemed the better way to touch the knees of Laërtes' son, Odysseus. He laid his hollow lyre upon the ground, midway between the mixer and the silver-studded chair, ran forward to Odysseus, clasped his knees, and spoke imploringly these winged words:

"I clasp your knees, Odysseus! Oh, respect and spare me! To you yourself hereafter grief will come, if you destroy a bard who sings to gods and men. Self-taught am I; God planted in my heart all kinds of song; and I had thought to sing to you as to a god. Then do not seek to slay me. Telemachus, your own dear son, will say how not through will of mine, nor seeking gain, I lingered at your palace, singing to the suitors at their feasts; for being more and stronger men than I, they brought me here by force."

What he had said revered Telemachus heard, and he quickly called to his father who was standing near: "Hold! For the man is guiltless. Do not stab him with the sword! And let us also spare Medon, the page, who here at home used to have charge of me while I was still a child,—unless indeed Philoetius or the swineherd slew him, or he encountered you as you stormed along the hall."

What he was saying Medon, that man of understanding, heard; for he lay crouching underneath a chair, wrapped in a fresh-flayed ox's hide, seeking to shun dark doom. Straightway he rose from underneath the chair, quickly cast off the hide, sprang forward to Telemachus, clasped his knees, and cried imploringly in winged words:

"Friend, stay your hand! It is I! And speak to your father, or exulting in his sharp sword he will destroy me out of indignation at the suitors, who wasted the possessions in his halls and in their folly paid no heed to you."

But wise Odysseus, smiling, said: "Be of good cheer, for he has cleared and saved you; that in your heart you may perceive and may report to others how much more safe is doing good than ill. But both of you leave the hall and sit outside, out of this bloodshed, in the court,—you and the full-voiced bard,—till I have accomplished in the house all that I still must do."

Even as he spoke, the pair went forth and left the hall, and both sat down by the altar of great Zeus, peering about on every side as still expecting death. Odysseus too peered round his hall to see if any living man were lurking there, seeking to shun dark doom. He found them all laid low in blood and dust, and in such numbers as the fish which fishermen draw to the bowed shore out of the foaming sea in the mesh of their nets; these all, sick for the salt sea wave, lie heaped upon the sands, while the resplendent sun takes life away; so lay the suitors, heaped on one another. And now to Telemachus said wise Odysseus:

"Telemachus, go call nurse Eurycleia, that I may speak to her the thing I have in mind."

He spoke, and Telemachus heeded his dear father and, shaking the door, said to nurse Eurycleia: "Up! aged woman, who have charge of all the slave-maids in our hall! Come here! My father calls and now will speak with you."

Such were his words; unwinged, they rested with her. Opening the doors of the stately hall, she entered. Telemachus led the way. And there among the bodies of the slain she found Odysseus, dabbled with blood and gore, like a lion come from feeding on some stall-fed ox; its whole breast and its cheeks on either side are bloody; terrible is the beast to see: so dabbled was Odysseus, feet and hands. And when she saw the bodies and the quantity of blood, she was ready to cry aloud at the sight of the mighty deed. But Odysseus held her back and stayed her madness, and speaking in winged words he said:

"Woman, be glad within; but hush, and make no cry. It is not right to glory in the slain. The gods' doom and their reckless deeds destroyed them; for they respected nobody on earth, bad man or good, who came among them. So through their own perversity they met a dismal doom. But name me now the women of the hall, and tell me who dishonor me and who are guiltless."

Then said to him his dear nurse Eurycleia: "Then I will tell you, child, the very truth. You have fifty slave-maids at the hall whom we have taught their tasks, to card the wool and bear the servant's lot. Out of these women, twelve in all have gone the way of shame, paying no heed to me nor even to Penelope. It is but lately Telemachus has come to manhood, and his mother has never suffered him to rule the maids. But let me go above, to the bright upper chamber, and tell your wife, whom a god has laid asleep."

Then wise Odysseus answered her and said: "Do not wake her yet; tell those women to come here who in the past behaved unworthily."

So he spoke, and through the hall forth the old woman went, to give the message to the maids and bid them come with speed. Meanwhile Odysseus, calling to his side Telemachus, the cowherd, and the swineherd, spoke to them thus in winged words:

"Begin to carry off the dead, and bid the women aid you; then let them clean the goodly chairs and tables with water and porous sponges. And when you have set in order all the house, lead forth these slave-maids out of the stately hall to a spot between the round-house and the neat court-yard wall, and smite them with your long swords till you take life from all; that so they may forget the love they had among the suitors, when they would meet them unobserved."

He spoke, and the women came, trooping along together, in bitter lamentation, letting the big tears fall. First they carried out the bodies of the dead and laid them by the portico of the fenced court, piling them there one on another. Odysseus gave the orders and hastened on the work, and only because compelled, the maids bore off the bodies. Then afterwards they cleaned the goodly chairs and tables with water and porous sponges. Telemachus, the cowherd, and the swineherd with shovels scraped the pavement of the strong-built room, and the maids took up the scrapings and threw them out of doors. And when they had set in order all the hall, they led the serving-maids out of the stately hall to a spot between the round-house and the neat court-yard wall, and there they penned them in a narrow space whence there was no escape. Then thus began discreet Telemachus:

"By no honorable death would I take away the lives of those who poured reproaches on my head and on my mother and were the suitors' comrades."

He spoke, and tied the cable of a dark-bowed ship to a great pillar, then lashed it to the round-house, stretching it high across, too high for one to touch the feet upon the ground. And as the wide-winged thrushes or the doves strike on a net set in the bushes; and when they think to go to roost a cruel bed receives them; even so the women held their heads in line, and around every neck a noose was laid, that they might die most vilely. They twitched their feet a little, but not long.

Then forth they led Melanthius across the porch and yard. With rustless sword they lopped his nose and ears, pulled out his bowels to be eaten raw by dogs, and in their rage cut off his hands and feet.

Afterwards washing clean their own hands and their feet, they went to meet Odysseus in the house, and all the work was done. But to his dear nurse Eurycleia said Odysseus: "Woman, bring sulphur, a protection against harm, and bring me fire to fumigate the hall. And bid Penelope come down with her women, and order all the slave-maids throughout the house to come."

Then said to him his dear nurse Eurycleia: "Truly, my child, in all this you speak rightly. Yet let me fetch you clothes, a coat and tunic. And do not, with this covering of rags on your broad shoulders, stand in the hall. That would be cause for blame."

But wise Odysseus answered her and said: "First let a fire be lighted in the hall."

At these his words, his dear nurse Eurycleia did not disobey, but brought the fire and sulphur. Odysseus fumigated all the hall, the buildings, and the court.

And now the old woman passed through the goodly palace of Odysseus to take his message to the maids and bid them come with speed. Out of their room they came, with torches in their hands. They gathered round Odysseus, hailing him with delight. Fondly they kissed his face and neck, and held him by the hand. Glad longing fell upon him to weep and cry aloud. All these he knew were true.

BOOK XXIII

The Recognition by Penelope

So the old woman, full of glee, went to the upper chamber to tell her mistress her dear lord was in the house. Her knees grew strong; her feet outran themselves. By Penelope's head she paused, and thus she spoke:

"Awake, Penelope, dear child, to see with your own eyes what you have hoped to see this many a day! Here is Odysseus! He has come at last, and slain the haughty suitors,—the men who vexed his house, devoured his substance, and oppressed his son."

Then heedful Penelope said to her: "Dear nurse, the gods have crazed you. They can bewitch one who is very wise, and often they have set the simple in the paths of prudence. They have confused you; you were sober-minded before this. Why mock me when my heart is full of sorrow, telling wild tales like these? And why arouse me from the sleep that sweetly bound me and kept my eyelids closed? I have not slept so soundly since Odysseus went away to see accursed Ilios,—name never to be named. No then, go down, back to the hall. If any other of my maids had come and told me this and waked me out of sleep, I would soon have sent her off in disgrace into the hall once more. This time age serves you well."

Then said to her the good nurse Eurycleia: "Dear child, I do not mock you. In plain truth it is Odysseus; he is come, as I have said. He is the stranger whom everybody in the hall has set at nothing. Telemachus knew long ago that he was here, but out of prudence hid his knowledge of his father till he should have revenge from these bold men for wicked deeds."

So spoke she; and Penelope was glad, and, springing from her bed, fell on the woman's neck, and let the tears burst from her eyes; and, speaking in winged words, she said: "So, tell me, then, dear nurse, and tell me truly; if he is really come as you declare, how was it he laid hands upon the shameless suitors, being alone, while they were always here together?"

Then answered her the good nurse Eurcyleia: "I did not see; I did not ask; I only heard the groans of dying men. In a corner of our protected chamber we sat and trembled,—the doors were tightly closed,—until your son Telemachus called to me from the hall; for his father bade him call. And there among the bodies of the slain I found Odysseus standing. All around, covering the trodden floor, they lay, one on another. It would have warmed your heart to see him, like a lion, dabbled with blood and gore. Now all the bodies are collected at the court-yard gate, while he is fumigating the fair house by lighting a great fire. He sent me here to call you. Follow me, then, that you may come to gladness in your true hearts together, for sorely have you suffered. Now the long hope has been at last fulfilled. He has come back alive to his own hearth, and found you still, you and his son, within his hall; and upon those who did him wrong, the suitors, on all of them here in his home he has obtained revenge."

Then heedful Penelope said to her: "Dear nurse, be not too boastful yet, nor filled with glee. You know how welcome here the sight of him would be to all, and most to me and to the son we had. But this is no true tale you tell. No, rather some immortal slew the lordly suitors, in anger at their galling insolence and wicked deeds; for they respected nobody on earth, bad man or good, who came among them. So for their sins they suffered. But Odysseus, far from Achaea, lost the hope of coming home; yes, he himself was lost."

Then answered her the good nurse Eurycleia: "My child, what word has passed the barrier of your teeth, to say your husband, who is now beside your hearth, will never come! Your heart is always doubting. Come, then, and let me name another sign most sure,— the scar the boar dealt long ago with his white tusk. I found it as I washed him, and I would have told you then; but he laid his hand upon my mouth, and in his watchful wisdom would not let me speak. But follow me. I stake my very life; if I deceive you, slay me by the vilest death."

Then heedful Penelope answered her: "Dear nurse, it is hard for you to trace the counsels of the everlasting gods, however wise you are. Nevertheless, let us go down to meet my son, and see the suitors who are dead, and him who slew them."

So saying, she went from her chamber to the hall, and much her heart debated whether aloof to question her dear husband, or to draw near and kiss his face and take his hand. But when she entered, crossing the stone threshold, she sat down opposite Odysseus, in the firelight, beside the farther wall. He sat by a tall pillar, looking down, waiting to hear if his stately wife would speak when she should look his way. But she sat silent long; amazement filled her heart. Now she would gaze with a long look upon his face, and now she would not know him for the mean clothes that he wore. But Telemachus rebuked her, and spoke to her and said:

"Mother, hard mother, of ungentle heart, why do you hold aloof so from my father, and do not sit beside him, plying him with words and questions? There is no other woman of such stubborn spirit to stand off from the husband who, after many grievous toils, comes in the twentieth year home to his native land. Your heart is always harder than a stone!"

Then said to him heedful Penelope: "My child, my soul within is dazed with wonder. I cannot speak to him, nor ask a question, nor look him in the face. But if this is indeed Odysseus, come at last, we certainly shall know each other better than others know; for we have signs which we two understand, signs hidden from the rest."

As she, long tried, spoke thus, royal Odysseus smiled, and said to Telemachus forthwith in winged words: "Telemachus, leave your mother in the hall to try my truth. She soon will know me better. Now, because I am foul and dressed in sorry clothes, she holds me in dishonor, and says I am not he. But you and I have yet to plan how all may turn out well. For whoever kills one man among a tribe, though the man leaves few champions behind, becomes an exile, quitting king and country. We have destroyed the pillars of the state, the very noblest youths of Ithaca. Form, then, a plan, I pray."

Then answered him discreet Telemachus: "Look you to that, dear father. Your wisdom is, they say, the best among mankind. No mortal man can rival you. Zealously will we follow, and not fail, I think, in daring, so far as power is ours."

Then wise Odysseus answered him and said: "Then I will tell you what seems best to me. First wash and put on tunics, and bid the maids about the house array themselves. Then let the sacred bard with tuneful lyre lead us in sportive dancing, that men may say, hearing us from without, 'It is a wedding,' whether such men be passersby or neighboring folk; and so broad rumor may not reach the town about the suitors' murder till we are gone to our well-wooded farm. There will we plan as the Olympian shall grant us wisdom."

So he spoke, and willingly they heeded and obeyed. For first they washed themselves and put on tunics, and the women also put on their attire. And then the noble bard took up his hollow lyre, and in them stirred desire for merry music and the gallant dance; and the great house resounded to the tread of lusty men and well-dressed women. And one who heard the dancing from without would say, "Well, well! some man has married the long-courted queen. Hardhearted! For the husband of her youth she would not guard her great house to the end, till he should come." So they would say, but knew not how things were.

Meanwhile within the house Eurynome, the housekeeper, bathed resolute Odysseus and anointed him with oil, and on him put a goodly robe and tunic. Upon his face Athene cast great beauty; she made him taller than before, and stouter to behold, and made the curling locks to fall around his head as on the hyacinth flower. As when a man lays gold on silver,—some skillful man whom Hephaestus and Pallas Athene have trained in every art, and he fashions graceful work; so did she cast a grace upon his head and shoulders. Forth from the bath he came, in bearing like the immortals, and once more took the seat from which he first arose, facing his wife, and spoke to her these words:

"Lady, a heart impenetrable beyond the sex of women the dwellers on Olympus gave to you. There is no other woman of such stubborn spirit to stand off from the husband who, after many grievous toils, comes in the twentieth year home to his native land. Come, then, good nurse, and make my bed, that I may lie alone. For certainly of iron is the heart within her breast."

Then said to him heedful Penelope: "No, sir, I am not proud, nor contemptuous of you, nor too much dazed with wonder. I very well remember what you were when you went upon your long-oared ship away from Ithaca. However, Eurycleia, make up his massive bed outside that stately chamber which he himself once built. Move the massive frame out there, and throw the bedding on,—the fleeces, robes, and bright-hued rugs."

She said this in the hope to prove her husband; but Odysseus spoke in anger to his faithful wife: "Woman, these are bitter words which you have said! Who set my bed elsewhere? A hard task that would be for one, however skilled,—unless a god should come and by his will set it with ease upon some other spot; but among men no living being, even in his prime, could lightly shift it; for a great token is carved into its curious frame. I built it; no one else. There grew a thick-leaved olive shrub* inside the yard, full-grown and vigorous, in girth much like a pillar. Round this I formed my chamber, and I worked till it was done, building it out of close-set stones, and roofing it over well. Framed and tight-fitting doors I added to it. Then I lopped the thick-leaved olive's crest, cutting the stem high up above the roots, neatly and skillfully smoothed with my axe the sides, and to the line I kept all true to shape my post, and with an auger I bored it all along. Starting with this, I fashioned the bed till it was finished, and I inlaid it well with gold, with silver, and with ivory. On it I stretched a thong of ox-hide, gay with purple. This is the token I now tell. I do not know whether the bed still stands

---

*The olive tree, which can give fruit for generations, symbolizes longevity.

there, wife, or whether somebody has set it elsewhere, cutting the olive trunk."

As he spoke thus, her knees grew feeble and her soul within, when she recognized the tokens which Odysseus truly told. Then bursting into tears, she ran straight toward him, threw her arms round Odysseus' neck and kissed his face, and said:

"Odysseus, do not scorn me! Ever before, you were the wisest of mankind. The gods have sent us sorrow, and grudged our staying side by side to share the joys of youth and reach the threshold of old age. But do not be angry with me now, nor take it ill that then when I first saw you I did not greet you thus; for the heart within my breast was always trembling. I feared some man might come and cheat me with his tale. Many a man makes wicked schemes for gain. Indeed, Argive Helen, the daughter of Zeus, would not have given herself to love a stranger if she had known how warrior sons of the Achaeans would bring her home again, back to her native land. And yet it was a god prompted her deed of shame. Before, she did not cherish in her heart such sin, such grievous sin, from which began the woe which stretched to us. But now, when you have clearly told the tokens of our bed, which no one else has seen, but only you and I and the single slave, Actoris, whom my father gave me on my coming here to keep the door of our closed chamber,—you make even my ungentle heart believe."

So she spoke, and stirred still more his yearning after tears; and he began to weep, holding his loved and faithful wife. As when the welcome land appears to swimmers, whose sturdy ship Poseidon wrecked at sea, confounded by the winds and solid waters; a few escape the foaming sea and swim ashore; thick salt foam crusts their flesh; they climb the welcome land, and are escaped from danger; so welcome to her gazing eyes appeared her husband. From round his neck she never let her white arms go. And rosy-fingered dawn had found them weeping, but a different plan the goddess formed, clear-eyed Athene. She checked the long night in its passage, and at the Ocean-stream she stayed the gold-throned dawn, and did not suffer it to yoke the swift-paced horses which carry light to men, Lampus and Phaëton* which bear the dawn. And now to his wife said wise Odysseus:

"O wife, we have not reached the end of all our trials yet. Hereafter comes a task immeasurable, long and severe, which I must needs fulfill; for so the spirit of Teiresias told me, that day when I descended to the house of Hades to learn about the journey of my comrades and myself. But come, my wife, let us to bed, that there at last we may refresh ourselves with pleasant sleep."

Then said to him heedful Penelope: "The bed shall be prepared whenever your heart wills, now that the gods have let you reach your stately house and native land. But since you speak of this, and God inspires your heart, come, tell that trial. In time to come, I know, I shall experience it. To learn about it now, makes it no worse."

Then wise Odysseus answered her and said: "Lady, why urge me so insistently to tell? Well, I will speak it out; I will not hide it. Yet your heart will feel no joy; I have no joy myself; for Teiresias bade me go to many a peopled town, bearing in hand a shapely oar, till I should reach the men that know no sea and do not eat food mixed with salt. These, therefore, have no knowledge of the red-cheeked ships, nor of the shapely oars which are the wings of ships. And this was the sign, he said, easy to be observed. I will not hide it from you. When another traveler, meeting me, should say I had a winnowing-fan on my white shoulder, there in the ground he bade me fix my oar and make fit offerings to lord Poseidon,—a ram, a bull, and the sow's mate, a boar,—and, turning homeward, to offer sacred hecatombs to the immortal gods who hold the open sky, all in the order due. And on myself death from the sea shall very gently come and cut me off, bowed down with the hale old age. Round me shall be a prosperous people. All this, he said, should be fulfilled."

Then said to him heedful Penelope: "If gods can make old age the better time, then there is hope there will be rest from trouble."

---

*The horses of the chariot that draws the sun.

So they conversed together. Meanwhile Eurynome and the nurse prepared their bed with clothing soft, under the light of blazing torches. And after they had spread the comfortable bed, with busy speed, the old woman departed to her room to rest; while the chamber-servant, Eurynome, with torch in hand, brought them to their chamber and then went her way. So they came gladly to their bed of early days. And now Telemachus, the cowherd and the swineherd stayed their feet from dancing and bade the women stay, and all lay down to rest throughout the dusky halls.

But while the pair reveled in their new-found love, they reveled in talking too, each one relating: she, the royal lady, what she endured at home, watching the wasteful throng of suitors, who, making excuse of her, slew many cattle, beeves, and sturdy sheep, and stores of wine were drained from out the casks; he, high-born Odysseus, what miseries he brought on other men and what he bore himself in anguish,—all he told, and she was glad to listen. No sleep fell on her eyelids till he had told her all.

He began with how at first he conquered the Ciconians, and came thereafter to the fruitful land of Lotus-eaters; then what the Cyclops did, and how he took revenge for the brave comrades whom the Cyclops ate and never pitied; then how he came to Aeolus, who gave him hearty welcome and sent him on his way; but it was fated that he should not reach his dear land yet, for a sweeping storm bore him once more along the swarming sea, loudly lamenting; how he came to Telepylus in Laestrygonia, where the men destroyed his ships and his armed comrades, all of them; Odysseus fled in his black ship alone. He told of Circe, too, and all her crafty guile; and how on a ship of many oars he came to the charnel-house of Hades, there to consult the spirit of Teiresias of Thebes; how he looked on all his comrades, and on the mother who had borne him and cared for him when little; how he had heard the full-voiced Sirens' song; how he came to the Wandering Rocks, to dire Charybdis and to Scylla, past whom none goes unharmed; how then his crew slew the Sun's cattle; how Zeus with a blazing bolt smote his swift ship,— Zeus, thundering from on high,—and his good comrades perished, utterly, all, while he escaped their evil doom; how he came to the island of Ogygia and to the nymph Calypso, who held him in her hollow grotto, wishing him to be her husband, cherishing him, and saying she would make him an immortal, young forever, but she never beguiled the heart within his breast; how then he came through many toils to the Phaeacians, who honored him exceedingly, as if he were a god, and brought him on his way to his own native land, giving him stores of bronze and gold and clothing. This was the latest tale he told, when pleasant sleep fell on him, easing his limbs and from his heart removing care.

Now a new plan the goddess formed, clear-eyed Athene, when in her mind she judged Odysseus had enough of love and sleep. At once out the Ocean-stream she roused the gold-throned dawn, to bring the light to men. Odysseus was aroused from his soft bed, and gave his wife this charge:

"Wife, we have had in days gone by our fill of trails: you, mourning here my grievous journey home; me, Zeus and the other gods bound fast in sorrow, all eager as I was, far from my native land. But since we now have reached the rest we long desired together, protect whatever wealth is still within my halls. As for the flocks which the audacious suitors wasted, I shall myself seize many, and the Achaeans shall give me more besides, until they fill my folds. But now I go to the well-wooded farm, to visit my good father, who for my sake has been in constant grief. On you, my wife, wise as you are, I lay this charge. Straight with the sunrise a report will go abroad about the suitors whom I slew here in the hall. Then go to the upper chamber with your waiting women. There remain. Give not a look to any one, nor ask a question."

He spoke, and girt his beautiful arms about his shoulders; and he awoke Telemachus, the cowherd and the swineherd, and bade them all take weapons in their hands for fighting. They did not disobey, but took their bronze harness. They opened the doors; they sallied forth; Odysseus led the way. Over the land it was already light, but Athene, hiding them in darkness, led them swiftly from the town.

BOOK XXIV

Peace

Meanwhile Cyllenian* Hermes summoned hence the spirits of the suitors. In his hand he held a wand, beautiful, made of gold, with which he charms to sleep the eyes of whom he will, while again whom he will he wakens out of slumber. With this he started them and led them forth; they followed gibbering after. As in a corner of a monstrous cave the bats fly gibbering, when one tumbles from the rock out of the cluster as they cling together; so gibbering, these moved together. Protecting Hermes was their guide down the dank pathway. Past the Ocean-stream they went, past the White Rock, past the portals of the Sun and land of dreams, and soon they reached the field of asphodel, where spirits dwell, spectres of worn-out men.

Here they came upon the spirit of Achilles, son of Peleus, and of Patroclus too, of gallant Antilochus, and of Ajax, who was first in beauty and in stature of all the Danaäns after the gallant son of Peleus. These formed a group around Achilles; to whom approached the spirit of Agamemnon, son of Atreus, sorrowing. Around thronged other spirits of men who by his side had died in the house of Aegisthus and there had met their doom. And the spirit of the son of Peleus first addressed him:

"O son of Atreus, throughout your life we said you were exceeding dear to Zeus, the Thunderer, beyond all other heroes, because you were the lord of many mighty men there in the land of Troy where we Achaeans suffered; yet all too early you were doomed to

---

*Cyllene, a mountainous region in Greece, was the birthplace of Hermes.

meet hard fate, which no one that is born avoids. Ah, would that, in the pride of your full power, there in the land of Troy you had met death and doom! Then would the whole Achaean host have made your grave, and for your son in after days a great name had been gained. Now you must be cut off by an inglorious death."

Then said to him the spirit of the son of Atreus: "Fortunate son of Peleus, godlike Achilles, who died at Troy, afar from Argos! Around you others fell, the Trojans' and Achaeans' bravest sons, battling because of you; while in a cloud of dust you lay proudly, all your horsemanship forgotten. All through the day we battled, and never would have stopped our fighting had Zeus himself not stopped us with a storm. And after we had borne you to the ships out of the fight, we laid you on a bier and washed your comely body with warm water and with oil. The Danaäns standing round you shed many burning tears, and cut their hair. Out of the sea came forth your mother, with the immortal sea nymphs, when she heard the tale, while over the water ran a wondrous wail, and secret trembling fell on all the Achaeans. Then all had hastened off and boarded the hollow ships, if one had not detained them who was wise in ancient lore, Nestor, whose counsel had before been proved the best. He with good will addressed them thus, and said: 'Hold, Argives! Do not flee, you young Achaeans! It is his mother coming from the sea with the immortal nymphs to look on her dead son.' By these his words the bold Achaeans were withheld from flight; while round you stood the daughters of the old man of the sea, lamenting bitterly, and with immortal robes they clad your body. Meantime the Muses, nine in all, with sweet responsive voices sang your dirge. Then not an Argive could you see but was in tears; the piercing song so moved them. For seventeen days, alike by night and day, we mortal men and deathless gods continued mourning. On the eighteenth we gave you to the flames. Many fat sheep we slew beside you, and many crook-horned cattle. In vesture of the gods you burned, with much anointing oil and much sweet honey. Many Achaean heroes moved in their armor round your blazing pyre, footmen and charioteers, and a loud din arose. And when at length Hephaestus' flame had made an end, at dawn we gathered your white bones, Achilles, laid in pure wine and oil. Your mother gave the golden urn; a gift, she said, of Dionysus, and handiwork of famed Hephaestus. In this your white bones lie, illustrious Achilles, mingled with those of dead Patroclus, son of Menoetius, and parted from Antilochus, whom you regarded more than all your other comrades, excepting dead Patroclus. Over them all the powerful host of Argive spearmen built a great stately tomb at a projecting point on the broad Hellespont, so that it might be seen far off upon the sea by men who now are born or shall be born hereafter. Your mother, having entreated the gods for splendid prizes, offered them in the funeral games to the bravest of the Achaeans. In former days you have been present at the burial of many a hero, when at a king's death young men steeled themselves and strove for prizes; but here you would have marveled in your heart far more to see the splendid prizes offered in your honor by silver-footed Thetis; for you were very dear to all the gods. Thus though you died, you did not lose your name; but ever among mankind, Achilles, your glory shall be great. While as for me, what gain had I in winding up the war? On my return Zeus purposed me a miserable end, at the hands of Aegisthus and my accursed wife."

So they conversed together. And now the Guide approached, the killer of Argus, leading the spirits of the suitors whom Odysseus slew. Amazed, the two drew near to see; and the spirit of Agamemnon, son of Atreus, perceived the son of Melaneus, renowned Amphimedon; for Melaneus of Ithaca was once his entertainer. Then thus began the spirit of the son of Atreus:

"Amphimedon, what has happened that you come to this dreary land, all of you chosen men and all alike in years? One who would pick the best men of a town would choose no others. Was it on shipboard that Poseidon smote you, raising ill winds and heavy seas? Or did fierce men destroy you on the land, while you were cutting off their cattle or their fair flocks of sheep, or while you fought to win their town and carry off their women? Tell what I ask! I call myself your friend. Do you not recollect how I, with godlike Menelaus, came to your house to urge Odysseus to follow us to Ilios on the well-benched ships? A whole month long we spent, crossing the open sea, and found it hard to win the spoiler of towns, Odysseus."

Then answered him the spirit of Amphimedon: "Great son of Atreus, Agamemnon, lord of men, all that you say, heaven-favored one, I recollect; and I in turn will very plainly tell how a cruel end of death befell us. We courted the wife of Odysseus long away. She neither declined the hated suit nor did she end it, because she planned for us death and dark doom. This was the last pretext she cunningly devised: within the hall she set up a great loom and went to weaving; fine was the web and very large; and then to us said she: 'Young men who are my suitors, though royal Odysseus now is dead, delay to urge my marriage till I complete this robe,—its threads must not be wasted,—a shroud for lord Laërtes, against the time when the hard doom of death that lays men low shall overtake him. Achaean wives about the land I fear might give me blame if he should lie without a shroud, he who had great possessions.' Such were her words, and our high hearts assented. Then in the daytime would she weave at the great web, but in the night unravel, after her torch was set. Thus for three years she hid her craft and cheated the Achaeans. But when the fourth year came, as time rolled on, when the months waned and the long days were done, then at the last one of her maids, who knew full well, confessed, and we discovered her unraveling the splendid web; so then she finished it, against her will, by force. When she displayed the robe, after weaving the great web and washing it, like sun or moon it shone. And then some hostile god guided Odysseus,—whence I know not,—to the confines of our country, where the swineherd has his home. There the son of royal Odysseus also came, returning by black ship from sandy Pylos. And when the two had planned the suitors' cruel death, they entered our famous town; Odysseus later, Telemachus coming on before. The swineherd brought Odysseus, who wore a sorry garb, like an old and wretched beggar, leaning upon a staff. Upon his back were miserable clothes, and none of us could know him as he suddenly appeared, not even our older men; but we assailed him with harsh words and missiles. A while he bore with patience this pelting and abuse in his own house; but when at last the will of aegis-bearing Zeus aroused him, he and Telemachus gathered the goodly weapons and put them in the store-room, fastening the bolts. Then, full of craft, he bade his wife deliver to the suitors the bow and the gray steel, to be to us ill-fated men means for our sport and harbingers of death. Not one of us could draw the string of the strong bow; we fell far short of power. But when the great bow reached Odysseus' hands, we shouted all together not to give the bow, whatever he might say. Telemachus alone urgently bade him take it. Then long-tried royal Odysseus took the bow in hand, bent it with ease, and sent an arrow through the steel. Advancing to the threshold, there he stood and poured out the swift arrows, glaring terribly around. First he shot prince Antinoüs, and then on others turned his grievous shafts, with careful aim, and side by side they fell. Soon it was seen some god was the men's ally; for straightway rushing down the hall, with all their might they smote us right and left. Then went up moans, a dismal sound, as skulls were crushed and all the pavement ran with blood. Thus we died, Agamemnon; and still uncared for in Odysseus' halls our bodies lie. Our friends at home have had no tidings, or they had washed the dark clots from our wounds and laid us out with wailing; for that is the dead man's due."

Then answered the spirit of the son of Atreus: "Fortunate son of Laërtes, ready Odysseus! You won a wife full of all worth. How upright was the heart of true Penelope, the daughter of Icarius! How faithful to Odysseus, the husband of her youth! Wherefore the story of her worth shall never die; but for all humankind immortal ones shall make a joyous song in praise of steadfast Penelope. Not like the daughter of Tyndareus* did she contrive vile deeds and slay the husband of her youth. Of her a loathsome song shall spread among mankind, and bring an ill repute on all the sex of women, even on well-doers too."

So they conversed together, where they stood within the house of Hades, in the secret places of the earth.

---

*Clytaemnestra.

But Odysseus and his men, after departing from the town, soon reached the rich well-ordered farmstead of Laërtes. This place Laërtes had acquired for himself in days gone by, after much patient toil. Here was his home; round it on every side there ran a shed, in which ate, sat, and slept the slaves who did his pleasure. Within, there lived an old Sicilian woman, who tended carefully the aged man here at his farm, far from the town. Arriving here, Odysseus thus addressed his servants and his son:

"Go you at once into the stately house and slay immediately for dinner the fattest of the swine. But I will put my father to the proof, and try if he will recognize and know me by the sight, or if he will fail to know me who have been absent long."

So saying, he gave his armor to his men, who then went quickly in, while Odysseus approached the fruitful vineyard, to make his trial there. Dolius he did not find, in crossing the long garden, nor any slaves or men; for they were gone to gather stones to make a vineyard wall, and Dolius* was their leader. His father he found alone in the well-ordered vineyard, hoeing about a plant. He wore a dirty tunic, patched and coarse, and round his shins had bound sewed leather leggings, a protection against harm. Upon his hands were gloves, to save him from the thorns, and on his head a goatskin cap; and so he nursed his sorrow.

When long-tried royal Odysseus saw his father, worn with old age and in great grief of heart, he stopped beneath a lofty pear-tree and shed tears. Then in his mind and heart he doubted much whether to kiss his father, to clasp him in his arms and tell him all, how he had come and found his native land; or first to question him and prove him through and through. Reflecting thus, it seemed the better way to try him first with probing words. With this intent, royal Odysseus walked straight toward him. Laërtes, with his head bent low, was digging round the plant, and standing by his side his gallant son addressed him:

---

*Conceivably the same Dolius who fathered Melantho and Melanthius.

"Old man, you have no lack of skill in tending gardens. Of these your care is good. Nothing is here—shrub, fig-tree, vine, olive, or pear, or bed of earth,—in all the field uncared for. But one thing I will say; be not offended. No proper care is taken of yourself; for you are meeting hard old age, yet you are sadly worn and meanly clad. It is not as if for idleness your master had cast you by, and nothing of the slave shows in your face or form. Rather you seem a royal person; like one who after taking bath and food might sleep at ease, as is the due of age. Come, then, declare me this and plainly tell whose slave you are, whose farm you tend. And tell me truly this, that I may know full well, if this is really Ithaca to which we now are come, as the man said just now who met me on my way. He was not too bright, however; for he did not deign to talk at length, nor yet to hear my talk, when I inquired for my friend, and asked if he were living still or if he were already dead and in the house of Hades. But let me speak of that to you, and do you mark and listen. In my own country once I entertained a man who had come there; and none among the traveling strangers was more welcome at my house. He called himself by birth a man of Ithaca, and said his father was Laërtes, son of Arceisius. I brought him home and entertained him well and gave him generous welcome from the abundance in my house. Such gifts I also gave as are fitting for a guest: of fine-wrought gold I gave him seven talents, gave him a flowered bowl of solid silver, twelve cloaks of single fold, as many rugs, as many goodly mantles, and as many tunics too. Further, I gave him women trained to faultless work, any four shapely slave-maids whom he himself might choose."

Then answered him his father, shedding tears: "Certainly, stranger, you are in the land for which you ask; but lawless impious men possess it now. Vain were the many gifts you gave. Yet had you found him living in the land of Ithaca, with fair return of gifts he had sent you on your way, and with a generous welcome; for that is just, when one begins a kindness. But come, declare me this, and plainly tell: how many years are passed since you received this guest, this hapless guest, my son,—if really it was he, ill-fated man!—

whom, far from friends and home, fishes devoured in the deep or else on land he fell a prey to beasts and birds. No mother mourned for him and wrapped him in his shroud, nor father either,—we who gave him life! Nor did his richly dowered wife, steadfast Penelope, wail by her husband's couch, as the wife should, and close his eyes, though that is the dead man's due. Tell me, however, truly, and let me know full well: who are you? of what people? Where is your town and kindred? Where is the swift ship moored which brought you here, you and your gallant comrades? Or did you come a passenger on some strange ship, from which they landed you and sailed away?"

Then wise Odysseus answered him and said: "Well, I will very plainly tell you all. I come from Alybas, where I have a noble house, and am the son of lord Apheidas, the son of Polypemon. My own name is Eperitus.* God drove me from Sicania and brought me here, against my will. Here my ship lies, just off the fields outside the town. As for Odysseus, five years ago he went away and left my land. Ill-fated man! And yet the birds were favorable at starting and came on his right hand. So I rejoiced and sent him forth, and he rejoicing went his way. Our hearts then hoped to meet again in friendship, and to give each other glorious gifts."

So he spoke, and on Laërtes fell a dark cloud of grief. He caught in his hands the powdery dust and strewed it on his hoary head with many groans. Odysseus' heart was stirred. Up through his nostrils shot a tingling pang as he beheld his father. Forward he sprang and clasped and kissed him, saying:

"Lo, father, I am he for whom you seek, now in the twentieth year come to my native land! Then cease this grief and tearful sighing; for let me tell you,—and the need of haste is great,—I slew the suitors in our halls, and so avenged their galling insolence and wicked deeds."

Then in his turn Laërtes answered: "If you are indeed my son,

---

*Literally, Apheidas means "not restrained"; Polypemon, "Everygrief"; and Eperitus, "Attacker."

Odysseus, now returned, tell me some trusty sign that so I may believe."

But wise Odysseus answered him and said: "Examine first this scar, which a boar inflicted with his gleaming tusk upon Parnassus, whither I had gone. You and my honored mother sent me thither, to see Autolycus, my mother's father, and to obtain the gifts which he, when here, agreed to give. Then come, and let me tell the trees in the well-ordered vineyard, which you once gave, when I, being still a child, begged you for this and that, as I followed round the garden. Among these trees we passed. You named them and described them. You gave me thirteen pear-trees, ten apples, forty figs. And here you marked off fifty rows of vines to give, each one in bearing order. Along the rows clusters of all sorts hang, whenever the seasons sent by Zeus give them their fullness."

As he spoke thus, Laërtes' knees grew feeble and his very soul, when he recognized the tokens which Odysseus truly told. Round his dear son he threw his arms, and long-tried royal Odysseus drew him fainting toward him. But when he gained his breath, and in his breast the spirit rallied, finding his words once more Laërtes said:

"O father Zeus, surely you gods still live on high Olympus, if the suitors have indeed paid for their wanton sin! And yet I have great fear at heart that all the men of Ithaca may soon attack us here and may send tidings through the Cephallenian cities."

But wise Odysseus answered him and said: "Be of good courage! Let not these things vex your mind! But let us hasten to the house which stands beside the orchard. There I sent Telemachus, the cowherd and the swineherd, that there they straightway might prepare our meal."

So talked the two, and walked to the fair house. And when they reached the stately buildings, they found Telemachus, the cowherd and the swineherd, carving much meat and mixing sparkling wine. Soon in his room the Sicilian servant bathed brave Laërtes and anointed him with oil and round him wrapped a goodly cloak. And Athene, drawing nigh, filled out the limbs of the shepherd of the people, and made him taller than before and larger to behold. Out of the bath he came, and his son wondered to see how like the immortal gods his bearing was; and speaking in winged words he said:

"Certainly, father, one of the everlasting gods has made your face and figure nobler to behold."

Then in his turn said wise Laërtes: "O father Zeus, Athene, and Apollo, would I were what I was when I took Nericus, the stately citadel of the mainland, leading my Cephallenians; and would that thus I yesterday had stood beside you in our hall, my armor on my shoulders, beating back the suitors! Then had I shook the knees of many in the hall, and you had felt your inmost heart grow warm!"

So they conversed together. Meanwhile the others, after ceasing from their labor of laying out the meal, took seats in order on couches and on chairs. They all were laying hands upon their food, when in came aged Dolius and his sons, tired from their work. Their mother, the old Sicilian woman, had gone and called them; for she provided for them, and diligently tended the old man now that old age was on him. When the men saw Odysseus and marked him in their minds, they stood still in the hall, astonished; but Odysseus kindly accosting them, spoke thus:

"Old man, sit down to dinner and lay aside surprise; for eager as we were to take our food, we waited long about the hall, ever expecting you."

He spoke, and Dolius ran, both hands outstretched, and seizing Odysseus' hand kissed it upon the wrist, and speaking in winged words he said:

"Dear master, because you have come home to us who sorely missed you and never thought to see you any more,—but gods themselves have brought you,—hail and rejoice! Gods grant you blessings! And tell me truly this, that I may know it well: does heedful Penelope understand that you are here, or shall we send her tidings?"

Then wise Odysseus answered him and said: "Old man, she understands already. Why should you think of that?"

So he spoke, and Dolius took his seat upon a polished bench.

Likewise the sons of Dolius, gathering round renowned Odysseus, greeted him with their words and clasped his hands, and then sat down in order by Dolius, their father. Thus were they busied with their dinner in the hall.

Rumor, meanwhile, with tidings, ran swiftly through the town, reporting the suitors' awful death and doom; and those who heard gathered from every side, with moans and groans, before the palace of Odysseus. Out of the house they each brought forth his dead, and buried them; and all that came from other towns they gave to fishermen to carry home on their swift ships. Then they went trooping to the assembly, sad at heart. And when they were assembled and all had come together, Eupeithes rose and thus addressed them: for he cherished in his heart a sorrow for his son that could not be appeased,—his son Antinoüs, the first whom royal Odysseus slew. With tears for him, he thus addressed them, saying:

"O friends, this man has wrought a monstrous deed on the Achaeans! For some he carried off in ships,—good men and many,—and then he lost his hollow ships and lost his people too; and now he has come home and killed the very noblest men of Cephallenia. Up then! Let us set forth, before he swiftly goes to Pylos, and sacred Elis where the Epeians rule, or we shall be disgraced henceforth forever; for it will be a shame for future times to know, if we take no revenge on those who slew our sons and brothers. Life to my thinking then would be no longer sweet. Instead, I would die at once and join the men now slain. But forth, before they escape from us across the sea!"

Tears in his eyes, he spoke; pity touched all the Achaeans. But Medon now drew near, and with him the sacred bard, from the palace of Odysseus; for slumber left them. They stood still in the midst, and wonder fell on all, while Medon, a man of understanding, thus addressed them:

"Listen to me now, men of Ithaca; for not without consent of the immortal gods Odysseus planned these deeds. I myself saw a deathless god stand by Odysseus, in all points like to Mentor. And this immortal god appeared before Odysseus, cheering him on; then to the consternation of the suitors he stormed along the hall, and side by side they fell."

As he spoke thus, pale fear took hold on all. But to them spoke the old lord Halitherses, the son of Mastor; for he alone looked both before and after. He with good will addressed them thus, and said: "Listen now, men of Ithaca, to what I say. By your own fault, my friends, these deeds are done; because you paid no heed to me nor yet to Mentor, the shepherd of the people, in hindering your sons from foolish crime. They wrought a monstrous deed in wanton willfulness, when they destroyed the goods and wronged the wife of one who was their prince, saying that he would come no more. Let then the past be ended, and listen to what I say: do not set forth, or some may find a self-sought ill."

He spoke; but with a mighty cry up started more than half,— together in their seats remained the rest,—for his counsel had not pleased them. Eupeithes they approved, and they straightway ran for weapons. Then when they had arrayed themselves in glittering bronze, they gathered in a troop outside the spacious town. Eupeithes in his folly led them. He thought to avenge the murder of his son, yet was himself never to come back more, but there would meet his doom.

Meanwhile Athene said to Zeus, the son of Kronos: "Our father, son of Kronos, most high above all rulers, speak what I ask: what is your secret purpose? Will you still further stir up evil strife and the dread din of war, or establish peace between the two?"

Then answered her cloud-gathering Zeus and said: "My child, why question me of this? For was it not yourself proposed the plan to have Odysseus crush these men by his return? Do as you will; I tell you what is wise. Now royal Odysseus has avenged himself upon the suitors, let a sure oath be made and he be always king; while for the death of sons and brothers we bring about oblivion. So shall all love each other as before, and wealth and peace abound."

With words like these he roused Athene, eager enough before, and she went dashing down the ridges of Olympus.

Now when the men had stayed desire for cheering food, then

thus began long-tried royal Odysseus: "Let some one go and see if our foes are drawing near."

He spoke; and out the son of Dolius ran, as he was bidden, and went and stood upon the threshold, and saw the men all near. Then straight to Odysseus in winged words he called: "Here they are, close at hand! Quick, let us arm!"

As soon as he spoke, there sprang to arms the four men with Odysseus and the six sons of Dolius. Laërtes too and Dolius put on armor; gray though they were, still warriors at need. Then when they had arrayed themselves in glittering bronze, they opened the doors and sallied forth, Odysseus leading.

But Athene now drew near, the daughter of Zeus, likened to Mentor in her form and voice; whom long-tried royal Odysseus saw with joy, and to Telemachus his son he at once said: "Now shall you learn, Telemachus, by taking part yourself while men are battling where the best are proved, how not to bring disgrace upon your line of sires; for they from ancient times were famed for strength and bravery through all the land."

Then answered him discreet Telemachus: "In this my present mood, dear father, you shall see me, if you will, bring no disgrace upon our line, even as you say."

So said he, and Laërtes too was glad and said: "Oh, what a day for me is this, kind gods! Truly glad am I. My son and son's son strive in valor."

And standing by his side, clear-eyed Athene said: "Son of Arceisius, far the dearest of my friends, call on the clear-eyed maid and father Zeus; then swing your long spear and straight let it fly."

With words like these Pallas Athene inspired him with great power. He prayed to the daughter of mighty Zeus; then swung his long spear and straight let it fly, and struck Eupeithes on the helmet's bronze cheek. This did not stay the spear; the point passed through. He fell with a thud; his armor rattled round him. On the front ranks Odysseus fell, he and his gallant son, and smote them with their swords and double-pointed spears. And now they certainly had slain them all and cut them off from coming home, had not Athene, daughter of aegis-bearing Zeus, shouted aloud and held back all the host:

"Hold, men of Ithaca, from cruel combat, and without bloodshed this instant part!"

As thus Athene spoke, pale fear took hold on all. Their weapons all flew from their trembling hands and fell upon the ground, as the goddess gave her cry. To the town they turned, eager to save their lives. Fearfully shouted long-tried royal Odysseus, and gathering his might swooped like a soaring eagle. Then too the son Kronos cast his blazing bolt, and down it fell by the dread father's clear-eyed child. And now to Odysseus said clear-eyed Athene:

"High-born son of Laërtes, ready Odysseus, stay! Cease from the struggle[39] of uncertain war! Let not the son of Kronos, far-seeing Zeus, be moved to anger!"

So spoke Athene. Odysseus heeded, and was glad at heart. Then for all coming time between the two a peace was made by Pallas Athene, daughter of aegis-bearing Zeus, likened to Mentor in her form and voice.

ENDNOTES

Book I

1. (p. 1) *O Muse*: The invocations of the muse that begin the *Iliad* and the *Odyssey* set the pattern for the epic tradition to follow, in both the Roman world and the European. The muses were the nine daughters of Zeus, and they personified artistic inspiration in all fields, from dance to history. Calliope was the muse of epic poetry. The earlier Near Eastern epic *Gilgamesh* begins with a similar description of its hero's epic journey.

2. (p. 2) *Our father, son of Kronos*: According to the ancient Greek poet Hesiod, Zeus, the youngest son of Kronos, usurps his father's place as chief god and frees his siblings, who include his brother Poseidon and his sister/wife, Here, from Kronos's stomach. Zeus and Leto produce the twins Apollo and Artemis, while Zeus gives birth to Athene, goddess of wisdom, out of his own head. As punishment for supporting Kronos, Atlas must hold up the pillars of the earth.

3. (p. 4) *a stranger . . . before his gate*: Telemachus immediately shows his worth by observing the conventions of hospitality, which dictated that strangers were to be safely harbored and guests honored with gifts. Such customs were regarded as the will of Zeus and, in the absence of any police, courts, or even body of laws universal to the Greek-speaking world, they afforded travelers a small measure of security and reinforced the host's social standing.

4. (p. 5) *sailing over the wine-dark sea . . . to Temesê, for bronze*: Temesê, today called Tamassos, is a city on the island of Cyprus. Bronze is an alloy of copper and tin, and at the time the *Odyssey* was composed, the mining of copper had already been an important industry on Cyprus for many centuries. The web of Mediterranean trade in Homer's time drew the Greek-speaking world into close contact with Egypt and Phoenicia, as the poem reflects.

5. (p. 6) *no skill in birds*: Soothsayers interpreted the flight of birds, particularly of the predatory variety, to foretell the future throughout the ancient Greco-Roman world; see, for instance, page 15.

Endnotes

6. (p. 7) *nor has she power to end it*: In Homer's world, only men could inherit property. Penelope and her son, then, face a dilemma: Telemachus cannot control his father's property without acknowledging the man's death, but to do so would remove Penelope's protection from a marriage that would force her to leave her own home for her new husband's.

7. (p. 9) *slave-maids followed her*: Slave labor was fundamental to the Greco-Roman economy. Slaves were generally foreign-born, and most were captured in raids or warfare. Men were relegated to field work and women to the home. Women slaves were often the sexual chattel of the house's patriarch, as Homer's praise for Laërtes' gallant behavior toward Eurycleia indirectly indicates on page 11. Slaves could own property; Eumaeus even buys his own slave; see page 179.

8. (p. 9) *the distaff*: A distaff is a stick used for spinning thread. Historically, women in the Mediterranean and throughout Europe were so identified with the production of cloth—a domestic task, performed inside the household—that the word "distaff" came to stand for the feminine realm or perspective in general. In the *Odyssey*, even the nymph Calypso tends the loom. Women had very little scope for a life outside the domestic sphere.

Book II

9. (p. 12) *early, rosy-fingered dawn*: Epithets such as this one, repeated frequently throughout the text, reflect the original oral composition of Greek epic poetry. Rather than memorize a long text word-for-word, a poet intimately familiar with a particular epic story would employ many such formulaic phrases to improvise a fresh version of the tale on each new occasion, so that the telling would never be exactly the same twice.

10. (p. 12) *summon to an assembly*: Homer includes only a sketchy picture of the form of government practiced in what to him was the long-past world of epic heroes. While Odysseus serves as Ithaca's king, the council Telemachus attends—which apparently includes only older citizens—seems to exercise some leadership function. At any rate, no new king has been anointed despite the hero's twenty-year absence.

11. (p. 15) *Tyro, Alcmene, and crowned Mycene*: All three of these women evidently bore human or partly human children to gods. Tyro founded the line that leads to Nestor with Poseidon, and Alcmene bore Heracles after union with Zeus. Mycene's story has not survived, but since her name is the root of Mycenae, Agamemnon's city, one may assume that she, too, favored some divinity with offspring.

Endnotes

Book III

12. (p. 24) *Peisistratus*: The disproportionate attention paid to Peisistratus, son of Nestor, may reflect a reported attempt by the Athenian ruler Peisistratus (sixth century B.C.) to collect and regularize all the manuscripts of Homer then in existence. The Athenian Peisistratus claimed ancestry from Nestor (called the Neleid line, after Neleus, son of Tyro and father of Nestor).

13. (p. 25) *as the pirates roam the seas*: Like the Vikings, the early Greeks considered sea raiding a legitimate, if dangerous, means of acquiring wealth. Odysseus earns his epithet "spoiler of cities" by many more depredations than the sack of Troy, as the plundering raids on the Ciconians and Laestrygonians, described in books IX and X, demonstrate.

14. (p. 27) *safely, too, Philoctetes*: Greek warriors maroon the archer Philoctetes on the island of Lemnos after he suffers a snakebite that festers to an unbearable pungency. But Odysseus and his comrades eventually retrieve the archer because a prophecy connected with his bow prevents Troy from falling in his absence.

15. (p. 30) *his gentle arrows*: The Greek world often pictured the arrows of Apollo or Artemis as inflicting death by what the modern world understands as disease. In the *Odyssey*, Apollo strikes suddenly, in the fashion of a heart attack or stroke, while Artemis effects more gradual and gentler ends.

16. (p. 30) *to Egypt*: The association of Egypt with the accumulation of wealth also figures in the tale Odysseus concocts to hide his identity after he returns to Ithaca (book XIV) and in the biblical story of Joseph; the element of bondage unites the latter two stories as well. The stability and prosperity of Egyptian civilization was long unique in the ancient Mediterranean.

Book IV

17. (p. 36) *Hermione:* According to some ancient sources, Hermione eventually marries Orestes, the avenging son of Agamemnon. The *Odyssey*, however, does not specifically allude to such an outcome.

18. (p. 40) *child of Zeus*: Homer does not specify the manner of Helen's descent from Zeus. Other sources explain that Zeus took the form of a swan to rape Helen's mother, Leda, resulting in the birth of four children from eggs: Helen, Clytaemnestra, Castor, and Polydeuces. The two males became symbols of loyalty (see p. 138) and the two females of betrayal, illustrating the fundamental male bias of ancient Greek culture.

Endnotes

19. (p. 49) *son-in-law of Zeus*: That Menelaus merits immortality as the spouse of semidivine Helen suggests that fragments of earlier, less patriarchal belief systems may underlie the mythic universe Homer inherits. In the ancient Near East, for instance, kings frequently affirmed their standing by a "sacred marriage" to a representation of a female divinity associated with fertility—often a priestess of the goddesses Inanna or Ishtar, the predecessors of Aphrodite.

Book V

20. (p. 57) *Tithonus*: According to texts a few generations after Homer, Tithonus is a human beloved by the goddess of the dawn. She grants him eternal life but forgets to preserve his youth. Consequently, he dwindles to almost nothing; in some versions of the story his faint voice becomes the chirp of the cricket.

21. (p. 58) *charms to sleep*: Hermes' most famous exploit was the killing of Argus, the many-eyed watchman. The goddess Here had set Argus to guard Io, with whom Zeus wished to make love. Hermes, on his ruler's orders, charmed all of Argus's eyes asleep at once (doing so in many versions by telling stories, which makes the function of the wand or rod Homer mentions puzzling) and cut off his head. Here preserved the eyes in the tail of the peacock.

22. (p. 60) *Jason*: The reference here is not to the Jason who leads the Argonauts, but to the mortal being (whose name is usually transcribed as "Iasion") who marries the fertility goddess Demeter. He fathers the god of wealth, Plutus, before his destruction at the hands of jealous Zeus; the whole tale likely relates to rites of the sort described in book IV, note 3, above.

23. (p. 66) *Ino*: She is the daughter of Cadmus, founder of the cursed royal line of Thebes. By a plot of Here, a lightning bolt annihilates one of Ino's sisters, Semele, yet another of Zeus' lovers. Later, Zeus and Semele's divine child, Dionysus, inspires Ino's sister Agave to tear her own son, Pentheus, to pieces. Ino, driven mad by Here, eventually leaps into the sea, but a merciful Zeus turns her into a nymph.

24. (p. 68) *whoe'er thou art!*: Odysseus offers a prayer to the god of Scheria's river, whose name he does not know. In Greek mythology, every location boasts a minor deity as its presiding spirit.

Book VI

25. (p. 73) *like a lion*: Such extended similes—direct comparisons by use of "like" or "as"—so characterize Homeric poetry that they have come to be known as

Endnotes

"epic similes." Every later writer of epic influenced by Homer, from Virgil to Milton to Derek Walcott, has imitated the technique.

Book VII

26. (p. 80) *Eurymedon . . . giants*: Zeus faced two wars to establish his dominance, one against the gods of his father's generation, known as Titans, and one against an army of earth-born giants. Hesiod tells the story of both wars fully in his *Theogony*, but, writing within thirty to fifty years after Homer, he identifies the leader of the giants as Typhoeus, not Eurymedon. Later writers tend to conflate the two struggles.

Book VIII

27. (pp. 89–90) *how they once quarreled*: The quarrel between Odysseus and Achilles to which the poem refers is a shadowy incident, never mentioned in the *Iliad* itself. Later texts claim that the argument concerned the means by which Troy was to fall, through an Achillean frontal assault or an Odyssean strategy, but Homer offers only the limited information found in this passage.

Book IX

28. (p. 105) *Cyclops*: The origin of the Cyclops myth may lie in misread bones. It has been suggested that the Greeks came across the skeletons of elephants and, being unfamiliar with the living animal, assumed that the cavity in the center of the gigantic skull, to which the trunk is attached, had once contained a single, monstrous eye. Unicorns, similarly, may have been inspired by the remains of the narwhal; the males of this whale species have a long, twisted ivory tusk.

Book X

29. (p. 120) *the sorcerer Aeëtes*: The Aeëtes identified here as Circe's brother may conceivably be King Aeëtes of Colchis, from whom Jason wrests the Golden Fleece. (Aeëtes' daughter, Medea, was also a noted enchanter.) That both characters named Aeëtes are the same, however, cannot be proven.

30. (p. 129) *the prophet blind*: Teiresias, the most famous seer in the ancient Greek tradition, foretold the death of Pentheus and identified Oedipus as the source of the plague afflicting Thebes. Later sources relate his transformation into a woman and back into a man; when Zeus and Here ask him which gender

enjoys greater sexual pleasure, Teiresias answers "women," pleasing Zeus. Piqued, Here blinds the man, but Zeus repays him with the gift of prophecy.

Book XI

31. (p. 136) *great men's wives and daughters*: Homer's catalogue of famous women is too long for full annotation here. Suffice it to say that none of these figures gains immortal repute for her own deeds, but for her relation to men—to sons and husbands in particular. The text neglects even to mention that Leda also bore Helen and Clytaemnestra, noting only her heroic sons.

32. (p. 144) *his wrath*: Most commentators agree that the section beginning with the words "Yet then, despite his wrath" and ending with "back he went into the house of Hades" (p. 146), does not date to the Homeric composition of the poem in the eighth century B.C., though it was added early in the text's history.

Book XII

33. (p. 148) *Jason*: Heir to the throne of Corinth, Jason needed to retrieve the Golden Fleece from the Black Sea city of Colchis, on the edge of the world known to the early Greeks, in order to wrest the kingdom from the usurper Pelias. He accomplished both tasks with the aid of Medea, whom he subsequently divorced for political gain, an act for which she revenged herself by the murder of their children.

Book XV

34. (p. 187) *lineage of Melampus*: Theoclymenus has impeccable credentials as a reader of omens, his ancestor Melampus having been renowned for understanding the language of beasts and birds and for his skill as a physician. Telemachus does not hesitate to shelter a wanted murderer, demonstrating the degree to which personal loyalty outweighed civil responsibility in the heroic world Homer describes.

Book XIX

35. (p. 236) *under his righteous sway*: Belief in the unity of the king with the land he ruled has a long history. Crops fail in Thebes when Oedipus violates the natural progression of time by marrying his mother; the God of Genesis curses

the land for Adam's sake; the Fisher King of the medieval Grail story rules an autumnal land because he can neither cure his thigh's deep wound nor die.

36. (p. 246) *one day blindly slew*: Pandareos's daughter, Aedon (which means "nightingale"), intends to kill the son of her sister-in-law, Niobe, who brags incessantly about the boy, but in the dark mistakenly kills her own child, Itylus. Zeus pities her and transforms her into the eternally grieving bird. Post-Homeric stories of the transformation of an entirely different character, Phil-omel, into a nightingale, and of the death of Niobe's children at the hands of Apollo and Artemis, have outlasted this now-obscure tale.

Book XXI

37. (pp. 260–261) *bend the bow*: A similar test of the bow appears in the Indian epic *The Ramayana*, when Rama must lift, bend, and string Shiva's bow to prove himself worthy to marry Sita.

38. (p. 266) *Lapithae*: The war between the Lapithae, a Greek tribe from Thessaly, and the Centaurs, narrated perhaps most memorably in book XII of Ovid's *Metamorphoses*, involved many of the earlier heroes of Greek myth, including Theseus and Nestor. The irony, of course, is that Antinoüs himself behaves like the Centaurs, to whom he compares Odysseus in this passage.

Book XXIV

39. (p. 306) *Cease from the struggle*: Athene's intervention to cut short an apparently endless blood feud anticipates the role she plays in Aeschylus's *Oresteia*, in which she removes the guilt that plagues Orestes for the murder of his mother, Clytaemnestra, an incident to which the *Odyssey* frequently refers. Aeschylus marks the advent of civil government by casting Athene's involvement in the form of judging a trial.

INSPIRED BY THE *ODYSSEY*

The *Odyssey*, now more than 3,000 years old, has been retold many times and continues to inspire storytellers. The Romans reappropriated Greek mythology freely, and the great poet Virgil used the *Odyssey* as the basis of his *Aeneid*, an epic that chronicles the adventures of Aeneas, second-ranking commander of the Trojan army, on his fated journey to become the founder of Rome. The first six books—which follow Aeneas's wanderings from the ravaged and burning city of Troy to the Libyan coast, where he meets the widow Dido—closely resemble the *Odyssey*; the latter six books describe Aeneas's triumphant war against the Rutuli tribe and follow the style of Homer's *Iliad*. Virgil not only appropriated specific passages from Homer, but he often translated some of Homer's original language into Latin.

Arguably the most innovative adaptation of the *Odyssey* is James Joyce's novel *Ulysses*. Published in 1922, *Ulysses* also mirrors the Homeric epic in structure, yet all of the action transpires in Dublin during a single day, June 16, 1904. (The playwright Tom Stoppard made Joyce and *Ulysses* the subject of his play *Travesties*, in which he comments that the only two sources from which the novel draws are the *Odyssey* and the Irish telephone directory.) Joyce finds his Ulysses, or Odysseus, figure in Leopold Bloom, a Jewish advertising canvasser who spends the day wandering dispassionately around Dublin. Joyce's correlation between this antiheroic character and Odysseus becomes decidedly ironic. Bloom's wife, Molly, is a concert singer and is also ironically different from her Homeric equivalent, Odysseus's wife, Penelope. While Penelope demonstrates her fidelity by convincing suitors she will accept their overtures only when she has completed a funeral pall that she weaves every day and cunningly unravels every night, Molly is an indulgent adulteress. Joyce gives the role of Telemachus to the youthfully pedantic Stephen Dedalus, who in a slightly different incarnation was also the hero of the author's earlier *Portrait of the Artist as a Young Man*.

While the Romans may have been guilty of the rote renaming of Homeric characters, Joyce's treatment of the epic is playfully inventive. Joyce employs techniques such as interior monologue, a form of stream-of-consciousness narrative, to lend epic qualities to his storytelling. As a result, *Ulysses* simultaneously depicts modernity as a pathetically unheroic age while translating the quotidian into the grandiose. Now considered to be one of the most influential books of the twentieth century, *Ulysses* was banned in the United States until 1933 and in Britain until 1937.

COMMENTS & QUESTIONS

In this section, we aim to provide the reader with an array of perspectives on the text, as well as questions that challenge those perspectives. The commentary has been culled from sources as diverse as reviews contemporaneous with the work, letters written by the author, literary criticism of later generations, and appreciations written throughout history. Following the commentary, a series of questions seeks to filter the Odyssey *through a variety of points of view and bring about a richer understanding of this enduring work.*

Comments

ARISTOTLE

Unity of plot does not, as some persons think, consist in the unity of the hero. For infinitely various are the incidents in one man's life which cannot be reduced to unity; and so, too, there are many actions of one man out of which we cannot make one action. Hence the error, as it appears, of all poets who have composed a *Heracleid*, a *Theseid*, or other poems of the kind. They imagine that as Heracles was one man, the story of Heracles must also be a unity. But Homer, as in all else he is of surpassing merit, here too—whether from art or natural genius—seems to have happily discerned the truth. In composing the *Odyssey* he did not include all the adventures of Odysseus—such as his wound on Parnassus, or his feigned madness at the mustering of the host—incidents between which there was no necessary or probable connexion: but he made the *Odyssey*, and likewise the *Iliad*, to centre round an action that in our sense of the word is one. . . . The story of the *Odyssey* can be stated briefly. A certain man is absent from home for many years; he is jealously watched by Poseidon, and left desolate. Meanwhile his home is in a wretched plight—suitors are wasting his substance and plotting against his son. At length, tempest-tost, he himself arrives; he makes certain persons acquainted with him; he attacks the suitors with his own hand, and is himself preserved while he destroys them. This is the essence of the plot; the rest is episode. . . . Epic poetry must have as many kinds as Tragedy: it must be simple, or complex, or 'ethical,' or 'pathetic.' The parts also, with the exception of song and spectacle, are the same; for it requires Reversals of the Situation, Recognitions, and Tragic Incidents. Moreover, the thoughts and the diction must be artistic. In all these respects Homer is our earliest and sufficient model. Indeed each of his poems has a twofold character. The *Iliad* is at once simple and 'pathetic' and the *Odyssey* complex (for Recognition scenes run through it), and at the same time 'ethical.' Moreover, in diction and thought he is supreme.

—from *Poetics*, translated by S. H. Butcher (1911)

JOHN KEATS

 Much have I travell'd in the realms of gold,
  And many goodly states and kingdoms seen;
  Round many western islands have I been
 Which bards in fealty to Apollo hold.
 Oft of one wide expanse had I been told
  That deep-brow'd Homer ruled as his demesne:
  Yet did I never breathe its pure serene
 Till I heard Chapman speak out loud and bold:
 Then felt I like some watcher of the skies
  When a new planet swims into his ken;
 Or like stout Cortez, when with eagle eyes;
  He stared at the Pacific—and all his men
 Look'd at each other with a wild surmise—
  Silent, upon a peak in Darien.

    —"On First Looking into Chapman's Homer"

S. H. BUTCHER AND A. LANG

There would have been less controversy about the proper method of Homeric translation, if critics had recognised that the question is a purely relative one, that of Homer there can be no final translation. The taste and literary habits of each age demand different qualities in poetry, and therefore a different sort of rendering of Homer. To the men of the time of Elizabeth, Homer would have appeared bald, it seems, and lacking in ingenuity, if he had been presented in his antique simplicity. For the Elizabethan age, Chapman supplied what was then necessary, and the mannerisms that were then deemed of the essence of poetry, namely, daring and luxurious conceits. Thus in Chapman's verse Troy must 'shed her towers for tears of overthrow,' and when the winds toss Odysseus about, their sport must be called 'the horrid tennis.'

In the age of Anne, 'dignity' and 'correctness' had to be given to Homer, and Pope gave them by aid of his dazzling rhetoric, his antitheses, his *netteté*, his command of every conventional and favourite artifice. Without Chapman's conceits, Homer's poems would hardly have been what the Elizabethans took for poetry; without Pope's smoothness, and Pope's points, the *Iliad* and *Odyssey* would have seemed tame, rude, and harsh in the age of Anne. These great translations must always live as English poems. As transcripts of Homer they are like pictures drawn from a lost point of view.

—from the preface to Butcher and Lang's translation of
the *Odyssey* (1917)

SAMUEL BUTLER

This translation is intended to supplement a work entitled *The Authoress of the Odyssey*, which I published in 1897. . . . I have nothing either to add to, or to withdraw from, what I have there written. The points in question are:

(1) that the *Odyssey* was written entirely at, and drawn entirely from, the place now called Trapani on the west coast of Sicily, alike

as regards the Phaecian and the Ithaca scenes; while the voyages of Ulysses, when once he is within easy reach of Sicily, resolve themselves into a periplus of the island, practically from Trapani back to Trapani, via the Lipari islands, the Straits of Messina, and the island of Pantellaria;

(2) that the poem was entirely written by a very young woman, who lived at the place now called Trapani, and introduced herself into her work under the name of Nausicaa.

—from the preface to Butler's translation
of the *Odyssey* (1900)

Questions

1. Aristotle praises Homer for focusing on specific and diverse events in the life of Odysseus, rather than attempting somehow to unify his adventures. How does this episodic treatment create a sweeping epic? By investing each scene with such vivid detail, does Homer make Odysseus's life feel realistic? Can this stylistic technique be construed as modern?

2. How do Keats, Butcher, and Lang argue for a plurality of translations of the *Odyssey*? Does this constant retranslating of Homer's work mirror its own oral history?

3. In literature, "unrealistic" events, distortions of actuality, and fantastic characters often make a point precisely by their deviations from the commonsense reality we think we live in. How, for example, do Polyphemous's monstrous differences help to reveal Odysseus's virtues, or at least, his definitive traits?

4. Are Odysseus's defining traits admirable or deplorable?

5. Odysseus's slaughter of the suitors and the servants who went over to them would be reprehensible in real life, no doubt. But does that mean we should be ashamed of enjoying it in literature? Do you think that this

kind of violence in literature encourages people to be violent in their own lives?

6. Does Homer imply that the reader (or originally, the listener) should emulate Odysseus?

7. To what do you attribute the *Odyssey*'s 2,500 years of popularity?

FOR FURTHER READING

The Context of the Homeric Epics

Drews, Robert. *The Coming of the Greeks: Indo-European Conquests in the Aegean and the Near East*. Princeton: Princeton University Press, 1988. An absorbing, balanced account of the evidence surrounding the questions of who the Myceneans and Dorians were, where they came from, and when they arrived in Greece.

Finley, M. I. *The World of Odysseus*. 1954. Revised second edition. New York: Viking Press, 1965. Now somewhat dated, but still a comprehensive introduction to Homer's world for general readers.

Freeman, Charles. *Egypt, Greece and Rome: Civilizations of the Mediterranean*. Oxford and New York: Oxford University Press, 1996. A comprehensive history of the ancient Mediterranean that puts Greek civilization firmly into the context of neighboring cultures.

Pomeroy, Sarah B. *Goddesses, Whores, Wives, and Slaves: Women in Classical Antiquity*. 1975. Reprinted with a new preface by the author. New York: Schocken Books, 1995. An excellent survey of the roles of and attitudes toward women in the ancient Mediterranean.

Steiner, George, ed. *Homer in English*. Edited with the assistance of Aminadav Dykman. London and New York: Penguin, 1996. A history of how Homer has been translated into English, with representative excerpts from all the major translations.

For Further Reading

Older Criticism of Continuing Interest

Auerbach, Erich. "Odysseus' Scar." In his *Mimesis: The Representation of Reality in Western Literature*. Translated by Willard R. Trask. Princeton: Princeton University Press, 1953. The classic statement of the ancient Greek aesthetic, especially as it contrasts with the Bible's method of narration.

Kirk, G. S. *Homer and the Oral Tradition*. Cambridge and New York: Cambridge University Press, 1977. A look at the oral context by one of the leading critics of mythological texts.

Lord, Albert B. *The Singer of Tales*. 1960. Second edition, edited by Stephen Mitchell and Gregory Nagy. Cambridge, MA: Harvard University Press, 2000. Based on the research of the late Milman Parry, this book explains the oral-formulaic principle of the poem's composition. Recent edition includes an audio and video CD Parry made of Balkan tale-singers.

General Current Criticism

Clay, Jenny Strauss. *The Wrath of Athena: Gods and Men in the* Odyssey. Lanham, MD: Rowman and Littlefield Publishers, 1997. An adept, detailed reading of the poem.

Griffin, Jasper. *Homer, the* Odyssey. Cambridge and New York: Cambridge University Press, 1987. A good, brief introduction to the poem's themes and background.

Latacz, Joachim. *Homer: His Art and His World*. Translated by James P. Holoka. Ann Arbor: University of Michigan Press, 1996. Probably the best general guide to the poem for the nonexpert.

Schein, Seth L., ed. *Reading the* Odyssey: *Selective Interpretive Essays*. Princeton: Princeton University Press, 1996. Essays that offer an advanced introduction to themes of current critical interest in the poem.

For Further Reading

Topics in Current Criticism

Cohen, Beth, ed. *The Distaff Side: Representing the Female in Homer's Odyssey*. Oxford and New York: Oxford University Press, 1995. A collection of essays dealing with female characters in the poem from the perspectives of a variety of disciplines.

Dimock, George E. *The Unity of the Odyssey*. Amherst: University of Massachusetts Press, 1989. A recent contribution to the debate about the authorship of the work.

Doherty, Lillian Eileen. *Siren Songs: Gender, Audiences, and Narrators in the Odyssey*. Ann Arbor: University of Michigan Press, 1995. Combines narrative-based, audience-oriented, and feminist approaches to illuminate the gender dynamics of storytelling in the poem.

Haubold, Johannes. *Homer's People: Epic Poetry and Social Formation*. Cambridge and New York: Cambridge University Press, 2000. An examination of the interrelation of Homeric epic and the production of social norms.

Louden, Bruce. *The Odyssey: Structure, Narration, and Meaning*. Baltimore: Johns Hopkins University Press, 1999. An analysis of the "ring structure" used to organize many levels of the poem's narrative.

Malkin, Irad. *The Return of Odysseus: Colonization and Ethnicity*. Berkeley: University of California Press, 1998. An attempt to understand the mindset of early Greek colonizers by drawing on a variety of evidence, notably the *Odyssey*.

Nagy, Gregory. *Poetry as Performance: Homer and Beyond*. Cambridge and New York: Cambridge University Press, 1996. A discussion of the epic emphasizing its qualities as performance.

Snodgrass, Anthony M. *Homer and the Artists: Text and Picture in Early Greek Art*. Cambridge and New York: Cambridge University Press, 1998. Revealing look at how early Greek pottery painting does not merely illustrate Homer, but preserves many variants of his stories that once circulated in oral tradition.

INDEX

A

Acastus, 177
Achaeans, 3
  assembly of, 12–18
Acheron, 129
Achilles, 25–26, 89, 293
  Odysseus talks with, in
    Hades, 142–143
Acroneüs, 90
Actoris, 289
Adraste, 39
Aeacides, 142–144
Aeaea, 120, 147
Aeëtes, 120, 148
Aegae, 67
Aegisthus, 1, 2, 8
  murdered by Orestes, 30
  murder of Agamemnon, 28,
    29, 48–49, 140
Aegyptius, 12
Aeolia, 117
Aeolus (King of the Winds),
  117–119
Aeolus (father of Cretheus),
  136
Aeson, 137
Aethon, 238

Agamemnon, 1, 26, 27, 48, 90
  murdered by Aegisthus, 28,
    29, 48–49, 140
  Odysseus talks to, in Hades,
    140–142
  recounts Achilles' funeral,
    293–295
  talks with Amphimedon, 295–
    297
Agelaüs, 256–257, 274, 276,
  277
Ajax (son of Telamon, Greek
  fighter at Troy), 25, 142,
  144, 293
Ajax (son of Oileus), 48
Alcandra, 39
Alcinoüs, 70
  assistance given to Odysseus,
    88–89, 158–159
  dancing, 94, 97
  description of house and
    garden, 81–82
  father of, 80
  feasting and games, 90–94
  gifts given to Odysseus, 97–
    99, 158–159
  Odysseus is welcomed and
    promised safe passage
    home, 82–87

Index